MY LIFE WITH GOYA

ALSO BY ANDREW POTOK
Ordinary Daylight

MY LIFE WITH GOYA

a novel by

ANDREW POTOK

ARBOR HOUSE / NEW YORK

Library of Congress Cataloging in Publication Data

Potok, Andrew.
My life with Goya.

I. Title.
PS3566.0688M9   1986   813'.54   85-22867
ISBN: 0-87795-789-4

The author remembers with affection and would like to acknowledge
Goya: Rebellious Genius by Marion Chapman, published in 1938 by
Egmont Press.

Designed by Richard Oriolo

For Charlotte

1

*D*uring the whole war and for some years after it had ended, my uncle Bolek and I lived at the Buckingham Hotel. We moved in a few hours after we stepped off the ferry from Ellis Island.

The hotel was a half-block from Prince Casimir Furs, now the center of Bolek's empire. But it wasn't merely the short walk to his office that made us stay, it was its transience, its air of wantonness that made the hotel irresistible.

When I wandered in the hallways late at night—the many nights Bolek was out—I sometimes ran into portly old gentlemen I hadn't seen before, with young girls on their arms, fidgeting with keys to rooms on our floor. "Rich men," Bolek told me, "keep more than one apartment."

On the other hand, the man with thick glasses who lived down the hall said as I was starting off to school one morning: "This is it, sonny, this is home sweet home." But though Bolek and I had lived here for four years, we never called it home, always "the hotel."

In the small, garish lobby—brass sconces hung on smoked mirrors and royal blue carpets cut in broad-leaf patterns covered the floor—Bolek was like a Napoleon on Elba. Short, trim, and pigeon-chested, with his navy-blue cashmere coat flung over his shoulders, he strode from the elevator, clapped the keys down on the front desk, took my arm, and marched us out into Fifty-seventh Street. On this Friday in December, as every Friday, we were going out to dinner, just the two of us. "Toots Shor's," he told the cabby in front.

Even though I was fourteen, there was no one I would rather have been with than Bolek.

"Tomorrow we shall drive into America," Bolek announced in the restaurant as we waited for our shrimp cocktails. "Fresh air," he said magnanimously, unfolding his napkin, "real American fresh air."

Even in Poland, Bolek had measured success by the purity of the air he could provide. It was like gold itself, this invisible air, especially when it smelled of pinecones in Zakopane or the sea in Zopot, where I was often sent with my governess.

My father never took vacations. He traveled only to supervise the building of his roads or bridges. It was always Bolek, my mother's brother, who would come to install us in the *pensions* and then call us from Warsaw to urge us to stay an extra week. "It takes time to cough up the filth of Warsaw," Bolek would insist. "But please, Mr. Boleslaw," the governess would beg, "Adam should be back in school." "School, school," Bolek would yell over the crackly phone line, "I spit on your Polish school."

Now, across the small white table at the restaurant, Bolek outlined the plan for Saturday. "Weinglass wants us to try out his new car. Do you know why? I'll tell you why, darling. Not because he is so good and kind, our Weinglass. It is because he cannot bear being the only one who owns such an expensive machine. Ach, what a salesman." Bolek was selling, too; otherwise he would have come to the point more quickly. "And while we are driving," he finally said, turning around to hail the waiter, "there is a house Sophie wants us to see."

Sophie, our closest friend in America, had been trying for

four years to get us out of the hotel, "so you can live a normal life like everyone else." Sophie dragged us to look at duplexes across from the Met, rambling high-ceilinged apartments on West End Avenue, estates in Riverdale. But Bolek and I managed to hang on to the Buckingham.

"A house?" I said. "We don't need a house."

"Adam, Adam," Bolek said, "the house is nothing. We will have a look just to keep Sophie happy. We will be going for a *drive*, a wonderful drive in the American countryside."

"I see the American countryside all the time," I said. "At camp every summer . . ."

"That's different," he said. "You go and you stay. You don't *see* anything."

"We walk in the woods, we swim in the lake. . . ."

Bolek leaned across the table to lift a lock of my hair from my eyes. "You have a beautiful forehead," he said, "so let us see it."

"I don't mind driving. It's the house—"

"No more, Adamek. This is enough. We will drive in Connecticut, do you understand?" To Bolek, Connecticut was like Xanadu. "And we will take Magdalena with us." Now he knew I could not refuse to go.

The next morning on a nearly deserted Fifty-seventh Street, Weinglass's Lincoln Continental sat ready. Weinglass was one of Bolek's partners, the richer of the two men who put up the money to start Prince Casimir's in New York. Weinglass was decked out in his weekend finery—the nubby tweed and twill, the sporting cap, the coat with fur collar. But the clothes contest Weinglass could not win. Bolek, only a few years in this country, was already considered one of New York's best-dressed men. He always wore a suit. Social occasions were defined by the distance between pinstripes. Even on this Saturday morning in December, his white linen handkerchief peeked elegantly out of his breast pocket.

Weinglass stood beside the navy-blue car, polishing the door on the passenger side with his own white handkerchief. A thin red stripe ran beneath the car windows and was broken only on the driver's side with the initials ZW, Z for Zyga.

"Adam, darling," Weinglass said, enveloping me in his thick arms, "you are going to fall in love with this car, I promise you. It is a perfection." His steel-gray hair was brushed back, pomaded, stiff, his eyes were rheumy. He settled himself behind the wheel. "I will explain to you everything," he told Bolek. "Pay good attention." Weinglass pressed the starter button and the long, elegant machine began to purr softly. "It is like a cat," he said. "If you are not looking, you cannot hear it coming."

I sat in back. Bolek handed me the seal coat he had taken along for Sophie to wear. He had also brought three ermine tails to pin on Magdalena, Sophie's daughter. I laid the coat down carefully, found an empty page in my sketchbook, and began drawing.

As Bolek studied the dashboard with a certain awe, I drew the two pilots absorbed in the shiny arithmetic of the instrument panel. Moving slowly uptown, Weinglass lovingly identified each dial and gauge. We drove through the park, time for the car's technology to be fully appreciated. They were appropriating it for their own. Like other Americans before them, they were planting their flags in Detroit, South Bend, Gary. This machine, this marvelous American machine, intoxicated them both.

As we were about to emerge from the park at Seventy-second Street, we found ourselves blocked by a parade—it must have been a high-school football band gone astray—heading down the avenue. It was a sight put there by heaven. Bolek and Weinglass were staring at a hundred high-stepping children pounding on the drums strapped on harnesses circling their backs, blowing on horns and clarinets, clashing cymbals. At the head of the long column, a pair of American flags was held high in the brisk winter air for all the world to see. Tears appeared in both men's eyes. They coughed, and dabbed at their moist faces. The parade moved slowly, stopped to march in place.

"That's what we need," Bolek said, breaking the patriotic silence. "We need music. Yes, the show needs music. . . ."

"What music? What show?" Weinglass wanted to know.

"What show?" Bolek said. "What you think? *My* show, Weinglass. It will be fantastic."

"*Your* show? Are you mad? Tell me, are you all right?"

"Listen to me, Zyga. We are in business together, may God help me. You have the funds, I have the genius. I want an orchestra—"

"An orchestra? You want maybe Toscanini?"

"Imbecile," Bolek snarled, "we must give America a spectacle. What do they know of such things? You are rich! What do you care?"

"Never! Never!" Weinglass yelled. He had refused money before. One year ago, an immaculately dressed German Jew— Weinglass insisted the man was a Polish Jew—had come to Prince Casimir Furs to ask both men for money with which his organization could barter for the lives of European Jews headed for the camps. Bolek had emptied his pockets and his bank account. Not Zyga Weinglass. "This is terrible," Weinglass had said. "I will not do it. How will it look in the newspapers? Jews, *again Jews,* banker Jews, moneylending Jews, are paying, *paying,* to save their own kind. This is the very reason Hitler is killing Jews!" he had screamed in Bolek's office behind the showroom.

The band of boys and girls had passed. The bleating of car horns behind him jolted Weinglass. We turned uptown on Broadway, behind a trolley now. The color had faded from Bolek's lips. He was making himself rigid. Weinglass was breathing hard, his chronic congestion producing deep growling sounds. He twisted his body away from Bolek.

"*I will have it,*" Bolek exploded. "You think last year was good? Last year was nothing. The world has never seen a collection like this. I *will* have an orchestra! I *will* have the Plaza ballroom! I *will* hire Claudette Colbert—"

"Not with my money," Weinglass said. "I will never permit it."

"I am not a rag peddler, Weinglass. I'm showing furs, you horse prick! Do you know what it is, *furs?* Mink and sable! That is furs." Bolek was howling like an animal. "This is not shawls," he sang, "this is not dish towels. *It is furs!*"

"You think I don't know furs? A Weinglass not know furs? It is in my blood, *my blood*, do you hear? For generations—"

"Generations? You? You have scarcely cut your *paes*—"

"And *you*, you are not exactly J. P. Morgan, Mr. Boleslaw *Man-del-baum*." Weinglass articulated each syllable of Bolek's old name, no longer used, not even known. It was on the advice of his partners that Bolek had changed it. "You can't have a business in America called Mandelbaum's," they told him during a bridge game at the Dakota. "In Warsaw, it had to be. In America, you have to make pretty boxes, a little crown over *Prince*, a little lion, perhaps a leopard, ha-ha."

"Back to the ghetto, rag merchant!" Bolek screamed at Weinglass now.

I kept drawing. They could threaten to kill, they could jump up and down, banging their fists. A stranger might think they were about to pull knives or call lawyers. In fact, they were about to give each other expensive gifts for Christmas. They would continue to share bank managers, accountants, tailors. And if Weinglass's wife, Basia, should need a coat to wear to the opera, Bolek would come up with just the perfect little ermine or chinchilla. He would fit her, he would flatter her, he would touch her monumental breasts with a wandering finger as he shaped the coat to her body.

As we approached Eighty-fourth Street, where Sophie and Magdalena lived, Weinglass didn't even bother to pull over to the curb. He jumped out of the car in the middle of Broadway, slammed the shiny striped door, and walked across the avenue to hail a taxi going downtown. "The car! You are responsible!" Weinglass shouted from the other side. A cab stopped and he got inside. "The car is perfect! Remember that, Mr. Mandelbaum!" he yelled out the open window.

"May your prick be marinated in brine!" Bolek yelled back, and, trembling, he slid behind the wheel and lurched the car over to the curb. As soon as the whitewalls squeaked against the sidewalk, I got out and ran the block and a half to Sophie's, our real home, our home away from the hotel.

Maggie, Sophie's daughter, with her honey-colored hair and thick eyebrows, was my age. She had arrived in New York a year before us. Maggie and I had played together in Warsaw, crawling out of our prams in Lazienki Park, trading chestnuts, pulling hair. Toward the end, our games became riskier, more illicit, as we found excuses to discover each other's bodies.

On our very first reunion in America, on a sunny day in Battery Park, the instant that Bolek and I stepped off the ferry from Ellis Island, I saw Maggie as alien, no longer like me. She had become an American while I, with the din of bombs and bullets still in my ears, was a foreigner in her land. Those few murderous months had made all the difference. I gaped at Maggie's strangeness, the way her feet were firmly planted, the extra space she seemed to command with her arms behind her back, her chest protruding. Maggie—my personal immigration officer—examined me, inspecting curiously with her special look, with her chin down and only the smallest moon segments of her eyes visible. She, too, was studying a stranger, an intruder in her paradise.

At that time, I still wasn't clear about who got out and who didn't, who got all the way out, who was plucked en route and dumped into one mass grave or another, who was crushed, who disappeared, who was left unscathed. Now I know, more even than I want to know, but then I knew only that Maggie and her parents left before the bombs.

Kor, the father, was with them in Battery Park that day. A large, imposing man with a cape around his shoulders, he stood behind Sophie and Maggie, aloof, distracted. His hands were clasped behind his back, he was looking up at the passing clouds. "Do you remember Mr. Kor?" Bolek asked me. "He is an artist, like Goya."

On that first day, driving to their place, squeezed into a single taxi, I had difficulty breathing. And when a plane flew overhead on its peaceful descent to some nearby friendly airport, I reacted like a trapped bird knocking about from window to window, desperate to get out. Maggie had been frightened. "What's he doing?" she sobbed, holding my arm, pulling at me. "They have come from the war," Sophie had said.

Now, as I returned with Maggie and Sophie, Bolek was once again composed, the color back in his face. He had walked to

15

Eighty-sixth Street, where he'd bought a large box of pastries. The act of buying was Bolek's most effective therapy, his cold shower, his good night's sleep. Gifts smoothed all his rough edges. Once he had the butcher deliver to Enid Swope's office at *Mirabelle* a large, juicy crown roast of lamb with all the little bone ends shod in white paper booties. When my friend Melvin had his bar mitzvah, Bolek had sent a vat of herring in sour cream to the grand ballroom of the Mayflower. Today, I was relieved to find only pastries in the front seat of the car.

Maggie snuggled up to the window opposite mine and looked out. I took up my sketchbook again. "What are you drawing?" Maggie asked almost immediately.

"Wait and see," I said.

She tried to follow the quick lines I was making. She moved toward me. "What is it, Adam?" she asked.

"Can't you tell? I'll kill myself if you can't tell."

"But you weren't even *looking* at me," Maggie said, so pleased that she dug her chin into my shoulder.

"I can draw you in my sleep," I told her.

I loved bringing drawings and melodies to Maggie. I drew better when she was there. I memorized fragments of opera, since Bolek and I had already begun to go to the Met regularly, and I brought these fragments to Maggie. As we sped toward Connecticut in Weinglass's Continental, I hummed a tune from Richard Strauss. After much difficult humming, Maggie was perplexed. She looked at me from down under, her eyebrows arched. *"Der Rosenkavalier,"* I said as I watched her try to lock the melody into her mind. "Richard Strauss," I added as Maggie smiled.

Bolek hogged the middle of the highway all the way up to Westport. Although this had once been the expression of his world view, now it was simply bad driving. In Poland, only Bolek and Marshal Smigly-Rydz, the commander of the Polish Army, had owned powder-blue Packards. Smigly-Rydz had a motorcycle escort in front and behind, wherever he went. He didn't care whom he ran off the roads. Bolek, in the name of democracy, felt this privilege should be his as well, and he took enormous risks speeding recklessly down the few passable

Polish roads. But in America he felt humble. He was willing—in fact thrilled—to be taken for just another American.

"You should let the cars behind you pass, darling," Sophie said. Bolek moved over and a line of cars went by, their drivers glaring. Bolek smiled, glad to be alive, glad to be sharing the American highways. A moment later he took his place in the middle again.

It was a miracle that Bolek was transporting us without incident. Someone must have always watched over him. He got out of jams as magically as he found treasures. In New York, Prince Casimir Furs grew like a sunflower, and who knew why? It was Bolek, charmed and charming, Bolek with his clear blue eyes and boxer's bumpy nose, his sweeping gestures, the sudden hand slap to his high forehead, the chin raised in a Mussolini-like arrogance, the unexpected smile. Bolek had gotten us out of that burning, stinking Europe, "out of the oven," he had called it, even before we learned what that really meant.

Magic hung over our lives, like the magic of my swallowing this American language whole, with its improbable syntax, its nonsensical spelling and pronunciation. Even Bolek, who loved seeing me so quickly Americanized, could hardly believe it. He stared wide-eyed, hoping to discover the trick, as my Polish became flawed, as my tongue could no longer twist into the gymnastic diphthongs and triphthongs, as I was finally left with only the barest Polish vocabulary, unable to express myself without the aid of English. I don't think Bolek ever knew that it hurt my mouth to say some English words. My tongue never tapped my palate gently enough to master the American *L*. Anyone who listened to me carefully could hear my Slavic childhood. My best conjuring act was in the sketchbooks, where I could make *anything* appear.

"Let's see what my favorite artist is doing," Sophie said, reaching for my sketchbook. She began leafing through it, stopping here and there to show Bolek. The pad was full of portraits, including my own, trying to look like Clark Gable, though I had just a trace of fuzz sprouting on my upper lip, and eyebrows that grew together in the middle. "Looks and brains and talent," Sophie said. "How did you manage to have it all, my precious?"

Sophie's English was much better than any other grown-up in the émigré group, and like an advanced swimmer among beginners, this Esther Williams of the language stroked through the frills and flourishes of English prose, making herself the envy of all the dog-paddlers, like Bolek. Languages were her livelihood. She was fluent in some dozen of them, including Czech and Hungarian. She read great Russian novels in the original and translated war documents for a secret office of the American government, which added immensely to her allure in the eyes of Weinglass and old man Spektor, Bolek's other thick-tongued partner.

Sophie had her very special allure for me, too. She had a soft, full figure with breasts that Bolek called his treasures. Especially after I had read a book called *French Aunt*, which my friend Melvin and I bought in a hole-in-the-wall bookstore near Times Square, my Sophie fantasies were sanctioned, even ennobled, by a great European tradition of teacher-aunts.

"You will follow upon the footsteps of the sublime Raphael, the mighty Rubens," she said to me. "Oh, my God, if only you were a little older. Who could resist you?"

"Oh, mother," Maggie said with disgust.

We entered the state of Connecticut. The day was clear and cold. Inside the car we baked pleasantly. Bolek smiled and hummed, sometimes mimicking the grand sweep of the lovely parkway with a gesture. Maggie asked for an apple, which Sophie had managed to cram into her fine alligator handbag. She polished it with a small embroidered handkerchief.

Maggie reached across to touch Bolek's shoulder. "This shall be precisely the ideally suited house for you and Adam," she assured him sweetly.

Sophie turned to hand Maggie the shiny apple. "Darling," she said, "that's a stiff way of expressing yourself. Try to find something less formal. . . ."

Maggie moved back to her window. She took a loud bite out of her apple. She hated having her language corrected by Sophie, and Sophie could not stop correcting us all—all except

Bolek, who seemed hopeless. I couldn't always tell whether it was Maggie's Polish language, like mine, that intruded, injecting a stilted phrase from time to time, or her need to speak like Bette Davis. Bette Davis was Maggie's favorite actress. Maggie adored Bette Davis. I tried to like her, too, but to no avail. Bette Davis made me feel bad.

Maggie handed the apple core back to her mother, who put it inside a paper napkin, then into her handbag again.

It was well after noon when we found the Westport house. Enormous elms and maples stood around it, encircling the gabled Victorian structure, which looked like a ship in a bottle. A brown stubble of grass poked through the snow-covered field to one side, where groups of children pulled sleds up into the pinewoods above, then weaved down through the trees.

Bolek parked the big Lincoln on the street and we began to make our way up the slippery path, Bolek in his paper-thin handmade shoes, Sophie in the seal coat and high heels. Bolek slid, kept himself upright, arms and legs working like a windmill. "He was a champion ice skater," Sophie whispered, hanging on my arm to keep herself from falling. I was already the tallest of them, as well as the warmest, always steaming, unbuttoning, loosening. Bolek said I was like a bull, an image I cherished.

"Look at that," Sophie said, pointing at the house. We all knew right away what astonished her. There were no shades on the windows and the curtains were drawn back. We could clearly see two people fussing around a Christmas tree inside.

"In America, there is nothing to hide," Bolek pronounced. "Not in the real America."

Maggie was the first to reach the front door with its holly wreath and brass knocker. The bell chimes brought the couple to the door, their arms outstretched and welcoming. He was tall, in a long cardigan sweater with leather buttons. She, half his size, was gray-haired, with gold-rimmed eyeglasses hanging from a chain around her neck.

"Mr. Casimir, is that right, sir?" Mr. Carlson said in a booming voice, pumping Bolek's hand. Sophie introduced the rest of us.

It was not until we were well inside, surrounded by the maple furniture and the flowered slipcovers, inside that pumpkin-colored glow, that we stood like a band of gypsies who knew only the interior of their own wagon. Family portraits hung on the walls, which were busy with the gay patterns of stenciled paper. There was a cat, there was a dog, a big black Labrador who nuzzled his wet nose into our hands and wagged his long tail happily, hitting Bolek's suit, thud, thud.

Mrs. Carlson was holding Sophie's hands, proposing that they inspect the kitchen. Mr. Carlson tried to interest me in his stamp collection.

"Do you know these people?" I whispered to Maggie.

She looked at me strangely. "Of course not," she said.

"What are we doing here?" I asked Bolek, who shot me a stern look. I went out into the car for my sketchbook, and when I returned, everyone was upstairs touring the house. I sat myself down by the window facing the sledding hill and began sketching.

They came down the stairs, chattering like family. Maggie stepped behind me to watch my landscape unfolding. "It was wonderful," she said. "They even showed us the inside of their medicine cabinets."

"Sounds great," I said.

"You grump," Maggie said, and touched the back of my neck with her warm fingers.

Maggie paid attention to every detail. She was full of questions about the house, about the Carlson family. "My God," she whispered to me, stepping away from the group, "they were all *born* in this house."

"The news doesn't thrill me," I said.

But Maggie would have been happy curled up, with Fred the Labrador at her side, on this glowing American hearth. Mrs. Carlson provided her with the family photo album. "I just love your family," Maggie told her.

Bolek displayed his entire repertoire of courtly manners—not much language, just grand gestures of appreciation and understanding—showing empathy, love, conviviality, entering into a wordless confederacy with Mrs. Carlson on every subject. At one point, Bolek took her hand and kissed it. Mrs. Carlson was totally charmed.

"We don't have to stay any longer," I whispered to Bolek.

But now it was Mr. Carlson's turn. He took Bolek by his elbow, me by mine, and led us out the kitchen door, down a couple of stairs. "I'm sure you have a hobby, Mr. Casimir," he said. "This, sir, is mine." We were in an unfinished shed with a cracked cement floor. Dried-up remnants of leaves gathered in the corners. I recognized some oil cans, brooms, and flowerpots. Over rough wooden shelves hung strange-looking tools, some like oversize forks, some like spoons, scissors mounted on poles, shears made for giants. Neither Bolek nor I had a clear notion of what we were looking at. "Of course, if you decide to rent, we will leave it all," Mr. Carlson said, "including the lawn mower." He beamed with pride, the lord of this weird domain. "And what is your hobby, Mr. Casimir?"

I didn't know how to translate the word into Polish. "He wants to know what you do when you're not working," I told Bolek.

"When I'm not working? I am thinking of work. I go out with women—"

"That's not what he means," I said. "He means something like stamp collecting."

"What about the opera?" Bolek asked me. "No," he corrected, "tell him I race cars."

"That's fascinating," Mr. Carlson said. "Where do you race cars, Mr. Casimir?"

"Tell him in Poland. I have no time here." Sophie had told me the story of Bolek's big moment at the Monte Carlo Grand Prix. He was actually signed up to drive a Polish hand-built machine and was saved just in time by the arrival in Warsaw, two days before the big event, of the king and queen of Rumania, who wanted to be fitted at Mandelbaum's.

Mr. Carlson urged Bolek to find a new hobby. "It is the reason we Americans live long lives," Mr. Carlson said.

Back inside, Mrs. Carlson, Sophie, and Maggie were putting out coffee and tea, brown gritty bread, butter, and homemade jams. We sat down to eat and I could see that Bolek was not only restless now but upset at being caught empty-handed. We had finished the box of pastries in the car and now he had *nothing,* no ermine tails, no bottles of Worth perfume, no eclairs. The business of giving was *his* game, but these Americans were beating him at it. Suddenly, noticeably, he stopped being polite. He was ready to go.

The Connecticut sky was streaked with purple and pink and the sledders on the hill had gone home. Inside Weinglass's Lincoln, Bolek, Sophie, and Maggie were jabbering like parrots. Maggie was leaning forward, holding hands with her mother.

Sophie said, "Maybe we could all move in together."

Bolek kissed her hand.

"What about school?" Maggie asked.

"There must be schools in Westport," Sophie said.

"It is too long to drive to New York," Bolek said.

"Let's go to the train station to ask about New York trains," Sophie said.

Then I shut them out of my consciousness.

I was drawing a figure. In the fading light, my pencil dug into the sketchbook as if it wanted to hurt it, etching in my lines, shading with a spastic fury. It was as if my hand and my mind were possessed, obeying some dark imperatives of their own, and the image that was emerging took me by surprise.

The face on the page looked wild, frenetic. Its nose was so small that it looked absent, skull-like. The mouth was open, gaping, with its animal teeth bared, and the eyes were huge black disks in a sea of white, a look of pure terror. I had seen this face before and its terror had touched off my own.

"What are you doing?" Maggie asked.

"Nothing."

"Are you drawing?"

"Yes."

"Can I see it?"

I closed the sketchbook.

"Is it something you saw at the Carlsons' or are you making it up?"

"I'm making it up."

Maggie moved to the edge of the seat again to join the conversation in front.

Even though the sky was black now, my pencil found the terrified face and continued drawing the neck and shoulders. The arms of the figure swept upward, the left hand's palm opened, the right clenched into a fist. The pencil dug into the page and broke. I closed my eyes. I saw the park, a cloudy warm day. My stomach had felt empty. I had just skinned my knee on the cobblestones beside the Prado.

"It will be cool and peaceful inside," Bolek had said.

"I don't want to go inside," I had told him.

"Inside we can forget everything," Bolek had said.

And so we had entered the cool dark rooms full of paintings. We were practically alone, the first respite after a month of running. The walls were full of gold and shiny dark surfaces with limp figures hanging on crosses.

We had walked into a room with two enormous paintings in it. In front of one, a woman dressed in black had stood weeping. A little girl clung to her legs.

"Let's go," I had said to Bolek, but he pulled me toward the painting. The man stood screaming in the center of the painting, the light of a lantern pointed directly at him. He stood there in terror, this man who was drawing himself in my lap on the Merritt Parkway. It was the moment of his death, the triggers of the firing squad already squeezed. Others in his group lay dead at his feet, and still others were marching through the darkness toward him. I had stared at him and had begun to feel his terror in my body. Like him, I had screamed, and the word that had come out of my mouth was *Papa*.

"What are you saying?" Bolek had said quietly, kneeling beside me and pulling me to him.

"Papa," I had said, the word muffled by Bolek's chest.

"Don't be a silly boy," Bolek had said, "it's only a painting."

In my mind, after that, this great Goya painting of an execution on the third of May remained confused with my father, my father who had also been shot, like that, whose face must have also formed into the pleading terror-stricken scream.

My broken pencil was pushing the sketchbook down until it

fell through my legs to the car floor. The noise woke Maggie, who had snuggled up against the window.

"What's the matter?" she asked sleepily. "You've been so strange."

"No, I haven't," I said.

"You're shaking. What is it?"

"I've been thinking. . . ."

"About what?"

"Nothing."

"Come on, tell me."

"About the war, about Spain."

"Spain?" Maggie sat up. "When were you in Spain? I didn't know you were in Spain." She knew. She knew every place we'd passed through on our way out.

"It was the last place."

"You've been *everywhere*," Maggie said petulantly.

The parkway was crowded, a long stream of headlights returning to the city. Bolek straddled the midline divider as he and Sophie talked quietly in front. Cars honked at us as they passed.

"I hated that house," I said.

"What's the matter with you, Adam?" Maggie asked.

"I don't know."

"I think I'd die if I didn't have *my* parents," Maggie said suddenly.

"I've got Bolek," I said.

She moved closer to me. "Do you want to tell me how you got to Spain?" She was whispering as if we were talking dirty. "Do you want to?"

"Yes."

The headlights on the parkway actually reminded me of crossing the border, except that then there had been a million of them. "We got out of Poland at Kuty," I began, perhaps for the twentieth time.

"Where's that?" she asked, pushing over some more.

"It's the last place before the Rumanian border. It's the last place where anyone got out. Half the Polish army got out through Kuty. Plus a lot of important people."

"Like who?"

"Like Marshal Smigly-Rydz."

"Who's he?"

"The commander of the army."

"He left Poland?"

"He even rode with us in our car."

"He did?"

"In Rumania, a couple of days later."

"Why with you? Did Bolek know him?"

"We were the only ones with gasoline. Bolek traded a fur coat for gas."

"A fur coat?" Maggie said. Sophie turned, happy to see us talking. "He gave away a real fur coat?" Maggie whispered. "How could he?"

All this made Maggie dreamy. She populated each country with her movie stars. She made everything into movies.

"Did you meet informers? Did you see partisans?"

How I wanted to provide her with the story she needed. I was sure she was thinking of Bette Davis. "Not really," I said. Maggie turned away.

"Did I ever tell you about my cousin Marek?"

She shook her head.

"He was a few years older than me. My mother said we looked alike. He tucked a hand grenade into his belly and threw himself under a German tank."

Maggie sat up. "He blew himself up?"

"And the tank."

"Did you see it?"

"Sure."

"Was he Jewish?"

I'd never thought about that. "Sure he was," I said.

Maggie leaned back and closed her eyes. As Bolek swerved in and out of the passing lane, Maggie's head with all its beautiful dark blond hair landed on my shoulder, where it stayed all the way to Eighty-fourth Street.

That night at the Buckingham, I woke up in terror. This same dread came from time to time, but that night I had gotten up before it started and smelled it coming. I walked out into our living room, wanting to wake Bolek to warn him, but I didn't. I sat on a cold chair by the window and the chill of the smooth fabric shot up my body, sending me back to bed shaking. When I woke up again, I was soaked with sweat, screaming.

The sequence in the dream was more familiar than the real events. In the dream, I am flying above my house on my bicycle. Planes are flying toward me. My face looks up, the pilots' faces down, and the bombs hurtle past me, little winged pins shining in the first rays of sunrise. One of them lands on the handlebars. It is tiny and beautiful. I flick it off. Then the house below collapses. I see people plummeting through the center of the house. My father is sitting on the stone bench in the garden.

Through the film of my tears, I saw my room at the Buckingham, ablaze with light and, in it, Bolek's face. As his mouth opened to speak, it changed into my father's face. "We are in America," Bolek was yelling through the haze. "It can't happen in America." I watched him rub his face, his whole head, rubbing it hard, wiping it all away.

"The house! The house!" I cried.

"I know, I know. It's over now."

"Mama! Mama!"

"Yes, yes," Bolek chanted through his own tears.

"It's there. Is it there?"

"Yes, yes."

"Where? Where?"

"Fucking Germans," Bolek cried.

"Mama!"

"No more. It's over."

"No more," I sobbed. I choked and coughed.

"Fucking Russians. Fucking Poles. Fucking Europe," Bolek said. I was still crying and Bolek began to chant: "May shit flow in the Vistula, in the Danube, in the Rhine . . ." He had invented this to make me laugh. And I began to laugh. He added rivers: ". . . in the Bug, in the Dnieper, in the Oder. . . ." He sat by my side in his plum-colored, monogrammed pajama top from Sulka. He never wore the bottoms.

His hand was playing with his balls. "Blood of a dog," he said. "It comes at us in dreams."

There was a movement of pink at the door. I looked up and saw Sophie in her nightgown. Bolek wiped the sweat from my forehead as Sophie took his place beside me. She leaned over to kiss me and I saw her breasts hanging grand and free inside. She sat up and I did, too. She pulled my head down to rest on her chest. "Zosia," I heard Bolek say, a reprimand. She turned to him but stroked my hair and let me stay. She smelled rich and earthy.

"Zosia," Bolek said again. Sophie stood up. She kissed me on the forehead and went back to Bolek's room. "I will take Sophie down to a taxi," Bolek said. "It's all right now?" He took my face in his hands and kissed me. Then he followed Sophie into his room to change.

With Bolek and Sophie out looking for a cab, I opened my closet door to get a sketchbook. As a rule, I slept with the closet door ajar so that the stacks of my drawings that stood like talismans on the closet floor could protect me from my dreams. These thick pads of newsprint were filled with images of *real* things, of Central Park landscapes, the horses and carriages that lined up on the south side of the park, portraits of Bolek and his friends, interiors, things with length and breadth and height, things I could see and touch.

My whole bedroom was alive with signs and symbols. Even its smell was created by me. To Bolek's horror, I kept a rag soaked with rectified turpentine inside my sock drawer. This intoxicating fragrance defied Bolek's colognes and he tried to free me of my noxious addiction. "You smell like a garbage," he would say. "It's only paint," I would tell him, protecting my sock drawer as a dog protects a bone. "Ach, my little Goya," Bolek would sometimes say.

My pencils, chalks, and erasers were lined up like soldiers on top of my dresser while above it hung rags in several shades of gray, each having seen service in the smudging of charcoals. Goya reproductions were tacked to the wall above my bed.

Bolek returned and got into his pajama top again. He brought back the seal coat he had lent Sophie for the day and wrapped it around me. He often lent his women stoles and jackets, for the opera, the theater, a weekend in the country, and he always remembered to collect the furs afterward. "It looks like it was made for you, darling," Bolek told me.

We sat in the living room. An occasional car sped up or down Sixth Avenue below. "It's peaceful downstairs," Bolek said, holding his balls with one hand. "We are lucky. We are starting from the beginning. We have beautiful America, movies and baseball, California and Roosevelt. We are in paradise."

"What about the house in Westport?"

"It's beautiful, too," Bolek said.

"It's not for us, is it?"

"Don't worry, darling," Bolek said. "We will stay right here."

I put my arms around his neck and kissed him.

"I was dreaming of our house," I said.

"I know. You must try to get that out of your mind. All that is over."

"My father sat in the garden reading the paper."

"Your father? No, he wasn't there—"

"Yes, he was. With his newspaper."

"Yes?"

"We had a beautiful garden, didn't we? Blue pansies. Those tools in Mr. Carlson's garage were garden tools," I said.

"I didn't see tools."

"I remember Tadzik, the gardener."

"Yes, a sweet boy from the village."

"I saw him cut in two."

"I know."

"Did we have paintings on the walls?"

"The family portraits were in Warsaw," Bolek said. "In the country we had French landscapes."

"Pani Fela was in the house, too. Three people died."

"Fela," he said with distaste. "Well, she loved you, that's sure. But you can't trust the Poles. She had a German boyfriend."

"She did?"

"She may have brought the planes."

"Why? What do you mean?"

"She was flashing a mirror."

"But she was inside. The planes killed her, too."

"Who knows what's true?" Bolek said. He got up, yawned, and stretched. "But that's all ancient history," he said. "I'll make tea."

I followed him into the kitchenette, the seal coat wrapped around me. I was suddenly starved. On a pad of paper napkins inside our tiny Frigidaire lay a few hardened canapés from a party at Prince Casimir's, the bits of caviar like bird food, the Nova Scotia stiff at the edges and glistening with oil. I took a round matzoh from the shelf above. In the morning I would make my Sunday run to the bakery.

We drank tea with lemon in glasses. Bolek picked up a *Vogue*, looked through it, showed me the Prince Casimir ad. The name was, as always, scrawled in Bolek's big, loose handwriting. "Can you draw this coat, darling?" Bolek asked. "Let's see if all that talent is good for something." I took up the magazine and, with an unsteady hand, copied carefully, wanting to impress him. "More loose, more free," Bolek said as he watched me draw.

When Bolek got up to go to the bathroom, I followed him in. He peed, then flushed by lifting his foot to press the plunger. I had seen him do that countless times—with his fancy shoes, his slippers, his neatly pedicured bare feet—and always something about the act moved me to think that Bolek could do anything, do it anywhere, that he could learn new ways, that his nature was forever youthful, gay. It seemed to me to be an American gesture, an American way of flushing. The European way was ponderous, with pulling, pushing, hauling.

How different Bolek was from my father. My father was so careful, so methodical, everything in its place. I couldn't imagine my father as a young man, taking shortcuts, being stylish. So set in his ways, my father would have bent over this toilet, studied the plunger, pushed and observed, and in an instant he would have mapped, in his head, the water path from the river to this valve.

"What was wrong with my father?" I asked. The subject was always painful.

"Nothing was wrong. He was a quiet man. Why do you think something was wrong?"

"He didn't spend much time with us."

"He loved you, you can be sure of that."

"Why did he leave us?" I asked.

"He didn't know what he was doing." Bolek paused. "Maybe he didn't want to leave your mother."

I had thought this same thing, over and over, in the middle of sleepless nights. It always hurt so much to think it.

"Sometimes a man can be driven crazy," Bolek said.

"Was he crazy?"

"No."

My father came with us as far as Kuty, and there, as we inched our way forward with the immense number of cars waiting to cross, he touched my hand, then got out of the back seat, closed the car door gently, and slowly disappeared among the crowd of cars and wagons. As if paralyzed, I watched his full head of curly black hair for a while until it vanished. A few days later, as we rested in a small town inside Rumania, one of Bolek's friends in the Polish government told him that my father had been captured by Polish peasants. He said my father was shot, but I didn't believe it. I'd known then, as I knew now, that he was alive, walking east.

It was three in the morning and Bolek and I were wide awake. Outside, the noise of garbage trucks and the occasional drunk reeling along Fifty-seventh Street carried in the sharp, clear air as if it were happening just outside our windows, not twelve stories down. In this room, where four years of living did not contribute a single personal touch to the oversize table lamps, the pale thin carpets, the rayon-covered chairs, Bolek stretched out on the couch, two pillows under his head. He closed his eyes and told me of the huge mahogany table in his office in Warsaw, covered with umber pelts of mink, the fine hairs of the fur sliding on the lustrous wood, smooth as glass. He talked of the beauty of sables draped on blue velvet Empire chairs, on his deep red Persian carpet. He told me about the

Leningrad fur auctions, where his friend, the head auctioneer, would take him in before anyone else and where, on entering the great hall, he would inhale deeply the rancid stench of dead animal skins as if they were the breath of life itself.

He told me of the feel of furs, and as he did, his penis grew. He began to talk of women, the feel of women, his love of women. "Adam, Adam, it is like heaven on earth to feel the smooth skin, to feel it swell, so gently, to breathe their breath, to hear their music . . ." He stroked himself. "And, darling, what it is like between their legs . . ." He became embarrassed, put a cushion on his belly. "Are you warm, darling?" I nodded. "Then bring me the seal coat."

The streets below were beginning to gray with the coming of dawn. "Let's have a look at this coat. Bring it closer." Bolek examined it, stroking the pockets, taking the sleeves in his hands. He closed his eyes, running the soft black fur across his face. "Come here, darling," he said quietly, pulling the seal toward us, black as pitch with the table lamps behind it. He brought it closer to his mouth and gently blew on it, the air darkening the delicate hairs even more, like a pool of spreading black ink. "Touch it," he said, inhaling and capturing all the seal smell. He looked at me. "It is so beautiful, so supple," he said. I stroked it as he had done.

We slept late on Sunday. When the desk called up after noon announcing Mr. Traister, it woke us. "Traister," I heard Bolek saying, "do me a favor, my friend." There was a pause. "What? In English?" A longer pause, then: "Traister, bread . . . yes, yes, *bread. . . . In the bakery,*" he said triumphantly.

Every Sunday Mr. Traister, a small bald man with thick glasses, came to give Bolek an English lesson. These sessions seldom ran smoothly. Bolek was suspicious of Traister's English, persuaded that to speak it would prove embarrassing. Still, he was too loyal to dump Traister, once persecuted by the University of Krakow. Traister tolerated Bolek's abuse because he couldn't find better work. "Who needs a Mickiewicz scholar in America?" he would shrug.

Bolek sat up on pillows in bed while Traister sat across the room in a chair, drilling him. He was trying to get Bolek to remember the past tense of some important verbs. "I say, I said," said Traister. "I go, I went. I am, I was." But Bolek had learned about the auxiliary *did* and would not repeat Traister's examples.

"I say, I did say," Bolek said. "I go, I did go. I am, I did am."

"Mr. Casimir," Traister interrupted, "you may not do that—"

"May not? Why may not? You imbecile, you horse! Fucking bone of a dog!"

"Mr. Casimir, your rampage is to avoid," Traister said, pronouncing the word *rampage* as if it were French, and giving *avoid* three syllables.

Bolek sprang out of bed, his penis hanging out, rampaging around Traister's chair.

"Please to stop, Mr. Casimir. You are grown-up person."

Bolek just didn't have an ear for English, though English was not the only language he managed to botch. Most Polish merchants—especially those like Bolek who did a lot of business outside Poland's borders—were adept at languages. But not Bolek. His Polish was elegant, descriptive, even poetic, but he bungled French, German, Russian, and English indiscriminately. It took him ages to tune his ear to English, and during these learning years his language muddles were becoming legend in the New York fashion world.

One Saturday I had witnessed Bolek fitting a fur coat with the help of his *directrice*, Mlle. Sacha. They were both fluffing and rearranging the coat on Elsa, the model, pulling at the sleeves, patting down the shoulders. Mlle. Sacha, a tall lady from Wilno who faked a French accent, had said, "Eet ees a leetel—*comment dirais-je?*—asymmetrical."

"What?" Bolek had said.

Mlle. Sacha had wiggled the fur to accentuate its unevenness. "Eet ees asymmetrical," she had repeated.

Bolek turned white. He stared at the long, bony Elsa, straight from a handbook of Aryan types, wagging his finger threateningly. "Who is this anti-Semitical? *Who is anti-Semitical?*" he screamed. "You, you cunt?"

When Traister left, Bolek got back into bed and I continued drilling him gently. But now he wanted some slang, "Some argot," he said. I found a promising article in the *Times* about the 101st Airborne Division besieged at Bastogne. "General Anthony McAuliffe," the *Times* reported, "surrounded on all sides by an overwhelming German force, replied to the enemy commander with the single word 'Nuts!' " I was overjoyed.

"Nuts," said Bolek, "what is this 'nuts'?"

I told him as best I could in Polish. He laughed so hard he cried. As he caught his breath, he said, "You know, darling, this is a real Polish answer. It is Polish humor and Polish balls. What is this general's name again?" I repeated it. "Makoliev," Bolek said. "It could be a Polish name, you know." He thought about it for a moment, smiling. "Could be a Jew originally, a Polish Jew. Here, anything is possible, even a Jewish general." Bolek put his arms behind his head. "I am so moved by America," he said.

That evening Bolek asked me to go to dinner with him and Enid Swope. With people like Enid, who spoke no Polish, he needed a translator and who safer than his nephew?

As we sat at Leon and Eddie's, my initial job was to avoid silence. Enid and I talked of my school, we talked of the war, we talked of Poland. Enid was the editor of *Mirabelle*, and, Bolek said, "from the best American family." A black veil hung in front of her pretty face, her small upturned nose, her limpid blue eyes, her full lips painted scarlet.

Bolek had never heard the name Enid before. He had me pass on this confession to her. "You can call me Didsy," Enid said, "my best friends do."

Bolek said he couldn't. I knew I couldn't either.

"Tell me about 'Bolek,' darling, and about 'Casimir,' " Enid said, lifting her veil to sip her manhattan.

Bolek pronounced both names in Polish for her, Boleslaw Kazimierz, and I began translating in earnest. "He was named for Boleslaw the Bold," I said.

"Really?"

"Tell Miss Enid," Bolek instructed, "that the Bold Boleslaw made war on the Germans . . ."

"But it isn't a Jewish name, is it? Don't Polish Jews—"

"Tell her," Bolek interrupted, obviously understanding the gist of the English, "that it is possible I was named for another Boleslaw, Boleeslaw the Pious." I did. Enid was puzzled. "That Boleslaw," Bolek said, "gave a charter of rights to the Jews in his domain, and Casimir the Great—the reason I am Casimir—took those rights and gave them to all the Jews in Poland."

"The Jewish people I know on Seventh Avenue have such different names," Enid said, accepting a thin Turkish cigarette from Bolek.

"In our family, never," Bolek said, "not for generations. We are very cosmopolitan."

"I am named after Adam Mickiewicz, the great Polish poet," I volunteered, sensing Bolek's discomfort with the subject of Jewishness.

"We love Mickiewicz," Bolek explained. "He kept the spirit of Poland alive."

"It's a beautiful name," Enid said.

"Adam and Magdalena," Bolek reflected, smiling over his private memory. "It wasn't every one of us who could give his children those names. It cost us plenty."

Enid Swope looked enchanted. She was being swept through the steppes, the dark forests of a mythic landscape. "There is so much to learn in this world," she said. "Who took the money?"

Bolek looked trapped, as if he weren't sure he should divulge such information. "The rabbi of Warsaw," he said confidentially.

Enid smiled. She understood. Apparently in her religion, too, one could buy such things. She buttered a roll. "Tell me, Adam," she said, "who is your favorite painter?" I told her. "Goya?" she said, surprised. "Ah, Francisco de Goya y Lucientes," she said, stressing the Castillian c's in a way I'd never heard before. "He made such darling children in little red costumes, such adorable faces. A delicious painter," Enid said.

Bolek raised his wine and they clinked glasses, smiling.

"Tell your uncle," Enid said as she looked into his eyes, "that I will be in Southampton next weekend. Alone. Be sure to say alone." I did as I was told. Bolek took her hand and lingered over it, nuzzling it. "Tell him he can drive with me or take the train, whichever he prefers." Bolek preferred to drive with Enid.

"Ask Miss Enid if she would like to come with me to the opera," Bolek told me.

"The opera?" I asked, my dissatisfaction evident. The opera, like our Friday dinners, was *ours*.

"The theater," Bolek corrected.

"Yes, darling," Enid said. "I'd love to. What will we see?"

Bolek turned to me. "What is playing?" he asked under his breath. "Say something."

"*Oedipus at Colonnus*," I said. It was the one play I had seen with my class that year.

"*Oedipus?*" asked Enid Swope, having expected, I suppose, something more romantic.

"With Jed Seacliff," I assured her.

"Doesn't he only play gangsters?" Enid asked.

"He's a terrific Oedipus," I told her.

"I don't think it's for us," Enid said.

Toward the end of the week, they went to the *Ziegfeld Follies*, much more to their liking.

And Monday morning, as I was getting ready to start my long trek to school, Bolek was on the phone, arranging with Schuller, the assistant foreman at Prince Casimir's, to drive up to Westport with three dozen yellow roses, a basket of assorted fruits, and a note written by Sophie informing the Carlsons that we would not be able to take the house.

2

Bolek went through cars as if they were handkerchiefs. I don't know if it was his third or his fourth Lincoln that transported us to Enid's place in Southampton, a trip I'd avoided for nearly three years.

On the Manhattan side of the river, Maggie and I sat silently in back, not wanting to distract Bolek from finding the entrance to the tunnel. As soon as he emerged on "the fresh-air side" and Enid began helping him thread his way through the Island's parkways, everyone relaxed. Bolek opened his window and stretched. Maggie whispered to me: "Bolek and Enid look so good together, like a prosperous American couple off for a day in the country."

The back of Bolek's bald head shone in the sunlight. Enid traced her scarlet fingernail lightly across his neck. She seemed solidly installed, happy and pretty in her red beret and sand-colored suit. I had never felt quite right with them, a fashion-industry couple, a warlike match, the emperor and his Maria Louisa. But this time Enid made it hard for me not to go by asking Maggie to come, too. I knew she couldn't have been exactly thrilled about spending a weekend with Sophie's daughter.

"I feel disloyal," I told Maggie.

"That's okay. Mother's away, too," Maggie said. "In New Canaan, at Count Kaczka's."

"Are they sleeping together?"

"Of course not, Adam," Maggie said. "Count Kaczka is married. Besides, he's ancient." She looked at me with a mischievous little smile.

"He's not *that* old," I said. "That man would do it to his own grandmother."

"Adam," Maggie said, "that man's family goes all the way back to the Piast dynasty." I put my hand on Maggie's and felt the touch of it down to my toes. "But Enid," Maggie said, "Enid suits Bolek."

"I don't know why you say that."

"Bolek needs an American woman," Maggie explained. "Mother will keep him in Warsaw forever."

Just as I tried to hold on to every little bit of my Europeanism, my vaguely Polish accent, my dreams alive with Polish terror, so Maggie encouraged her own melting into the American pot with her quick opinions, the big space she made around herself, her "real American" speech, liberated by her elocution teacher even from her turgid Bette Davis-isms. I went with Maggie often to her acting classes, her speech classes, her dance classes, both modern and ballet. Maggie, ever more womanly, was being coached, groomed, handled, assaulted with increasing zeal by all her teachers. Even stooped, cleft-palated Mr. Matuchenko, once a taskmaster for the Ballets Russes, could not keep his hands off her. "I can get up there myself, thank you anyway, Mr. Matuchenko," Maggie would say as Matuchenko's shaky fingers traveled up and down her strong, shapely torso, pretending to hoist her to her toes.

In the front seat, Enid was directing Bolek from expressway to expressway. This new Lincoln was like the others, except that it was cream-colored, the cream of sweet desserts. Its soft leather interior was a delectable fruity shade, *fraise des bois,*

Enid called it. In his first Lincoln, which he bought shortly after our Westport trip, Bolek didn't quite make the left turn off the Fifty-ninth Street bridge. Coming back to the city late one Sunday night, he crashed through the plate-glass window of the Allen Carpet Company. Luckily, only the car and the store were demolished. Bolek, with magic clinging to him like a glove, walked out with minor cuts.

We were in the country now and I could smell the sea breezes. It was May and green fuzz blanketed the trees. I played with Maggie's fingers, one finger at a time. "It's so easy to be an American," Maggie said. "It feels so right. Don't you feel free here?"

"Free?"

"I feel it," Maggie reported. "I don't mean free like free from prison, more like carefree. . . ." She looked me straight in the eye. "I mean loose, unbuttoned. . . ." I wanted to pick her hand up from the seat, bring it to my lips, kiss it in a show of Warsaw gallantry, but I squeezed it instead.

Bolek let me drive the last twenty miles, while he sat stiff and scared next to me. We were passing freshly plowed fields, ramshackle collections of cottages and bungalows, the feudal debris that accumulates around the rich, whose estates, like Enid's, were out of sight behind tall hedges.

At the end of a tree-lined driveway, Enid's house, the Petit Trianon, stood stark and alone, a tidy white box packed with small rooms, some of which were recent extensions that spilled out of the original structure on the beach side. Bolek and Enid fit the house well, while Maggie and I, now practically the same height, had to stoop under the low door lintels. For Bolek, not quite five-foot-six, all America was a land of giants. "It is unhealthy," he had told me once in the elevator going from the Boys Department to the University Shop at Saks. "The heart has to pump too hard. Blood never gets to the feet."

We were helped into our rooms by a family of caretakers, a gray-haired couple and their son. They seemed particularly fond of Bolek, who piled their arms high with cheeses, wines, and fruit from the city. By the time Maggie and I came downstairs, everyone, including the Murchesons, Enid's Southampton neighbors whose ancestors had settled the town, was standing around in a lovely small conservatory, still hot from the day's sun. The conversation was loud and lively, with Bolek, who was not a real drinker, leading the group in Polish toasts. "Down with the Fur and Leather Workers Union," Bolek was saying, to the apparent delight of all present. Emboldened by consensus, he forged ahead. "To our President Truman who has defeated the coal miners." No dissent here, either. The vodka was being poured freely, everyone's cheeks rosy, mouths stretched into happy grins. "And to poor President Roosevelt, the great dead god of war," Bolek said.

Maggie, frontierswoman, unbuttoned American, joined in before we even sat down. "If you toast him, Bolek, you should also toast Mrs. Roosevelt."

"You are right, Magdalena," Bolek said, raising his glass once again. "She was a very good wife."

Maggie bristled. "A good wife? If not for her, none of us would be here. She was the goddess of refugees."

Mr. Murcheson, a chunky man in a seersucker suit and white buckskin shoes, was unable to keep his eyes off Maggie. He slid over to stand beside her. "My dear," Mr. Murcheson said, "how is it possible that you have no Polish accent?"

"I was little when I came," Maggie told him.

His small dark eyes scanned Maggie's body top to bottom. "Yes, you are quite grown up now," he said, a film of sweat appearing under his eyes. "I am told that you want to be an actress. A risky profession," he said in a scratchy voice, "one in which you must be ready to do *anything.*"

Mr. Murcheson's wife, a wide, flat-chested woman sheathed in an abundance of green silk, headed toward me. She sipped her vodka as she came and draped her arm around my shoulder. "Tell me about the war," she breathed into my ear. "Tell me what you think about in the middle of the night." Her hair was like straw, nearly colorless, with just a touch of Naples yellow. "I love *your* accent," she said.

"Speaking of accents," Enid said, taking Bolek's hand in hers, "just listen to the improvement in this man's English."

"I have lost everything *but* my accent," Bolek quipped. "But

I have now the best teacher in America. And the most beautiful."

"European men," Puss Murcheson said in my ear, loud enough for all to hear. "I adore European men."

"My gallant European *chevalier*," Enid said to Bolek.

"My tip-top Zizi," Bolek said. It was the first time I had heard Bolek call Enid "Zizi," not to even mention "tip-top." It turned out to be his way of saying Didsy, as close as he wanted to come to a name he'd thought ridiculous. "Tip-top Zizi" made Maggie choke on her wine. Schuyler Murcheson happily pounded Maggie's back.

"It was all so dull before you came," Puss Murcheson told Bolek.

"Ah, it is always so in the country, madame," Bolek said.

"I mean the fashion world, Monsieur Casimir," Puss Murcheson said.

"We have been waiting for years and finally this man has brought Europe to America," Enid said.

"Fashion is not everything, Zizi," Bolek instructed her.

"I understand you had quite a business in Poland," Schuyler Murcheson said. "You people certainly are making this country a livelier place."

Maggie shot up from the piano bench we were sharing. "Who do you mean by 'you people'?" she challenged.

"I'm referring to the refugees," Schuyler Murcheson explained. "Especially the Jewish refugees. I welcome them. I welcome you, Mr. Casimir, and *all* the Jewish people. You are a remarkable people, a people who can feel at home in anyone's country."

Maggie stiffened. Bolek smiled courteously, but it was a pale smile. Schuyler Murcheson changed the thrust of his inquiry. "How did you manage such a success in so short a time, Mr. Casimir?" he asked.

Puss Murcheson had not stopped sipping from her crystal glass. The housekeeper's son, in shirt sleeves and apron, walked around refilling everyone's glass. Puss Murcheson sipped and said, "God helps small businessmen."

"What an irony, Mr. Casimir," Schuyler Murcheson continued, "that you, a man on the move, a wandering Jew, a refugee, should choose to make such transient shapes. . . ."

"What did he say?" Bolek asked me in Polish.

"That the fashion business is a strange one for Jewish refugees," I told him.

Bolek ran his hand over his head. He was struggling to remain civil, this man of short temper and big passions. "Mr. Murcheson, if you please," Bolek started, leaning forward in his wicker chair. "We are not exactly refugees as you know them." Bolek took a sip of his vodka. "I am not leaving the ghetto, Mr. Murcheson. In my showrooms on Marszalkowska—the Fifth Avenue of Warsaw—I am leaving in the Frigidaire a thousand sables and minks. I am leaving a penthouse overlooking our beautiful Vistula. I am leaving a villa in the country with a Watteau, two Canalettos, and servants." Maggie held my arm and squeezed it. Bolek was more and more engrossed in his story. "I am not like other refugees, Mr. Murcheson. We come as invited guests. Many people ask me to come to many places. My friend Balenciaga wants me in Paris, King Gustaf wants me in Stockholm, the Banco Braziliano wants me in Rio."

He lit a cigarette as we waited.

"What do I do, Mr. Murcheson?" Bolek went on. "Where do I go? To America, only to America. And in America, only to New York. And in New York, only to Fifty-seventh Street." Puss Murcheson's head dropped to her chest. Her glass of vodka remained upright. "I walk all over New York, Mr. Murcheson," Bolek said as he brushed imaginary hairs from the lapels of his suit jacket. "I walk so much I must stop to buy for myself another pair of shoes, ready-made shoes right from the store window. Then I walk to Seventh Avenue where the cutters cut, the pinners pin. 'Never!' I say to myself, 'never I will be on Seventh Avenue.' I walk to Fifth Avenue, past all the big stores, the beautiful stores, and I say to myself, 'Not here, not on Fifth Avenue, squeezed between those giants.' I know from the beginning where I will be, and that is where I am."

Puss Murcheson applauded. Bolek glared across the darkening conservatory at her. She fingered a large topaz broach pinned to her dress at the collarbone. "Fifty-seventh Street," she said, "home of the Automat."

"Home of Tiffany's," Maggie snapped angrily in Bolek's defense. She got up again. "The race is not given to the swift, nor favor to the wise, but all things depend on time and chance," she recited.

"The difference, madame," Bolek said, "between Prince Casimir and all the rest is art."

Enid's housekeeper, now in uniform, came to announce dinner. Bolek and Enid led the way and the rest of us followed. Puss Murcheson was surprisingly steady, even in the small dining room where we had to squeeze between the table and the sideboard. We took our places, two to a side, with Bolek and Enid at either end. Two silver candelabra lit the table. Between them stood three low crystal vases crammed with daffodils. Lithographs of old steamships and early etchings of Southampton hung on the dark green walls.

Everyone looked rosy with drink, but the heat I managed to trap beneath the jacket Bolek made me wear was unbearable. I thought I would faint. "You two look like brother and sister," Mr. Murcheson said to Maggie as he uncorked a second bottle of French wine that lay in a rack behind him. Maggie took my hand under the table.

"They're both wonderful artists," Enid announced. "Adam inherited all of Bolek's genius—"

"And you, Magdalena?" Schuyler Murcheson asked. "Your mother must be a beauty."

"My father's an artist," Maggie said.

"Her father," Enid said, "is none other than the renowned R. Z. Kor."

"Another success story," Schulyer Murcheson marveled. "I take my hat off to all of you."

"This Mr. Kor is not a serious man," Bolek suddenly told us. "He *plays*. He is like a child." Bolek looked at me. "Not like Goya," he added with a smile.

Maggie put down her knife and fork and stared at Bolek. She didn't look so much hurt as dumbfounded. I loosened my tie. "What are you doing? Why are you doing this again?" I asked Bolek. "You don't even *know* Kor's work."

"I don't know it? What is to know? Of course I know it," Bolek said as he took a second helping of the delicate spring lamb and tiny peas, not touching the bright green mint jelly.

"Kor is a surrealist," I said. "Do you know what *that* means? He is a friend of Max Ernst and Dali."

Bolek said nothing.

"Is Goya still your favorite painter?" Enid asked me.

"My father *loves* Adam's work," Maggie said, glaring at Bolek.

This information hit me like a bolt of lightning. "He's seen it?" I asked.

"Of course he's seen it," Maggie said. "I showed it to him. He was very moved. He *loved* it."

"*Life* magazine will be publishing an article about Mr. Kor," Enid said. Her eyes were on Bolek, apologetically and with such gentleness that he finally looked embarrassed about his petty jealousy. More than anything, though, I couldn't wait to get Maggie away from them, to ask her what she showed Kor, when, what exactly he'd said. As my mind raced with the possibility of knowing him, being guided, *initiated*, by him, the others turned to what someone must have thought to be a less quarrelsome subject, the rebuilding of Europe. But every route they took seemed to be mined.

"I'm not sure I approve of such largesse," Mr. Murcheson said, "especially after the enormous cost of fighting their war."

"I hate him," Maggie whispered in my ear. Then, aloud, "Not *their* war, Mr. Murcheson, *our* war, *my* war." I saw Maggie, with Mrs. Roosevelt at her side, as Delacroix's *Liberty.*

"Schuyler," Enid chided, "helping others is a Christian thing to do." Sweet Enid blushed. "Of course charity isn't exclusively Christian," she added.

"We are all Christians under the skin," Puss Murcheson said.

"I am surprised by you, Mr. Murcheson," Bolek said. "All Europe is rubble, so many million dead. I thought America is always wonderful to underdogs." *Underdog* and *comeback* were becoming Bolek's favorite words in English.

Schuyler Murcheson was whispering into his wife's ear. I was so hot that I stood up to go outside. Everyone had lost the nerve for conversation, and Enid moved us into a small wood-paneled den next to the dining room, where Schuyler Murcheson presided over liqueurs. Enid and Bolek talked softly to each other. Maggie and I held hands. "Can we take a walk?" I asked.

"A wonderful idea," Enid said. "The beach must be splendid." We filed out, and even Puss Murcheson, with the inexplicable reserves of some drunks, took off her shoes and stumbled down the grassy slope.

A bright moon hovered over the tip of the island and we began walking toward it. Maggie and I took off our shoes and went on ahead, dipping our feet into the cold surf. The others walked slowly, and were nearly out of earshot when we heard them shouting that they were turning back. I was happy to share the sand and ocean with just Maggie.

I took her hand as we walked on the hard sand near the water. "Did your father really say those things?" I asked.

"Yes."

"Tell me what he said."

"I showed him a whole sketchbook. It had pictures of me and a lot of Goya stuff. I didn't tell him who did it."

"He doesn't know?"

"Of course he knows, but he didn't know till after. He looked through them carefully, then he asked me who made them."

I let go of her hand. I felt like a comet, flying through the sky alone. "So, you told him," I said.

"He was surprised."

"Why?"

"Because of Bolek," Maggie said. "He said that it must be your father's genes—"

"My father?"

"You're not going to like this, Adam," Maggie warned. "He said that coming from Bolek's family, he would have expected feathers inside your head."

"You'd be surprised," I said. "Bolek's not so dumb."

"*I* know that," Maggie assured me. "I can't figure out why they don't like each other."

"Maybe because of Sophie," I said. "Do you think that's the reason?"

44

"Maybe because they're both artists . . ."

"Bolek's not an artist," I said.

"He has an artistic temperament."

"He does love opera," I said.

"He sure does," Maggie said. She hated never being invited to go to the opera with us. It was the one thing we shared with no one else.

"You know what he once did at *La Traviata*?" I asked. "When Alfredo's father told Violetta that he wanted better for his son than her, Bolek yelled down from our box, 'May cholera take you, you swine!'"

"I love Bolek," Maggie said.

"I feel so torn," I told her. "It may be the beginning of a tug-of-war," I added hopefully.

"My father isn't pulling," Maggie reminded me.

"I think of him all the time," I said. "Bolek must be afraid that Kor's the real genius."

"I guess you're right," Maggie said.

"And not just a fashion-world genius, either," I said. "What does Bolek know? The right moment to pad a goddam shoulder or sew the perfect lining, for Christ's sake."

"Bolek's great at what he does," Maggie said.

"And your father isn't just another refugee, either. He's too close. He's a Polish Jew, almost in Bolek's own circle." I suddenly hated Bolek. What did Bolek know of Tristan Tsara? Or Max Ernst? Nothing. Their Dada pranks, their politics, their poetry, were as foreign to Boleslaw Casimir, né Mandelbaum, as Einstein's search for a unified theory. On top of it all, R. Z. Kor—no longer Kornfeld, like Maggie and Sophie, not even Korn, but Kor—had more tricks up his ragged sleeve than the impresario of haute couture himself. This *other* magician, perhaps the better magician, was now to appear in *Life*, as he had already done in the pages of *Mirabelle* and *Women's Wear Daily*, Bolek's press. "It's all happening too close to home," I said, "right there on Fifty-seventh Street."

A cloudy ring formed around the moon and a tiny boat light appeared on the horizon. I took Maggie's hand again and felt its warmth travel through my whole body. "Never mind them," I said. "What about us? What about this summer?"

45

"I don't know," Maggie said, looking out to sea.

"Will you go to Vermont?"

"Oh, I don't know," Maggie said with a sigh. About a month earlier, Bolek had driven us to Vermont so Maggie could have a look at a drama camp run by one of her English teachers. Vermont felt strangely like home to all of us. Bolek said that it was like the Tatra mountains.

"Will you go?" I asked again. "I guess you will."

"I guess so," Maggie said.

"Don't you want to?"

"Don't you know anything, Adam? I want to be with *you*."

I stopped, and my shoes, which I was carrying in my hand, dropped to the sand. Maggie put her cold sandy feet on top of mine. I pulled her close.

"What about you?" she asked. Our faces were almost touching. "You're going back to camp."

"I should."

"You see?"

"They're counting on me," I said, "but I don't have to go."

"Oh, Adam," Maggie said, and buried her face in my neck. She inched her way up my feet as close as she could get and locked her arms around me. Then she touched my lips with her fingers and then with her tongue. As we tasted each other's mouth, I walked us over to a dry spot of sand. "Adam," Maggie said as we collapsed in a heap, "let's do it. If you want to."

"I want to."

"And I want to," Maggie said.

"Are you sure you want to?"

"I don't know," Maggie said.

"I think you're sure," I told her.

"Yes."

I unbuttoned her blouse. Maggie sat up and I tried to unfasten the hooks of her bra. Maggie put her arms behind her back and helped me. Then she covered her breasts with her hands and lay back on the sand. "Let's just lie here for a while," Maggie said, looking up at the starry sky. I lay on my side next to her. "It's wonderful like this," she said.

I put my hand on top of hers and we stayed like that, without moving, until I began to make spaces between her fingers so I could touch her breasts. Maggie sighed and dropped her hands. "You know what I can't wait to do?" Maggie asked.

"What?"

"To be in a play." She moved onto her side, facing me. "I've been reading a lot of plays. I'd give anything to be Emily in *Our Town*." I put my fingers to her mouth to stop her from talking, but Maggie went on. "There's a part in it where Emily and George are finding out that they want to be together, that maybe he shouldn't go away." Maggie turned on her belly, her face in her hands. "He was going to go to State Agricultural College. . . ."

"He was?" I moved close to her and ran my hands over her smooth, cold back.

"It's like you and me going off for the summer," Maggie said. She got to her feet, then settled herself down cross-legged in front of me, her hands on her knees. She was George asking Emily if she would write him a letter from State Agricultural College. Then Maggie raised her voice to become Emily. " 'I certainly will, I certainly will, George,' " Maggie declaimed. " 'It certainly seems that being away three years you'd get out of touch with things.' Then George tells her how important her letters will be. 'Just the same, three years is a long time. Maybe letters from Grover's Corner, wouldn't be so interesting after a while. Grover's Corner isn't a very important place when you think of all New Hampshire.' "

"Maggie," I begged, "please—"

"There's no end of theater in English," Maggie said. "And not just English, Adam, but *American*, too. This is such an incredible opportunity," Maggie said. "If there hadn't been a war, if we had stayed in Warsaw, nobody in the world would have understood me."

"Nobody? What does that mean?"

"Only Poles," Maggie said.

"That's not *nobody*."

"Well, you know what I mean."

More than the darkness of the night, our conversation was obscuring the fact that Maggie was half naked and I ached to express my love. "I *don't* know," I said impatiently.

"We would be speaking *Polish*, Adam. The theater would be all in *Polish*," an exasperated Maggie said.

"The Polish theater was really good and Polish actors were the best in the world," I said.

"Who told you *that?*" Maggie asked.

"Bolek."

"Bolek?" Maggie said, annoyed. "Bolek's a furrier."

"That's what he said."

"The whole world can understand *this* language," Maggie said. I sat up and began patting sand together into rows of hills, like a child. "Just because *you* don't need language, Adam, you shouldn't act so dumb."

Suddenly Maggie was up on her feet again, this time ripping the rest of her clothes off and running into the ice-cold Atlantic. I did the same and we splashed in the freezing water. I was numb inside a minute and tore out of there yelling like a cossack. Maggie thrashed about for another few minutes, then she, too, ran out, arms flailing, teeth chattering. Naked and cold, we hugged and rubbed each other's backs. Neither of us spoke. We danced around to get warm, we got dressed, then we raced back to Enid's house.

It was dark and quiet. We heard the tinkle of Enid's laughter from a second-floor bedroom, then the hum of Bolek's voice. Maggie and I climbed the three flights to our rooms, still dripping and nearly blue from the cold. I heard Maggie running the bath next door, and then she came into my room, wrapped in a big white towel. "We'll both have a bath," I suggested.

"Yes," Maggie agreed, and as we tiptoed into the bathroom, she turned the light off. Maggie got in first, then I did, and we sat at opposite ends of the tub, our knees up, my feet on top of hers.

I fished for her foot. "Mine are bigger," I said.

"No, they're the same," Maggie said, touching my feet, then her own.

"Let's turn on the light," I said, rising out of the water.

"Oh, Adam."

As I got up to do it, Maggie slid into the tub, though she couldn't hide all of herself. I thought I'd be shy, too, all exposed like this with my penis at right angles to my belly, but I wasn't. Before I got back into the tub, I put my right foot on the rim. Maggie lifted one of her feet out of the water and, heel to heel, sole to sole, we measured. "You see?" Maggie said. She was *big*. Not only her feet but everything. She had perfect breasts—how could she not, being Sophie's daughter?—but her shoulders seemed immense, like a football player's. We put our hands together and agreed that mine were bigger, though not by much. My hair was darker, but hers had darkened in the last few years, now the color of buckwheat honey, maybe molasses. We did look alike, our bodies lanky, mine all knobby, elbows and knees, Maggie's graceful and smooth. We examined each other's belly button, making believe that our genitals weren't nearby. I stuck my hand inside Maggie's mouth, feeling her gums and tongue and teeth, and she did the same to me.

"Did you ever do it?" Maggie asked. "I mean *everything*."

"No. Except in a whorehouse."

"In a whorehouse," she repeated. "Damn boys, you can do anything you like. Was it great?"

"Awful."

Maggie leaned forward. "Why, Adam? Tell me everything."

"She was very hairy . . ."

"Where?" Maggie asked.

"You know, all the way up to her belly button. She was covered with hair."

"What difference does that make?"

"I don't know. It was like grass." Maggie laughed. "Grass growing on a marble floor."

"Why did you choose her?"

"She was pretty," I said. "She didn't show me *that* at first."

"Was she the only pretty one? Didn't the others try to get your attention? You'd be surprised, Adam. The more an actress knows about people, the better an actress she is."

"A lot of them were busy. They rub up against you. They dangle their breasts right in front of your face."

Maggie touched her own beautiful breasts, not like the overused, mangled breasts of the whores. "Were they all big?" Maggie asked.

"Not all."

"What were they wearing?"

"Bathrobes."

"Ugh," Maggie said. She turned on the hot water. It trickled into our tub. "Let's go to my room," Maggie said. We got out of the tub and dried off. "Let's not do everything, Adam. Not tonight. Let's put our underpants on."

In her bed, Maggie climbed on top of me and lay there perfectly still, like Jane Russell in *The Outlaw*. We spent the night like that, with our underpants on, our arms around each other, breathing each other's breath, tasting each other's mouths. As we lay there, I realized something about the two of us. I knew that Maggie was right there, in my arms, but I also knew that she was elsewhere, hovering above us, watching us, posing us. For me it was the same. I, too, was watching. I was watching us and watching Maggie watching us.

Maggie fell asleep while I lay awake most of the night. I had just read *The Fountainhead* and wondered if Maggie would have liked to be forced into making love, like Dominique. Howard Roark *raped* Dominique, and their love reached unparalleled, spiritual heights after that. I worried about it but I knew I couldn't have done it. I realized that Howard Roark was an asshole. But what did worry me was the possibility of some other Howard Roark, a slimy Howard Roark, in Maggie's life.

Bolek and Enid spent most of the next day at the Southampton Country Club. Maggie and I went back to the empty, chilly beach. I had a clean sketchbook, and Maggie curled up next to me with a bunch of Clifford Odets plays. While I drew whatever was nearby—the beach grasses, shells, debris thrown up on the high sand by winter storms—Maggie's alto voice recited her favorite passages from *Golden Boy* and *Awake and Sing*.

There were still untouched mysteries, deeds not done, the *real* depths of Maggie unexplored, yet I did see Maggie differently now, no longer my celestial Aphrodite but a long, lithe snow leopard stalking the North American continent. She was more and more *my Maggie,* with crooked bottom teeth, a goddess with wide shoulders, large hands and feet.

Midmorning, Maggie said, "You know what I think?" She stretched out sensuously on the cold, soft sand, way up by the tufts of dune grass that fluttered in the spring wind. "I think artists are like conquerors. They make real-estate claims, like Zyga Weinglass or Columbus or Alexander the Great."

As usual, I felt that she'd put her finger right on it. I felt just like that about my drawing, as if my lines were diminishing the outside world as they enlarged mine. "I'm not going to leave the world intact," I said. "You'll see. I'll change it all. One day it'll look different because of me." I lay down next to her and pulled her close. I kissed her hair. "You're going to be a great actress," I whispered.

Maggie's face was buried in Clifford Odets as I rubbed her neck and back. "We'll *both* make it, Adam," she said lazily but with conviction. "I've never been more sure of anything."

"They'll come from all over to see you," I said.

"And you? What about you? The great Krinsky exhibit. *Adam Krinsky, American Painter,*" Maggie said.

I turned over on my back. "*The New World According to Krinsky,*" I said.

"Part of a series called *The Giants of the Twentieth Century,*" Maggie said.

"*Modern Giants,*" I ventured, "*from Goya to Krinsky.*" Suddenly I turned Maggie over and put my hands on her breasts. "Maggie," I said, "I'll never love anyone except you."

"I won't either," Maggie said. "All my life."

"We should make love," I said. "It'll be something that's just ours, our secret."

Maggie took my face in both her hands and kissed me hungrily, licking the whole inside of my mouth. "For now our secret will be that we *didn't* make love," she said.

That night at Enid's, we did almost everything else. We felt indelibly marked with a special stamp in our passports, for not doing it, for doing everything but. We said that we never needed to actually do it at all, that this way we could always be different.

*   *   *

Before Maggie went off to Vermont for the summer and I went back to my camp in Massachusetts, we gave each other gifts. The cash Bolek had slipped into my pocket to pay for summer clothes, I took to Tiffany's, where I bought Maggie pearl earrings, the highest-quality pearls put together by Viennese craftsmen. I also gave her a collection of European plays. I didn't know any of them, but after hearing about George and Emily, I thought it was important. Maggie gave me the *Treasures from the National Gallery* and a biography of Goya called *Lusty Genius*. In the end, we didn't mind going our separate ways. We both looked to the summer as another rehearsal, another test, another chunk of time to prepare ourselves for our art and for each other.

3

*I*n this, my sixth summer at Camp Kee-Nah-Wah, I was Mr. Seligman's assistant. This was both an honorary position and one burdened with all sorts of odd jobs. I was expected to teach some arts and crafts, to help out at the waterfront, and sometimes even to wait on tables in the converted cow barn at the south end of the meadow that separated the boys from the girls. Camp Kee-Nah-Wah was in a scrubby part of western Massachusetts. The yellow fields and small spruce trees that surrounded it turned a lush green around Lake Pocahontas where Mr. Seligman, the director, had made a small beach and where, every summer, he battled the creeping weeds that threatened it.

Camp Kee-Nah-Wah was never classy. It didn't compare with the trim, woodsy places where some of my Alexander Hamilton friends spent their summers, navigating their canoes down Maine rapids, riding horses bareback through Connecticut hills and dales, nor did it have the single-minded purpose, until this year, of Maggie's theater camp in Vermont.

Mr. Seligman was partial to his refugees, like me, whom he had collected and nurtured since the beginning of the war. Now that the war had been over more than a year and the photographs from the concentration camps had been published, he turned his love and energy to the plight of the Jews and the struggle for a Jewish homeland. When Bolek first saw the pictures from Auschwitz, the mass graves and the nearly dead survivors, he searched for my mother. "It is always possible," he had said. "Anything is possible." I didn't want to look. If she was there, he would tell me. For the first time in my life, Bolek dragged me to a synagogue, where we spent nearly a whole day, just sitting.

Mr. Seligman's conversion was profound, transforming Kee-Nah-Wah into a hotbed of Zionism. His zeal for good simple food and waterfront activities turned into scheming for a Jewish victory, his brisk whistle that had set a martial tone for camp life finally found its real purpose: a passionate call to arms. He hung portraits of Theodor Herzl and Chaim Weizmann on every available knotty-pine board in the big barn, in the converted milk house, the old horse barn.

At the waterfront, I swept the dock, raked the sand, burned brush, and painted new names on the canoes: *Hatikvah, Ben Hecht, Moledeth,* named for the boats that were making refugee runs to Palestine.

In my postcards to Bolek, I never mentioned the camp's new missionary fervor, for I knew it would have bothered him. "Why do you need to fill your head with all that garbage?" he would have said, especially since Sophie had assured him from the beginning that nothing could be more American than Kee-Nah-Wah and Lake Pocahontas.

While the campers lay quietly in their bunks, observing rest period, I now sat leaning against a canoe with my sketch pad, my *Treasures,* and my copy of *Lusty Genius* spread before me. Since Maggie had given me the Goya biography, I had taken it in, guzzled it, swallowed it whole. It gave me another view of Goya to sit beside the grim painter of the *Executions of the Third of May.*

I had copied his portraits of the Duchess of Alba and the

Condesa de Chinchon. I dreamed that I was in Saragossa, fighting the bulls that grazed in the pastures and captivating the eager girls at the *fonda*. Goya's life became mine. More than once, during the first week, I wandered around the rows of jerry-built bunks not knowing where I was or where I was going.

On the little piece of lakefront belonging to us, I imagined myself on the banks of the river Ebro. *Francisco's fierce, penetrating eyes, black as onyx, were as brilliant as the domes of El Pilar. He heard someone move to his right. Like an animal at bay, he spun around and saw her. His rage oozed away as he stared at her undulating along the riverbank. Suddenly he was rich in sensation. . . .* My heart pounded as I looked up from the book. Campers were sitting in rows on the sand. I hadn't heard them come down the weather-beaten stairs. *She mocked him, leaning forward. "What a wench!" he said. "Who in the devil's name is she? Her dark gaze would melt a stone saint from his niche."*

Carla Popescu was at the head of one line, looking at me. We had been campers together all these summers, the oldest of Mr. Seligman's refugees. Carla wasn't Jewish, but Mr. Seligman's compassion stretched to Communists, socialists, and Gypsies. Carla was Rumanian and looked like a Gypsy, dark and shining, with a mole on one cheek and eyes the slightest bit crossed. She hadn't entirely lost her Rumanian accent. *His nostrils dilated. With brutal curiosity he took in every line of that desirable body while a savage eagerness scorched his senses. He looked at her small brown feet, the copper-fleshed legs, braced far apart.* Carla had matured over the winter. She herself was a junior counselor now with a gentle cleft that appeared between her developing breasts. My own eyes grew large, my mouth felt dry. *Her eyes, black as charcoal, wet with dew, opened obliquely on him, blinking with animal innocence. Her brown breasts were thrust provokingly forward. "Jesucristo!" he exclaimed.*

I smiled at Carla, and Carla smiled back. Little stars glittered from her braces, which were not quite ready to be retired. In groups of two, her girls were splashing in the water, some beyond the dock, swimming to the raft, others paddling inside the crib area. *Spasms of sensual pain stabbed his throat. Throwing back her head, she laughed defiantly. The fiery blood in his veins pounded from knees to thighs. And then his fine, sensuous mouth widened to a smile as he sprang toward her, shouting. . . .* Carla came out of the water, her black hair glistening, her towel stretched behind her back. She faced me and began jumping on one foot to shake the water out of her ear. The little beach was crammed full of girls. When their bunk numbers were called, they swarmed around the crib area waiting their turn to try out for the deep water. Carla turned to me again, her smile now sultry fire, her walk self-conscious and clumsy. It was a sign, and that evening I wrote a letter to Maggie, my premature guilt shining through between the lines. Throughout my hastily written, nervous text, I expressed my fear that *she*, Maggie, was bound to attach herself to some budding John Garfield in the Vermont woods.

As for me, seventeen and as horny as an Andalusian bull, I *knew* what was going to happen right here on the banks of Lake Pocahontas. I was sitting on the dock right after lunch, my feet dangling, my *Treasures* open to Bronzino's *Allegory of Passion* in which a Venus was being felt up by a small, precocious Cupid. When I squinted, she was a double for Carla, her body shapely and slender, with boyish hips, eyes slightly protruding, and a Roman nose. From the other side of the lake, I heard the muffled sounds of hammering, a motorboat engine starting. And then I heard the dock creak behind me.

"It's so hot, Adam," Carla said. "I thought I'd sneak down for a dip."

"I've been waiting for you," I said.

She covered her smile with her hand. "I left my kids," she said, "so I can't stay long. Still, we are the chosen here." She began taking off her Kee-Nah-Wah grays. Her bathing suit was underneath.

"I'll watch," I said. "I don't have my bathing suit."

"Oh, come on, Adam," Carla said. Then she climbed down the ladder and, without a sound, slipped underwater, surfacing a few feet away.

"I guess we tricky Europeans could get away with anything," I said.

Carla blinked the water out of her eyes. "We've got panache," she said, and disappeared underwater.

I walked over to the deep water as she made her way quietly through the slimy maze of piers that held up the dock. She found a rotted-out place in one of the thick black piers, stuck one hand into it for support, and, with the other, pulled down the straps of her bathing suit. Her small breasts were already pale in contrast to her tanned body. She pulled herself up to show them to me.

"Do you smoke?" she asked in a husky voice.

"Sure," I said.

"I do too," Carla said.

"Holy Mother," he yelled, "stay . . . just so. . . ." His fingers fondled her full brown breasts. "I would sketch your wonderful body!"

"I'd like to draw you," I said.

"Now?"

"No, but soon."

"I think I'd make a good model," Carla said, pulling herself up and down in the water.

"You will be perfect," I assured her in my "European master" voice.

The rest of the week, I sat on the dock waiting for Carla, who didn't come. I cooled myself off in the water and wandered around the little beach with my sketchbook in hand, ready for action.

At the end of the week, I got sick. It was tonsillitis and poison ivy and blue balls, the latter undiagnosed by Dr. Wilcox, the town doctor who spent an hour or so a day at camp. I ached and itched and had a fever.

Mr. Seligman came to visit. He sat on a spindly wooden chair by the window. "Shalom, Adam," he said. "How's the fur business?" Mr. Seligman was a short man with an aquiline nose and a thick, coarse moustache. His biceps were enormous, hard as steel. A whistle hung from his bull neck. "Will we see your uncle this summer?" he asked.

"I don't think so," I said.

"Pity," he said, "we could use him."

"Use him?"

Mr. Seligman's eyes seemed to lengthen; they looked feline, almost Oriental. "I heard that you and Carla are seeing a lot of each other."

"You did?"

"A fine girl and a pretty girl. She has had a difficult time herself." His voice had developed a rabbinical resonance that hadn't been there previous summers. He paused and looked into my eyes. "She isn't Jewish, you know. Not that it matters," he added, "though you must be careful, do you know what I mean?"

I didn't and told him so.

He ran his fingers along the colorful lanyard that held his whistle. "It's easy to make mistakes, and then . . ." He gripped the whistle and pulled at it, snapping the lanyard against the back of his neck. "More than ever," Mr. Seligman said, "we have a responsibility, a moral responsibility, to help each other, to stick together." He looked at me deeply and long, so long that I turned away. "And what will you do, Adam?" he asked.

"When?"

"With your life."

"With my life? I guess I'll finish school first, then I'll go on drawing, do art, be an artist. . . ."

Mr. Seligman blew his nose into a very large handkerchief, folded it back into his pocket. "But is this anything for Jewish people to do?"

"Not for Jewish people?"

"Especially now," he said. "It is for others to beautify." He spoke as if he were quoting scripture. "It is for us to sanctify. To build and sanctify."

"Why shouldn't Jewish people make art?"

"Thou shalt not make unto thee graven images or any likeness of anything that is in heaven above or that is in the earth beneath or that is in the water under the earth," Mr. Seligman said.

"Well," I said, "I'm not much of a Jewish person. I mean I

don't really pay much attention to that. Neither does my uncle."

"Now more than ever," Mr. Seligman said, "you have to pay attention. You must be a Jew, Adam, like it or not."

"We've never been religious," I protested.

"Religion is one part of it only, important, yes, but being Jewish doesn't just mean being religious. It's being a people, a special people, with a special task. Right now that task is to survive."

"Why shouldn't Jews survive? The war is over." My stomach began to hurt. "Some will survive, some won't, like everyone else."

"With Jews, it's different," he said. "Hasn't your uncle taught you anything about being Jewish? The two of you have been through so much. . . ."

"I don't think he really knows about Jewish things. Anyway, he never talks about it."

So Mr. Seligman began talking about it, telling me about the prophets, about the just, about the importance of a Jewish state. "Nowadays," he confided, "that is my one goal, my one dream." He blew his nose again. "You are an exceptional young man," he said. "You have all the advantages now. You should do something *useful* with your life. Boys your age are going over to fight for Israel. You can help build Israel. A scientist, an engineer . . ."

I tried to think of myself as Jewish. It felt strange. What would Bolek think? He was whatever his customers wanted him to be, and I don't think it included being Jewish. But *I*, I could become Jewish: Krinsky, the Jew; Krinsky, the Jewish artist. *All night Francisco painted like a madman. One painting after another, to avenge Spain's wrongs. Kill evil by creating beauty, he thought. Rid the world of sloth, hypocrisy, disease. . . .* "Art can save the world," I said.

"I thought you were smarter than that," Mr. Seligman said.

"I will be an artist," I said quietly and deliberately. "I *am* an artist. I will not be a furrier or an engineer. My father was an engineer—"

"You see—"

"I can't even do math."

Mr. Seligman took my hand. "You must do what is *right*," he said. "You have to know who you are, what you come from. Whatever you do, *that* you have to know." He massaged my hand. "You could be my son," he said.

"My father was killed for being Jewish."

"All the more reason . . ."

"Reason for what?"

"For fighting for Israel."

"I won't. I'm an artist, I told you. All right, I'm a *Jewish* artist."

"There are no Jewish artists," Mr. Seligman said.

"No Jewish artists?"

"Not to speak of. Plenty of Jewish engineers, though."

Mr. Seligman spotted something out the window. He got up, walked out of my room to the outside door, where he picked up his megaphone and said, "Barry Mendelsohn, Barry Mendelsohn, do not throw stones down to the waterfront. Civilized people do not act like that."

I thought that camp activities would claim him now, but he came back.

"Adam," he said, "I've been thinking. I want to make our summers here more meaningful, to give more purpose to camp life." He patted down his thinning hair. "We've always had fun at camp with sports, fun with swimming, with archery, with baseball. Well, I'd like us to get more serious." He wanted to divide the camp into leagues, which, he said, would breed loyalty and toughness. He made a note on a pad he carried in his back pocket. "I will order baseball caps from Feitelson. What do you think? The Youth of Zion and the Workers of Zion. Red for Workers, green for Youth." He pulled his chair over even closer. "Adam, listen," he said, "do you know what is the Irgun?" I shook my head. "It is a secret organization of commandos. Most of them are young—"

"I'm not going over there," I said.

"Who said anything about going over there? No one said that. I'm talking about little training groups here at camp." He sat back. "The real ones blow up things—railroad stations, ammunition dumps . . ."

My throat began to hurt again. I lay back on the pillow. I remembered how the Sunday before camp started Bolek and I ran into Weinglass and his wife in Central Park, walking their dog, a well-groomed poodle with a ribbon on top of its head.

Mr. Seligman was droning on: ". . . oil refineries in Haifa . . . the King David Hotel . . ."

"A *dog*, Zyga?" Bolek had said.

"Why not a dog, Bolek?" Basia Weinglass said. "You had a dog. You were so comical, so afraid the dog would jump from your terrace into the Vistula."

"But look at that ribbon," Bolek teased.

"So?" Zyga Weinglass said. "Nothing is wrong with dogs and ribbons. It is stupid superstition that Jews should not own dogs. What do you think? That we are more Jewish than you?"

What is this thing, this being Jewish? You couldn't be an artist, you couldn't own a dog? Maybe I wasn't really Jewish, I thought. I didn't know about any of those things.

I woke up well after midnight. My supper, on a tray, lay on the chair where Mr. Seligman had sat. I ate a few bites of cold meat loaf and carried the tray into a room down the hall that served as Dr. Wilcox's office. The room was nearly empty except for a few kidney-shaped bowls, some boxes of tongue depressors, and a dozen bottles of calamine lotion. On a long shelf behind the card table that was Dr. Wilcox's desk stood a set of medical encyclopedias, some Red Cross manuals, and a *Textbook of Anatomy*. I borrowed the anatomy book and copied muscles and bones for the rest of the night.

When, a couple of days later, Dr. Wilcox pronounced me well, I took the anatomy book back to the staff house with me. To my surprise, it commanded the bunk's immediate attention. What my art books, with their Bronzinos, Titians, and Rubenses, were unable to provide as my share of the bunk's salacious material, the *Textbook*, with its long section on the vulva, could. It wasn't for everyone, though. Everyone ached to be a student of the female organs of generation, but only some had the imagination to transform those schematic sections, the finely crosshatched diagrams, into steamy, pulsating flesh.

Late at night, Teddy Shapiro, who slept in the cot next to

mine and planned to be a doctor, gave my bed a shake. "Hey, Krinsky," he said, "wanna hear about the *labia pudendi?*" Teddy Shapiro was selective. Neither the ovaries nor the fallopian tubes nor the uterus itself produced the desired effect. It was the *mons veneris,* the *labia majora* and *minora,* and especially the arousable *erectile* tissue that found their way directly to his jaded heart. Teddy claimed to have experienced it all at Bronx Science. Under a diagram labeled "a plexus of veins enclosed in a thin fibrous sheath," he penciled the words "yum, yum, the best part." Others weren't as adept at interpreting the cutaway sections. "For C-Christ's sake, K-K-Krinsky," Stu Levinson said after hours of hectic study, "if this is supposed to be the top of her leg, and the p-p-perineal membrane stretches all the way to the, you know, asshole, then where the f-fuck is the v-v-vestibular bulb?"

One cool night, after her little campers were tucked into bed, Carla and I walked down to the waterfront. We sat on the sand, leaning on the *Ben Hecht,* facing the lake. Just a sliver of moon shone through hazy thin clouds. "This is a strange place this summer," I said.

"I feel a little out of place," Carla said.

"He's so preoccupied. . . ."

"I know."

Then I bent Carla's head back against the gunwhale of the canoe and kissed her with my mouth open.

"I hate these braces," Carla said when we disentangled. I licked my lips and tasted blood. By slow degrees we slid down the side of the canoe until we were lying side by side on the damp sand. I slipped my hand inside her Kee-Nah-Wah shirt and explored the gentle swell of her new breasts as carefully as an archaeologist fingers an amphora. A heavy necklace hung from Carla's neck. It clanged like cowbells as I moved it to one side. "It was my mother's," Carla said, and to demonstrate my respect, I touched each bangle on the coarse chain. "So were these earrings," Carla said, turning her head to the side.

"They're very beautiful," I said.

"They had great jewelers in Bucharest," Carla said with a sigh.

These things, these *heirlooms,* bent into shape by goldsmiths hammering somewhere in the Carpathian mountains, excited me. I pushed my hand through the brassy metal to Carla's nipples, which were stiff as young Concord grapes. My hand darted from the one to the other. Carla began to squirm and rub her knees together and to wail softly, a kind of "wa-a-a, wa-a-a" I hadn't heard before.

"Shhh," I warned, but Carla went right on wiggling and moaning, her arms spread out as far as they could go, her fingers filtering sand through them. My own hand, like a sandpiper, alighted everywhere, from her breasts, which Carla had exposed to the moonlight, to her lips, to her *mons veneris*.

And then the worst thing I could think of happening happened. Someone was coming down the stairs to the waterfront. We stopped everything and watched a powerful flashlight illuminate the lush poison ivy that licked the sides of the steps. The flashlight came slowly and deliberately. Quite clearly, I saw this moment as a turning point. Whatever was left of school, of family, *of life*, would now be forever changed. Like the young Francisco, I was about to be branded as a full-fledged renegade.

At the bottom of the stairs, the beam of light turned right, away from us, and in its path I saw the flash of a knife blade. Carla and I held our breath. At the other end of the beach, the light was now placed on the sand facing the woods, making the knife blade, a machete blade, seem to catch fire. *Out of the night flashed a sword, but Francisco's own knife struck first, piercing the heart. He wiped his blade and made off for the fonda. There, by the light of the candle, he drew the dead man on the tail of his shirt. . . .*

"It's a machete," I whispered. "It's got to be Mr. Seligman."

"Mr. Seligman?"

"It was his brother's. From the war." Mr. Seligman's brother served in the Philippines under General MacArthur.

Mr. Seligman picked up the machete and traced circles in the air. He spoke some gutteral words and sat down on the sand, rocking back and forth.

Carla burrowed her face into my armpit. "What's he doing now?" she asked. She had one arm between her legs.

Mr. Seligman unbuckled his heavy leather belt and stepped

63

out of his pants. In his boxer shorts, with the light in one hand, the machete in the other, he entered the thicket of trees and bushes that threatened his beach.

"Come on," Carla said, "let's get out of here."

"I want to see," I said.

Mr. Seligman began cutting gently, attacking only the ends of leafy branches, announcing his presence, warming up. After a while, his strokes became freer, surer. Small lance-shaped leaves flew like the downy tufts of milkweed. He began to take on the young willows, the spreading alders, which bent, cracked, and fell into the tall ferns and blueberries.

"Listen," I said, "he's saying something." We heard a kind of mumble, like a prayer, before each clout of the machete. Mumble, mumble, crack, mumble, mumble, crack. Then we began to make out the shout that accompanied each blow. Mr. Seligman was naming names: Himmler, Hoess, Bevin, Webb.

"I've watched my father," Carla said in a shaky voice, straightening her body and moving closer.

"You did?"

"With his girlfriends."

"You saw them?"

"Yes."

Mr. Seligman was making a racket, slashing and cursing.

"What did you see?" I asked, rubbing against her.

"You know, making love." Her voice was hoarse. We were both rubbing, grinding, pulling at each other. Then Mr. Seligman came out of the bushes again.

"*Madonna*," Carla said. "Do you see that?" Mr. Seligman's hairy legs were matted with blood. I saw that this was not the first battle with the interior of his thicket. His new wounds shared the sacrificial surface of his legs with scars that shone like the tails of comets. "Why doesn't he wear his pants?" Carla asked.

I don't know why she thought I'd know, but I did know, for this insanity struck a deep, familiar chord. "He doesn't want to take unfair advantage," I said.

"Unfair advantage?" Carla asked. "Of what?"

"Of the bushes."

"Adam," Carla said. "Is this something *Jewish?*"

At that moment I saw Carla as a stranger, someone from another planet. Perhaps being Jewish had little to do with artists or dogs. Perhaps it had to do with *this*. It didn't even matter whether it was between people. Could it really be between people and *plants?* It seemed ridiculous, yet I detected the similarity of Mr. Seligman's action and my father's at the Polish-Rumanian border. "Yes," I said to Carla, "this is Jewish."

We stopped touching, we put a little distance, a little sand between us. Carla began buttoning her Kee-Nah-Wah shirt. "Tell me what it means," she said.

"It means that you pay back what you take," I explained, "that you offer something in return."

"Like Abraham and Isaac?" Carla asked, tucking her shirt into her pants.

I didn't know anything about Abraham and Isaac, but I said yes. "It's like my father," I said.

"What did your father do?" Carla asked.

I saw my father close the car door quietly, just a few hundred yards from the little bridge that led into Rumania. I saw him walk back into where the bombs were falling, where the tanks were rumbling. "He went back to Poland to be killed," I said.

"He did?"

"Yes. They said he was shot, but I don't believe it."

"Why did he go back?" Carla asked.

"Because—I think because he thought he killed my mother."

"Did he?" Carla asked, reaching now for my hand. Her hand was very cold.

I remembered the day. It was just before the first bombings. I was in bed, still feverish from croup. My mother came home from Mandelbaum's, which she ran with Bolek. In my room, she unpinned her wide-brimmed flowery hat so she could touch her lips to my forehead to check for fever. My father had stayed home to listen to the radio all that day, pacing in and out of his study.

"We must leave Warsaw," my father said as he stepped into my room. "The Germans are on the border." He was unshaven

65

and pale. No one spoke until our old butler shuffled in. He had served in the Imperial household in St. Petersburg and still wore white gloves. He brought us tea.

"They will bomb Warsaw first," my father finally said. "Take Adam to the country, I beg you."

My mother sipped her tea. "Do you think the business runs itself?" she asked my father.

"Marysia," he said to her, "I beg of you. There will be no business. Maybe there will be no Warsaw. Save yourself and save our son."

"And what about you?" my mother shot back. "You are too busy?"

"I will come the moment they cross into Poland."

"I won't go," my mother said, and my father, with a single motion, cleared the table of tea and dishes and everything. My mother ran out of the room, out the front door, out of the building.

Bolek took us to the country, where the bombs also fell. I never saw my mother again.

We didn't know how she died, whether in the bombing or later, but when my father walked back into Poland, leaving me, it was to sacrifice a life for a life.

Mr. Seligman, with better odds, went back into his brambles and thorns. He went deep into the woods this time, so deep that we no longer saw his light. We only heard the crack of the machete, the snap of branches, the heartrending cries naming the enemies of his beach, the enemies of the Jewish state, the enemies of humanity.

We watched Mr. Seligman perform his grim duties until well after midnight. We saw him drag himself wearily up the long stairs back to where the whole camp slept. Carla and I parted more like the crusty veterans of a battle than like lovers.

On another part of the camp's hundred acres, I discovered a lovely clearing with raspberry bushes all around and a large flat rock close to its center. I began going there daily, skipping meals when I could, trying to avoid Mr. Seligman. I became engrossed in a project stirred up by Bronzino and his *Allegory of Passion*. From the beginning of my affair with Bronzino's Venus, I was uneasy about her impossible pose, appearing to sit with all her weight on one ankle. Not only that but her other ankle supports the weight of a cherubic little being representing Folly. Anyone else would have writhed in pain. Even though it *is* only a picture, I could not bear her discomfort. In my sketchbook, I stood her up, I stretched her out, I settled her into a more tolerable position. Once she was erect, with her long boyish torso, her firm young breasts, her downy *mons veneris* fully upright, I felt as powerful as Dr. Frankenstein. Oblivious to the mosquitoes that devoured me, I twisted and turned her this way and that while old Father Time— whom Bronzino had hovering aimlessly above her—leered lasciviously. Soon my wonderful Venus was performing unspeakable acts upon all of them, on little Cupid and Folly and on Time himself.

The Bronzino led to others. I tackled crowd scenes full of giants and centaurs, groups cavorting in forest glades or marble baths, though I preferred the intimacy of a lone nymph, maenad or Nereid giving herself fully to someone who, I must admit, more often than not, looked like me, with an abundance of black hair hiding much of his forehead, with thick eyebrows that met in the middle, with a hungry but sensitive look.

I was very encouraged by the reception these sketches got in the staff house. It was better by far than the *Textbook of Anatomy*, certainly better than the Varga calendars and stained nude snapshots that circulated endlessly. "Jesus, Krinsky, did you really do that?" "Holy shit, Krinsky, you're good." "Hey, who helped you?" Larry Golub, who taught lanyard-making and baseball, said, "Lemme have that fat one for tonight," and Irv Finkel, swimming and drama, offered money, my very first sale. With Morty Turoff, the archery counselor from Colorado, who drove into Duckworth every few days for supplies, I traded for magazines, wine, and condoms.

In the clearing, I took on Goya's *Clothed* and *Naked Maja*, adding an element of devotion to my lust. I discovered that I couldn't do proper justice to these hallowed figures, though.

Stretching out the Maja's limbs was not the problem. It was Goya who eluded me. The Maja herself stopped at nothing. She was lewd and aggressive. But making images of the Master was hopeless. Goya sat pale and wooden, while she, astride his lap, tried to breathe life into him.

Although Mr. Seligman had cast a pall over both Carla and me, after a week's respite we launched into flashing each other signs of our continuing interest. As Carla walked a line of her girls into the barn for lunch one day, I caught up with her.

"Can you get away during rest period?" I asked.

"Where to?"

"I found a marvelous place in the woods."

"Oh, yes?" She smiled. "Nowhere near the beach, I hope."

"Way back of the girls' bunks," I told her.

"To study nature?" Carla asked.

"To draw."

"Maybe," she said.

"You must see it, Carla. I've fixed it up just for you."

I waited for Carla in back of her bunk until her girls were quiet. Carla walked barefoot beside me. When we reached my haven, I swept aside the drooping branches of a wild willow tree as if it were a stage curtain. Carla gasped. "It's beautiful," she said. I had clipped some of the bushes, scythed paths, squared things off. "You've made it so homey." Carla sat down on the rock, took out a crumpled pack of Chesterfields, straightened a couple of them out, and offered me one. We both lit up. Carla inhaled and blew a neat stream of smoke. She spit out a fleck of tobacco. "Goddam these braces," she said. She opened my sketchbook to a page that had the Maja kneeling between Goya's legs. Carla took a deep drag on her cigarette. "*Madonna*," she said.

"That's the Duchess of Alba," I said. "She posed for Goya."

"Like that?" Carla cried. *She was covered by a many-colored costume, a Maja's bolero, gown, and sash.* "Now, my Francho," *she said with urgency.* "Oh, my White Flower," *he said as he fell upon her.* "Openly, my Crusader," *she said, taking off her Maja's costume,* "paint me as I really am. . . ."

I showed Carla the two Maja paintings in my book and told her about the famous love affair.

"Do you want to paint me?" Carla asked.

"Yes."

She stubbed out her cigarette and I did the same. "Your drawing has gotten so good, Adam. Where did you learn?"

"I didn't really learn," I said. "I just do it a lot."

"Have you read *The Fountainhead?*" she asked. I told her I had. "You should illustrate *that*," Carla said. "I really loved that book."

"You did?"

"You're like the architect," Carla said.

"Howard Roark."

"Yes."

"Did you like it when Howard Roark attacked Dominique?" I asked.

"Yes."

"He raped her," I said.

"Except she *wanted* it," Carla said.

"To be raped?"

"Yes."

"He hurt her," I said.

"Yes," Carla said, closing her eyes as she pointed her face to the sun. "But he knew she wanted more. They just *knew* a lot about each other."

The sun beat down on us. We were both sweating. "Are you going to be an artist?" Carla asked. "I mean *always*."

"Yes."

"You're so much like Howard Roark," Carla said. "You really are. To me anyway." I started playing with her bare toes. "Free like an eagle, doing what you want to do, not caring if it upsets people, *just doing it . . .*"

"I know," I said. "Let's take our clothes off."

"Both of us?" Carla asked.

"Yes."

"Will you draw with your clothes off?"

"It's better that way."

We both got undressed slowly, not looking. Naked, we sat down, faced each other, with our knees up, our arms wrapped around them.

"Dominique liked it so much that no one could ever do it to

her again, not like that." Carla leaned back on her elbows, stretched out one leg, and pointed her toes, like Betty Grable. An ant raced across her belly and she flicked it off. She had a mole under her belly button. I put my hand on her thigh just above the knee. "You're going to have a wild life," she said. "I don't know how I know that but I do."

I sat up straight and stuck the fingers of my other hand between her toes. She flexed and stretched them like a cat. "Sometimes I wonder . . ." I said.

"What do you wonder?" She put her hand on my belly. "Look how white your stomach is," she said. "What do you wonder, Adam?"

Her hand felt so good that I closed my eyes. "I don't know," I said.

"Yes, you do. Tell me."

"Forget it." I put my hand on her belly.

"Come on, tell me."

"I need to live more, to experience more. . . ."

"You've lived so much, Adam," Carla said.

"Look at us, still going to *camp*. This place is ridiculous."

"I know," Carla said. "Mr. Seligman scares me."

"At least he's different," I said. "He's crazy, but I feel crazy, too. I have visions sometimes. I get into trances. . . ."

Carla began moving her hand on my belly. Her fingertips traced an arc from a point on my hipbone, up over my belly button, then back down again on the other side. She moved her hand slowly, methodically. "I feel I know too much about you," Carla said. I couldn't speak. "I *know* you'll have a spectacular life and a spectacular death," she said. "You'll be blown to bits in a gigantic explosion. People are going to *hear* about you."

Carla's skin was hot and oily. "Let's go over there," I said, pointing out a mossy, shady place I had fixed up.

"Don't forget your sketchbook," Carla said.

I picked it up.

"What about your charcoal sticks?"

I bent down again to get the charcoal.

We walked over, holding hands, and stretched out on our backs. It felt soft and spongy and cool.

"She's so developed," Carla said.

"Who?"

"You know, the Duchess." I put one arm across her small breasts. "I'm too skinny. It wouldn't be the same drawing me."

"You look like her," I said.

"I do?" She turned to her side and moved closer. I put my fingers inside her. She was so wet, it was like sticking a hand into compote, into peaches and pears in syrup. Here, finally, were the sebaceous follicles, the vestibular bulb, the whole *corpora cavernosa*. I rolled over and tried to guide my penis inside her, but Carla stiffened. "I don't want to get pregnant," she said, and backed off as I pawed the ground for my pants with their stash of Morty Turoff rubbers.

"It's over there," I said, pointing to the rock where we had left our clothes.

"Adam, maybe we shouldn't," she said, sitting up. "Adam, why don't you draw me—draw me first." *Submissive, inquisitive, superstitious, she watched the quick movement of his hand gliding across the paper. He showed his sketch to her. Her eyes opened wide and she crossed herself. Under the weight of his body, she cried out with each spasm of joy.*

I grabbed Carla's arm and pulled her through the uncut raspberry bushes back to our clothes. "It must have dropped out of my pocket. . . ."

"Adam, it's okay, let's not . . ."

With one hand I raked the tangle of thorns, searching frantically. With the other I held on to Carla.

"Come on, Adam, let go, you're hurting me. . . ."

On my hands and knees, I groped insanely in the undergrowth, cutting my arms and legs, panting like a dog.

"Adam, please, we'll do it some other time," she said. "I promise. Adam, we're going to get caught. I'm going to lose my job—"

"What are you talking about? Nobody cares what we do. We're *exiles*. Do you know what that means? Like Rosa Luxemburg, for Christ's sake."

I held on to her with all my strength and miraculously I found the wallet and the rubbers. I pulled Carla back to our mossy bed. She was struggling, near tears. I pushed her down and pinned her with my knees as I figured out how to unravel the condom. Her eyes were closed now, her mouth open, the silver shining inside. "No," she whispered as I entered, exploding as I did, afraid that the rubber would rupture with the force of my coming. *What a strange fellow, she thought, but one who knows how to love. The saints in Paradise know no such bliss. . . .*

I lay spent on top of her. "Carla," I said, "you are so wonderful, so perfect." When I looked down at her, I saw that she was trying not to cry. She put her arms around me and held me. "You're going to be the best model. You don't know how much I need you." I kissed her gently. "I would be lost without you."

The clearing became our little cottage in the woods, our artist's garret. For Carla, it was home. She trimmed the hedges, cleared the thorns around the rock, clipped the excess leaves from the willows. She even made what she called "closet space" under a cluster of drooping ferns where we sometimes left our sneakers.

With Mr. Seligman preoccupied, crazed, obsessed, we felt safe in our remote clearing. The only way our activities could have reached his tuned-out ears was if he himself strayed from his own battlefield and wandered into ours. However inadvertently, Mr. Seligman had transformed camp from a well-regulated, responsible home-away-from-home into a libertine heaven, not only for Carla and me but for others as well. Couples were forming everywhere. Almost everyone in the staff house had found a mate and at night the beach was as carefully divided as in a game of mumblety-peg. Morty Turoff, who slouched when he stood and spat when he talked, had developed more than a passing interest in Carla, but instead of intruding on us, he took first option on every drawing that I put up for sale.

Carla was a good model, though preferring more demure poses than I would have liked. We were on our fourth *odalisque*, in which Carla was propped up against a mound of earth, with one hand behind her, the other shielding her pubic region. "Will you take me to museums in the city?" Carla asked.

"Move your hand away from there," I said.

She moved it to her waist. "I can't wait to see Goya with you," she said, trying to blow a fly off her nose. "My aunt and uncle have an art gallery in Switzerland."

"Carla," I said, "you're a great model, but there are plenty of *odalisques* in the museums. I love *odalisques*, I really do, but I'd love it if you posed in other ways."

"What other ways?" Carla asked.

"Ways you can't find in museums." Carla sat up. "I just think we have a lot to show each other, a lot to teach each other. We can do anything we want to." Carla lit up a cigarette and coiled herself into a ball, her knees up, her arms around them. "I want to make some drawings with your legs apart." Carla said nothing. "We have to experiment. . . ."

"What else?" Carla asked.

"Oh, I don't know. . . ."

"Adam, this isn't right," Carla said.

"What isn't right?"

"I don't know. . . ."

"Carla," I said, a little annoyed, "these are *artistic demands*. People like us—you know, artists, Europeans, survivors—we have to do what we have to do."

"But it's all for *you*, Adam," Carla protested. "I don't think you really care for me."

"I do care for you," I said. "We are discovering things together. We're learning, we're trying new things, we're caring about each other."

Carla began to cry. "I don't know what I mean," she sobbed. "I don't know what I want."

"What about Howard Roark?" I asked.

"I was wrong about Howard Roark," Carla cried. "I don't think I like people like Howard Roark."

"I've never liked Howard Roark either," I said. I took Carla's hand. "What I really like about you is your whole history. That makes you special. You weren't just born yesterday. You've lived in those mountains forever."

"What mountains?"

"Your mountains, the Carpathians. You *civilized* those mountains."

"I don't know about that," Carla said.

"You will always have an accent," I went on, "just like me. You can't forget. You are sophisticated. You have to try *everything*. We need spice. That's what makes us interesting."

Reluctantly, Carla did just about everything I asked. I drew and pastelled with more passion than ever. I sketched myself in next to her, on top of her, below her. Like some kneeling Titan grasping the pink thighs of a sylvan nymph, I knelt before Carla, inhaling her dank, earthy smells. Carla made all the mousy grays and muddy browns in the woods explode like firecrackers. I had never seen the world like this, a lush new palette of reds and greens and brilliant yellows. The contrasts were dazzling. Nobody but the lusty Francisco had ever let on that getting laid would totally change *the way you see*.

"You're going too fast," Carla said. "Everything I predicted is happening *right now*."

Carla began to find excuses for not coming to the clearing. I saw her with Morty Turoff. She seemed to cling to him as to a raft in midocean. Morty was furious with me. "I'll never force her to do *anything*," he said. "She's too fine and delicate, Krinsky."

During the last month, camp became even more insane. It was apparent to everyone that anarchy reigned. Little kids, abandoned by their counselors, formed into small bands of wanderers who seemd to be foraging for food among the plentiful berry bushes of late summer. Mr. Seligman managed to organize some of the older boys into masked, though unarmed, Irgun commando units. They practiced ambushing campers, usually taking small amounts of their pocket money or an occasional penknife. But Seligman outdid himself, coming close to the end of his usefulness as a camp director when he took an elite group into the barn of a neighboring farm and brought back a cow. The poor animal bellowed for days since no one at camp seemed to know how to relieve it of its swelling udders. "You see," I heard Seligman tell Barry Mendelsohn, who'd become his most trusted ally, "we must eliminate all sentimentality. We are at war with devils."

Most every evening, either during supper or before evening activities in the big barn, Mr. Seligman gave talks celebrating some Jewish action in the Holy Land. "Shalom, Youth and Workers," he would begin, as the first couple of rows, occupied by the little kids, were already half asleep. "Our cause is just, our war is holy . . . we shall transform the desert into gardens . . . a Jewish paradise. . . ." Sobbing, dabbing at his eyes, he would tell about the boys who bombed, the martyrs who robbed, the Americans who manned the boats with their human cargoes. Mr. Seligman looked more and more drawn. He was counting the days until camp was over.

One week before the end of camp, the baseball tournament was in a critical phase. The field had been freshly mowed and the baseball cage patched with chicken wire. In the spirit of democracy, all the campers, even the smallest, played on one team or another. They roamed the outfield like sheep, their thumbs in their mouths, or on all fours looking for toads. They seldom retrieved balls hit deep into the tall grass around the bunks where they foraged, and the scores of games were astronomical.

I was a pretty good baseball player. At school in the city, I had made the jayvees. I played first base, partly because I was the only one at the Alexander Hamilton School for Boys who owned a three-fingered baseball mitt. Bolek, of all people, had given it to me, not because he knew anything at all about baseball. One day, as he flew by Mlle. Sacha in the showroom of Prince Casimir Furs, he had pressed a twenty-dollar bill into her bejeweled hands. "Go, go, darling," he had said, "and buy for Adam something *American*." And she, like Balboa stumbling into the Pacific, found her way to Davega's, where she was sold this trifurcated piece of cowhide, now oiled and aged into the shape of a wilted lettuce leaf. It assured me unquestioned hegemony over the first-base slot.

My league, the Youth, was near elimination, but with Teddy ("Dizzy") Shapiro pitching for us, we felt we still had a chance. In the third inning, with the score tied at 14 all, Morty Turoff was at bat for the Workers. In Morty's fat hands, the bat looked like a toothpick. Mindy Katz and Danny Oppenheim were on base because of throwing errors. Teddy fired a sizzler by Turoff for the first strike. When he tried the same pitch again, Morty sliced a low liner directly over first base. I lunged for it, my three-fingered mitt, like a Venus's-flytrap, ready to snare. In my midair extension, I saw two people high-stepping over the freshly cut barbs of grass. The man wore a white suit, straw hat, red and blue necktie; the woman a long, loose summer dress. As my foot dragged across the bag to double Mindy off first, I realized that it was Bolek and Enid. I landed hard on my belly and dropped the ball.

"That was wonderful what you did to catch the ball," Bolek said between innings.

"I dropped it, Bolek."

"No, no," he insisted. "I saw it."

After the game, Bolek, Enid, and I drove to Duckworth. Bolek was quiet as he navigated the big car over the rutted dirt roads that led into town.

"We are going to hear music in the mountains," Bolek said. "Zizi looked at the map and right next door was your camp."

"Music under the stars," Enid said.

"Yes," Bolek said, "tell me why in camp are all the Stars of David? I didn't know this was a Jewish camp."

"It's a rather appalling place, Adam," Enid said.

"It looks like Silesia," Bolek said.

"There are no horses," Enid added.

The Duckworth Inn, where Enid and Bolek were staying the night and where we were eating dinner, wasn't the St. Regis either. The dining room, which had four tables squeezed into it, was hot and stuffy. A roll of flypaper hung near the window.

"Your uncle is a great celebrity in Paris," Enid said. "Everyone says that he is the world's most fabulous furrier."

Bolek was picking at his chicken. "They all love Zizi, too," he said. They looked at each other devotedly.

We were the only guests in the dining room. Our waitress, the owner's teenage daughter, was leaning on the doorjamb, watching us. Beyond her, in the little lobby, her father had fallen asleep with the newspaper on his lap.

"The new Paris couturiers are *unbelievable*, Adam. They're making a revolution in fashion." Enid glanced at Bolek. "What an artistic business it is! With your talent and your genes, darling, you are *made* for it."

We were all trying to squeegee the white sauce from the chicken. "A wonderful business," Bolek said. "They are a genius over there . . ."

"Over there?" Zizi said. "What modesty! The greatest talent is right here in this family."

"No, no," Bolek protested. "Christian Dior is our Picasso—"

"And Dior says that it is Bolek."

Bolek pulled the cuffs of his shirt out from under his jacket and fingered the fluted gold cuff links. "And our Mr. R. Z. Kor," Bolek laughed, "he is like a little Jewish tailor."

"There he goes again," I said. "He knows *nothing* about Kor."

"I don't know? Yes, I know," Bolek said. "He is like a pig doing the mazurka."

"Why is he saying this, Enid?" I asked.

"He only wants the best for you," Enid said.

"He does?"

"You mustn't say bad things about Mr. Kor," Enid said to Bolek.

"All *your* friends are named Christian," I said, feeling a new solidarity with Mr. Seligman. "Don't you know what all the Mr. Christians have done?"

"Nothing is wrong with that name," Bolek said.

"This is not the way to interest me in your stupid business," I said.

"Yes, darling," Bolek said. "You are right."

"Rich uncles can be useful, you know. Their nephews can become artists. This is nature's way to make artists," I said.

"He is a philosopher now," Bolek said, laughing.

"You can buy your way into immortality," I said.

"And you don't think we can find a little immortality through the fur business?" Bolek said.

"The fur business!" I said, laughing. "Can you picture it, Enid? Someone is going to write a book a hundred years from now about his revolutionary new sleeves."

"You may laugh, Adam," Enid said, "but his creations belong to the museum. And they'll be there one day."

"Art is a hobby," Bolek said, "like garden tools."

"All the people who don't know anything about art lecture me about it," I said.

"Really?" Enid said.

"Mr. Seligman says Jewish people can't be artists."

"Can't be artists?" Bolek said, turning white.

"Mr. Seligman said that?" Enid asked.

Bolek sat up straight. He asked me to repeat in Polish *exactly* what Mr. Seligman said. When I did, Bolek put his two fists on either side of his plate and sat in silence with his eyes closed. "And what did he say Jewish people should do?" Bolek asked, his lips hardly moving.

"What a foolish thing for Mr. Seligman to say," Enid said. "What about Modigliani, what about Pissarro? They were Jewish, weren't they, darling?"

"I don't know," I said.

"Also Soutine," Enid said, "and Chagall . . ."

"They're all Jewish?" I asked.

Bolek started to say something and stopped. He tried again, but nothing came out. "And what should Jews do?" he finally managed to repeat.

"They should fight for a Jewish homeland," I reported. "They should make laws and religion. They should decide what is right and what is wrong."

Bolek bit his lip. "Is that what he thinks, that pigshit?" He pushed his chair back and, with his arms held rigidly close to his body, left the table.

"He has been very upset about just these kinds of things lately," Enid whispered. "He has even gone to temple with Mr. Weinglass. He couldn't sleep when he saw the photographs from the concentration camps. And now there's Kielce. . . ."

"What happened? What is Kielce?"

"It's in Poland," Enid said. "Bolek said that Jewish survivors who went back home to Kielce were massacred by the Poles."

"When?"

"Last month," Enid said. "While we were in Paris."

"Last month? The Poles?" The whole Jewish business was

beginning to settle on me like one of those long black overcoats I'd seen Orthodox Jews wear in New York.

Bolek came back, paid our waitress, bowing as he did. We went outside and began walking through the village. "Jews must join everyone else," Bolek said. "As our family always did."

"It didn't help them much," I said. "They were all killed, no matter who they joined."

"That will never happen again," Bolek said. "All that is behind us. Now everyone must shave his beard and join the modern world."

"America needs everyone," said Enid. "Jews and Christians alike."

"God bless America," Bolek said.

We passed the First Methodist Church of Duckworth with its white paint peeling off. Bolek walked with his hands behind his back, his linen jacket draped over his shoulders. "What I don't like," Bolek said, "is when someone is *too* Jewish, *all* Jewish. It is like a slap in the face."

"Would you like it if we weren't Jewish?" I asked.

"It's a curse," Bolek said, looking pained. "Look what it has done to us, to your mother and your father. God punishes people by making them Jews." The sidewalk had turned to dirt. "But why all this interest in Jewish things, darling?" Bolek asked. "Jewish people take with them the memory of their mothers' cooking. Your mother never cooked even an egg!"

"I have never understood why the Jewish people wanted to stay in Poland," Enid said.

"Yes, but we were not like that," Bolek said. "You see, we were *Poles*. Our family defended Poland. They were patriots. Our family helped to finance the uprising of 1831. That was a *Polish* revolution."

"And the Poles were nice to you?" Enid wanted to know.

Bolek was having a hard time explaining it. "They left us alone," he finally said.

"What does that mean?" I asked.

"How can you understand, you two who are Americans?

79

You don't know what it is, corruption. Rich Jews behaved badly. They thought that they could do anything, that they were better than the Poles. And if not the rich Jews, then who? Poor Jews stayed by themselves, they never spoke Polish, or when they did, they murdered the language. What did they know about the greatness of Polish theater, Polish music? They were noisy, dirty, *primitive*."

"I have always thought that the Jews were special because they wanted to educate themselves. They contributed so much to the arts, to science, to business," Enid said.

"Everyone wants to educate themselves," Bolek said. "Everyone wants to be special. In America you can be whatever you want to be. That's the miracle of America."

"I want to be an artist," I said.

"That is not work," Bolek said. "But no matter what you will do, first you must be—finished—elegant—"

"I must be *elegant*?"

"Darling, we must do what we can to make everything more beautiful. It's only decent," Enid said. "I know some very elegant painters," she told Bolek. "There is Max Ernst, Salvador Dali. There is Peggy Guggenheim—"

"Peggy Guggenheim?" Bolek said. "I know Peggy Guggenheim. She is not a painter, she is a customer."

"I know, darling, but all around her is a group of elegant European painters, right on Fifty-seventh Street."

"On Fifty-seventh Street?" Bolek said. "They are painters?"

"They are perfectly dressed, they understand—manners, class . . . they know the value of publicity."

"Just look at Kor," Bolek said, unable to contain himself. "No suit fits Kor."

"No more about Mr. Kor," Enid said, sliding her long, sleek fingers from Bolek's shoulder to his hand. "No one is rich anymore, darling. Everyone is just in love!"

"So," Bolek said to me, "you can be an elegant painter?" He stopped, slapped his forehead. "An elegant *Jewish* painter?"

"A Jewish painter can't be elegant?" I exclaimed. "What are you saying? Maybe a Jewish *person* can't be elegant. Is that what you think? And what about you?"

Bolek's face suddenly relaxed into a smile. "Painters are

smelly," he said, laughing. "They put dirty paint rags everywhere." He told Enid about my paint rags. "Anyway, you have to be a genius to be a painter." He wiped his brow. "You know, darling, you have to be a genius to make furs, too." He put his arm on my shoulder.

A tractor pulling a load of hay made its way slowly past us. Bolek stared at the machine until it disappeared behind a gray clapboard building. Then he lifted his nose like a bear and took a deep breath. "It is good clean air," he said.

Back at the inn, I told them that I wouldn't wait for camp to be officially over. "I'm leaving early. I'll take the train to the city."

Bolek turned to Enid. "He makes all his own decisions now," he said with more pride than remorse.

"Would you like to come with us, Adam?" Enid asked. "I can call ahead for tickets. No opera, darling, but a lot of Beethoven this weekend."

That night I told Mr. Seligman I was leaving. He nodded but wasn't really listening. I asked Morty Turoff to explain in case Mr. Seligman asked what happened to me. "Will you also tell Carla for me?" I asked. He said he would.

"Her father's a diplomat, Krinsky," Morty said. "I'm going to stay with them in New York."

"Oh, yes?"

"I'm nuts about her," Morty said. "I want her to come to Colorado with me."

"Doesn't she want to finish school?" I asked.

"After school," Morty said. "I'll wait." His eyes glowed with love and hope. "Next year she gets rid of her braces."

In the morning, as the sun was coming up, I took my last peek at the waterfront, the canoes that once again were in total disrepair, the weeds that were beginning to grow through the sand.

Camp Kee-Nah-Wah was sold that winter. But even before the sale was finalized, Mr. Seligman sailed for Palestine, where, good and passionate man that he was, he fought bravely for his dream, and where, just before the state of Israel was proclaimed, his jeep, with him in it, was blown up by a land mine.

4

Maggie came over to the hotel
the day after she got back from Vermont. I'd gone out early in
the morning for a haircut and came back upstairs looking too
shorn and smelling of witch hazel. I paced from room to room.
I played a Mozart quintet over and over again. It seemed
appropriate for Maggie to walk in on its bittersweet strains.
When she finally did come, it was noon and I was worn out.

Standing on the threshold was a different Maggie, a Maggie
transformed. Her hair was swept back so severely that it pulled
at her eyes, which, over her gleaming high cheekbones, looked
like Mongol eyes. Her small, exposed ears were bare, free of
the pearl earrings I had given her. Her gray cotton dress was
shapeless, her shoes black old-lady shoes. I closed the door
behind her and as the Mozart continued to play in the background, we kissed. I searched her eyes, but they were opaque,
closed to me.

We sat on the couch. "Do you have any Shostakovich?"
Maggie asked. I had no Russians and told her so. "I had the

most wonderful summer," Maggie said. "I learned so much. I've become a more serious, a more *sober* actress." I thought for a moment that I could smell hay, manure. "We did Clifford Odets's *Awake and Sing*. It expanded me, Adam."

"Are you thirsty?" I asked. It was very hot.

"I'd love some water," Maggie said.

I went to get it and let the water run for a long time. My head felt empty.

"I became a little wiser," Maggie went on. "Clifford Odets is a playwright of the people." Maggie replaced a stray bobby pin. "Goya was like that, too. Didn't you find the biography a little extravagant?"

"Yes," I said.

"I see so many things differently," Maggie said. "Do you know the Social Realists?"

"How do you feel, Maggie? I mean about *things*." Maggie took out a cigarette from a metal case and offered me one. "When did you start smoking?" I asked.

"Adam," Maggie said, "I became sort of attached to an actor. He played Moe Axelrod. In the play, he's a little dark and evil, but he liberates me from a bourgeois existence. He's really like that, very sensitive to working people, to all the world's oppressed."

I went into my room, turned off the Mozart, brought out my summer's work, and sat down next to Maggie. She smelled of laundry soap. "Look," I said, leafing through a bunch of drawings. "These nudes—that's *my* friend. We made love all summer, *all summer*."

Maggie picked up the sketchbook and studied the nudes. "Who is she?" Maggie asked.

"She taught me a lot," I said. "She's Rumanian." I saw a shadow of discomfort, if not jealousy, in Maggie's face. "A Gypsy," I added.

"I'm sorry I didn't answer your letters," Maggie said. "You can't imagine how hectic the summer was."

"What about us?" I asked.

She turned toward me. "You are my most precious friend," she said, sounding like Sophie.

"A couple of months ago, we just about swore eternal love. We mentioned the word *forever*. Remember the *forever*?"

"I need to work," Maggie said. "I need to be free."

"Did you—I mean, did he—"

"Adam," Maggie said, "that's not important." She looked at her watch. "I have to meet mother at Bloomingdale's," she said.

"Right now?"

"I'm sorry, Adam," Maggie said, and with her head tipped to one side, she gave me a very genial look. She breezed past me and stopped at the door. "I must run," she said. "We'll be in touch."

Later that day, I tried to be in touch, but Maggie was out and I got Sophie instead. "Sweet Adam," Sophie cooed. "Are you in pain?"

"In pain?"

"Maggie told me."

"What did she say?"

"That you were suffering terribly. I am so deeply sorry, darling, but don't despair. She is so young, so impressionable."

"Did she tell you about the actor?" I asked.

"Well, not very much, darling. . . ."

"But she mentioned him?"

"Yes. Maggie and I have no secrets."

"No secrets? What do you know about the actor, Sophie?"

"Well, his name is Julian. Julian Roy. It used to be Roy Punsky, but he changed it, thank God. Punsky sounds awful, don't you think?"

"Roy Punsky," I repeated joyfully. "That's the best thing I've heard today. Are you sure, Sophie? You're not kidding around, are you? How old is he?"

"Adam, I should divulge no more."

"Is he in college?"

"He's in his last year at Syracuse," Sophie said with a touch of contempt. "But that's not the point, darling. This Julian is here for the blink of an eyelash. You are here forever."

"How do you know that?"

"I've already said too much," Sophie said coyly.

I imagined Roy Punsky's hairy dark mitts crushing Maggie's body, the body I thought was mine forever. Swarthy, lumpish Roy Punsky defiling Maggie's flesh. Simian, slobbering Roy Punsky handling Maggie like pork, mauling and mangling as he told her tales of the Party, braying proletarian songs from the banks of the Volga.

New York was in the middle of a heat wave. The sun appeared like a forty-watt bulb through a sheet of dirty gauze. The women on Fifty-seventh Street bustled about on spike-heeled shoes with their full skirts nearly down to the ground, paying little heed to our sooty, debilitating inferno.

I went over to Bolek's air-conditioned office. He was already informed of my situation by Sophie, and between customers he offered me his advice. "Magdalena is like your sister," he said.

"She's not my sister," I said.

"There are plenty of other minks on the farm," he observed.

"You know just how to make me feel better," I said.

"You are young, darling. You have school, you have your whole life ahead of you."

"Don't even mention school, Bolek. They can't teach me anything."

"It's the best school in New York. What are you telling me? You are too smart for them?" He dug around his top drawer for an English cigarette. "He doesn't want school, he doesn't want business," he said. "He will be a cossack."

By late afternoon I had made my way downtown, as if my course had been prescribed, and found myself knocking on the door of R. Z. Kor. I was probably the last person he expected to see, and I thought for a moment that he was about to slam the door shut when he suddenly brightened with recognition. "Adam," he said, "what a surprise this is! Adam," he repeated warmly, his long, chiseled face dissolving into soft circles, like a clown. "You are welcome, you are welcome," he sang as he put his arms around me and kissed me. He held me at arm's length and, still grinning, examined me carefully. I was nearly as tall as he, though I felt in the grip of a powerful, *physical* man, a mountain of a man. "My God, what time is it?" Kor asked. "I have been torturing a little painting all day." He wiped his forehead with a handkerchief the size of a pillowcase. "It is unbearably hot," he complained, his accent, in contrast with the other Polish émigrés, more French than Polish.

Kor had left Sophie a year after Maggie was born. Though Maggie was a mistake, Kor and Sophie got officially married to give her the legitimacy Sophie insisted upon. Kor left to live in Paris, where he was quickly recognized as a brilliant surrealist. André Breton, who didn't know that Kor was a Jew, called him *"mon Chopin sauvage."* Kor always had a special smell for danger, Sophie had told me, and after Hitler marched into Czechoslovakia in 1938, Kor marched back to Warsaw to get his family out. They lived in Paris for a short while, making do in Kor's messy quarters in the fifteenth arrondissement, "a studio," Sophie had said, "that was like a Hungarian bordello." When Kor realized that the new persecution of the Jews would not be limited to one country, they packed their bags. They arrived in New York on the *Normandie* in early 1939, a year before Bolek and me.

"You know what is strange?" Kor now asked. "No one in New York thinks this climate is tropical. I am always amazed that the streets are not full of people in white suits. Come in, *mon cher*, come in. I am glad to see you. How is Magdalena? How are you?"

Like others of Kor's artist friends, he lived in a small apartment near Gramercy Park, which they all thought was more like Europe than any other part of the city. An easel was pushed up against the wall, while a long desk under the windows served as Kor's principal work space. Above it hung a postcard of an eerie Cycladic figure, a drawing of Apollinaire in a flier's suit, and a photograph of André Breton, Tristan Tzara, and a young Kor with their arms around each other.

Kor brought two plates from the kitchenette, felt around the fruit bowl for two of his best apples, and put one in front of each of us. "So, Adam," he said, "tell me why you are here."

"I just wanted to say hello."

"Listen to him," Kor said. "Your English is perfect, like a real American." He found knives, forks, and napkins and as I deliberated whether or not I even wanted to eat my apple, Kor peeled and quartered his with the speed and precision of a surgeon. The transformed fruit, cleanly dissected, lay like an open chrysanthemum in the center of his plate. "You want to say hello, *chéri?* Well, here we are, saying hello." He deftly sliced his quarters into paper-thin sections and began stuffing them into his mouth. "I haven't eaten all day," he explained.

"I saw Maggie this morning," I said.

"Ach, what a summer she had in Vermont," Kor said. "Do you think she is an actress?"

"Did she tell you about Roy Punsky?" I asked. "Or Julian Roy?"

"They are actors?" Kor asked, his mouth full of apple.

"Maggie's boyfriend," I reported.

"Why should she tell me about her boyfriends?" Kor said, taking my untouched apple and performing the identical procedure on it. "I am a bad father," he confessed. "You don't want an apple, *chéri?*" He stuffed my apple slices into his mouth as well. "You are not jealous, are you? Is that it? Tell me, are you infatuated with my daughter?" His voice mocked a stern patriarch. "I would be very pleased if that were the case. What did you say is this boy's name?"

"Punsky," I said. "Roy Punsky."

Kor laughed and rubbed his belly. "Punsky," he repeated. "I don't think you need to worry about the Punskys, *mon cher.*" He puffed and snorted like Pan himself, big yet delicate as a magician, glowing with life.

I told him about Maggie and me. I told him about my summer infidelity, I told him how Maggie and I fed each other's art.

"Maggie was always ready to devour the whole world," Kor reminisced. "Even in her baby carriage, she sang to the birds, her little hand flapping above the pram. And when people looked down into her nest, there she was, smiling and cooing, inviting them in."

"She is still like that," I said mournfully.

"An American, even in Warsaw," Kor said. "Sophie was like that, too, an exquisite woman. When I first met her, she was like the sixteen-year-old Hélène de Froment giving herself so nicely to old Rubens." Kor chuckled and belched, then walked over to the window from which you could see a corner of

Gramercy Park. "Nothing remains young and beautiful except art," Kor said. Something down below caught his eye. He motioned me over. "Look at that," he said, pointing to a young Negro man walking, *loping*, down the street, swinging his chain. "That is the heart of America," Kor said, "and thank God for it, because without this man, there is nothing here. Look at him, he is like you and me. He has no family, he is an outlaw." Kor walked us back to the table. He found his cigarette holder, put it in his mouth, and sucked on it. He seemed to do everything at once, to notice everything. His mind and his eyes worked so swiftly that the rest of him seemed clumsy by comparison, always lagging behind. He told me about the lives of Cellini and Caravaggio. "Brawlers, madmen, renegades," he called them. "Artists are criminals who, thank God, have found art to relieve them of their antisocial tendencies. Without art we would steal and murder, for we must take risks."

I felt like a medieval supplicant being given the keys to the guild. Mr. Seligman had wanted to give me the keys to the temple, and I had held them gingerly, then put them aside. I was no Zionist, just barely a Jew. Kor's keys were the ones I wanted. I wanted them more than anything. And yet these artists seemed to have something in common with the nervous rabbis of Wilno and Bialystok that Mr. Seligman had told me about, rabbis who tore at their beards and sucked boiled chicken feet as they waited for the Messiah.

"There is a direct line between the possession of great gifts and the temptation to abuse them," Kor continued. "Artists are madmen. I speak to you of our common illness, *cette maladie qu'on appelle génie.*"

Our common illness? *Genius?* I took an apple from the bowl, peeled and quartered it, and stuffed it into my mouth.

"This is the lesson then," Kor said. "An artist cannot live *en famille.*" Kor put his hands behind his head, leaned back in his chair, and looked up at the cracked ceiling. "This is profoundly sad," he went on. "Perhaps because of my rotten behavior, my daughter will crave to live in a real house, a place where she can take off her shoes, wash the curtains, kiss the dog." Kor rocked back to the table, his face close to mine. "I am telling you this because I am sure you are like me. You do not blow bubbles, you are not stuffed with feathers, not even mink, thank God. You *tempt* Magdalena and you *terrify* Magdalena." Kor got up to stretch. "You see, that is why we have this Punsky," he said, "and he is not her last Punsky, either. But between Punskys there will always be you. I know this, Adam. Ah, it is all because of her father who left her—not for a woman but to make art." He sat down again. "We are renegades and outlaws. There are not many among us like that good Rubens, who was a great artist *and* a perfect gentleman. Most of us live on the edge, dangerously."

"But I am not like you," I blurted out, surprised by my ready tears. "I am not like any of you. I take no risks. I have no vision."

"No vision?" Kor said, then began to laugh. "How can anyone your age have a vision? You cannot have a vision when you are seventeen. Not even your Goya had a vision until late in life. Your job is not to have visions. Your job is to work hard, to observe, to look everywhere. Nothing is wasted. Your losses—all our losses—will come back to the center of your work one day." Kor looked at me with evident pleasure. "You know what I did when Magdalena brought me your sketches?" He touched the bags under his eyes. "I cried. Yes, I cried. But don't misunderstand me, *mon cher*. It was not because I was discovering a young Rembrandt. A Rembrandt you are not, at least not yet. But your sketchbook was full of the *Third of May*. This is a boy, I said, who may be able to do it."

Kor got up to pace. "The death camps have made art an absurdity. Yet as I looked into your sketches, I thought, Ah, maybe this boy will *use* them, *transform* them, for you are tied to them and to all that happened there. You could be the ideal observer, the mad Caravaggio who gives us a new art." I took another apple and bit hard into it. "You are hungry? Come with me. We will go to meet Lala, my beautiful Lala. Nothing wrong with beautiful women, eh?"

Before we left his apartment, I looked at the collage he had been working on all day. Scattered around the desk were European images—palaces on the water, dungeons, equestrian statues—their edges curled or torn from all the pasting, removing, pasting again. He was trying to fit these images into a vast pristine landscape, flat as Kansas.

We left the apartment and walked downtown toward a Rumanian dairy restaurant. As we stopped at corners, Kor peered down the side streets.

"Ah, Nineteenth Street," he said, storing away some secret detail. On Fourteenth Street, he showed me a manhole cover he particularly liked. "One day I shall return to take a rubbing," he said. "Chirico told me about these things, also about fire escapes." He looked to see if I was listening. I wasn't only listening, I was memorizing his every word. "Look at the life stories of artists," he said on St. Mark's Place. "You will always find the biographer trying to exalt *his* artist's landscape, *his* artist's confluence of this and that river, always the ideal breeding ground for art, the banks of the Rhine, the Seine, the Arno, the meeting of north and south, east and west." We were paying little attention to traffic. A quiet bus nearly hit us. "Imagination is born of the thick layers of blood in the soil," Kor was saying, "and where is it thicker than in Europe?" We looked down an open bulkhead in front of a hardware store. "Art must never again be parochial or regional," Kor said. "Artists must always reach for the absolute."

We took a table in a bright, busy restaurant. Kor looked happy to be there. We drank a glass of prune juice and then greeted his friend Lala, a tall woman with red hair and green eyes who was waving a brand new *Life* magazine before us. She put it down in front of Kor. "You never told me about this," she chided him. "I found it quite by accident."

Kor leafed through the magazine. He pushed it between us so that I could read it with him. The title was "Life Goes to an Artist's Studio." It spoke of the European influence on postwar American art, especially that of the surrealists, "a rakish band of sophisticates," who managed to attract the attention of some of their New World colleagues. "For better or for worse," the *Life* writer said, "our vigorous American regionalism is being fertilized by cosmopolitan Europeans. These 'modern masters' who escaped the war in Europe dispense their wisdom like papal indulgences."

There were wonderful photographs of Kor, with his rakish friends and alone in his Gramercy Park studio. There were two reproductions of Kor's paintings, one a full-page spread of *The Polish Rider*, much like the small Rembrandt in the Frick Collection. In Kor's version, Kor himself sits naked astride a big brown workhorse. Kor's private parts are partially obscured by his large belly. His hairy legs, in stirrups, jut out awkwardly from the animal's flanks. The caption underneath read: "In modern art, nothing is sacred."

We ordered blintzes and tea. "You will be a rich man now," Lala said. "You won't need me anymore. I will be abandoned."

"Yes," Kor said absently, "we shall buy a boat and sail back to Europe where I belong."

Lala took his hands and looked at him lovingly. "We?" she asked.

"Of course *we*," Kor said. "I shall not share you with anyone. You are *my* heiress." Kor flipped through *Life's* pages and found what he was looking for. "Look here, *mon cher*," he said to me, pointing to a half-page ad of rubber heels and soles. "This is my Lala's family business. She is cobbler to all America."

After tea, we shared a cab uptown. Kor and Lala dropped me at the Buckingham on their way to Peggy Guggenheim's. As I went up the elevator to the twelfth floor, I thought of hiding the *Life* from Bolek. How could I get him ready for this? Surely this time it was going to lead to a stroke.

Most of my school friends lived on the west side of Central Park, the more scholarly families uptown near Columbia, and some, the older money, on the East Side. I was the only one below Fifty-ninth Street, the murky region of actors, dancers, prostitutes, and artists.

Now that I was seventeen and Kor had opened up the gates to art, I began to notice the chasm that existed between the Alexander Hamilton School for Boys and the dangerous, criminal world, the art world. Until this, my senior year, school was just school, a way of marking the slow, orderly progression of my minor accomplishments, a way of pleasing Bolek, who loved to study my report cards. He kept them with his passport and citizenship papers in the top drawer of his bureau, next to a leather box of cuff links. "A businessman must be educated these days," he often said. "Well educated."

In fact, I did my schoolwork well, I was liked by my teachers, I played baseball well enough for a foreigner, I smoked with my friends behind the cement football stands, I was vice-president of my class. Only recently had I begun to notice the Art Students' League, which I passed daily on my long trek to Riverdale.

The League was a couple of blocks from the hotel. Most mornings, groups of young artists talked and smoked outside, paint rags hanging out of their back pockets, the veins in their hands protruding as on the hands of surgeons, though for the most part these art students looked unspectacular. The men needed shaves, the women's ponytails were held together with rubber bands. I sometimes stopped to look at the paintings displayed in the windows and to listen in on their discussions. It was clear that, like Bolek, most of their families could not accept the quiet enterprise of art, especially in the lush, teeming garden of postwar America, spilling over with more rewarding opportunities.

My heart raced as I approached the League—intending to stop, to throw in my paint rag with theirs—but each day I walked by, then rode the two hundred blocks on the subway to school. I was still not the free spirit that Carla had seen in me, that Kor prescribed for me, that I desperately wanted to be.

When the subway arrived at its bucolic Riverdale destination, I trudged up the steep hill to school, weighed down by my stuffed book bag and surrounded by boys.

Even though my life plans with Maggie were in disarray, Maggie's very existence was cutting me off from school, from the study of Virgil, French proverbs, from the Wednesday-morning sing. Maggie and I had penetrated the unexplored caverns of our souls, and Carla and I had poked our fingers into every crease and crevice of our bodies, all of which elevated me beyond Alexander Hamilton's dreary grind.

My Old Masters drawings were doing very well in school. Every boy, from the lowest grades to the top, was augmenting his meager Alexander Hamilton education with a perfunctory knowledge of art, at least art according to Adam Krinsky. I even took specific orders and listened to complaints about the inaccessibility of art.

"You know that Venus with the stringy hair standing on a clamshell, Krinsky?"

"Yeah, I guess so."

"She doesn't look *real*, you know what I mean?"

"No?"

We discussed and negotiated as if I were their tailor.

"Why not try giving her a pageboy?"

"Really?"

"Put lipstick on her."

"Okay."

"And why don't you lay her down inside the shell? Hang her legs over the side, you know what I mean?"

I was making good money and began riding to school in a taxi with a fellow renegade, my new friend Paul Kaitz. Not long after the beginning of the school year, we became partners in delinquency. Toward the end of French class, I leaned over to Paul as Mr. Barry wrote the last idiom of the day on the blackboard. "Come on, let's get out of here," I whispered. We'd begun sitting next to each other without saying a single word until now. Somehow we'd smelled each other out, two men among boys. "I can't take it anymore," I said.

"I didn't think you did things like this," Paul said. "You're always in the middle of everything." Paul himself was different. He was a loner, a brilliant, arrogant loner who didn't seem to care if he had friends. His splendid detachment filled me with admiration. When on occasion he made an appearance at some party, he spent the time at the piano, pounding out boogie-woogie or improvising on show tunes. Tamarack School girls in cashmere sweaters and tartan plaids crowded around him, humming along.

"I'm leaving," I said. "Now."

Mr. Barry had written, "*Quand on crache en l'air ça retombe sur le nez,*" and turned to us looking sheepish. "Kaitz," he said with boyish anticipation. "Translate."

Paul looked the sentence over. "When you spit in the air it falls on the nose," he said.

"Wrong," Mr. Barry all but shrieked with delight. "Krinsky."

"He's right," I said just as the bell rang.

Mr. Barry wagged his stubby finger at me. "To each his own," he translated. "Think, Krinsky, think."

On the subway downtown, Paul said, "You getting laid?"

"Sure."

"Me too," Paul said.

"It's just you and me in the whole goddam school," I said.

"My father pays for mine," Paul said matter-of-factly. "She's a call girl. She gets so lonely in the middle of the day that she calls school saying she's my mother. I go down to her place to keep her company. I think she's in love with me."

"No shit?"

"How about you, Krinsky?" Paul asked.

I told him about Carla. "It was terrific with Carla, but we're not seeing each other anymore." It was easy to talk to Paul. I hadn't talked to *anyone* about these things. "Then there's Maggie," I said. "Maggie's like no one else. With Maggie it's forever."

Paul looked down at his shiny cordovans. "Forever?" He seemed a little embarrassed. "We're pretty young."

"Maggie and I have been together since we were little kids. Babies."

"In Poland?"

"And here."

"Have I seen her?" Paul asked.

"She's at Tamarack," I said. "Sometimes we go up on the train together, but she gets rides from her English teacher, who lives on her block." The train hurtled into the dark tunnel just below 125th Street. "It's all screwed up," I confessed. "She's found someone else."

"She has?"

"I can't really explain it," I said. "It's probably going to be like this for the rest of our lives."

94

"It is?"

"We're a little like a brother and a sister," I said. I got up, took a deep breath, sat back down again. "But that only adds to it. We can't keep our hands off each other. My uncle and her mother are like that, too."

We got off at his stop at Seventy-second Street and walked toward the park. "A fucking den of iniquity," Paul said, putting a hand on my shoulder. "A nest of crafty Europeans," he added.

As the fall progressed, Paul and I made fewer and fewer appearances at school. Instead, we cruised in a cab until we decided on something to do. Often, we walked in the park, spent part of a day at the Forty-second Street Library, or sat talking for hours in the lobby of the Plaza, Pierre, or Sherry-Netherland. As a rule, my cab stopped across the street from the San Remo, where Paul lived with his mother. The doorman, looking out for me, would call upstairs on the house phone and Paul would come down quickly, carrying his book bag, looking more like a young businessman than a schoolboy.

One morning, in the Palm Court of the Plaza, Paul told me about his father. "Tell me the truth, Krinsky," he said. "Didn't you ever hear of Lou Kaitz?" He searched my face carefully.

"No," I said. "Why should I?"

"He's pretty well known. Van der Orp and Dunne sure know who he is." Van der Orp and Dunne ran the Alexander Hamilton School for Boys.

"Why all the mystery, Kaitz? What's it all about?"

"He's also known as "Spider" Kaitz. Doesn't *that* sound familiar?"

"Is he a mobster?" I joked.

"A mobster? That's a funny word. He's a businessman, really." Paul looked down. "He's a mobster," he said.

I didn't know what to say. "Is he here in the city?" I asked.

"In Miami and Las Vegas mostly. Building casinos."

"He's a builder. What's the big deal?"

"Big deal?" Paul said. "Fuckin'-A it's a big deal. Don't be a *putz*, Krinsky. My father's a killer."

We were leaning over our white wicker chairs whispering as groups of foreign dignitaries gathered to start their day and Upper East Side ladies were beginning to meet for coffee.

"What do you mean a killer? You mean he actually *mows people down?*"

"No," Paul admitted, "not like that."

"Listen, Kaitz," I said, "this may not make sense to you, but some men are just too big to live a normal life. I can name you artists, well-known artists, who have killed." Paul looked puzzled. "And that would be just the beginning. What about politicians, what about businessmen?"

"Krinsky," Paul said patiently, "maybe there's something you missed, maybe I didn't make myself clear."

"Very often," I said, "a man becomes an artist precisely because he finds art a substitute for his antisocial feelings. I'm talking about men of great power and vision—"

"What the fuck are you talking about?" Paul asked.

"If an artist can be a criminal, then a criminal can be an artist. I know, Kaitz, that this doesn't necessarily follow the rules of logic, but we're not talking logic here, we're talking *the sublime.* I don't know your father. He could be just a petty criminal—"

"*That* he's not," Paul said.

"Of course he's not. He's a man bursting with imagination and power who needs to *express* himself."

Paul looked at me with affection. "Well," he said, "it's always possible. . . ."

"That's just it. We don't know."

"He hasn't been particularly nice to my mother."

"Paul, Paul," I said. "That's just it. We're not talking about a family man. We're talking about a man for whom family is prison."

"That's right, Krinsky. It's no fun for his wife and son."

"I know, I know. People suffer. Maggie could have used a real father."

"What about you, for Christ's sake?" Paul asked.

"That's different," I said. "They didn't *choose* to leave."

"Your father?"

"We're not talking about that," I said, meaning that I didn't want to talk about that. "We're talking about the courage to go after your own destiny."

"You think my father saw it that way?" Paul said.

"Have you ever heard of Cellini?" I asked.

"From Chicago?"

"From the Renaissance," I said. "He wrote an autobiography where he *admits* doing all this stuff."

"Oh, you mean *that* Cellini. It was different in the Renaissance," Paul said. "The laws weren't the same. Maybe it was okay to cut someone up."

"No, it wasn't okay. These guys got in real trouble. Artists like Cellini and Caravaggio were in and out of jail. They were chased all over goddam Europe. But the people who knew about those things—*and this is the point*—the *smart* people, the popes and princes—they knew that these crimes were nothing compared to the art these guys were creating. They collected their art, Kaitz, and they bailed them out of prison. It's what you have to do for special people." I could see that Paul was trying out a new image on his father. I for one couldn't wait to meet Lou Kaitz.

But now I wanted to show Paul the Cellinis, the Caravaggios, the Goyas at the Met. We paid for our coffees and took a cab up Fifth. In the cab, with our book bags between us, I asked him if he'd ever read *The Fountainhead*. "It's full of people like your father," I said. "Free spirits."

"Hey, Krinsky," Paul said. "I read that book. Those guys aren't free spirits, they're sons of bitches. That's a dangerous book. That book's about how strong people shit all over weak people. You think that's good? That's shit, Krinsky." Paul had been weakened by respiratory ailments when he was a kid and read *everything*. He knew baseball players' averages, surrealist poetry, the Oedipus plays. When he said he'd read *The Fountainhead*, he'd really read it.

The Goyas at the Met seemed uninspired after what we were talking about. "You know," I said, thinking I now understood, "life and art can be the same goddam thing."

We stood in front of pretty little Don Manuel Osorio de Zuñiga in his bright red suit and silver sash. "That's a cute little kid," I said.

97

Paul looked for a long time. "Cute?" he finally said. "You think that little pecker's cute?"

I looked some more. Don Manuel, dressed to kill, was parading a magpie on a leash in front of three cats crouching in the background.

"He's torturing the cats," Paul said. "I know it, you know it, the goddam cats know it. The moment they pounce on that bird, that kid's going to kick the shit out of them."

Paul astounded me. I thought *I* had given *him* a new way to see, a new way to look at his father, but it was Paul who forced my eyes below the sacred surface. And then there were other, more complicated layers. I was embarrassed by how I'd accepted Enid's love of the cuteness of this painting, its dazzling colors, and nothing more. Paintings had signposts, meaning beneath meaning. I had to *work* to see how a brushstroke could be brave and new, what it demolished of the past, what it announced for the future. I couldn't wait to see everything anew, to delve into the mysteries, not just the immediate majesty of a painting, not just the pleasure of recognizing a shared mood or action. I had to penetrate its complexity, understand its structure, its mathematics, its historical cunning.

We left the Met and walked into the park. We sat down under a tree, where I began sketching Paul. "We're like Goya and that lawyer, what's his name?" Paul said. The lawyer was Don Sebastian Martinez, proud, haughty, the general treasurer of the financial council in Cadiz. I liked that. Goya and Martinez. Krinsky and Kaitz.

I took the sketch back to the hotel and worked it up in pastels. In it, Paul sits in silk coat and knee breeches, with an impeccable wig on his head. The day I brought the finished portrait to school with me, Miss McIntyre, our librarian, handed me a letter from the headmaster, Dr. Sander van der Orp. It outlined my history at the school, from the time "you reached our shores as a young refugee chap" until the present. "For several years, my trust in you was not misplaced," he wrote. I searched for the point, and in the last paragraph I found it. It began with this sentence: "I fear that the recent war has brought much depravity to our republic," and continued with a brief description of *my* depravity, which included my increasing absence from school but focused on "a series of filthy drawings which are now in my possession, and which are, I am told, only the tip of an immense pornographic iceberg." He asked that Bolek and I appear on the given date in his office, to make a "final disposition of this sorrowful case."

Bolek was not at all pleased by the news from school, insisting that those people had made room for us, that if it had not been for the likes of them, we would have fried in Europe.

A few days before the scheduled meeting, Bolek asked for a postponement because of a fashion show, "the greatest America has ever seen," he had Mlle. Sacha write Dr. Orp.

I stopped going to school altogether. Paul and I continued our daytime activities, adding the Frick, the Museum of Modern Art, and the Hispanic Society to our tours of the city. Paul was now so convinced of the possibilities of artists and delinquents being one and the same that he began to look on me more and more as a man of vision. "You're lucky," he told me. "Getting kicked out of school can work to your advantage. What can those idiots teach *you*? I *have* to continue. I'm thinking of going to law school. That'll be a big help to my father in his business"

Though I tried to stop him, Bolek sent Schuller up the West Side Highway with two sets of antique bookends for Dr. Orp's office. "You are bribing him," I said as we sat in Bolek's office at Prince Casimir's.

"You need help," Bolek said glumly. "I am helping."

Just then, Sophie called with a suggestion of her own. We each took a phone. "Why not bring Kor into the picture?" Sophie asked.

"Kor," Bolek pronounced with great annoyance. "He is not exactly my best friend."

"*Your* best friend?" I said. "He is *my* friend."

"Really," Sophie said, "Kor is not an ogre. He is a greatly admired artist, and, after all, art is at stake here."

"It's not exactly high art," Bolek said. "It is pornography."

"How can you say that?" Sophie reprimanded. "Nothing Adam does can be called pornography."

"Zosia," Bolek said, "what in God's name can Kor do?"

"He can go up to Adam's school and plead his case," Sophie said.

"They have not even heard of Kor," Bolek insisted.

"Of course they have," Sophie said. "They are educators. Everyone has seen the *Life* article."

"What will he wear?" Bolek asked, his hand on his forehead, tired of the whole discussion. "Tell him I will lend him a suit."

A week later we ran into Kor at Tamarack, where Maggie was playing Emily in *Our Town*. He sat with a group of his friends on the opposite side of the small auditorium. They were shielded from our view by students who were interviewing him.

When the performance started, Sophie and I whispered into Bolek's ear to explain what was going on in Grover's Corners. "Magdalena is the perfect American," he said, "so young and innocent. And, please, where is this Gruber's Corner?"

Between acts we stepped outside. "Frankly," Sophie said, "I'm a little surprised at how good Maggie is."

"Don't worry," Bolek said. "It doesn't mean she has to be an actress."

"I do want her to be happy," Sophie said.

"And so do I," boomed a voice behind us. It was Kor, looking like a magician in a black cape with a blue lining. His arms were outstretched to encompass us all. "Marvelous," he said, "though if this play takes place in the mind of God, as we are told, then our future looks bleak."

Beautiful Lala came behind him, on the arm of Salvador Dali, while Dali's wife followed behind, talking with a student.

"Sophie, Sophie," Kor sang, throwing his arms around her. "Your daughter is a born actress, a perfect American." He looked across at the rest of us. "And, Bolek," he said heartily, taking him by the elbows, "let me look at you." Bolek looked uneasy, but he grabbed back, so that each of them held the other's elbows. From Kor's yellowing teeth protruded his gold cigarette holder with no cigarette. "And here is our notorious Adam," Kor said, winking at me. "Our own Caravaggio. We shall petition for a pardon, perhaps even an apology."

Dali broke away from several Tamarack girls who were shouting questions at him. He stared bug-eyed between Sophie's breasts. "That coat," he said, "it is magnificent. I must put it on Dali."

"Certainly," Sophie said, slipping Bolek's chinchilla off her shoulders.

Dali wrapped it around himself with a flourish. "You must make one for me, Prince Casimir," he said to Bolek. "Dali must have furs."

Bolek was sizing Dali up, taking silent measurements. "Perhaps a Persian lamb, Mr. Salvador," Bolek said. "Perhaps a fur lining . . ."

"Yes, Prince," Dali said, "a Persian lamb for a Spanish lion."

Later, as Maggie delivered her goodbye speech toward the end of *Our Town*, Kor's side of the auditorium began to hum, interrupting the flow on stage. We could see Kor trying to quiet Dali, who could no longer contain himself. In a monotonous singsong, getting louder and louder, he chanted: "Help me, help me, this Town is driving me sane."

"Goodbye, world, goodbye, Grover's Corners, mama, papa," Maggie said, as Sophie, on our side, sobbed quietly. "Goodbye to clocks ticking and Mama's sunflowers and food and coffee and new ironed dresses and hot baths and sleeping and waking up. . . ."

"Goodbye, goodbye," Dali wailed back as Kor attempted to gag him. "Go back to the cemetery, dear girl. Your Town needs a dose of paranoia."

When Schuller finally drove us all up to school in Bolek's Lincoln, Kor looked marvelous, wearing not only his cape but spats over his well-polished shoes—something I hadn't seen since my father wore spats in Warsaw.

Kor's presence surprised Dr. Orp. But this event brought him several surprises, not least among them the mention in a *Mirabelle* end section of "an upcoming art trial at the Alexander Hamilton School for Boys." And as Bolek, Kor, and I entered the main school building, I noticed some boys in the stands at one end of the football field, gathered around a thin, shabby man who, I was to learn later, was a city reporter from the *New York Times.*

Inside Dr. Orp's office, the heavy drapes had been pulled back. It was as if the midocean floor were being exposed to light for the first time. The American flag on one corner of Dr. Orp's desk looked positively garish within the monkish drabness. Bolek's bookends were nowhere in sight.

In the center of the room, Bolek and Kor greeted Dr. Orp and Mr. Thomas Dunne, the school treasurer and hatchet man. Orp was wearing tweeds while Dunne, as always, wore a black suit, silver tie, and enormous black shoes. Dr. Orp's thick glasses made two milky circles in front of his eyes. Everyone smiled, bowed, clicked their heels, like civilized generals before the battle. I realized that the two academic gentlemen held all the cards. From high up on the cliffs overlooking Van Cortlandt Park, these nobles, these descendants of the early settlers, looked out on the upper reaches of Manhattan, which was *their* turf, *their* tract of land.

Dr. Orp expressed his regrets for not being as conversant in contemporary art as he felt he should be. "Art is," Dr. Orp stated, "a radical process. It is, as I see it, an ongoing revolution, always stirring up trouble."

"On the contrary, sir," Kor corrected. "Art is essentially conservative." Kor had a theory for everything. There was no bottom to his well of knowledge or imagination. "It preserves, memorializes, eternalizes—"

"Yes, of course," Dr. Orp said, dismissing his original point of attack and locking his fingers together. "You are the expert in those matters. And most likely, sir," Dr. Orp said with a good-natured smile, "you are not entirely at home in the field of education."

"No, I am not an expert," Kor admitted, "although it pains me to witness the neglect of art in your school. I might tell you, sir, that since the fifteenth century, art has been firmly entrenched, together with poetry, the theoretical sciences, *all* intellectual pursuits. As a matter of fact, I would consider myself living in an ideal society if art were the foundation of a school's curriculum."

"Perhaps so, Mr. Kor, perhaps in an ideal world," Dr. Orp said, "but we live in an imperfect world, a vale of tears, as you well know." Kor acknowledged the point with a tilt of his large head. "And the reason we are here at all this afternoon," Dr. Orp continued, "is to discuss how this world has been further defiled through the efforts of your young friend."

I pulled at my shirt collar to let air in. I was seated on a hard little chair against one wall, while Kor and Bolek shared a leather couch.

"If you please, sir," Kor said then, stepping to the desk like an attorney to the bench. Orp and Dunne flinched as their space was being invaded. Kor looked about the desk. "If you please," he repeated, "do you have the drawings in question?"

Dr. Orp opened a bottom drawer, then looked down into it, hoping, I was sure, the sheets of smut would levitate without the help of his fingers. Slowly, reluctantly, he pulled out the Majas, the Kee-Nah-Wah Majas, now in the collection of Melvin Harris, a third-form student.

Kor plunged further into Orp's space by walking around the desk to see the Majas in Dr. Orp's hands. Orp seemed not to know if he should give them up, fearing perhaps that in one rash gesture this European libertarian would tear them to shreds. He held them at arm's length, just the right distance for Kor to see without his glasses. Kor looked at them and smiled.

"Ach, Adam," he said, "you have chosen the astonishing Maja. What an interesting choice. And my good Dr. Orp, you were right." Every one of us was silent. "This man, this Goya, he is one of those rare birds, a revolutionary artist, and in the very sense you meant. Here you have the first truly profane nude in Western art. You, my good sir, knew what you were talking about." Kor chuckled. "Ach, Adam, she is exquisite. And how she teases us!" Then in Polish, "Bone of a dog, not bad, not bad."

Notoriety stuck to the *Clothed* and *Naked Maja*, not only because of the somewhat questionable identity of the sitter, but because whoever she was, she looked like a real woman, perhaps a housewife, perhaps secretly spending the afternoon in the painter's studio while the cleaning lady scrubbed at home. Perhaps this was the cleaning lady herself, "smelling of the corset," as the French say. She stared boldly from the canvas, daring you to look. *My* Maja, on several sheets of drawing paper, transformed herself from the Clothed to the Naked as she stretched, scratched, removed her sash and bolero. It was Carla at her best, just before she stopped posing.

Bolek, who had been keeping silent, leaned over to me. "Ask him, darling, if I could see the drawings." I was so absorbed in Kor's oratory that I didn't answer. "Why not?" Bolek yelled out in Polish. "Blood of a dog, why not?"

Kor said, "The young man's uncle wishes to see the drawings, sir."

As if handling a rock of glowing radium, Orp handed them to Dunne, who handed them to Bolek. Bolek crossed his legs. "This is good, darling," he said.

"Sir," Kor said after taking the series from Bolek to study it, "these drawings show talent. Furthermore, they are within a historical tradition. You fail to understand—"

"Fail to understand?" Dr. Orp at last exploded. "Fail to understand? Sir," he declaimed, "if a painting arouses base instincts, then it is false art and bad morals . . ."

Kor matched Dr. Orp's outburst. "If you please," he shouted, "the depiction of the unclothed female body naturally arouses desire. If it did not, it would be *bad art* and *false morals*." The elegance and precision of his English thrilled me. I think it surprised Dr. Orp.

"I think, sir," Dr. Orp said, very flustered now, "that you should not be here in this office. You are yourself a well-known pornographer. You yourself should learn to bury your prurient impulses."

Kor was shocked into speechlessness.

"What did he say?" Bolek asked.

"That Kor makes dirty pictures, too," I translated, bringing a big smile to Bolek's face.

"We must exercise control, sir," Dr. Orp continued, "or our society will crumble. Don't forget, sir, we are talking about a school for gentlemen. We are not talking about the street or the garret. Your friend here is a schoolboy—"

"Who knows? Perhaps he is the hope of his generation," Kor said. "You run the risk of rejecting Rembrandt—"

"Rembrandt?" Dr. Orp guffawed. "Rembrandt, ha-ha! Let me tell you, in case you don't know, Rembrandt was a God-fearing man, a man of simple taste, a man who glorified the home and the hearth—"

"You are a fool," Kor said, and walked back to the couch, taking the arm opposite from Bolek.

Orp flinched but continued. "Your self-portrait was not fit to be printed in a national magazine. It is a reflection of the immoral times we live in, times that your war precipitated." The self-portrait that Dr. Orp referred to was, of course, Kor's now famous version of *The Polish Rider*.

Bolek, sensing that violence was brewing, got up and began to speak, partly through me, partly in his own English. "I came to America because I love America," he began, putting one hand in his jacket pocket, the other illustrating his words. "I had offers from Brazil, from Sweden, from Australia. But America has the biggest heart." He stopped and looked at all of us in turn. "Adam needs America now," Bolek said. "He needs to go to university, to be polished. These drawings are dirty, but they are good," Bolek said. "Don't cut him off from your world, I beg you. Teach him to be a better citizen. After all, haven't we all, as men, felt these same stirrings, testing our boundaries, finding out what is right and what is wrong?" I had never heard Bolek so eloquent.

"It will take a great deal of rehabilitation, I'm afraid," Dr. Orp said.

"But you can play with the rules," Bolek said, "everyone plays with the rules. The world is made by exceptions."

I was afraid that Bolek would offer money, but he didn't. Kor got up from the couch. "No," he bellowed. "No, no, no! We will not bend any rules. It is not a matter of your idiotic rules. There are *principles* here, basic principles." He went to the desk again and slammed his fist on it. "The erotic is our deepest impulse," he pronounced at the top of his lungs. Art yearns for the erotic!"

"I was against America entering the war," Dr. Orp said, as if from a bad dream. "We were a hybrid people but a great people. We had an opportunity, a calling." He turned to the wall on his right. "Leave us alone," he begged, his thick glasses moving nervously, flashing the bright light from outside his windows.

Kor lowered his head so that he and Orp were nose-to-nose. "You, sir, are everything that is puckered, shriveled, *Sanforized!* You, sir, are an asshole!"

Kor took us all by surprise. My face flushed. Bolek leaned forward, his eyes open wide. Mr. Dunne rushed out of the room, presumably to find reinforcements, while Dr. Orp sat with all the color gone from his face. He looked chiseled out of white marble.

"Have you never been with a woman?" Kor taunted. "Savonarola! Pig turd!"

Dr. Orp seemed paralyzed, though he did not fold, he did not go down. Bolek ran over to try to salvage something, who knew what. He tugged at Kor's sleeve. "A woman is ecstasy," Kor shouted as Bolek pulled him away. "To fuck is divine."

Mr. Dunne rushed back in with Miss McIntyre, our librarian. I took the center of the floor for the first time. "This is not a school," I proclaimed. "You teach nothing important here. You teach only manners, you teach behavior for stockbrokers. I will never come back to your rotten school. I spit on your stinking school!" I was shaking my fist. "Never!" I swore to the astonished company. "Never!" There was no turning back now. I was colleague to Caravaggio and to Lou Kaitz. I was brother to Kor.

The *New York Times* reporter rode downtown with us. Schuller told a joke about a Jewish furrier meeting the Pope, but no one laughed. Bolek stared at the river all the way down.

"That school is a scandal," Kor eventually said. "They would not recognize art if it was put in front of their nose. And it was," he added with feeling.

The reporter, who smelled of whiskey, asked to see samples of my work. I sketched a portrait of him with his eyelids heavy, his hair mussed by the breeze from Bolek's open window. It wasn't my best effort, for my hand shook, and, as Francisco said so well somewhere in *Lusty Genius,* "the touch of a hand must be as light as the fluttering wing of the dove."

Two days later, the *Times*'s local news column ran this story:

A student at the Alexander Hamilton School for Boys in Riverdale was expelled for what the headmaster, Dr. Sander van der Orp, called "the vilest pornography."

"A school like this one," Dr. Orp said, "the best in the city, cannot tolerate the propagation of smut." The student, Adam Krinsky, sold these drawings to other boys in the school, according to Dr. Orp. "We do not train pornographers, brokers, or salesmen," Dr. Orp said.

Mr. R. Z. Kor, the renowned artist, recently showing at Peggy Guggenheim's Art of the Century Gallery and featured in a *Life* magazine article, maintained that Adam Krinsky, an Alexander Hamilton senior, is not only an excellent student but "a great talent."

I began to have bad dreams again. Twice in one week, I woke up screaming as our country house crumbled. Bolek had a hard time reconciling himself to my delinquency, though Sophie helped every chance she got. As we sat around in her dining room after dinner, she cited all the examples she could muster of artists who never went to school, those who dropped out of school, even those who blew up their schools. "Listen, darling," she said to Bolek, "artists should study with other artists."

"School is not for me," I said, gauging Maggie with the corner of my eye. "I have too much to learn, to see, to feel. I need to find myself."

"He wants to find himself?" Bolek said, exasperated. "What is this to find himself? On what money does he intend to find himself?" He turned to Sophie, ready to do battle. "Would you like it if Magdalena stopped going to school?"

"Maggie is an artist," I said. "Her allegiance should be to her art."

Maggie lifted her eyes and smiled. I recognized in the down-from-under look a revitalized interest, perhaps desire. "Adam has been booted out, Bolek," she said, *"booted out,"* she repeated with relish. "There is no turning back."

5

*A*t the end of Bolek's day, he slumped exhausted on his satin couch in the showroom. The entire third floor was silver and blue, enlarged by a wall of mirrors, scented by huge vases of freesias and calla lilies.

Bolek took a cigarette from a leather case on a side table. He lit it, puffed, but didn't inhale. "I am working too hard," he said. "I need a rest." For the first time, he looked old. His navy-blue suits made his face look more sallow, but the gray shadows under his eyes wouldn't go away with a change of clothes.

During these quiet moments together, I would have loved to paint Bolek. I was taking classes all day at the League with George Grosz and Reginald Marsh, but it wasn't enough. I would have been happy to paint around the clock. I wanted to paint the streaks of blue—the blue of Poussin's distant mountains—under Bolek's strong cheekbones, the iridescent glow of his warlike cranium.

"A lot of people today?" I asked.

He nodded and looked out the window.

The patternmaker in his long white coat came into the show-room with canvases draped over his shoulder. Bolek called for Elsa and they began fitting.

Bolek and Weinglass now owned the five-story building, for which Bolek supervised the buying of antiques and paintings. The street floor was almost entirely show space, so that win-dow-shoppers could see sables and leopards draped over gilt-framed chairs and couches, or laid out on the Oriental carpets. A dwarf elevator man in a pillbox hat and sky-blue uniform stood in front of the imported French elevator. All of it was as glorious and inviolable as Versailles.

"Ah, Adam, darling," Mlle. Sacha said in a voice loud enough to bring Jacques the salesman. "You look terrifeec—*très* sexy." She inhaled deeply. "What is that smell?" she asked. "What have you been doing?"

"Paint?" I suggested.

"Ah, yes? Have you been painting in school?"

"Hasn't Bolek told you? I'm no longer in school."

"No?"

"I have been—how to say?—kicked out."

"No," she said. "Eet cannot be."

"Yes," I assured her. "Eet ees."

Mlle. Sacha and Jacques didn't know what to say. They had beamed at me all my life, all the Mlles. Sacha, Sabrina, Basia, all the salesmen Jacques and Janek and Pierre, all the models from Kiki through Elsa. They had tickled my chin, squeezed my cheeks, clucked adoringly over me ever since I was a baby. My mother or Bolek would bring me to the factory in Warsaw to parade me through the aisles as white-coated women leaned from their machines like pendulous trees over a country road, touching my head, offering me chocolates.

"Yes, I paint all day now, right here on Fifty-seventh Street," I told Mlle. Sacha and Jacques.

"But you are such a good student," Mlle. Sacha said, her face all loose, unhinged by my news. Bad news was not easily tolerated in the showrooms.

"I was caught making feelthy peectures," I said.

"No!" she exclaimed.

"Is that so?" said Jacques. "Nude girls?" He smiled and his gray eyes twinkled.

"Doing weird things," I told him.

Jacques beamed as if he had been waiting for this moment. "We must play squash together at my club," he said.

Bolek called my name. He was making graphite lines on a canvas that hung on Elsa. She stood like a statue, staring into the mirror. "Go into my office and look at the paintings on the floor," Bolek told me as Elsa slipped into the next canvas.

In Bolek's ornate office—all leather and gold and silver— three small landscapes in baroque frames leaned against a wall. They were beach scenes, each with a turquoise sea, each with strollers in large beribboned hats, carrying parasols, strutting on white sand.

"Which one?" Bolek asked when I returned to the show-room.

"None of them," I said.

He stuck a pin into Elsa's side and she slapped his hand. "None?" he said.

"That's chocolate-box painting," I said.

He stopped pinning and turned to me. "You think you know all about painting? You don't know *anything*. One of them is a Dufy. You know what that means, a *Dufy?* All you know is dirty pictures! These are masters."

"They have nothing to do with art."

"Oh? He knows so much about art now. Dufy is not good enough for him."

"It's not Dufy. It's Dufy's brother."

"It is the same thing," Bolek shouted. "It is a family of artists, like the circus—"

"Max Dufy," I said, "means nothing."

"That is not his name. It is not Max. It is Maurice!" He stormed out and I took refuge in the model's cubicle with Yvette, who sat in front of the mirror tugging at her eyebrows with a tweezer, a towel thrown over her shoulders, the top of her black dress down at her waist. "What's the matter weeth heem?" Yvette asked, glancing at me in the mirror. "He has been like a greezly bear."

I leaned back in my chair and let my head sink into a rack of minks. I rubbed my face in it. "I must paint you, Yvette," I said.

"You naughty boy," she said. "'Ow you like me to pose? Weezout my dress probablee."

Mlle. Sacha peeked in. "Customer," she sang, and Yvette scurried to get herself together. I went to the elevator, where Bolek found me. "You are right," he said, "they are not for here, those paintings. Here we need paintings of flowers." Bolek put his hands on my shoulders. "We will go to eat together."

"I can't," I said.

"You can't? What this means, you can't?"

"I've already promised Paul—"

"Paul? I know who he is, this Paul. Why do you never tell me who he is? People like that will destroy us."

"What are you saying, Bolek?"

"Do you know who is his father? Do you know? He is a gangster, a Jewish gangster, a killer like a regular Pole."

"He's a businessman like you," I said.

"Like me? You are crazy, you, you shit smear—"

"Lou Kaitz is a hardworking man."

"Don't say his name in this place," Bolek warned, his eyes large blue disks, his lower jaw thrust forward.

This time *I* stormed out. "Lou Kaitz," I cried as Dick the dwarf shut the fragile glass door, *"he is a real man!"*

I met Paul downstairs and we walked to the Warwick, where Paul knew the bartender. We drank beer and smoked cigarettes. "My father's coming in from Miami," Paul said. "He's going to meet us at the Trip Deuces." We walked down Sixth Avenue. Everything in the world was out there to be painted. We went over to Broadway to the penny arcade, where we shot beams of light into the glass shoulders of Mussolini, Tojo, and Hitler. The place smelled of popcorn and vomit. Record stores along Broadway blared "Mammy" from *The Jolson Story.* I wanted to stick it all on canvas, the noise of the music, the popcorn, the empty faces, the gum wrappers on the sidewalk. Everything that had been given a name and a value for me by Bolek, by Alexander Hamilton, by the radio, the stores, the magazines and movies, I had to rename, revalue. We wandered back uptown, gaping at the whores. On Fifty-second Street, a doorman in a dirty brown uniform asked us if we wanted to get laid. "Fuckin'-A," Paul said, guiding me past him, then down a few steps into the Trip Deuces, Lou Kaitz's place.

Though it was still early, a few people sat at small tables. We stayed at the bar, where the bartender polished glasses. "Your dad is coming to town," he told Paul. The pretty hatcheck girl came over to tease Paul and brush our jackets. A black piano player walked by. "How ya doin', boss?" he said, then went over to an upright to the right of the stage and began playing a medley from *Call Me Mister*. Sandwiches and beer were put in front of us. "That's them," Paul said as a group of black men walked into the kitchen. "Just wait till you hear."

The Trip Deuces was beginning to stir. The carriage lights on either side of the stage were turned on, the doors to the kitchen swung open and shut, tossing out eerie bursts of bright light. Smoke curled up into the powerful beam of a spotlight that lit the stage. Paul took his glass of beer and disappeared in one of the dark corners of the room. I began to see the grand diagonals of Goya's space, those slapdash backgrounds come to life. And when a group of partygoers in little pointed party hats came in laughing, Goya's space filled with Goya's grotesques from the *Caprichos* and *Disparates*.

On the bandstand, a couple of the musicians took their places. They unpacked and polished their instruments, making incidental brassy sounds. There were five men on the stage, and they began to play, making sweet music, slow and melodic. They slid up and down tunes I recognized, teasing them, slipping off them into pretty little twists and turns. The more they played, the bolder they got.

Paul elbowed his way through the crowd at the bar followed by a small, dapper man rubbing his hands together vigorously. "Finally," Lou Kaitz said, putting out both arms, "I meet the famous Adam." In this dark, beer-soiled place, the air around him was perfumed, fresh as a garden. He looked immaculate, as if he had just stepped out of a steam bath. He was bronze from the sun, his flesh smooth and shiny, sparkling with health. Paul helped him off with his overcoat. Lou Kaitz stood straight, knowing how good he looked. A tall drink with slices of lime and orange was put into his hands as people gathered around him. Rose, the hatcheck girl, brushed his jacket, then took his arm. Then they were all swept away from me and the sounds of the music took over.

The saxophone wailed with a human voice, deep and throaty, an extension of the lazily swaying man whose lips were wrapped around it. Long melodic lines fragmented into doodles, collided, coalesced. This raw, intense sound filled my whole body. It stabbed, then healed, stung and pacified. It was like watching Goya push through the resin on his copper plates, like watching the images appear for the very first time, watching the golden thread of a winged bat, a butchered body, a priest with a donkey's tail.

I got up from the barstool and nearly fell. I'd paid no attention to all the beer. Paul was there to steady me. "You want to meet them?" he yelled into my ear. "We'll go backstage." He steered us through the packed club to a back door. The music was everywhere, thick as the smoke. On the other side of the door, it was quiet, a brutal change. We walked into a dingy room with a few chairs and a single bare bulb hanging over a stained round table. "Sit down," Paul said, pushing a chair under me. "We'll wait here for the set to end." He pulled over a chair and sat next to me. "This stuff's pure joy," he said. "Haven't you ever heard of Charlie Parker?"

The musicians came in, wiping their sweaty faces, blowing spit out of their instruments. "That's Lou's son," one of them said, and everyone grumbled, "How ya doin'?"

I'd gotten up and stood off to the side, leaning against the wall. Paul introduced me. He knew them all: Bud and Max and Jimmy and Oscar and Charlie. "Adam's an artist," Paul said.

"Oh, yeah?" someone said. Paul and I stood in silence as they lit up, poured whiskey into their glasses. "You fellas want a drink?" someone asked.

"We better get some air first," Paul said, taking my arm.

"Sure thing," the musicians said, more or less in unison.

Paul and I went out the back door into a grimy alley full of garbage cans. "You look white," Paul said. We took out our cigarettes and smoked. It was cold and still, the city's noises muffled by the buildings all around us. Then the metal back door opened and one of the musicians came out. "That's Charlie Parker," Paul whispered.

Charlie Parker lit up a skinny cigarette and took deep drags on it, swallowing air. "How's your old man?" he grunted, trying to hold his breath. He looked up at the ribbon of starry sky between buildings, then took off his jacket and laid it down neatly on top of a garbage can. "If you'll excuse me, gentlemen," he said as he kicked over two garbage cans, pushed them together, and lay down on top of them. He rolled back and forth, arching his back like a cat. Paul and I kept out of his way. He picked himself up and began riding one of the garbage cans. He yelped like John Wayne riding a log in the river. Out of breath, he stopped, stuck the butt end of one of his cigarettes into his mouth, and smoked some more. "That's better," he said. We said nothing. "Limbering up," he said, "doing scales." He began to laugh so hard that he coughed and spit. "You gotta loosen up, man, then you can do *anything*." He lifted his head to the sky. "I can do fuckin' *anything!*" he roared. He wiped his face and put on his jacket. The air was thin and cold, yet the alley reeked of rotten meat. I couldn't put it all together. How could *this man*, this wild man riding garbage cans, make *this music?*

Paul's eyes filled with tears, probably because of the cold. "My father," Paul said, "he'd do *anything* for you."

Charlie looked surprised. "I dig your old man," he said. "That's one mean son of a bitch." He laughed. "Lou lives right out there. He doesn't *like* you, he *loves* you. And if he really doesn't like you, look out."

From outer space, I said, "Where did you learn music like that?" My eyes opened wide. I would have turned myself inside out for this man.

"Who is this kid?" Charlie Parker asked.

I said, "Is it different all the time? Is it written down?" I had to know.

"It do come naturally," Charlie Parker said in an exaggerated drawl, "jes' like suckin' on ribs."

I wanted to tell him that I'd gone to this dumb school, this ridiculous gentlemen's academy, that I lived half in the fashion world. I felt dizzy.

"Where the fuck you think I come from, kid, the jungle?" Charlie asked. I ran over to one of the garbage cans, flipped the lid, and threw up inside. Charlie laughed. "You know something about music?" he asked.

The smell was almost unendurable now. "A little," I said.

"What's this?" Charlie asked. He whistled the waltz from *Der Rosenkavalier,* which I knew. I whistled *Petrouchka,* which he got immediately. Then he whistled something very weird. He went on and on. "You think I'm just improvising?" he asked. I didn't know. So Charlie whistled the whole piece over again, exactly like the first time. I had no idea what it was and told him so. "*Wozzeck,*" he said. "It's an opera." He slapped me on the back, then got up and put a piece of gum in his mouth. He chewed it for a minute, took the gum out, stuck something into it, then put it back in his mouth. "Gotta get goin', boys," he said, and we followed him in. He grabbed his saxophone, caressed it like a wild pony, looked back at us, laughed, and joined the other musicians, already on stage.

Paul and I went in to sit at Lou Kaitz's table near the front. "I fucked up," I said gloomily.

"He liked you," Paul said.

"He couldn't have."

"He knew he knocked you out with his music."

"I don't know anything," I said. "I don't even know where it all comes from."

"Where what comes from?"

"*Art.*" I exhaled the word as a dragon exhales fire.

"From the gut," Paul said.

"If he were white, and rich, could he make music like that?" I wanted to know.

"I've never seen you like this," Paul said. My questions felt as if they'd been lying around somewhere deep inside me. They felt strange and familiar at the same time. "You all right?" Paul asked.

"What he does comes from what he is," I said, not knowing how to say it, "from his life."

Paul looked around us. His father was still at the bar. "Just like you," he said.

"No, I don't *feel* mine," I said. I had a terrible taste in my mouth, like hot aluminum, the acrid smell of my dream. "You know my dream that keeps coming back? No one in it bleeds. The house that crumbles is made of popsicle sticks. . . ."

"Adam, you're my friend," Paul said, "my real friend."

I looked into his face, just like mine, his eyes like black coals, full of love, full of promise. Paul put his arm around my shoulder and I squeezed his hand.

Lou Kaitz came back with his entourage and the music began again. Lou Kaitz was full of good cheer, promoting the sun, the sea, the good life on the American frontier, where, he said, everything was possible. Paul looked positively proud. "In the sun," Lou Kaitz was saying, "you eat good and you sleep good." He leaned over to me, enveloping me in his aura of sweet cologne, and said in my ear, "And you fuck good, you know what I'm saying, Adam?" He squeezed my arm and offered me a private laugh. Paul was thrilled. Lou Kaitz told the table that he was dating Rita Hayworth, that Tyrone Power was a fairy. He told us about the hotel he was putting up in Las Vegas. Then he turned to Rose, who stood behind him, leaning on his shoulders. He whispered something in her ear and reached into his wallet for a hundred-dollar bill—everyone saw it—which he stuffed into the palm of her hand. When, an hour later, Paul and I got up to go, Rose met us at the door. "Your dad asked me to show you a good time," she said, taking both our arms.

Outside the Trip Deuces, Charlie Parker was talking with the other musicians. All but Charlie took off in a white convertible, and Charlie walked with the three of us to the corner of Sixth. As we approached the White Rose Bar, a tall blond woman ran up to him, threw her arms around him, kissing him drunkenly. He grabbed her ass and they squirmed under the streetlamp. "See you folks some other time," Charlie said, and Rose, Paul, and I started up Sixth Avenue. Rose put her hands inside our pockets. We walked briskly. The cold night air was doing me good. "You boys are pretty damn cute," Rose said.

Paul and I each had an arm around her until Paul skipped away from us to look back at Charlie and the blonde. There was scaffolding in the middle of the next block, so we walked along the street side of a line of parked cars. "That's some guy," Paul said, "the greatest alto sax in the world." He walked out into the middle of the street to have another look back. "Hey, Krinsky," he suddenly yelled. "Come on out here."

Rose was moving her hand inside my pants pocket. "I'm staying with you," I told her. "What's the problem?" I yelled out to Paul, who had already started running back.

"There's trouble," he yelled.

"You just come up when you're ready, honey," Rose said, and scribbled her address on the back of an envelope.

Reluctantly, I followed Paul, walking slowly, turning back to look at Rose, whose high heels were clicking hurriedly uptown. Beyond the construction on Fifty-third Street, I saw a huge sailor in white poking a fist into Charlie's chest. The blond woman was yelling for the cops. As I was about to cross the street, Charlie took a knife from his pocket and was swiping at the sailor. Paul was at their side, yelling, "Stop, stop!" when two more sailors swaggered over from across the avenue, bottles in their hands.

"Fuckin' nigger," the first sailor drawled as Charlie's knife ripped a long tear in the front of his shirt. "That's a white girl you're fuckin' with." One of the other sailors smashed his bottle on the lamppost, spraying the sidewalk with beer. Paul screamed, "Get the cops!"

"I'm going to kill this gorilla," the sailor with the broken bottle growled.

I stood across Fifty-second Street paralyzed, trying to move. "Adam!" Paul yelled when he saw me. As I ran across the street, Charlie, in the moment's distraction, took off in the opposite direction, down into the subway. They all disappeared down the stairs except for one sailor, who jumped out at me from a recessed storefront. His fat fist connected with my nose, "that pretty little *goy* nose" that Bolek was so fond of. The sailor hit me again and again until I crumpled to the sidewalk, my nose gushing blood, my face feeling split open.

Below me, my Polish Jewish blood stained the cement of Sixth Avenue. I held my face together in my hands like thousand-year-old shards pieced together into a bowl. I heard shouting voices resound off the tiled walls of the subway somewhere under me. And then they all appeared again, running, in a jumble, until a siren wailed its way up Sixth. The sailors took off. Paul gasped when he saw me, and Charlie pulled me up and into the shadows of Fifty-second Street.

"We gotta get you to a hospital," Charlie said, panting, his arms crossed on his chest. He gave me his perfumed handkerchief to stop the bleeding.

"Those cops," the blond woman said, "let me get those cops."

"No cops," Charlie said. "A cop on the scene means a nigger in jail." He hailed a cab and we drove to Lenox Hill, where an emergency-room doctor stuck the metal handle of some instrument into my nose and pushed until the bone lined up. Then he stuffed it with cotton, stitched around it and down my cheek, bandaged the whole thing, taped it, and gave me a handful of pain pills.

Outside on Lexington, I began to feel the various parts of my face as distinct pieces belonging to me. My front teeth felt loose and my jaw ached, making a weird cracking sound when I opened my mouth.

"We better get you home, kid," Charlie said.

"I'll go with you," Paul said.

"I want to hear more music," I said, and Charlie howled.

"This kid wants to hear more music," Charlie said, "we are going to hear more music." The four of us piled into a cab, Paul and I in the jump seats, Charlie and his friend Connie in back. Charlie took out another thin brown cigarette, asked the Negro driver if it was okay, and lit up. "What do you boys say to a short spin through the park first?" Charlie offered us all drags on his cigarette. "You boys never had no weed?" He laughed. "Just suck it in, then pass it on."

I suddenly remembered that we were supposed to meet Rose. "Another time," Paul said. "She'll keep."

"Yeah," Charlie said, pulling Connie close. "Some keep, some need immediate attention."

The city around the park sparkled, like decorations on Christmas trees. I looked up to see a sky filled with stars. It was like the Hayden Planetarium, like traveling through the Milky Way. In spite of my eyes beginning to swell shut and my ears ringing like sleigh bells, I felt on top of the world.

"How did you learn to do it?" I asked Charlie.

"Do what?" he said, his hand inside Connie's dress.

"Do what you do." I felt like I was floating.

"Who taught me? No one taught me." Connie's hips were moving slowly.

"Do you practice all the time?" My face throbbed.

"All the time," Charlie said as Connie's breathing got heavy.

I was leaning back with my eyes closed when the cab began to shake with Connie's motion. "You know," I said, as the movement became frenzied, "I just swallow your music without chewing it. Wap, it's all gone, like that. I don't know all the little things you worked out, everything you know, all the stuff you thought about." Connie was making her own music now, the way Carla did in the Massachusetts woods. Even with my eyes closed, I was full of sensations, the smell of the weed, of sweat, the taste of blood. "It's probably like you looking at paintings," I said. "All the things that go into them. You don't even know, there's so much, so much." The inside of the taxi became quiet. I heard a hansom cab's bells jingling as we passed it. "What about when you were a kid?" I asked. I waited patiently for Charlie to answer.

"Even then," he said.

"What about school?"

"Don't need no school for it."

"No school," I said contentedly.

Paul was dozing. Connie straightened herself up and said, "This man always knew how." She looked at him. "It all started in Kansas City," she said.

I said, "Where's Kansas City?" knowing damn well where it was. I had no idea why I said it, but it made Charlie howl.

"Where the fuck you from, the moon?" he said.

I thought that was very funny and I laughed, too.

It seemed like hours later when the cab pulled up to the Hotel Cecil in Harlem. Even though it was very late, the club inside the hotel was packed. Most of the people were black, though some were white. As we walked along the tables toward the front, the whole place buzzed with greetings for Charlie. He sat us down near the stage and disappeared. I began to feel that I was at one end of a long tunnel, and when Paul asked if I was all right, his words echoed off the tunnel walls. I ran my hands down my ribs, feeling their thickness. When I looked up, I saw smiling black faces with bright white teeth looking at me. They crowded the frame like people trying to get into a photograph. My head throbbed. I felt greased and shiny, a projectile ready to be shot out of a cannon. Then my head dropped to the table. I was vaguely aware of it splitting apart again, like a rotten pear. Someone was shoving me into another taxi. My face ached with the cold, my bandages stiffened, and my eyes locked shut like windows frosting over. When I next opened them, I was in a hospital and Bolek was pacing at the foot of my bed, his suit crumpled, his cigarette being shuffled from hand to hand. His relief at seeing me awake lasted but an instant.

"So you are becoming a fighter," he said. "I thought we left all that behind."

"There are things about America you don't know," I said, my mouth opening with difficulty, my voice resounding painfully inside my skull.

"What does that mean?" Bolek asked.

"There are cossacks everywhere," I managed to say, "even in your wonderful America."

"Of course it happens in America, too," Bolek said. "Poor America, it is open to the world's garbage." He tightened his necktie. "How can it not happen when you associate with gangsters and Negroes?" He rubbed his eyes. "I don't know you anymore." He walked to the window, put out his cigarette in a saucer already full of half-smoked butts. "The doctor says you will need two new teeth and your nose will look like a turnip." He kicked the radiator. "A filthy Silesian turnip."

"Always?"

"Who knows always? Long enough, for one night's entertainment. You are lucky to be alive." He stomped his foot. "What is this? You should live in Katowice or Kielce."

"Who told you I was here?" I asked.

"Who told me? Your friend. The killer's son."

I tried to sit up a little. The movement hurt unbearably. "As always, you're confusing things," I said. "The Negroes are the victims. . . ."

"Look at you," Bolek said. "Your whole face is purple. Thank God your mother doesn't have to see you like this."

"The Negroes are like Jews. Everybody hates them. An American sailor was going to kill him. A white American sailor punched me in the face."

"It's his country," Bolek said. "You are a guest."

"You were a guest in Warsaw?" I asked him. "It belonged to the cossacks?"

Bolek sat down, exhaled loudly, and closed his eyes. I saw that in some way he had conceded and looked relieved to have this point settled. "Magdalena wants to see you," he said.

"How bad do I look, Bolek?"

Bolek went out into the hall and came back with a small mirror. I was shocked. The exposed part of my face was one enormous bruise. The white bandages made me look grotesque, like a shaman mask. "Let her see me like this," I said. "It's the real me." My head felt like an empty room with the shutters banging. "I never heard anything like that music. The musicians are all Negroes."

"Primitive men," Bolek said.

"The music isn't primitive, Bolek. It's complicated and powerful—"

"Jungle music," Bolek said. "They know how to beat their drums."

"Bolek, you've got to listen to me. It's not like that. You would be stupid if you really believed that. It's more like *your* kind of music than you think. I don't understand how it happens."

"Anyone can make music," Bolek said, "even birds."

"Bolek, we both thought that you had to be educated to make art. I even thought you had to be European. You must come with me to hear this man—"

"This is nonsense," Bolek interrupted. "For them it is like boxing—"

"And what about Jews playing violins?"

"They're not like Jews," Bolek pronounced, and punctuated the thought by noisily unfurling the *Women's Wear Daily* he had carried inside his breast pocket. There would be nothing in those pages about Negroes or artists, just fatuous, pale, hysterical morons chirping about clothes.

I stayed in the hospital just long enough for another set of X-rays, and then, swaddled in head bandages and feeling sorry only that Maggie hadn't come before I was discharged, I tried to walk home. My legs pounded the sidewalk like sledgehammers on an anvil, and after two painful blocks down Lexington, I took a cab.

Paul and his father were waiting for me in the lobby of the Buckingham. Between them they held a huge basket of fruit wrapped in cellophane. Lou Kaitz was in a solemn mood. "I'm going to find out who those cavemen were," he said as I unlocked the door, "and unless we get satisfaction, I guarantee you, Adam, the navy's going to pay for this." We sat quietly as Lou looked out the window.

When Lou left, Paul said, "I feel terrible. It was all my fault."

"That's not true. It was a gift," I said. "It expanded me."

"Your uncle doesn't think so," Paul said. "I don't think he likes me."

All I was thinking about now was Maggie. I tingled with anticipation, knowing that the Punskys would lose this one. "Sure he likes you," I said, "though he doesn't know you well enough yet."

"I decided to stay in school," Paul said, "and go on to college." I wondered if I should call Maggie to tell her I was home. "Maybe I'll go on to law school," Paul said. "I think eventually I'll work for my father, you know, join his business."

The call came from downstairs, the desk announcing Maggie. When I opened the door, Maggie covered her mouth with her hand. "You look *terrible*," she said through her fingers. Then she curtsied, bowing her head low. Her hair was tied in a ponytail. She was in her favorite skirt, with enough fabric in it for a sail on a sailboat. On her feet she wore her dancing shoes.

A tight leotard clung to her body under an unbuttoned man's shirt.

"My mother said you were pretty good with your fists," Maggie said as she leaped into the room.

I looked at Paul. "I walked into it, that's all."

"Actually, Adam saved the day," Paul said.

"By letting Charlie Parker escape," Maggie said. She seemed to know the whole story and then some.

"There were no heroes," I announced, "just a lot of interesting experiences."

"I love Charlie Parker's music," said Maggie, who always surprised me by seeming to know something about everything. "It's people's music."

"According to Roy Punsky?" I asked.

"His name's Julian Roy, Adam." Maggie sat on the floor with her back rigid and the excess material of her skirt gathered between her legs. The heels of her Capezios touched while the toes pointed away from each other, making an obtuse angle. "He's been a help pointing things out that I wouldn't have known about. But I do have a mind of my own, you know."

"We'll have to hear Charlie together," I suggested. "You can bring Punsky if you want to."

"I don't want to," Maggie said sternly. "Julian and I are just friends."

I wanted to kneel at her feet, to wrap my arms around her legs. Instead, I went into the kitchenette to make tea. Lou Kaitz's fruit basket had nuts and jams and figs as well as apples and pears. I brought out plates and silver and napkins. "I've never had marijuana," Maggie was telling Paul. "I can get high without it."

"You should try it," I said. "You should try *everything*."

"My opiate's the theater," Maggie said.

"For Christ's sake, Maggie, it's no big deal," I said. I sipped tea, for I couldn't eat hunks of things like apples. The phone rang and Maggie jumped to get it. My things—my dreams, my adventures, even my telephone—were hers again. "It's Charlie Parker," she said, her eyes aglow.

Charlie wanted to know how I was. "Stick to your art," he

advised. "You gotta do it all the time. Do you do it all the time?"

"Yes."

"You do that and you'll do okay," Charlie said, "if you keep out of fights."

Paul left in one elevator and Bolek came up in the other. "He is like a Polish count, Magdalena," Bolek said. "He just sits here and everyone comes to him." His mood changed for the worse when he saw the fancy basket of fruit. He looked at it with fire in his eyes, the way he'd glare at a cheap fur coat. Maggie kept his mind off the fruit, telling us about her classes, her reading, her thoughts. "I'm learning Greek," she said.

Bolek looked more annoyed than amazed. He asked her why.

"To read Aeschylus in the original," Maggie said.

Bolek had always been impatient with Maggie's endless curiosity, the words that never stopped coming from her mouth. "She should be more like Sophie," he told me later, "more soft, more feminine."

When Bolek went into his room to take a nap, Maggie asked to hear about my night with Charlie. "Tell me everything," she said, sitting on the floor again now, with her legs crossed, the skirt, like an open rose, all around her.

I knew what Maggie wanted to hear. She was thirsting for the grand sweep of the scene, the gestures, the shape of our speech, the rolling, churning *feelings* behind everything. Surprisingly, I didn't want to tell her that. I didn't need to. "It was elegant, Maggie, that's what it was. All that night I tried to find other words for it, but this is the right word, *elegant*, the way being crystal clear is elegant. I've always heard Bolek calling things elegant. Everything he loves, everything he wants for me, is elegant. Oh, God, Maggie, I don't know."

Maggie got to her knees and came over on all fours. She put her head on my lap and her hands took my hands. "I've gotten to hate that word, too," she said. "It's such a Fifty-seventh Street word."

"In the hospital I was thinking that I have a history that is the subject of what I do. It brings my own feeling to what I do.

124

I have to know it better. I have to find a way to tame it. The way those musicians did it was so full of grace, I wanted to cry." Tears came to my eyes now. "I could see all his rage, and I could feel my own, just the tip of my own."

"You'll use yours the same way he uses his," Maggie said.

I stroked her hair. I couldn't wait to start painting again. I was burning to illustrate terror, injustice, stupidity, cruelty. I wanted to open everyone's eyes, to make them rise, as one, in outrage and indignation. As my hand pushed its way through Maggie's thick hair, it began tracing the outline of a nude in spite of myself.

My bruised and swollen face deflated quickly, then reassembled itself. My nose had returned to its original shape, and soon only Maggie, feeling the inside of my mouth with her tongue, was aware of my two new porcelain teeth.

She met me often at Grosz's class at the Art Students League. Grosz had been particularly attentive to me, spending extra time at my easel. "If you don't get all mixed up in art movements and manifestos," he said, "you can be as good as Norman Rockwell." He had a special scent about him, a cologne used by European men, one I thought indispensable to my own Old World identity. "I see a fire in your eyes, kiddo," Grosz said, "and you are blessed as few are with a light touch. Go to the West, pal. See the real America. Go paint the cactus and the turtles." When Maggie was sitting next to me, Grosz could not be pried away with a can opener. He talked to us of everything: his flower garden on Long Island, his exercise classes at the "Y," and all the time he ogled Maggie, top to bottom, bottom to top. In the crowded studio, with a brown-skinned nude lying serenely in one corner, George Grosz, once the great mocker of the fat, German bourgeoisie, looked down the length of his pipe at Maggie and divulged his favorite foods, pipe tobacco, shaving cream. As he dabbed at my canvas, he prescribed and he unburdened his émigré heart. "A little red in the knee and cheek doesn't hurt now, does it?" he said, performing for Maggie, "and below the breasts some ultramarine, just so." His own brick-red complexion turned a fiery crimson, making his eyes appear even bluer and lighter.

Unlike the other painters at the League, Grosz dressed elegantly. As he took up my brush and loaded it with pigment, his movements were careful, finicky, conscious of his three-piece suit. "Just so," he said, pushing some ocher around a nipple, "don't you think, darling, just so?" In Grosz's classes, I painted only nudes. I had set up a small easel in my bedroom at the hotel, where I tried my hand at remembered war images. Those stilted efforts I was too embarrassed to show Grosz.

"He's not the man I imagined George Grosz to be," Maggie said later as we drank orange juice at the Buckingham drugstore, "painting nudes in his natty suit, telling us about his diet."

"He's a different man in America than he was back there," I said.

"Yes, I guess so," Maggie said. "They say the same thing about my father."

"Grosz has a wife and kids now," I said.

"My father never worried much about *that*," Maggie said.

"I know. It's either kiddies or art."

"That's stupid, Adam," Maggie said. "Bach had twenty-one children."

Maggie had several part-time jobs, arranged for her by Weinglass and old man Spektor. She modeled mostly jewelry and gloves on Seventh Avenue. Weekends, she was an eager substitute for one of the regular ushers at the Belasco Theater. To my surprise, the money really mattered. Sophie's new job as a translator at the United Nations paid well enough, but Sophie liked to live well. Hardly a day went by when she didn't buy herself or Maggie some fabulous article of clothing, a scarf, a string of beads, some gloves, and always from Bergdorf's or Bendel's. Kor helped when he remembered or when he wasn't disturbed by where the money was going. "I will not fund Magdalena's dermatological preoccupations," he said, referring to the allergy doctors, the expensive salves and creams prescribed to remedy Maggie's skin conditions, skin I thought to be smooth as silk, though Maggie pronounced it to be "filthy with open pores and pimples." To the Kornfelds' well-being Bolek contributed fruit, meat, and champagne, while Sophie had a way of eliciting, without apparent shame, all sorts of donations from her other male friends.

Like Maggie, I wanted to make some money. I wanted to be independent of Bolek, but not enough to take time away from painting. It was Maggie who financed most of our concerts and theater trips around the city, trips Maggie intended for "the study of American life." We went to Far Rockaway or Brighton, where we sat in old-age homes or dingy neighborhood taverns observing gestures, facial expressions, body language. We rode the subways endlessly, watching, taking notes, sketching. We looked at women being made up at Helena Rubinstein's, then we watched the same women viewing the Douanier Rousseau on the walls of the Museum of Modern Art. Inside a Cunard Line pier on the West Side, Maggie would call my attention to some woman surveying her baggage, another being shipped off on a Grand Tour. "Look at that kid dreaming on his duffel bag," she would say excitedly, or "Look how miserable that lady is in her girdle," or "I'll bet you that poor lady is being stood up." Maggie catalogued everyone everywhere for future use.

Much of our pleasure together came in the theater, where Maggie immersed herself in the total theatrical experience. She folded her supple body, like a young leggy leopard, into Broadway's plush seats. She took title to the gracefully sloping balconies, the regal-looking stage boxes, even her part-time comrades, the dour ushers in their black dresses with white lace collars and cuffs. As the lights began to dim before *The Glass Menagerie* or *Born Yesterday* or *Another Part of the Forest*, and the genteel chatter of the audience subsided, Maggie's hand squeezed mine so hard that I could hear my knuckles pop. For days after each performance, she *was* Laurette Taylor or Judy Holliday or Patricia Neal.

Maggie had finished at Tamarack and sometimes I went with her to her acting classes in a loft on West Forty-second Street. She mesmerized me as she became a tree or an ice-cream soda or Anya in *The Cherry Orchard*. Nothing we witnessed on the streets together went to waste. Everything she did inside this Drama Institute loft looked unstudied, easy, just right. Her energy and talent shone in all her movements.

As the weather got nicer, we went to the park, where I sketched her over and over, her appetite insatiable, for each time I found something new in her: the woman of the people, the Amazon lover, the simpleminded movie queen. "Draw me, Adam" was the constant refrain. It goaded me and satisfied me. "Draw me, draw me," she sang as the sun beat down on us and I whipped up another likeness of my Maggie. She shook with excitement as she tore the page out of my sketchbook and stuffed it into her pocket.

At the Met, we looked at Millet and Courbet and Delacroix, then on to the Goyas. Like a window-shopper in late-eighteenth-century Europe, Maggie studied the portraits of Doña Narcisa and Don Tiburcio, investigating ways, I thought, to have her own portraits enriched. We looked at *The Bullfight* with its double bullrings and at smart-ass Don Osorio with his imperiled magpie. We wandered over to the Frick to see Goya's *Forge*, which animated Maggie more than the other Goyas we'd seen.

"This is the Goya I'm really interested in," she said.

"This one? Why?"

"It's Goya the proletarian painter," Maggie said.

"That's Punsky talk," I said. *The Forge* is a monumental painting, though the labor it portrays is unglorified. It is simply and powerfully stated. The three workmen in drab costume swing their long hammers mechanically onto an anvil.

Maggie pulled me over to a bench. She couldn't keep her voice under control. "I don't want you to say things like that to me," she said. The few people in the gallery turned toward us. "These are my own ideas now. I like painting that talks about real things, about what is right."

"That's not what painting's about," I said, though I wasn't sure what it *was* about. "It's not about ethics, it's about aesthetics," I proclaimed anyway.

"What about your drawings in the hotel?"

"What about them? They just try to be good drawings, that's all."

"They're about inhumanity," Maggie said.

"They're about this, they're about that. Who knows what they're about? This one here is just three figures swinging hammers. And they're beautiful."

"They are not beautiful," Maggie said.

"Not them," I said, "the goddam painting."

"Look at them," Maggie said too loudly. "They're not royalty, they're not fat burgers, they're simple, poor laborers."

Even though Roy Punsky didn't exist anymore, I was jealous, jealous of the ideas he'd planted. I felt defeated by my own triteness and didn't recognize Maggie's. "You're just being sentimental," I said. "Good art is never sentimental. Bolek likes sentimental crap. What makes this Goya great is its diagonals, its force. It's like a curled-up tiger."

"I'm not being sentimental," Maggie whispered, loud enough to bring the guard from the adjoining gallery. She began to straighten her hair, tuck in her shirt. "You are being thick."

"You're not going to tell me what painting is about," I said.

"Somebody has to," Maggie said. She picked up her shoulder bag, stuffed full with skin creams, makeup, cheap jewelry, a change of underwear, books. She dug through it looking for bus fare, which she finally scraped together from the bottom. And then she rushed out of there, out of the calm, decorous Frick, her long, angry strides taking her around the corner by the time I followed her into the street.

I prowled around the city for the rest of the day. I was jealous of the Russian soldiers for whom Maggie had knit khaki gloves during the war, jealous of everyone who *labored*, jealous of the goddam Social Realists who painted factories and power stations. I passed a construction site on Fifth Avenue and dreamed of dynamiting Maggie's sainted laborers off the high girders. I stormed into the library, where I asked for all its Karl Marx. The librarian looked at me as though I were an idiot. "All?" she asked. "All," I told her. "I'll bring you one," she said. "You see if you like it." When I went back to the hotel, I sketched men hauling stones, plowing fields, pounding rails.

Within an hour, I was drawing still lifes and nudes again.

6

*B*olek himself suggested that we ask Paul to come with us to dinner. "He is a nice boy," Bolek announced. Friday evening, Paul met us at the hotel and, arm in arm, we walked east. Paul wore his gray flannel suit, made for him the previous year by Lou's tailor. The cuffs of his white shirt stuck out from his jacket and the vest was almost too tight. He looked very handsome in it, sprouting out of it, blooming, the picture of health and vitality. I wore a new sweater Bolek had just given me. He had stopped yelling at me about the suits and ties I refused to wear. His solution was to fill my drawers with cashmeres and the closet with chic windbreakers.

We stopped in front of Prince Casimir's. Bolek, who should have been immune to its charms by now, just *had* to examine the window display one more time. After all, he was approaching it from another perspective, as a passerby. He slipped on his glasses. "Not bad," he said. The carpets and chairs and couches were piled haphazardly, jauntily, with furs that looked as if they were dropped there by busy royal visitors. Bolek peered inside, trying it with and without his glasses. He said, "It is the elegance of Europe before the war. Yes, with the styles of absolutely today." We walked on briskly, stopping at other windows. "Pederasts," Bolek growled at Bergdorf's, "*Schmatas*" at Revillon Frères. Paul and I whistled the march from *The Marriage of Figaro* down Fifth Avenue, then, walking under the El on Third, "The Woody Woodpecker Song." Paul knew the lyrics to everything—"Hit Parade" tunes, Fidelio, Gilbert and Sullivan. Bolek joined us farther downtown, singing out his favorite numbers from *La Traviata*.

Zyga Weinglass had recommended this new steak house under the El called the Prairie Dog. Meat sizzled on several fires that lit the Prairie Dog like campfires on the Oklahoma plain. Bolek ordered three Irish whiskeys. "I can see that here we must drink whiskey," he said, then added, "and we must talk of horses and business." Sawdust covered the creaky floor and the smell of burning meat floated in the air.

"Horses and business," Paul repeated. "That's just what my father would say. I think you would like my father, Mr. Casimir."

Bolek preferred to disregard this. He raised his glass instead. "And beautiful women," he said. "Let us drink to beautiful women."

"To Maggie," Paul added, and the two of them drank.

"To the champion of working people everywhere," I said, raising my glass.

"Magdalena?" Bolek asked. "Do you speak of Magdalena?"

"Our very own Rosa Luxemburg," I said.

Paul leaned toward Bolek. "I have never known anyone like Maggie and Adam," he said.

"Long life to the new Americans," Bolek said, clinking glasses with Paul.

"They are remarkable," Paul said. "Rosa Luxemburg and Goya. They make you feel that whatever they do, whoever they are, it is the *only* thing to be."

"We're terrible egotists," I said, feeling embarrassed. "How can you bear us?"

"Your nephew is my friend," Paul said confidentially to Bolek, "my *real* friend."

"He is my whole life," Bolek whispered into Paul's ear.

Paul sat up straight, pulled at his fingers, cracking the joints. "Maggie must be almost like your daughter," he said.

Bolek sighed. "If she is my daughter, I will dress her in dainty things, like a princess. She can be very beautiful, our Magdalena. I would say, 'No more of your crazy ideas. All that is for old men with beards. You must take piano lessons, perhaps drawing lessons.' "

"You see," I said to Paul, "art and music are for girls. Bolek lives in another age."

We ordered slabs of meat and seltzer water to splash into our whiskey. Each of us buttered his breadstick. Paul said that he would love to find a girl like Maggie. "There aren't many Maggies around," he admitted.

"You are with your mother?" Bolek asked.

"Yes, my mother," Paul said. "It's not easy at home. She protects me from everything, especially my father." Bolek's look said: Little wonder. "She stays home most of the time." Paul drank a whole glass of water. "She plays canasta, she listens to the soap operas, she eats a lot."

The waiter brought our steaks. "And your father?" Bolek asked with difficulty.

"Well, you know about him. But he is a complicated man. He is very strong, he is well loved and respected. . . ."

Bolek really didn't want to hear more about Lou Kaitz, whom he now called "the Spider."

"My parents hate each other," Paul said. "When my father used to drop me off after a weekend, I'd beg him to leave me at Columbus Circle. I was afraid they'd kill each other if they met."

"One day," Bolek said, "you will find a beautiful girl and you will marry. It is the same for Adam. You will both live like normal people."

Paul shot some seltzer into his whiskey. "You were never married?" he asked Bolek.

"Ah, it is complicated," Bolek said. "One day I, too, will marry."

"Why didn't you ever marry Sophie?" I asked.

"You would have liked that, darling?" Bolek asked. "I love Sophie, but Sophie is my family. Sophie makes us a home wherever we are." Leaving his steak for a moment, he took out a cigarette and lit it. "Kor was married to Sophie," Bolek explained to Paul. "Mr. R. Z. Kor, the big artist." He puffed, making a thick cloud of smoke. "I cannot follow Mr. R. Z. Kor. It is impossible for me. Ach, it is impossible." The waiter brought another basket of soft rolls and breadsticks. "Probably I should have married," Bolek said, beginning on his steak again. "For Adam. So Adam could have a mother."

"You were as good as any mother," I told him.

Bolek stopped eating. He leaned over and, like in old times, he brushed the hair from my forehead. "No one could take your mother's place," he said. "She was a wonderful woman."

"How well do you remember her?" Paul asked me.

"She was tall and beautiful," I said. "She wasn't home much."

"She always had you in her mind," Bolek said. "She worked so she could give you everything."

"Anyway," I said, "it worked out fine, with Bolek and me together."

"Look at us, though," Bolek said, "still living in a hotel. We have no home. Adam has no school. I have no wife. We live like gypsies."

Paul said, "Your business is your home. And art is Adam's."

All the diners in the Prairie Dog were devouring meat, and the meat fueled their energy. Next to our table, a family of six was stripping hunks of beef from the bones. They laughed and teased. I watched their jaws work, blood and grease dripping from their chins. There was always one hand in the middle of the table, tearing off a piece of soft roll to dip into the wet plates. They worked as one, like a colony of ants.

I felt hot and a little nauseous. I went outside the Prairie Dog to breathe some air. A train made a terrible din on the tracks above me. Taxis honked as they swerved around the iron columns holding up the El. I took some deep breaths and went back into the vestibule to call Maggie. "I'm sorry," I said, wanting only to be with her again. "You're right about Goya.

He was so many different things. I didn't want to admit
it . . ."

"We're both right," Maggie said. "He was this and he was
that, but I've made plans for us for tomorrow. Can you give me
the whole day? We'll start at the Hispanic Society . . ."

"Oh, yes, Maggie, yes," I said, nearly in tears.

When I came back, Paul was telling Bolek about some of our
school friends. "They all drive each other nuts with all their
loving and hating. Meals are pandemonium. Like this place,"
Paul said.

"A circus," I said. "They feed each other, they scream at each
other, and when they're done, they all French-kiss."

It reminded Bolek of Weinglass, "Weinglass and Basia and
their little Francesca with all the pimples on her face." Bolek
sat back. "She sits and she says nothing. She cannot chew or
swallow her food because they are counting every spoonful.
They tease her like a baby. This is a family? Weinglass is stingy,
Basia is stupid, Francesca is ugly. But they are always together.
And why? Probably to raise dogs. They have one dog after
another. The dogs are fat and they die. Weinglass goes to the
hospital with his dogs, then to a store to buy new dogs." Bolek
brushed the crumbs off our table, then straightened the creases
in the tablecloth. "This is a family?" he asked again.

The Prairie Dog, the Weinglasses, all of us, we were the stuff
of Grosz's German satires, the slobbering couples, their fat
children, everyone getting fatter, slower, noisier. It was like
Goya's *Family of Charles IV*, the whole vapid lot of them. I
promised myself that I would always travel light.

Saturday, Maggie and I went to the Hispanic Society to see
the notorious duchess pointing to a place beside her tiny slippers where Goya had etched his name in sand. "I thought she
would be just like the Maja," Maggie said inside this mock
Iberian courtyard right on upper Broadway. "But I don't think
she is."

"Probably it wasn't her," I said.

"It's hard to tell with the Maja being in Madrid," Maggie
said.

"Someone that well known wouldn't have let him paint her like that," I suggested.

"You've got to admit, Adam, that was some wild court," Maggie said.

"Barbaric," I admitted.

"Antediluvian," Maggie said.

We walked back on Broadway. The weather had changed overnight. The day was balmy, a soft breeze blew up the avenue. Maggie wore a white angora sweater that I loved. Her school friends wore only cashmere, but what did they know about how angora felt to the touch, to *my* touch? Maggie kept her hands inside the pockets of her navy-blue coat with brass buttons. She swung them up and down like a bird. "Hey, Adam," she said as we sat down to rest on a bench at Broadway and Ninety-sixth, "you're getting out of the habit of drawing me."

At Eighty-fourth Street, we went up to her place. We stood quietly in the elevator, both of us towering over Rabbit, the elevator man. When we let ourselves into the apartment, Maggie told me that Sophie was in New Canaan for the day, at Count Kaczka's. I put my arms around her, but she slipped away, ran down the hall, and locked herself in the bathroom. "Just hold on, señor painter," she yelled through the door.

I loved this place. I loved the umbrella stand in the hall, a thick-walled ceramic vase decorated with birds. Several umbrellas in various states of disrepair and a couple of fancy canes were crammed into it. A tiny brocaded chair, too small for a person to sit in, and a drop-leaf table with a lace doily, all carefully collected from Connecticut gift barns, tried to resurrect our lives in Warsaw. All these things re-created permanence. It was like walking back into my childhood.

The place smelled of a roast, which Sophie must have put into the oven that morning. Our Warsaw apartment always smelled of baking rolls and cakes. It gleamed like horse chestnuts. Grandfather clocks ticked and chimed, maids shuffled in their carpet slippers on creaky parquet floors, polishing the silver and placing it in slate-blue flannel envelopes.

"Hey, aren't you done?" I yelled down the hall.

"Wait another minute," Maggie shouted back.

I sat down again at my place at the dining table, the first place I had come to in America, the table under which I had dived for cover, afraid of airplanes. I laid my cheek against the cool mahogany, its luster smooth as satin. Here I had always felt a special kind of peace.

"Okay," Maggie yelled.

I walked down the hall dreamily and through Maggie's half-open door I saw a warm red glow. A single standing lamp with a heavy yellow shade lit the room. In the amber light, I saw Maggie lying on her bed, her arms crossed behind her head. She was on her side, with her right leg drawn up a little more than the left. She was in costume, a yellow bolero over some light diaphanous material, half dress, half trousers. A pink sash circled her waist. She was the great Maja Vestida.

"It's a gift, Adam. No more bickering. No more ethics debates. We're both too smart for that."

"Yes," I said.

"I've been collecting this stuff for a while," Maggie said. "I've always wanted you to paint me like this."

"You're exactly like her," I said.

Maggie had covered her bed with a green cloth, nearly the hue of Goya's simple couch. The precarious pose, so delicately perched, almost floating, just like in the painting itself, was stabilized by big puffy pillows. And within this pretense lay Maggie, *my Maggie,* with her thick hair the color of honey, her feet not the delicate Spanish feet of the thirteenth Duchess of Alba but Maggie's own broad, sturdy feet with brightly painted toenails.

"I don't really care if it was her," Maggie said. "It was *someone.*"

"I don't care either," I said.

"It just seems like a great moment in history, no matter who it was," Maggie said.

"I always thought that the clothed Maja was even more sensual than the naked," I said, my eyes adjusting in the semidarkness.

"Let's do both," Maggie said. She had set up a canvas on an easel. Another blank canvas was propped against the closet door. Tubes of paint, brushes, oil and turpentine lay on a shiny new palette. "We need music," Maggie said.

"There must have been music down below, in the courtyard," I said. In Maggie's courtyard, between apartment buildings, I heard the super roll garbage cans to the street.

"I've got some Spanish music on the record player," Maggie said.

My hand shook a little as I put the needle on the record. "I don't think I can paint," I said.

"Why not?"

"I'm shaking."

"Adam," Maggie said in a husky voice, "put all that on canvas."

Her unguarded body, hidden only by transparent cloth, was daring me. Her breasts pushed out at me and the faint darkness of her pubic hair was making me giddy. "Maggie, I'll die. I want to make love to you."

"Wait," Maggie said. "The longer you wait, the better it will be."

I squeezed some color onto the palette. Maggie lay very still, and I began to block her in with thinned ocher. We were so alone here, inside the secret rooms in the Alba retreat at Sanlucar, inside Maggie's lair on Eighty-fourth Street between West End and Riverside. Maggie had insulated us with drapery, rugs, and tablecloths that she'd hung on the walls and windows. They shut out the gray daylight of the airshaft, the noise of the street. The little portable record player shielded us with lutes and viols and the tinkle of the harpsichord. I began to sketch in the murky background behind Maggie. Nearly lost in the textures and patterns of the drapery were photographs from school, a group portrait from camp in which, surely, Roy Punsky lurked, dark and serious. I saw parts of my sketches of her, and, pinned to the bottom of the corkboard, the tips of three ermine tails given to Maggie by Bolek.

Maggie's voice, soft and low, broke into this *tableau vivant*. "This is like a child's game," she said. "Did we play games when we were little?"

"Yes."

"Not like this," Maggie said. "This is adult theater." Maggie shifted her weight, and this Maja in motion sent a shock wave of pleasure through me.

"I can't stand it, Maggie."

It's what we do best," she said. "We can stand it. We're extraordinary. Should I tell you about the Napoleonic invasions of Spain?"

"No, Maggie," I begged.

"There are so many parallels with your life. All he went through," Maggie sighed. "Just imagine, first his world is shattered by deafness, then, as if that wasn't enough, the rotten French swoop down, brutalizing, murdering—"

"This doesn't help," I said. "Horror stories mean nothing to me."

"You're funny," Maggie said. "You're always so intense. You're not good at games."

"One thing at a time," I pleaded.

"I've got to take a break," Maggie said. She got to her feet, then up on her toes, her arms above her head. Then, taking tiny dancer's steps, she went out of the room. "I'll be right back," she sang from the hall. Like a dog, I stood outside the bathroom door. I listened to her pee. After she flushed, she must have studied herself in the mirror, for it seemed like an eternity before she came out, and when she did, I grabbed her, pulling her close. She shivered in my arms, pressed herself hard into me, then relaxed. Her body felt luxurious through the gauzy costume.

But Maggie wasn't ready yet. She led me back to her room, looked at herself taking shape on the canvas, and took her pose again. We worked for another hour, maybe two. Small areas of the painting began to be detailed—the left side of her face, some of the brocade on the bolero, one wonderful foot. Finally, I said that it was enough.

Maggie said, "We'll start the other one then," and she inserted one hand inside the knot of her pink sash and loosened it. She pulled it away from her waist in a swift motion like a tablecloth being yanked from a set table. Gracefully, she stepped out of the bolero and the robe under it. And then she threw it all off the bed. She was naked except for the painted tips of her fingers and toes. She took the pose again, and then, remembering, she reached behind her, found a lipstick, and touched her cheeks and lips with it. She smeared the color around with a finger, diffusing it into a blush. As I gaped helplessly, she held her breasts, one at a time, and applied the lipstick to each nipple, kneading the color in, spreading it in concentric circles.

"She did this, too," Maggie explained. She looked up. Her mouth was slightly open and her breathing heavy. She placed a hand, with all the fingers spread, between her breasts. "I've heard that if they're far apart like this, it's a sign of nobility." Maggie's nipples were like perfect amber droplets that form at the bottom of the Baltic Sea, and the distance between her breasts was as vast as the steppes. These were not Holbein's hard little apples between which a whole panzer division could have marched with lightning speed. This was the landscape of Eden, the lush valley of a warmer climate. I could hear bees buzzing around the marigolds, I could smell the white petals of almond trees. "Now, Maggie," I begged.

"Wait, Adam. Paint me. Paint our indescribable desire."

And so I labored, and it was painful labor. I began to understand the artist's urgent search for images of ideal form. It worked to relieve his nagging, ever-present lust. It explained artists' dalliance with cool symmetry, with the purity of mathematics, with fantasies of heavenly innocence. As I went on painting, I no longer felt like a painter, not even a man, but a painting dog, a howling, wild, insatiable dog.

"I feel weak," Maggie said. Her eyes were closed. I went over to the bed and knelt beside her. My hand lightly touched her face, then down her body to trace the gently rising surface of those breasts, that landscape of forgetfulness, that belly, the dark tangle of her pubic hair. She smelled like leaves and flowers and the rich red earth underneath. In a dreamlike motion, lazy and smooth, Maggie took her nipple in her fingers and directed it into my mouth. "Gently," she said, so quietly that I thought the word might have come unspoken from my own throat. I took her nipple in my mouth, keeping it, preserving it like a little raspberry candy. Her hands were in my hair and I felt the sweeping curve of her hips, the dip back down to the flat of her belly. Her pose didn't entirely collapse until then, but now her long body became soft and pliant, and a gentle keening sound, like a distant train whistle, escaped from her lips. Her thighs parted and between them my fingers entered her. She tried to pull me up, but she kept slipping as if she had no strength. I tore my clothes off and threw myself on top of her. Maggie put me inside, then held me hard against her. "Just like this. Oh, Adam, don't move." We lay like that, feeling the wetness building between us. And then she pulled me so hard, so violently, that I thought I would explode. But it was Maggie who was coming and I who watched, I, the giver of gifts, basking in her pleasure.

And then I heard the outside door slam, the voices in the hall. "Maggie, darling, are you home?" Sophie yelled down the hall.

Maggie's body was shaking, her hands on either side of her head. "Oh, God," she whispered through clenched teeth. "Mother," she screamed. "Wait!" Tears welled up in her eyes. "Jesus, mother, we're busy."

"Who's there?" Sophie said as she started down the hall toward us.

"Adam's here. He's painting me. Just wait. We'll be right out."

"Can I come in?" Sophie asked.

"No," Maggie shrieked, holding me with all her strength.

"Hello, Adam, darling," Sophie chirped from the other side of the door. "Hurry up, my precious children. Count Kaczka's with me. He'll be so happy to see you both."

Maggie found her skirt and white angora sweater and put them on. I was already in my clothes. "Oh, Adam," she said. "I'm so sorry." We held each other, both of us hot and glowing, like steamed chickens.

When we came out into the living room, Maggie had it all under control, trained as she was for moments such as this.

The Count embraced her warmly, then turned to me. "So this is Bolek's nephew," he said. "Sophie tells me you are a fine artist. I am a collector. I own several R. Z. Kors." He coughed. "I knew your father very well in Poland," he said.

Count Kaczka was from one of the oldest Polish families.

The Kaczkas traced their ancestry beyond the Casimirs and the Boleslaws, to the murky Polish past before Catholicism's icy grip, to a Duke Mieszko who bludgeoned his way to the Vistula and the Oder. Maggie had always called Count Kaczka "the Piast man," after the early Polish dynasty of that name. In fact, with his white hair plastered back without a part, his prominent brow and bony cheeks, he looked like a Visigoth. He leered at Maggie. "What were you doing in there, my dear?" he asked.

"Doing?" Maggie said. "When, where, Count Kaczka?"

"Zbygniew to you, my dear," he said so unctuously that even Sophie's face flushed pink. Kaczka riveted his narrow eyes on Maggie's nipples, which were poking through her white angora. In fact, I was sure I saw a halo form around them, the faint roseate glow of lipstick.

Maggie folded her arms over her chest. She said, "Adam and I were planning to go for a walk."

"Stay, Magdalena," the Count said. "I have a proposition for you." Maggie looked suspiciously at Sophie, who was smiling. Count Kaczka offered us thin cigarettes with gold filter tips. His hands shook as he attempted to light them. "I propose," he said as we sat down around the coffee table, "to introduce you to a very important friend of mine. I have told you about Madame Clothilde? She is the editor of the French *Vogue*. A charming and eccentric woman who collects artists and lives with a honey bear from Ecuador." He puffed on his cigarette, inhaling deeply. "You are a beautiful young woman, Magdalena. You cannot continue modeling cheap jewelry, not for *those people*."

"I do it for a little extra money, Count. I'm not a model, not really," Maggie said. "I'm not built like a fashion model, and besides, I'm clumsy," and, to prove her point, she pulled herself up on her toes and came down, flat-footed, with a thud.

Count Kaczka's cigarette hung from the corner of his mouth. A long ash was forming, ready to drop. He was mesmerized, delighted by Maggie. "Clothilde will form you," he said, his hands clasped in front of him in an attitude of ecstatic devotion. "She will make you into anything you wish to be."

"I should go," I said, triggering Count Kaczka into action.

With chivalric ardor, he jumped to his feet, clicking his heels. He extended his hand to me quickly, lest I change my mind. "A pleasure, Krinsky," he said. "Soon I must see your work." He remained standing at attention, waiting for me to move to the door.

"It's a very kind offer, Zbygniew," Maggie said. "I want to think it over. Thank you, really, thank you. I am grateful, very grateful." Maggie got up. "I must go with Adam now," she said.

Sophie was angry. "Count Kaczka has come all this way just to help you. Surely you can stay a little longer."

"If we hadn't made arrangements to meet Paul, mother, we would stay with great pleasure," Maggie lied.

Count Kaczka shrugged. "Youth," he said philosophically, "a glorious time."

Maggie took the Count's hands and looked into his sly eyes. "You will forgive us, won't you, Zbygniew?"

Count Kaczka sat down. "I shall move mountains for you," he said. He turned to Sophie dreamily and kissed her hands.

In the elevator, as Rabbit plummeted us down the eight floors, Maggie put her head on my shoulder. "Jesus, Adam," she said. "I don't know what to make of all that." We walked into the park. "I'm not a fashion model," she mused aloud.

"You're an actress," I said with an edge of anger in my voice.

"I guess it's a way to be seen," Maggie said.

"Only if you want to parade up and down in front of pigs," I said.

"I think he meant the magazines," Maggie said. "Photographs, publicity . . ."

"You have to be seen on the stage. You can't just stand there like a—like a goddam clothes hanger."

"I can be a clothes hanger if I want to," Maggie said, and she bent herself and drooped, a hanger with a full skirt and stained white sweater.

For a while we were inseparable, dreaming our private dreams together, building our egos, buttressing our strengths. Some afternoons we met in Maggie's room, others in the hotel, depending on which was vacated. We explored each other's bodies. We watched each other's orgasms, which we'd delay, prolong, deny. We would let ourselves cry tears of sadness, tears of joy, tears that came with the crazy kind of abstinence we imposed on ourselves, as before, to mark our power, celebrate our specialness. It was our imprint. It was our insurance, guaranteeing that we would long for each other always. Sometimes we wavered. "What does it matter?" Maggie would say, throwing her arms back in total abandon, her hot face lolling to one side. "Come now, Adam," she'd cry. But then I'd slip out and Maggie would take me in her hands so gently, so lovingly. At other times it was Maggie's will that had to be exercised. "We are special," we'd remind ourselves, "we are in control of our lives."

When word got to Bolek that Count Kaczka had offered to make a fashion model out of Maggie, he immediately called Enid. "We must do something, Zizi," he yelled into the phone. "We must stop that animal. He will sink his claws into Magdalena."

The same day, Enid telephoned Maggie. "I've just talked with Ernest Da Capo, darling," Enid said. "He would like to meet you, to take some trial shots of you. It's a wonderful opportunity, Maggie."

I went with Maggie to Da Capo's studio the following week. His place was stark white, with no props. Maggie was the only object and she needed no enhancement. She sat, she stood, she laughed, she danced, she told jokes, she recited poetry. Da Capo was charmed, moving around her, stopping the snap of his shutter only to change film. "Yes, Maggie, yes, that's it," he kept saying. "Oh, my goodness, Maggie, that's perfect." He showed us the delight of a man who had been spared—surprisingly—the boring discharge of an obligation. Maggie was no one's obligation. She was a source of everyone's delight.

I sat in a corner, eyeing the Rolleiflex as it eyed Maggie. It was shameless, caressing the body, perhaps even the soul. I was jealous of their dance, though grateful for the little black box through which they communicated, grateful that Maggie's image reached Da Capo via mirrors.

They took a coffee break, but when an energized Maggie, cup in hand, gave us a speech from *Golden Boy*, Da Capo got up again to shoot.

" 'Somewhere there must be happy boys and girls who can teach us the way of life,' " Maggie declaimed. " 'We'll find some city where poverty's no shame—where music is no crime—where there's no war in the streets—where a man is glad to be himself, to live and make his woman herself!' "

"Go on, Maggie, more," Da Capo encouraged, traveling around her, a bull around a buttercup.

" ' . . . we ride in your car, we speed through the night, across the park, over the Triboro Bridge. . . .' "

Toward the end of the session, Maggie asked if he would take a few pictures of the two of us together. In them, I am brooding, half angry, half jealous, as if I knew that Maggie was being propelled into another life.

When, a few days later, Da Capo called Enid, he was ecstatic. Enid immediately got on the phone to tell Maggie, but she got Sophie instead. Under different circumstances, the two women could have been friends, but with Bolek in the middle, they were somewhat guarded and cool. They had seen each other from time to time, always in passing, in the lobby of a theater, at a Prince Casimir fashion show, across the room at Rumpelmayer's. I was sure they suspected that in Bolek's life they served as each other's counterpart, their cultural differences providing him with everything he thought he required: the jaded, almost incestuous sensuality of Sophie, and the sharp tongue and fastidiousness of Enid.

Sophie reported their conversation with relish. "Dear Sophie," Enid had said on the phone, 'your gorgeous daughter is a hit. Da Capo says she is more than photogenic. She jumps right out of the picture at you."

"It's so good of you to look after Magdalena like this," Sophie had replied. "I am in your debt forever, darling."

Maggie's first appearance in the pages of *Mirabelle* evoked a stream of letters asking who she was. The photographs caught Maggie in full flight, her wings spread, her eyes sparkling, carefree and gay. The energy and intelligence she exuded would, I was sure, send women off to the stores to buy the same cut of cloth, the same French labels, hoping that they, too, might transform their sated lives into mirthful, joyous youth.

Two months later, Enid put an amazing Da Capo photograph of Maggie's face right on the cover. For the first time, Maggie's down-from-under look blitzed the waiting world. And it produced startling results. Within a week Enid's little Empire desk spilled over with stacks of cables, letters, and telephone messages. Among outbursts of love and admiration, there were six offers from the major studios for screen tests.

"I thought you were going to make a little extra pocket money," Sophie said, confused by the commotion, "but this— this is *awe-inspiring*."

Suddenly everyone had advice for Maggie. Sophie's co-workers at the United Nations, parents of Maggie's Tamarack pals, tenants from their building. People who had never cared much about this profligate European household clamored to be heard. Maggie should dye her hair, straighten the heavy curls, smooth its rough texture. She should pencil her eyebrows, hide her ears, wear only pink. Countess Kaczka phoned with the names of lawyers, accountants, and agents, all Polish. Basia Weinglass offered the name of a secret skin formula, "ground with the hand from Mexican tree bark."

Sophie herself began paying attention to Maggie's skin, seeing for the first time the rough spots Maggie had complained about. "And the teeth!" Sophie cried. "We should have insisted on braces." To prove Sophie's point, Maggie clamped her teeth together loudly. "A monstrous overbite," Sophie concluded.

Maggie couldn't sleep. She spent a lot of time in front of mirrors, and when we were out together, she behaved strangely around newsstands. On the corner of Fifty-seventh Street and Sixth Avenue, I'd try to drag her past the newsstand, and she, just as determined, pulled me back. There she would stand, fixing her hair or putting on lipstick, counting the number of *Mirabelle*s left in the pile. "No one buys this goddam magazine," she decided. Sometimes she acted as if she were being pursued, at other times totally neglected. She stared at passersby, gauging her impact on the world.

I *hated* what was happening and hid out at the Art Students League, busying myself with nudes, inhaling sweat and turpentine, talking art *with artists*. But my concentration was shot and I got myself into one aesthetic jam after another. I poked away at a canvas of a huge nude, unable to exercise that light touch Grosz had talked about.

Grosz was looking on from behind me. "So, kiddo," he said, "where is that beautiful friend of yours?"

"She's on her way to Hollywood," I said.

"To Hollywood?"

"To make movies."

"*Mein* goodness, a real beauty," Grosz said. "She will be a star?"

"Yes," I said, jabbing away at my nude. "What a mess I'm making."

"What mess?" Grosz asked. "You can always go west."

"What would you do?"

"I would pack my bags."

I stopped and turned to him. "You would?"

"I would follow her anywhere," Grosz said. "What have you to lose, pal? You are young, you have the touch—"

"You still think so?"

"Ach," he said, lighting his pipe, "maybe it's for the best. Look at me. I have a wife, she is fat. I have boys. I worry." He stared blankly at the mountain of flesh sitting on the platform in front of us. "Maybe it doesn't matter," he concluded.

Sunday morning Bolek and I prepared to go to Sophie's. "Maggie's fate must be decided right away," Sophie had said frantically on the phone. First, Mr. Traister had to be disposed of. His English lessons with Bolek had continued over the years, even though many of these Sundays were just a forum for catching up on the news from Poland: who perished in what camp, who wandered back to Warsaw from deep within the Soviet Union, who was there in the Party hierarchy; who was purported to be doing very well in Johannesburg or Sydney. Like everyone else now, Traister had his own opinion about Maggie's bonanza. "In life we must seek the truth," he told a wide-eyed Bolek, "and there is no truth in California." It was certainly the kind of statement that would have given Bolek apoplexy, but as he got out of bed, showing Traister his bare ass on his way to the bathroom, he simply muttered, "Little rabbi," and let it go at that.

We took four bottles of brut champagne and, stopping to load a taxi at the Sixth Avenue Deli, we sped uptown to Sophie's. The place was a mess, the result of all the unexpected guests. Both Sophie and Maggie had bags under their eyes, and their movements, usually so graceful, had become jerky. A stack of *Mirabelles* lay on the piano. Sophie had already sent copies to her surviving relatives in Poland, England, and France, and now all who entered got one, whether they already had it or not. There were flowers everywhere, an assortment of spring wildflowers on the coffee table, a floor vase of irises in a corner by the window, crimson and white peonies on the dining table.

Bolek paced up and down, rubbing his hands together. His opinion about Maggie's future was unambiguous. He had become her champion. "She will make more money than we have ever dreamed," he predicted. "She is a good girl. She will know what to do." Sophie put the salmon, the sturgeon, the cheeses, and caviar on platters, then she lay down on the sofa looking exhausted. Even in this state—it was one of the few times I had seen her without high heels—Sophie was soft and voluptuous, like a Rubens. Her hair was swept back in a French twist, now a little mussed, with haphazard strands of blond aimed in every direction.

Maggie pulled me into her room, then down on her bed.

"It's happening so fast," she said smiling. "Too fast."

I began to touch her, maul her a little. I pushed hard against her breasts. "These are mine," I said.

"Yes," Maggie said, pulling away.

I pushed my hand between her legs. "And this," I said.

"And this," she agreed.

"For Christ's sake, don't go," I said.

"Don't go? Are you nuts?" She sat up.

"That's no life out there," I said. "People go and never come back."

"I'll come back," Maggie promised, grabbing my hands and placing them gently on both sides of her face.

"It's not art out there," I said.

"I know," Maggie agreed.

"Art is *hard*, you know what I mean? Everything out there is easy. It's made for morons."

"I know," Maggie said.

I pointed to the Maja canvases propped up against a wall. "We have to finish these," I said.

"There'll be plenty of time," Maggie said.

"I brought a joint," I said, taking a pack of Chesterfields out of my pocket. The tobacco had been emptied and marijuana stuffed into the papers by a Las Vegas friend of Lou Kaitz's.

Maggie looked inside the package. "Where did you get them?" she asked.

"Never mind," I said. "Want to light one?"

"We should go back," Maggie said, "or they'll come bursting in here."

Bolek was sitting on the couch next to Sophie, holding her hand. "The star is back," he announced when he saw us.

We all sat down at the table to eat. "We will call Bolek's friend in Hollywood," Sophie said as she served. "We shall have it directly from the horse's mouth." Max Chwast, now Mike Craig, once a prosperous ham merchant from Lodz, had become Jack Warner's right-hand man, "a very serious vice-president," according to Bolek.

"We must talk to my father," Maggie said.

"He is furious," Sophie reported.

"He won't stay that way," Maggie said, "and he has friends out there, too."

"Kor has friends in Hollywood?" Bolek asked, an incredulous yet amused look on his face.

"He has friends everywhere," Maggie told him, an edge of annoyance in her voice.

Bolek took out a cigarette. "What do his friends do in Hollywood?"

"Never mind, Bolek," Sophie intervened, to avoid his commentary on Kor's friends. "Do you know what Zyga Weinglass said?"

"Weinglass?" Bolek said. "When did you see Weinglass?"

"Basia called Maggie," Sophie said. "They think I should go with Magdalena."

"Good God," Maggie said.

"Why not?" I asked.

"Stop it, Adam," Maggie warned.

"Out there," I told Sophie, "you can pick avocados right in your backyard."

As Bolek poured the second bottle of champagne into our glasses, Kor telephoned. "He wants to see Maggie," Sophie told us when she came back from her bedroom where she took the call. "He's coming right over."

Bolek sat up. "Kor is coming here?" he asked.

"Would you like us to meet him outside?" Maggie asked with blatant irritation.

Kor arrived within minutes. "I was with a friend uptown," he explained. He fixed himself a plate of caviar and black bread. I poured him a glass of champagne. "I want to talk about this," he said curtly to Maggie. It was a little frightening to see anger inside Kor's great frame, his imposing corpulence. He chewed slowly and carefully while we waited in silence, all of us except Bolek, who went back into the living room, picked up a copy of *Mirabelle* from the piano, and began leafing through it. Kor washed the bread and caviar down with champagne and poured himself another glass. He wiped his mouth, folded the napkin, and looked around the table at us. Then he focused on Maggie. "They are using you, Magdalena," he said, "manipulating you. They will chew you up, then spit you out. What do they care?"

Maggie looked astonished. "Why use me?" she asked. "Why should *they* use *me*? Supposing I use *them*?"

From the window Bolek said, without looking at us, "Magdalena can do it, too, such a smart girl."

Kor paid no attention to that opinion. "What does this have to do with talent?" he asked, turning his gaze from one to the other of us. "Nothing," he answered, "nothing at all. A screen test is simply to see if you photograph well."

"But that much we know," Sophie said. "The photographs are stunning."

"*Their* photographs come from every angle," Kor said, instructing us, a slow class in the behavioral sciences. "And I mean *every* angle. You have to protect everything. They prey upon people. If you are not careful, their cameras will crawl up your legs, invade under your skirt!"

"How can I turn it down?" Maggie asked, exasperated. "I can't say no without trying it first."

"You are an actress, Maggie," I said. "Acting happens here, in New York and across the Atlantic."

"Yes," Kor agreed, "out there, they breed only sentimentality, and we all know what that does to art."

Sophie said, "That's all nonsense. Of course they make stupid movies, but they also make good ones."

Maggie named names, not of movies but of the actresses she admired. Besides Bette Davis, she thought of Ingrid Bergman and Barbara Stanwyck. She stopped and tried to think of others, but Kor wouldn't wait.

"The only decent cinema is in Europe," he pronounced. "There is only Cocteau and Bunuel and now the Italians."

"If you please," said Bolek from the other room. He could no longer contain himself. "Who are your friends in Hollywood?"

"My friends?" said Kor as he swished the champagne around in his glass. "I'm not sure their names will mean anything to you, Bolek." He named Thomas Mann and his brother Heinrich, then Arnold Schoenberg and Billy Wilder. "They are exiles, Bolek. I know only exiles."

"In America," sighed Bolek, "one should know some Americans."

Kor began before Bolek had even finished his sentence. "No one in California—no one but the exiles—even knows that a war happened in Europe. It is too far. The weather is too good." Kor pushed his chair away from the table and stood up. "And what is art in California?" he asked. "It is the paint job on their motorcycles," he said, "and I am talking about artists' motorcycles. They do a marvelous job, I assure you, coat upon coat, so that it is like an Oriental lacquered box. This is their art. It is hardly an enriching experience."

Sophie, who had been agitated throughout the discussion, now wiped away the tears in her eyes. "I have heard enough," she said. "You are a hypocrite," she shot at her ex-husband. "Look at you, look at all of you. You are the most ambitious crowd ever assembled in one room. Your entire lives are devoted to success—success in art, success in business. And now with your cheap moralizing, you are doing your best to dissuade my daughter from some success of her own, success perhaps beyond your reach." Fuming, she stomped into the kitchen, followed by a flushed and worried Bolek.

"Success is not good for art," Kor said patiently. "Too much success eats at art from the inside."

From the kitchen, Sophie and Bolek put in a call to California. We heard Bolek shouting into the phone as if the mountains that divided the continent were a barrier to being heard. Kor tried to soothe Maggie's feelings. She was sullen, quietly cleaning off the table.

Maggie was called to the kitchen. She and Sophie and Bolek returned smiling. "Bolek and Maggie just talked with Mr. Craig," Sophie said. "I think they have made a choice."

Maggie looked at her father with more pity than guilt. The decision was made in spite of Kor's interference. "Mr. Craig and his wife want me to stay with them while I'm out there," Maggie said. "They urged me to accept his studio's offer." Kor and I were silent. "It's Warner Brothers," Maggie said. Her face was bright and happy as she stood behind Kor, her hands on his shoulders.

I stayed at the League for the rest of the summer, waiting for Maggie's departure to make changes in my life. Maggie was busy with preparations—buying clothes, signing contracts, writing letters—but we saw each other often, making love when we could, unable to deny ourselves those delicious pleasures. But even in the midst of our lovemaking, I—both of us—preserved an unspoken distance, keeping our new evolving selves secret, waiting to test ourselves away from each other.

In mid-September we took Maggie to Grand Central where the 20th Century would carry her to Chicago. There, she would change for the Super Chief—the sleek silver train we had seen only on postcards—and on to dreamland. I was neither sad nor happy. I was numb. We had made plans to talk on the phone, then, depending on how each of us was doing, to meet on the one coast or the other.

Maggie looked chic in a tailored wool skirt and silk blouse. Her shoulders were padded, making her look even broader than she was. When she sat down in her compartment, the skirt rode up her legs, exposing a sturdy stockinged thigh. Tears ran down her cheeks as she kissed all of us in turn. How could anyone keep his eyes, his hands, off her? Whatever was going to happen in Hollywood I didn't want to know about. I wondered how she was going to survive the cross-country voyage untouched and unmolested.

7

Dearest Adam,
　　Last night I dreamed about your mother. At least I think it
was your mother. I sat in a magnificent room, all gilded and
marbled (Mandelbaum's?), but instead of furs there were
mountains of shoes and your poor mother was trying to fit
me with a pair. She was frantic sorting through the piles,
trying to squeeze my monster feet. Every pair in the place
was too small! God, Adam, she was beautiful!
　　Here in the other dreamland, they're wrangling about my
overall size and the muscles that show. Some moron in the
makeup department almost tweezed my eyebrows out until
Hal Wallis himself stormed in and said: "I want her the way
she is!"
　　The Craigs are wonderful. Mike makes halfhearted passes
at me every once in a while but thank God never seriously.
Stefa is a darling, showing me off to all her friends—the
crème de la crème. As I wait for my movie (and God knows
what it'll be—I'm betting on Yugoslav partisans) I sit
poolside, reading, *devouring* Chekhov, or (when no one is

around) singing (they are making me take musical comedy!) and always thinking of you. I have fantasies of us living here, of my waiting for you to come home from your studio so we can make love in the grass around the pool. How I wish you would like this place, Adam, but no matter how I would love to make it all come out right, I know you won't, you melancholy Pole. It's simply too easygoing for you, the weather is too perfect and you have to *drive* everywhere. (Did I tell you that I was taking driving lessons? This weekend Stefa and I are going to buy me a royal-blue 1940 Ford, "in mint condition" according to the slimy salesman.)

Since I've been signed up, I make a neat little salary, nothing enormous like the top people but still $200 a week is not to sneeze at, especially since they're going to renegotiate after the movie. The reason I mention this at all—and don't get angry with me!—is that I think you should make money on your own, too, just to see how it feels. I know Bolek gives you anything you want, but it's not the same. I'm finding out how good it feels to bring a check home at the end of the week, a check big enough to buy a car. My darling, I don't mean to lecture you, but you sounded so blue in your last letter that I thought I'd impart some of this working girl's newly acquired wisdom.

You're going to love this: Yesterday at the commissary I ate lunch with Robert Montgomery, Ann Sheridan, Gary Cooper, and Jed Seacliff! But don't worry, I like this place now but I'm sure I'll tire of it quickly. One day I'll wake up and wonder what a nice Jewish girl like me is doing in a place like this. And the worst part of everything is that you're not here.

Maggie

Getting out of bed in the morning was like staging a new *Aida* daily. It was despair for sure, also rage and total distraction. Every day I risked walking under a bus, not intentionally but because I couldn't see or notice anything.

"Nothing *that* special's happened," I told Paul, who had started Columbia in September. "Maggie's gone, that's all."

"Yeah," he said. "A mere nothing." We were sitting on a

bench just inside the park. The smell of manure from the line of horses mixed with the car exhaust along Central Park South. I stared dismally at the gum wrappers, newspapers, and condoms bobbing around in the pond.

"She wants me to go to work," I reported.

"You mean like other people?"

"She thinks it'll be good for me," I said.

"Mmmmm."

"That's a bullshit American Protestant idea," I said, bouncing off the bench. "Who does she think she is, a goddam pilgrim?"

"Maggie, a pilgrim . . ." Paul smiled.

"Look at Cézanne," I said, "taken care of all his life."

"Artists are special," Paul said. "I've always known that."

"On the other hand, maybe I've got to earn my way. You know? Maybe the other way it's too easy."

"It doesn't look easy," Paul said. "But maybe you ought to leave the League, maybe you've got nothing more to learn from Grosz."

Right now I wasn't about to leave anything. Not leave and not be left, either. That much I knew. "I've got no place to go," I said.

Paul stuck his hands inside his pockets. He looked taller, more self-assured than ever. I straightened my shoulders. "There's always California," he said, "or what about Europe?"

"Europe?"

"You've heard of Europe," Paul said, looking at his watch. "I've got to go up to school."

"You don't *live* there, for Christ's sake," I snapped.

"A biology lecture," Paul said.

"Biology? You don't need biology. A big fucking help that's going to be to your father's business." Paul stood up. "Listen, Kaitz," I told him, "I don't have any goddam money for Europe."

"It's cheap and Bolek will give you anything you want," Paul said. He took a small notebook out of his pocket. "Notes," he told me. "Meiosis, mitosis, all that shit."

"That's just it," I said. "Bolek won't give me money for Europe. *That* he doesn't want." We began to walk toward Columbus Circle.

"What's wrong with Europe?" Paul asked.

"Nothing for *you*. He doesn't want it for *me*."

"Tell him real Americans go to Europe, too," Paul said. "Jesus, Krinsky, kids have been sent off to Europe to forget love affairs ever since they invented boats."

"I don't need to forget anything. Maggie's not the problem."

"Why are you shouting?" Paul said. He put his hand on my shoulder. "Go soak up some culture, Krinsky."

"That's for you! I *reek* of culture."

"Big fucking Polack Jew," Paul said, and smacked my chest. He ran down Central Park South.

I was right behind him. "Gangster!" I yelled.

He headed down the subway stairs, turning to give me a parting shot. "Homo artist!" he shouted from the semi-darkness, then took off to catch the train rumbling into the station.

Paul was making a life for himself at Columbia, Maggie was in Hollywood, Bolek was buried in work, preparing for a fashion show. He left the hotel early in the morning and often didn't come back, staying, I supposed, at Enid's Madison Avenue apartment or possibly at Sophie's, who, like me, was now alone.

Some mornings I didn't get out of bed, missing Grosz's classes. I read Nathanael West and despaired for Maggie on the movie lot—for desperate, lonely people everywhere. Often I sat at the bar inside the Warwick Hotel, where Paul's bartender friend, a blue-eyed Irishman, began to worry about my wasted life.

"You're a nice kid," he said. "You don't have to booze it up. You've got things to do. Take a trip, go to Europe."

The first time Bolek found me on my bed in the morning, fully dressed, reeking of alcohol, and snoring like a bum, he had a fit. Cholera was the best he wished me. "Where does it come from?" he wanted to know. "Where do *you* come from?" I saw revulsion in his eyes, and fear, as if traits not wholly unknown or unexpected were surfacing. "It's your father's black gloom," he muttered.

Feeling hopelessly boxed in by my meticulous drawing, by my traditional subject matter, I could not paint. I looked around the galleries and museums. Picassos were everywhere, and Giacomettis, too, which Enid called "fugitives from

Dachau." Over cocktails waiting for Bolek one afternoon, Enid gave me her list of favorite American painters: Marin, Hopper, Burchfield, and, above all, Ben Shahn. "He's Jewish, too, you know," Enid said.

"Something new is happening," I told her. "Go over to the Whitney."

"I've seen some of it," Enid said. "I'm quite attracted to vulgarity. It's the spice that makes the beautiful even more dazzling."

The new stuff—Pollock, Motherwell, de Kooning—threatened the American pictorial world. It threatened *my* world. I got an erection every time I looked at it. It was a frontal attack, the storming of the Bastille, the mutiny on the *Potemkin*.

At the League, I slowly began to destroy the boring nudes and still lifes I'd made in Grosz's class. I took my canvases one at a time and pulled curtains of color over them, obliterating them, expunging the fine detail, the delicate balance, the subtle tones. Only faint suggestions of bodies remained. In no time at all, I had dozens of monochrome rectangles, black and red and orange.

Grosz was furious. "What is this crap?" he wanted to know. "Maybe you know someone who is interested in this shit?"

"I can't stand it anymore," I said. I fished in my pocket for my little penknife with two sharp blades and a bottle opener. I opened it and slashed the canvas in a diagonal from upper right to lower left.

George Grosz paled. "What about Goya?" he said.

"Goya?"

"He had it all, pal," Grosz said. "He could draw."

"He had something to draw. He had a war, he was deaf. . . ."

"And you?" Grosz asked. "You have nothing? All of nature is nothing? You are the best, kiddo, *the best*. You can be a great illustrator. There is nothing better."

"I don't want to be an illustrator!" I screamed, and Grosz took my elbow and yanked me into the hall.

"Listen to me," he said, pulling me down the stairs. "You are hysterical. This is not right. There is only nature. Nature is *lawful*. Everything else is clowning, not normal, *unnatural*." He picked up his overcoat and hat and led me out into the street. "If the cavemen had a Kodak, pal, they would have used it. Believe me, art is imitation." Grosz dragged me across the street to the Automat, where he treated me to coffee. "You want some cake? Have some cake. You don't fool around with a gift like yours. You can be worth a lot of money."

"Money? I need money." I was panting like a crazy man. "I need money for Poland, for Europe."

"This is serious," Grosz said. "Come with me, pal. I am going to take you home." We rode the bus to Penn Station, then the train to Long Island. "Europe," he said on the train. "Why Europe? It's depressed, ancient, *kaput.*"

I called Bolek from Douglaston to tell him I would spend the night at Grosz's home. "Is this true?" Bolek said. He loved Grosz's German drawings—the fat, slobbering burgers, the complacent, murderous couples. "He likes you?"

I whispered into the phone. "He thinks I'm the best." Bolek would have had an easier time believing I was spending the night with the Vanderbilts or Greta Garbo. Those people he knew and understood. He served them, flattered them, entertained them. But as much as he didn't want me to join the dubious ranks of artists, it was the artists, totally outside his ken, who, finally, impressed him most. "This is the same George Grosz?" he asked.

"The ex-antifascist," I assured him.

"He thinks you will amount to something?" Bolek half asked, half stated. "Bone of a dog."

"He wants to show you some of his new work, Bolek. I told him how much you like his caricatures."

"He wants to show it to me? Yes, tell him I want to see it. I will buy something."

Dinner at Grosz's was pleasant, though a little strained. Grosz kept a tight lid on the conversation, which was polite, Presbyterian. Mrs. Grosz was the quintessential mom, doting on me, distracted by the absence of her boys away at boarding school.

After coffee, Grosz took me into his studio. "I'm miserable," I said. "I don't know what to do."

"Maybe you should go back to school," he said, "real school, like my own sons. It is where they belong. It may be that you belong there, too. You have great talent, pal, that is true, but what does that mean? What does it *really* mean?

Talent," he said, "big deal." He loaded his pipe and puffed until it hissed. "Go to law school," he counseled, "be a businessman, make a lot of money. Your uncle is well connected. Go west, live like a king, the king of the Rockies." This gave him an idea and he went into the hall closet to fish out a pair of cowboy boots. "Nice, eh? Touch them, pal, they're the real thing." He slipped them on and paraded in front of me. "Harvard, Yale, contacts with the best families, the pulse of government, a wise partnership—"

"I don't want to be in business. I hate business," I said.

"Don't be naïve, sonny boy," Grosz said. "Your uncle sits on a gold mine, right there on Fifty-seventh Street. You don't need all that stinking history, the blood of that rotten continent—"

"You know what Kor says?" I asked.

"Kor, Kor," Grosz crowed, flapping his arms like wings. "Your friend Kor is a hypocrite. I hate those people with their phony dialectics. If they don't like it here, why do they stay? I'll tell you why. To poison everyone else with their important talk." I got up, ready to do battle, to leave, to protest. Immediately Grosz became conciliatory. "Anyway," he chuckled, "you should not listen to Surrealists or old Dadas. We lie. With us, nothing is sacred."

"Kor says that all that blood in Europe makes the earth rich, makes art grow."

"That's a good one," Grosz laughed. "I like that one."

"I should go back to where I come from, to see it, to feel it."

Grosz exchanged his meerschaum for a little corncob. As he lit it, his brick-red face looked somber, his bright blue eyes troubled. "You don't know," he said, "but sometimes a cold wind comes to me from the east. I *smell* blood." He looked out the dark window, then suddenly he wheeled about, lunged toward a rack of his paintings, and pulled one out. "Look," he said, pointing to an image of a man struggling to extricate himself from a swamp. A sprawling city burned in the background. "There is your fucking Europe. I leave all that behind, and *you*, you want to run back." He began pacing up and down. "Look at these hell pictures," he said, pushing that one back, pulling out others at random, each one more gruesome than the last. "I am cursed with them for the rest of my life." I saw ruins licked by flames and infested by rats, old men driven mad by war and disease, marching with demented enthusiasm toward some distant battlefield. "'I can paint only devils," Grosz said, sitting down in a stuffed chair. He looked close to tears. "But *you*, sonny boy, if you must make paintings, paint angels, American angels." He pointed to a series of Norman Rockwell *Saturday Evening Post* covers that hung on one wall. "Like those sweet pictures," he said. "And money, pal, that is how to make money."

"My uncle wants to buy a painting from you," I told him.

"Yes?"

"Something from Germany."

"That crap nauseates me," Grosz said. "I don't even want my boys to see it. These images do not help to make good citizens."

I spent the night in a tiny guest room on the third floor. In spite of Grosz, Europe loomed large. On the orange crate that served as a bed table, the last visitor had left a packet of photographs, perhaps intending to use them to illustrate a book. Each photograph was of a destroyed city: Dresden, Warsaw, Stalingrad—picture after picture of rubble. On the back of the bombed-out Cologne, someone had written: "I feel at home only here, only in the ruins."

As my head fell back on the thin, musty pillow, I saw my father, crazed with passion, rebuilding cities. I pictured him in the Crimea, a sunny port, ships bedecked with fluttering flags, gold domes overlooking the deep blue water. My father's strong, callused hands were repairing water systems. Under his arm he carried rolled blueprints of bridges, dams, tunnels. I smiled, at last seeing something useful being added to the world. Then the *Third of May* appeared and my father was there again, on his knees, at the instant of his death.

In the morning I accompanied Grosz and his little Scotty dog, Punch, on a walk through the quiet streets of Douglaston. "I want to go to Spain, too," I said, "to see the Goyas, to see the *Third of May* again."

"Ach, your love affair with Goya," Grosz said. "Tell me, pal, why are your sketchbooks filled with images of the *Third of*

May?" A neighbor of his approached us and Grosz doffed his fedora, bowing courteously.

"Because of my father."

"Your father?"

"He was a Jew—"

"You are Jewish?" Grosz said. He stopped by a tree where Punch had pulled him, then he looked at me as if for the first time. "Ach so," he said, "a Jew." For a moment we were strangers, a space had opened up between us. Then he shook my hand. "Yes," he said as if everything were clear now.

"He was shot. . . ."

"It is a terrible thing, the story of our time. And we are told to love the proletariat. The masses are a rabble, I tell you. Radicalism was a delusion. The Germans deserved Hitler."

"The Poles did it."

"Yes, anyone can do it," Grosz said. We walked, still holding hands. "Goya *knew.* He knew it would happen like this. Those people in the *Third of May* are ciphers, we are all ciphers before the death machine." We walked in silence a while. "But he doesn't moralize, your Goya. Things simply *are*, even these things." Grosz turned toward the sea and, like Bolek in the country, he took a deep breath, obviously grateful that it was there, so clean and fresh and relaxing. He closed his eyes to savor his enjoyment. In that breath at least he could not have smelled the blood.

We waited for Punch to squeeze out another drop by another tree. Grosz let go of my hand and gave me a friendly swat on the back. "But what am I saying? I tell you not to be so serious and I make philosophy. Listen, my pal, Goya himself stopped trying to understand anything. Don't tell anyone I said so," he whispered into my ear, "especially not the swell Republican ladies of Douglaston, but life becomes harder and harder. Goodness, order, dignity . . ." He paused to spit. "Those things don't exist anymore." He looked up at the clouds. "Poor Douglaston ladies, how they pray and hope. Fine folks," Grosz proclaimed, "good citizens, prosperous and charitable. But," he said, looking around, "to have hope is idiotic." He yelled a cheerful "Hi, pal" across the street to a paper boy who addressed him by name. "You want to be an artist?" he said to me. "Okay, kiddo, be an artist. You will be fine. But don't let me hear that you want to save the world. Nothing will save the world, especially not art." He put his arm around me and squeezed me. "You are so earnest, you will give them your soul. If I see anything of Grosz in your work, I will destroy it. I want to see nothing Groszian, nothing Teutonic, nothing *original*. Remember Norman Rockwell."

As we approached his house, he said, "Goya's ordeal took him beyond caring, beyond style. With me, it is different." He took off his hat and performed a little gigue for me. "I still care—oh, how Grosz cares," he sang as Punch yapped around his heels. "Grosz loves the swell ladies of Douglaston, the rich bank president at his big oak desk, the pastor of this little church—"

"Your work moves me deeply," I said. "You are a great artist."

"You too have already lived a little," Grosz said. "That counts, pal. As for technique, no problem, you have it. Now you must observe, study, *think*. Europe is a cemetery, a cemetery of Jews and Gypsies and surrealists and dialecticians. America is the future. Here, no one thinks except how to make money."

On the train back to the city, I thought of Grosz's work. It represented a whole life, with a beginning, a middle, and an end, a life he had wrapped up and rejected. Even at my age, I'd left one whole life. It had its own morbid completeness, like an amputated limb that ached on cold rainy mornings. I was convinced that the severed part was back there somewhere under the rubble.

True to his fiduciary policy, Grosz called Bolek Monday morning and arranged to meet him at his dealer's. In the middle of the week, a small Grosz nature study was hung with some fanfare over the Buckingham's woolly couch. Enid was present with her assistant, Phoebe Clarke, a Holbein Eve on her Bennington work term. During the hanging ceremonies, accompanied by a bottle of Piper-Heidsieck and pâté on matzohs,

pear-shaped Phoebe did not take her light gray eyes off me. They followed me as I moved, studying me, taking my measure.

The Grosz painting of chestnut trees was nicely detailed and devoid of drama. Bolek seemed delighted with it. He sat himself down in a chair opposite the newly decorated wall, his chin in his hand, tilting his head this way and that. Pink from the champagne and pleased with himself, he called this a memorable moment, an illustration of the importance of money. "I can own the best of everything," Bolek proclaimed, another cautionary tale.

Except for Grosz's political work, which for Bolek translated only into a shared disdain for the Bosch, the two of them seemed to be in perfect agreement about the function of art. "This is beautiful," Bolek asserted. "I can smell the buds of that tree."

"You can go out into the garden to smell trees," I said.

"But it is the great skill of your teacher which brings the tree inside this place, inside a hotel."

This view of art was beginning to no longer interest me. It was indeed Grosz's skill and mine as well to be able to imitate, to reproduce. But Bolek's taste for the delectable in art I found boring and false.

At dinner at Longchamps, Phoebe talked to me passionately about Spengler's *Decline of the West* while under the heavy white tablecloth her hand rested on my thigh. "You're beautiful," she sighed into my ear as Bolek and Enid talked shop, "so dark and brooding."

"I don't feel beautiful," I told her, which put new life into her busy fingers.

"I hardly sleep at night," Phoebe said. "You look like you don't sleep much either."

"I'm in a rage," I whispered.

Her mouth was on my ear. "I want to see it, taste it, feel it," she said.

That night, in her railroad flat in the east Thirties, Phoebe could not stop talking. "I've read all of Freud, all of Reich," she said. "I spent a year in an orgone box, two years with the fucking Sullivanians, and still I don't *feel* anything. I've never had an orgasm."

"You're shivering," I told her. "You should try to relax."

Phoebe wrapped her arms around herself, her teeth chattered. She seemed dry as a bone. I went over to her and put my arms around her to warm her, but she stiffened more. I got down on the floor and rolled around like a madman, howling at the moon.

Phoebe laughed and sobbed, and though she stopped shaking, it was clear that she required full-time attention. "Oh, Adam, teach me," she cried. "I need artists—melancholy, agitated, *deranged* artists."

Saturday night I took Phoebe to the Cedar Bar, the *Deux Magots* of the Abstract Expressionists. She hung tightly on my arm, but it was clear from the moment we passed through the door that this crowd of frolicking artists took her breath away.

The air resonated with the sheer force of this conquering army, just as the tranquil hills around Rome must have quaked with the presence of Attila's feverish hordes. We worked our way through to a booth on the back wall. We ordered beer, then Phoebe made her way to the ladies' room, jostling everyone in her way, making heads turn. The noise was deafening, the smoke thick. People milled around the tables, the bar, the booths. I stood up to look around. Two booths down from us I saw Carla, sweet supple Gypsy, the secret sharer of our maiden voyage in the Massachusetts woods. I sidestepped over to her table and stood grinning at her. For an instant Carla looked at me blankly, then she cried out my name. She climbed over the chunky, moustached man sitting next to her, and we hugged, examining each other like the old friends we were.

"You look terrible," Carla said. "Are you okay?"

"Barely," I told her. Carla's eyes, so delicately crossed at Camp Kee-Nah-Wah, were now nearly parallel to each other, their hair's breadth of difference adding an ocean of mystery. And the little mole floating coquettishly a few centimeters above the corner of her mouth had been blackened into a perfect little circle. She opened her mouth and pointed to her straight white teeth. "No more metal," she said proudly.

I turned to check on Phoebe, who wasn't back yet. I squeezed into the booth beside Carla, forcing the squat fellow with a cigar in his mouth against the wall. "This is Abe Strawberry," Carla said as she made room for me. "And here," she went on, smiling at the couple across the table from us, "is my aunt and uncle, Draga and Timor Baku."

We shook hands all around. "We are looking for good location for a gallery," Timor Baku said to me as he must have been saying to everyone he met in New York. "I am Rumanian, you see."

"I am not," Draga Baku confided impishly. "Timor found me in Liechtenstein."

"Vaduz is a tax shelter," Timor explained.

"The Duke is my cousin," Draga whispered.

The Bakus were small people, dressed entirely in white, their hair plastered into solid blue-black sheets, like helmets. Their faces shone like polished apples and only when Timor Baku smiled did I notice the worm hole, the familiar imperfection, his uneven yellow teeth, sparkling with gold.

A trio of men now stood by Phoebe's booth. They wore army fatigues, one of them with a cowboy hat on his head. Phoebe waved to me and I waved back. With the fraternal understanding of two strangers in a whorehouse, we let the other know that the present arrangements suited us both. When, an hour later, we got up to leave, Phoebe, surrounded by deranged artists, came over. "What the hell," she said.

"May as well try," I told her, and kissed her parched lips.

Outside the Cedar Bar on University Place, Abe Strawberry invited us to his studio. The Bakus declined, promising to visit him another day. Strawberry shook our hands, lingered over Carla's, then went back inside. The four of us walked uptown, the Bakus, charmed by the city, walking ahead, chattering in Rumanian, Carla and I behind them, catching up on the past two years.

Morty Turoff had had just the briefest sojourn in Carla's life. "I'm afraid I hurt him," Carla said, and then, "the way you hurt me." The streets were quiet except for the resonance of the Bakus' hard leather shoes. "Before we'd even left camp, Morty

165

said he wanted to marry me," Carla said. "I was only seventeen, and anyway I'm really a city person. I didn't want to live
in Colorado."

"Morty wasn't right for you," I said.

"I suppose not," Carla agreed. "You were the one I couldn't
get off my mind. I started really looking at paintings that
winter. You are at least partly responsible for my being at
Barnard, studying art history."

"Carla, this is the nicest thing that's happened to me in a long
time."

"I don't want to start again," Carla added quickly.

"I don't mean that," I said. "We won't do that. I want you to
know how much you meant to me, still mean to me. We're
important in each other's life."

Carla took my hand. I raised her hand to my lips and kissed
it. "Anyway, there's Maggie," I said. "Maggie's always been
with me and I suppose she always will be, always spoiling
things."

"She was there that summer, wasn't she?"

"Yes." I wondered if Roy Punsky was real. Surely Maggie
couldn't have made the whole thing up. "I keep losing her," I
said. "It hurts, but it almost doesn't matter. What I mean is that
it seems mystical." Who's going to be next, I wondered, Robert
Montgomery? "I'm being too romantic," I confessed to Carla,
"too Germanic, Grosz would say. Sometimes I feel as if Maggie
and I are like a Wagnerian couple, part brother and sister, part
lovers, part mortal, part immortal, who go on and on and on
forever."

Carla laughed and I did too. At Twenty-third Street, the
Bakus wanted to take a taxi the rest of the way home. We hailed
one and they got in. "You and I will always be friends," Carla
said as she climbed in after them.

The next time we met, I brought Paul. The three of us began
seeing one another often, listening to jazz, going to readings at
the "Y," to chamber music at Town Hall. Once, at Birdland,
Charlie Parker sat with us between sets. Since Paul and I had

166

seen him, Charlie had gotten fat and puffy. In the twenty minutes he spent at our table, he drank three shots of whiskey. Before he left to play again, a pearl button popped off his dark blue shirt. It rolled into my lap without anyone noticing. I turned the little thing around in my fingers and decided to keep it, remembering Grosz's instruction about collecting. "Select, catalog, and file" was Grosz's motto. "Artists must have a collection of objects and illustrations to refer to." I didn't quite know how the button would serve me. It became the foundation of a stash of items picked up here and there, to be raised, one day, to a place of significance.

Mostly, Carla, Paul, and I sat around her aunt and uncle's rented town house on East Sixty-third Street, where something strange and wonderful always kept us amused and distracted. The Bakus transformed that proper house into a circus, a commodity exchange, "a charade ground," as Carla called it. There, people bought, sold, bartered, told stories, juggled, performed magic, played Schubert lieder or German cabaret songs on the Steinway baby grand. There were cats everywhere. The Bakus loved cats—cats with ribbons, cats with bells, exotic cats from the Orient, long-haired and short, two-tone and single-color cats. Sometimes Draga Baku would pick up one of her favorites, a sleek Persian, and wrap it around her neck. Xerxes, the Persian, must have been trained to do it, for she hung there, limp, like one of Bolek's silver foxes.

Above all, there seemed to be an unending supply of paintings that kept changing hands, among them a small Magritte with a bowler hat, a cryptic Tanguy whose pair of figures had bags over their heads, Modigliani nude drawings so fine as to be barely visible, plus fresh semiabstractions from Paris, dull and lifeless compared to the exuberant new work—the Klines, the Motherwells, the Pollocks—popping up in New York.

One night after Paul's final exams, the three of us went to the Cedar Bar. The moment we opened the door, Abe Strawberry, already in his cups, lifted his beer mug. "A thousand years of abstraction," he proposed, spotlighting Carla in his buffoonish leer. The Cedar Bar was unusually empty. "They're all at the club," Strawberry told Carla. "Lecture on Navajo blankets or some such shit." Somewhat reluctantly, we invited him to join us at a table. "I've got a better idea," Strawberry said, never looking at Paul or me. "Come to my place. I'll show you my work." He didn't bargain for all of us, but he got all of us. After one beer at the bar, we followed him downtown. Strawberry, not too steady on his feet, steered Carla with a hand that wandered over the small of her back. As we approached the Bowery, where he lived and loved and worked, bums shouted out at us from unlit doorways. Outside Strawberry's door, we had to walk over a man lying in a puddle of urine. Strawberry nudged him into the street with his shoe.

On the grimy stairs inside, Paul said quietly to me, "This guy's a total schmuck. We could beat the shit out of him if we wanted to."

"Let's see his painting first," I said.

Abe Strawberry's loft was huge and profoundly filthy. It must have been a printshop once, for the floor was still thick with printer's ink in which Strawberry's daily droppings, like compost, had been irrevocably buried. Paul, visibly revolted, stood by the door.

It made me furious. "Why do you have to live like this?" I blurted out. "The whole fucking world is trying to dig itself out of the rubble and the filth."

"What is this shit?" Strawberry said. He was half my size. "You some kind of a businessman?"

Paul came over and stood behind him. "He's saying that only dumb Americans *try* to live like this, that you don't *have* to live like this—"

"Oh, yeah?" Strawberry said. "Where do you think I come from, fucking Cincinnati? Strawberry's a fucked-up name some *putz* gave my grandfather at Ellis Island. . . ."

Paul was itching to take care of business, to give Abe Strawberry a lesson. I supposed it was Lou Kaitz's genes surfacing. I felt stupid and apologized. Carla looked relieved. Strawberry pulled a six-pack out of the refrigerator and opened four of them. Carla sat down on a folding chair at a card table piled with art magazines and empty beer bottles. Above Strawberry's bed—a mattress on the floor with gray, crusted sheets, partly under the card table—hung Raphael's *School of Athens* and a clipping of Babe Ruth saluting the crowd at Yankee Stadium.

"My aunt and uncle like your work," Carla told Strawberry. She bent over, took her shoes off. "New shoes," she said. "My feet are killing me." She slid down on her chair, stretched her arms above her head, her legs splayed out in front of her.

Like a shot, Strawberry was at her feet. He took them in his hands and began massaging them, sticking his stubby fingers between her toes, picking out lint like chimpanzees in *The National Geographic*. Paul and I looked at each other, then at Carla's feet again. I could see that Strawberry was close to salivating. He wanted to take those little pink toes in his mouth and suck them like chicken feet. It gave me a pang, remembering how I had played with them on our mossy bed in the clearing. Paul walked over and took Carla's hand, and Strawberry let go.

He went over to a long wooden rack and pulled out a well-stretched, framed canvas. He laid newspaper on the floor along the wall and placed his painting on it, leaning it back. "Before the war I felt real insignificant," he said. "Those Europeans made us feel like assholes. Well, let me tell you, we picked those bastards clean when they came here. It turned out that there was no big mystery. They didn't know it all, they only *acted* like they knew it all."

Strawberry's large canvas was alive with color, an explosion of pigment, wild and mean, as if jars of red, orange, and pink had been dropped on a cement floor. We all gasped, especially Paul. Abe went over to Paul, put his hand on his shoulder. "Like it?" he asked. "Not bad, eh?" He took a long swig of beer. "You don't paint what you see anymore," he said to me, his tone assured now, almost academic. "You paint what you are."

"Is this what you are, Abe?" Carla asked. "Splitting apart in all directions?"

"Yeah," he said. "They're orgasm paintings." He looked at Carla and blushed. "At the moment of the most exquisite awareness," he said, gaining confidence with every word, "I begin to see through the mist into specific colors and shapes. It's then that it becomes *mine*, like handwriting." The more earnest Strawberry seemed to be, the more I relaxed. "Take Picasso," he continued. "Picasso said that first you eat the fruit, then you paint it. You get it?" he asked. "Once it was different," Strawberry said. He began searching around the room for an illustration, found a postcard of Soutine's hanging turkeys. "This is the way it used to be," he explained, passing the blue and green putrid-looking birds from Carla to Paul to me. "You used to paint the thing in front of you; then, if it didn't rot, you ate the goddam thing or you gave it to a hungry friend." He put the Soutine down on the table. "With me, I don't paint nudes, I eat them. Excuse me, sweetheart," Strawberry said to Carla, "but first I fuck and then I paint. And this—"he pointed with a theatrical flourish in the direction of dozens of canvases stacked neatly in the rack—"this is what I paint."

Paul was wide-eyed. "Do they have names?" he asked.

"Numbers," Strawberry said. "I give them names, but they're just for me." He went to the big red one and looked behind it on the crossbar. "Judy Horowitz, August in Montauk," he read. He pulled out a gorgeous eruption of violets, blues, and madders. "Gail Diamond in the back of Kline's Chevy," he read off the back.

We had worked through our belligerence. The feeling inside Strawberry's loft had become convivial. Paul went to take a leak into a yellow, rusty toilet that I had already used. It stood in the corner of the loft, exposed to everyone's view. Carla was the only one who hadn't used it, though her long legs were now tightly crossed. Strawberry pulled out some more folding chairs from behind a torn curtain that hung over a back wall for no apparent reason. He opened more beer, delivered one to each of us. When Paul came back, he made a screen of the cool Gail Diamond so that Carla, too, could pee.

Strawberry propped up some ten paintings for us, each with a slightly different configuration of exploding colors, different in the hue, direction, and velocity of the spinning fragments. They were a little like Kandinsky's bursting biological debris, except that instead of weird sacs of amoebic, paramecial parts,

Abe's centrifugal junk was made up of squadrons of brave, well-fed, flying spermatozoa. Nevertheless these enormous stretches of canvas looked effortless, as if they had rolled off Strawberry's brush.

"Are you ever tempted to paint real things?" I asked.

"This stuff's real, as real as anything," Strawberry said.

"Don't you ever want to make statements about people's lives?"

"I'm not a social worker," Strawberry said.

"I mean like Goya or even Picasso."

"I hate that shit," Strawberry said. "It's either religious or theatrical. Take *Guernica*. All those horses with their guts spewing out, all those rolling eyes lifted to heaven."

"They call your attention to the horror all around," I said. "They commemorate it."

"Painting's about paint," Strawberry declared simply.

"Just about paint?"

"The rest is for journalists."

I thought it best to let Paul and Carla leave by themselves when they announced, in unison, that they were tired. I stayed with Strawberry, drinking more beer still, seeing all the dozens of paintings he hadn't pulled out before. I warmed up to them more and more, beginning to love their energy and freedom. At the same time, this work that celebrated the event of its creation sent shudders of terror down my spine. If this was the new painting, it left me far behind. Even at my age, it made me feel like a relic, the ancient trumpeter, attached to Goya, Rembrandt, the Renaissance.

In my mind I composed a letter to George Grosz. Dear George, it began. I need to be tested, I must take the path of *most* resistance, not the sure road to success. I don't want to be like Norman Rockwell. I don't want to paint like *anyone*. I need to take risks, I need to risk making awkward things, *ugly* things. . . .

I met Kor one afternoon in the garden of the Museum of Modern Art. Each of us was carrying a wedge of cheesecake to a different table until I saw him. We kissed as people who had obviously recognized Kor smiled at the uncomplicated human response of their surrealist hero. I was thrilled to see him for I desperately needed to discuss this Abstract Expressionism.

"Some of the new American painting is strong stuff," I said.

"There is a world of difference," Kor declared, "between plumbing the depths of neurosis and looking up one's own asshole."

"But no matter where the inspiration comes from, the painting is lively, interesting to look at."

"So is a puddle of vomit," Kor said.

I was not about to convert R. Z. Kor. "Can't there be a nonobjective art?" I asked, hoping that somehow, somewhere, there were rules that forbade its existence.

"Of course there can be," Kor said, "and there was, a long time before *this*. This is neither the first nor the best."

"I was just upstairs with the Kandinskys—"

"That was serious art," Kor said. "This is nothing but seduction. Who can turn away from this Bastille Day?"

"It's just fireworks?"

"Who knows? They will find something in it eventually. Critics spring up like jack-in-the-boxes to endow anything they choose with sacred meaning, primal energy. For me, it is skin-deep, and skin-deep is boring."

"But it's *about* the surface," I said, giving Kor what Strawberry gave me.

"Yes, yes, it is wrapping paper, and who can resist a good package, especially in America?" Kor polished off his cheesecake. "My God, darling, there is nothing but trivia all around us. Look at *my* work. I haven't made a piece I like for years. I make the same things over and over again. Have I shown you the canvas at Julian's?" I was about to tell him how much I liked it, but he wasn't interested. "Yes, yes," he went on, "I know it is going to the Atheneum, but have you really looked at it? It is nothing but nostalgia. And nostalgia for what? For that quarrelsome little continent, for the Raphael in the jungle."

The jungle or the desert as background for palladian palaces and rococo flourishes had preoccupied Kor for a long time.

"This is a monumental theme," I said. "Every time you explore it, it's more marvelous."

"I don't know," Kor said, lost in his sad thoughts. "Perhaps it is like this everywhere now. Perhaps Auschwitz has put an end to culture and to civilization."

"But new things are happening," I said. "Things aren't really that bad—"

"Oh, yes," Kor said, looking directly at me now, "things *are* that bad. There are no ethics. Look what is happening to people who fought for their principles. It is abominable. They are being hunted, stripped of their beliefs and identity, not to speak of their means of survival. Look at Magdalena's Hollywood. People are losing their jobs, ostracized, blacklisted. How many times did they refuse me citizenship?"

"Don't you think this will stop?"

"Adam, Adam, I came here not looking for a paradise, just a safe place to live. . . ."

"It *is* safe. Don't you think it's safe?"

"They are making their cold war. They are playing with atomic bombs. This is safe?" People with trays of food were standing waiting for tables. Kor looked around, then got up, ready to go. "It is frightening," he said, "and I think every day of going back, of at least being where I come from, where you come from, where our ancestors made art, where they are buried. I am dreaming about the mass graves. I am dreaming about Auschwitz and Treblinka."

I felt part of nothing. A raucous celebration was going on downtown where Abe's friends, in dingy little rooms, shrouded in total abandon, anchored to no one, held back by no past, no dreams, were splashing their paint over huge canvases. Big men, tall men, *American men*, carefree and lawless, in the plain garb of the frontier, the woods, the cow ranches, boozed and whored and danced in the streets.

Grosz was displaced, Kor was displaced, I was displaced. I couldn't go on, not now. I had to stop painting.

At the hotel, I held on to the furniture to keep myself

upright. I lay down on the floor and emptied my head of thought. I tried to see only the radiating phosphenes inside my eyelids as I pressed them with my thumbs. And late in the evening, when Bolek came home, I went into his room to lay out a new plan. Stumbling and stuttering, I proposed to go to work for him at Prince Casimir Furs.

8

*B*olek's fashion show had come and gone without my noticing it at all. There must have been parties, press releases, reviews. Bolek must have burdened his heart with worry, but I hadn't been looking and had seen nothing.

None of that mattered now. "So what is the difference?" he asked now that I had filled his heart with joy. He had already changed into his pajama top. He sat cross-legged on his bed. "I started in business when I was sixteen. So what is a few years? It is nothing. It is perfect."

My proposition flushed his cheeks a healthy pink, it worked magic on his furrowed brow. He bounced up from the bed like a clown on a trampoline. "Let us go out," he said. "We can't stay home on a night like this."

Quickly he pulled his pants back up. Unzipped, they fell to his ankles as he spun me around his bedroom in a little polka. Tripping to the phone, he called to reserve a table at El Morocco. Then he called Sophie, then Enid, and finally—it was already after eleven—he called Weinglass. "Zyga," he said in a voice as light as a summer breeze, "Adam is coming into the business."

I pulled at him. "Just to try," I reminded him. "Don't forget that, Bolek, just to try."

Undoubtedly Weinglass was not elated, for black clouds were gathering around Bolek again. "You are in the middle of a bridge game?" Bolek asked, astonished perhaps that Weinglass wasn't waiting for his call, expecting this news. "Why do you tell me that? Am I not telling you the most wonderful news? I should care about your bridge game!" He reached for a cigarette and lit it. "Yes, Mr. Weinglass, he will stay. Yes, Mr. Weinglass, he will work hard. No, it is not money down the drain, you swine. Do you know what this means? How can you know, you and your Bolshevik Francesca! Tell Basia, tell Spektor, bark the news to Fouffie." Bolek slammed the phone down and his mood changed immediately, those knitted brows relaxing into a sunny smile again.

At El Morocco, everyone knew Bolek. A bottle of champagne was waiting for us in a bucket on a side table. "To a thousand years of fur business," Bolek toasted, and even the turbaned waiter grinned.

The motif at El Morocco was zebra—zebra and potted palms. As Bolek and I celebrated a decision I could no longer take back, show girls with baskets of ersatz fruit on their heads pranced jerkily to the rhythms of tom-toms and brass. "You will see, darling," Bolek yelled above the din, "everything will now be yours. You will learn quickly. It is nothing for a smart boy like you."

"What will I do?" I asked. "Where will I work?"

"You will work with me. You will be *my person*."

"Your assistant?"

"Never I can trust anyone, and now I have you. It will change my life."

"Don't you want me to start upstairs in the factory?"

"No factory for you," Bolek said. "You are needed in the showroom with me."

"I'm not sure I can tell one fur from another," I confessed.

"Of course you can," Bolek laughed. "It is in your blood." We drank our champagne, so dry it was like licking silk. "Look over there," Bolek said, nodding in the direction of an elderly man sitting in the shadows with a buxom blonde. "That is Mr. Fillippo Fillippi—"

"The fascist?"

"The sewing-machine king," Bolek said. "He buys his wife two coats a year and two more coats for his whores." Bolek smiled. "You see, we are working even here. Nothing is lost. This is where your education begins."

I took a small sketchbook out of my jacket pocket and wrote, "Fillippo Fillippi, four coats annually."

At the hotel, Bolek couldn't sleep. He came out into the living room, where I was trying to write a letter to Maggie. "Your mother would be proud," he said. "And believe me, your art talent will not be wasted."

The next day we walked down Fifth Avenue to Bolek's tailor, a sad Viennese gentleman who made suits for the three partners as well as other rich, conservative Europeans. Mr. Rattner offered me his limp hand and mournfully showed us the grim possibilities for my new wardrobe.

"Lighter, Rattner," Bolek reprimanded. "he is not a half-dead underdog like the rest of us. Look at him, he is jumping with life, and handsome like a god."

The somber bolts of cloth at Rattner's were the foundation of three new suits. On the opposite end of the spectrum, Bolek's Lebanese shirtmaker provided light cottons with my initials sewn in Gothic letters on the breast pocket. These were the symbols of my reformation, the sign of my serious intentions.

We bought shoes and neckties, then expensive casual wear. We found cashmere sweaters with colors the salesmen called avocado, peach, and mulberry, sport jackets of fine tweed and subtle plaid. "Can I wear these at work?" I asked.

"Ah, this is for Southampton, for *their* country clubs, *their* golf, *their* boats. Wherever you are, darling, you never stop selling." He tugged at the back of my gray and blue jacket, then stretched my arm out to see the cuff.

"Do I really have to *sell?*" This I hadn't bargained for.

"I am not talking shoes, darling. I am talking a way of life. You are now a model of what is fine and expensive."

When, a week later, I arrived at Prince Casimir Furs at nine in the morning, decked out in my new finery, freshly barbered and manicured and smelling of Bolek's colognes, Mignon, the receptionist, blushed. No one knew what to make of it. Mlle. Sacha and Jacques made a fuss, pulling out my handkerchief another millimeter, straightening my paisley tie. They quickly ran out of things to do or say and retired to the showrooms to rearrange ashtrays. And slinky, flat-chested Yvette, fiddling with the cosmetics on her dressing table, offered me a half-smile. "So now even you weel work for a leeveeng," she said.

Bolek practically stopped all business activity in order to devote himself entirely to teaching. Elsa and Yvette trudged up and down in front of me while Bolek, sitting proud and silent by my side, tried to imprint upon me, as on a duckling who had strayed from the fold, the relative worth of crown sable, Russian broadtail, Alaska seal, mutation mink. A gesture or a gasp would inform me that the little ermine stole on Elsa's bony shoulders was a masterpiece. "Siberian ermine," Bolek said, "ballerina skirt of black broadtail." And then he began to announce each piece as if we were in the first row at the fashion show, touching the silver runway. "Triangle silhouette in champagne nutria. Blood of a dog, this is wild Labrador mink, full shirred skirt with pockets." I could hardly believe his extensive English vocabulary. "This darling is a hug-me-tight," he said, "and this—may cholera strike me if I lie—is a dolman sleeve." My eyelids felt heavy. "Cape of blue fox with deep yoke," Bolek continued, observing me carefully out of the corner of his eye. "But all this is nothing, darling. I did it all before, and years ago. But then, in Warsaw, the Philharmonic played and all Europe watched."

I had never known time to pass so slowly as at Prince Casimir Furs. The showrooms were often empty, a condition that had little to do with sales, for the business depended on a few enormous transactions rather than the democratic commotion of the large department stores. Jacques, and now Emile, the dashing new salesman spirited away from the fur department at Bergdorf's, spent a lot of the day looking for quiet, unobtrusive niches where they could rest their weary feet or browse through the paper, as far as possible from Bolek, our very own resident Vesuvius whose eruptions were always imminent. The only camaraderie of the salespeople centered on this game of hide-and-seek. They knew nothing about each other's life outside our Fifty-seventh Street mausoleum, nothing except rumors. Elsa maintained that Jacques was a Forest Hills pansy. Jacques said she was a cheap whore whom he'd seen parading in front of Lindy's. Emile was suspected of leather worship and sadism, and even poor Mlle. Sacha who devoted her life to her autocratic mother was said to have carried home bottles of good champagne and jars of caviar under her Paquin cape.

Relief from boredom and innuendo was furnished by the customers. Like fizz pills in cool water, the customers jiggled the pot, sending Jacques and Emile and Mlle. Sacha scrambling to the elevator, that wrought-iron box from which all good things sprang. It was there, in the plush vestibule under a photograph of Bolek helping Pope Pius XII into an ermine cape, that Jacques, Emile, and Mlle. Sacha faced the outside world. Madame in her new Dior suit just brought back from Paris, madame barely out of the turquoise sea at St. Tropez or the mud baths at Badgastein. Here, Jacques and Emile and Sacha claimed their territory. Here, the nature of the guerrilla actions they would conduct on each other was determined.

Bolek's territory was clear. He had his shahs and agas and maharanis. Jacques and Emile and Sacha shared the crumbs, mostly the new managerial class, just learning their manners. This ambience of intrigue, jealousy, and suspicion suited Bolek well for it kept the pot boiling. He presided over this tense domain like a shrewd impresario. He shared with the help and the customers alike their love for the ephemera of life, their faith in mood, color, and pretense. Yet underneath it all, buried within the bluster, I saw a man who had to work himself into a fever pitch to be sure of anything. Only when he was quiet did he have doubts. Only in his unguarded, unpossessed moments did I see the scared immigrant who stood in awe before all he had wrought. Seeing this made me love him all over again.

"This could not have happened in Poland," he said to me. "*You* could not have happened in Poland."

"What do you mean? You had everything you wanted."

"Yes, but we all had to watch our step. We were allowed to do what we did because we served those pigs like slaves."

"And here?"

"Here, darling, there are maybe some places they don't want us. Maybe we have to work harder than they do. But look at you. You do what you want. You are an American. They have to pay attention."

Bolek exercised his charms on me, luring me into the glamour, the drama, the *Aida* of his everyday life. When the showrooms were cleared out one afternoon so that Greta Garbo could have a private viewing, Bolek made sure that I was with them. "My nephew," he said proudly at the outset, "he is an artist, madame. He has perfect taste." He even dared to approach the inscrutable Garbo as if he were her confidant. "And he is not bad-looking, either," he said, winking a naughty eye. As the models brought out the season's best, Bolek said, "The little chinchilla would look splendid on Madame Greta, don't you think so, Adam?"

My presence genuinely energized him. Instead of the exhaustion that had become a part of Bolek's late afternoons, he now seemed able to keep going the whole night long. By six, when neither my legs nor my mind could take another moment in this place, Bolek would stand by the windows overlooking Fifty-seventh Street with a new bundle of pelts, shaking them playfully like a puppy with a bone. "Look, look, this is like a handful of emeralds," he said, and then, putting the bundle down on a chair, he eyed it happily, his hands behind his back, his body rocking back and forth. He called for Yvette, who was leaving for the day, shopping bags in both hands, a kerchief on her head. "Come here, darling," he said to her as she waited for the elevator. "Tell me, does Adam not please you? He is a good boy."

Bolek tried to tell me about all the important customers, but he didn't know what many of them did to make their money. But when Mrs. Walter P. Schmeck was to arrive the next morning, Bolek knew just what the Schmecks did, what they were worth. "I know them a long time," he told me, "even in Warsaw. The Schmeck family owns *everything*. Rubber in Malay, tin in Bolivia, copper in Chile, gold in Alaska." He chanted the minerals reverently. Then he leaned across his desk and squeezed my arm hard. "This year, darling, they buy the whole jungle around the river Amazon."

"Why?" I asked, thinking of how Maggie would have reacted.

"Why?" Bolek said, letting go of my arm and leaning back. "Paper, darling. The world needs paper."

In the morning, Mrs. Schmeck arrived with her daughter. Wally Schmeck was about my age, though she looked a lot older. Mrs. Schmeck was superbly coiffed and tailored. She had the breasts of an operatic contralto, but the green Balenciaga suit with its cinched waist made her appear formidably *a la mode*. It seemed that nothing could have helped poor Wally Schmeck, who looked troubled, her face sunken, her body frail. Among the oversize Chinese vases, the theatrical silver drapes, the floor-to-ceiling mirrors, Wally Schmeck was like a tiny lost bird with fractured wings.

Bolek and I took mother and daughter into the smallest of the three showrooms, used exclusively for "the biggest customers." Mlle. Sacha herself set out the silver tray with coffee, croissants, Swiss jams, paper-thin Nova Scotia, sliced Russian black bread, curlicues of butter. We sat around the laden coffee table and I instinctively began pushing the food toward the emaciated Wally Schmeck.

"Isn't it wonderful," asked Mrs. Schmeck, "to have your handsome nephew working with you, Mr. Casimir?" She clasped her hands together and looked down at Wally. "He is learning a trade," she said.

I leaned over toward Wally Schmeck, who looked as uncomfortable as I was. I whispered in her ear: "Pulling myself up by the bootstraps." Wally's thin, gray face brightened. Bolek looked at Wally and me and smiled. "Madame," he said to Mrs. Schmeck, his eyebrows raised, "to have Adam here is all I have dreamed."

"I have observed your uncle's career for years, even in Poland," Mrs. Schmeck told me. "He is one of the most creative men of our time. He has always understood the needs of society."

To my astonishment, Wally Schmeck was stuffing a croissant into her mouth as if she were as starved as she looked. While she chewed it, she picked up several slices of salmon with a silver toothpick and made a sandwich. Then, as if awakening from a dream, she looked up at us and wiped her mouth decorously. The sandwich followed the croissant into her mouth.

Mrs. Schmeck wanted something exotic from Bolek, something, she confided, that none of her friends could possibly own. "A rare combination, my dear Mr. Casimir, something so unique that perhaps we might make it up together right here, right now."

Bolek was willing. While Yvette showed Mrs. Schmeck the collection, Mlle. Sacha brought out pelts and skins, swatches of wool and chiffon. They played with combinations of seal and leopard, broadtail and mink, long hair and short, fur and hide. Yvette wore one coat after another. I went to help Yvette off with a long coat, and as I slid the sable down her bare arms, my nose inhaled a marvelously *human* smell. In this chill ether dripping with the frigid scents made by Guerlain, Ricci, and Worth, I got a luxurious whiff of Yvette's armpits. It made me dizzy with desire. "Yvette," I said into her ear, "I'm crazy for the smell of your armpits." For an instant she looked astonished, then she broke down laughing. As I held the sable, she doubled over with uncontrollable laughter. Bolek, like a furious Poseidon blowing up a storm, pointed to the curtained door. Her hand over her mouth, Yvette fled.

Wally Schmeck asked for the bathroom. Happy for an excuse to get away, I showed her the way, and while she did her business, I ran into Yvette's cubicle, where she was spraying deodorant under her arms. "No, Yvette, please," I begged. "I'm in love with your armpits."

She broke down again. "You love the armpeet," she managed to say.

"I want to smell them," I said, and lifted her arms.

"You are crazee," she yelped.

"Yvette—"

She pushed me away. "You are bad, you monstair. Do you hear me?"

I rushed out to meet Wally Schmeck, who was just coming out of the bathroom. I felt wonderfully refreshed. "Do you have a fur coat of your own?" I asked.

"Me?" she said. "What would I do with a fur coat?"

"I don't know. I just thought that one day maybe I could help you pick one out."

Wally Schmeck looked at me tenderly. "Yes," she said. "Why not? I'll ask my mother."

Bolek and the patternmaker were slipping a canvas on Mrs. Schmeck. They had come up with something together and Mrs. Schmeck's ample chest was being scribbled on and pinned while she looked happily into the mirror. "You are a naughty man, Mr. Casimir," Mrs. Schmeck said. "It's impossible to resist these beautiful things."

"Madame," Bolek said as he pulled at the canvas from the back, "I am blessed with wonderful customers who make it worthwhile my toil."

As the work continued around Mrs. Schmeck's body, they talked of the horse show at Madison Square Garden where the Schmeck family annually entered animals from their stables. Would Bolek come to see their princely horses? Of course he would, and he would bring his nephew, who, like our entire family, loved horses. Didn't Mr. Casimir agree that the Retired Actors Pension Fund and the Home for Unwed Mothers were worthy of everyone's time and money? Agree? Bolek more than agreed. He called for his checkbook and wrote out two checks for Mrs. Schmeck to deliver in our family's name.

When the Schmecks left, Bolek said, "Madame Schmeck is a wonderful woman, very elegant, *very* elegant." We left the salon together to eat lunch. "Her daughter is a little strange," he said, touching the side of his head, "but she is a nice girl, don't you think so, darling?"

"Yes."

"My English is getting better. Did you notice that?" Bolek asked.

"Much better," I said. "I was surprised."

Bolek put his arm around my shoulders. Our jackets were unbuttoned, flapping like flags in the breeze that blew across Fifty-seventh Street.

After lunch, I labored over Maggie's letter, probably in its third revision.

Dear Maggie,
I've given up painting and, like you, I'm making $200 a week. I'm writing you from my desk in a little cubicle the carpenter just made for me in the bowels of the loathsome furry kingdom, Prince Casimir Furs. Yes, I am working for Bolek.

I'm not sure I understand what this is all about. I was once this oddity who lumbered over here from beaten-up Europe wanting to make his little Goyescas, portraits of all that madness. Too young, everybody thought, to be saddled with the world's horrors. Well, now the horrors are Mlle. Sacha and the dread customers. I have entered a new madness. I may lose my grip entirely.

I ran into your father at the museum and he also seemed in bad shape, haunted by the mediocrity all around him, dreaming of times gone by. For me to give up painting is important only to me, for him to do it would be a catastrophe!

Do you remember Carla, Carla the Gypsy from my camp, at the time of Roy Punsky? Well, Paul and Carla are becoming a very serious number. If not for them, I don't know if I'd survive New York without you. There is also a clown, a very serious Abstract Expressionist clown, named—don't laugh—Abe Strawberry. Extremely gifted. Paints *orgasms*. I should let loose and paint my rage and guilt and sadness, but I'd poke holes in the canvas or make mud. I don't share their enthusiasm for psychoanalysis (boring!) or for primitivism (phony!).

Have you seen *Bicycle Thief* or *The Miracle* with Anna Magnani? Finally movies one can watch without embarrassment. Paul dragged me to see John Wayne in *Fort Apache*. What shit! And he is stiff as a board and a lot dumber. Maybe you should make movies in Italy.

Have you met any of your father's friends, like Bertolt Brecht? I don't think you should miss the opportunity.

When you come to New York, you must stop in at Prince Casimir Furs. Oh, Maggie, I don't know what I'm going to do without you.

Adam

I had a hard time enticing Yvette to go out with me. She shrugged it off. "Eet ees something I don't do," she said.

"What don't you do, Yvette?"

"I don't fraternize weeth the boss familee," she said. We were both facing the mirror in her cubicle. Yvette moved her arms self-consciously. She was either protecting her armpits or, I hoped, suggesting that they were not necessarily off limits. When she raised her arms to fix her hair, though, she remembered the pervert she was dealing with and flung them back down to hug her body again. "You are a nice boy," she said, and I got up to my full six feet plus and told her that I was nearly twenty and that it wasn't just her armpits that turned me on.

"I'm feeling a little lonely, Yvette," I said.

After that, I managed to get her out for a drink. I wasn't mad for Yvette, though drawn to find the erotic within these walls where everyone seemed to bask in the sensuality of money, fur, and the tall, skinny models who, legend had it, were there to service rich gentlemen. "You are family, Yvette," I said. "We've known each other a long time."

"Not familee," she said. "In the ménage onlee, like the cleaning ladee."

Finally I got her to come to El Morocco, where we drank a lot of champagne so she could forget that she was five years older than I and not the least bit interested in me. I insisted that she wear a lovely broadtail jacket I'd picked out from cold storage. "You are like your uncle," Yvette said. I bought her a Dunhill lighter, a gardenia corsage, and a photograph taken at our table by a photographer in a fez. But Yvette was tough, *rigid* on the dance floor.

"Maybe we should just be friends, Yvette," I said, "just good friends."

Yvette looked into my eyes for the first time. The thin, pursed lips, always intent on covering her protruding front teeth, eased into a smile. Yvette's body relaxed, too, and for the rest of the medley, performed by a band in orange jackets, she rested her head on my shoulder.

Nearly every night I put on my old clothes and went down to the Cedar Bar, where Abe Strawberry and I drank ourselves numb either on the premises or, in the company of Abe's eager art students, in some dirty little Lower East Side apartment. "You smell like a homo businessman," Abe said to me early on, so I scrubbed myself diligently coming and going, washing off the colognes before my trip downtown, then obliterating every trace of booze and women after getting back to the hotel early in the morning.

Some nights Paul and Carla came along. Even Phoebe came when she was in the city. I loved paying the bill for everyone. Paul said, "Bolek has a thing or two to learn from you." My pockets bulged with cash and I didn't want to keep any of it. I was developing a real taste for money, this money earned by patient survival in that animal depository, that elegant abattoir called Prince Casimir Furs.

Bolek was not anxious to have me snoop around in the factory. When he took me up to show me the progress of a coat, he also took me back down. The relationship of boss to up-stairs workers was becoming more and more adversarial, sometimes approaching violence. "It's their fault," Bolek said. "They do not need a union. I have never stolen from them. Aren't we all Polish Jews? How can they do this to me?"

Victor, the foreman, met us as we got off the elevator to check on Mrs. Schmeck's coat, an exotic combination of leop-ard and Alaska seal. Beyond him, the place hummed with industry. Stacks of flat boards leaned against the walls with strips of fur stretched in place.

Victor and Bolek chatted for a while. How's your family? How's *your* family? Isn't it wonderful to have Adam here, home at last? Splendid, Victor said. And Victor's nephew? The fur business is not for him, a geology student at Oklahoma State. Ah, America, Bolek sighed. Ah, life.

Victor held a couple of coats over his arm. His job was to follow the progress of the coats from the time they were ordered, through all the exacting work upstairs—the fittings, the cutting, the putting together, the refitting—right to the delivery, and then, after the season, the storage. He had worked for Bolek from the beginning in New York. He was a decent man, but his loyalty was split down the middle, proud of being associated with a house that was the best, the *very best*, but committed to the struggle of the union. The split caused him discomfort and pain.

"One day soon I will give you Adam so he can see for himself how it is done," Bolek said. Victor said that it would be his pleasure to help educate me. He ran his free hand carefully over his scalp. He was losing his hair, and what was left he combed over the balding middle in thin black strands. He looked at me and smiled warmly. "Probably I must get permission," Bolek said sardonically.

Victor said that he understood Bolek's sentiments. "I sympathize with your difficulties, Mr. Boleslaw," he said, "but permission is hardly necessary. This is family. The union is not a cold brute, the union understands."

In fact, the union, once proud and militant, was veering toward corruption. Some of the new officers were trying to muscle into positions of power in this and other fur businesses, trying to make deals with Weinglass and Spektor, though never with Bolek.

"The fifth floor wants peace, Mr. Boleslaw," Victor said, laying the coats down on a long table.

"Peace?" Bolek said incredulously. "You say this to me? How can I make peace when you are killing me? Peace we could have before."

"Everyone here loves this firm, Mr. Boleslaw. After all, we have here Europe's greatest fur workers, superb craftsmen all—"

"You see, you see?" Bolek said to me. "First they spit in my face, then they say they cannot live without me."

"That's not exactly what was said," I told Bolek, not really knowing how to restrain him. "Everyone has to live, Bolek, everyone has to look out for himself—"

"We want to live *with you*, not without you, Mr. Boleslaw," Victor said.

Bolek was working himself up into the realm of pure hysteria. I could see it happening, traveling down his body, from the glassed-over eyes to the pulsating toes, shuddering with rage. "He would be nothing without me," Bolek screamed, "and how does he treat me? Like pigshit."

Victor looked concerned for Bolek's health, an unhappy witness to this weird pathology. "Mr. Boleslaw," he said, "the workers love you *and* the union."

"And the union?" Bolek said, hardly opening his mouth. *"And the union?"* Bolek began to stomp his feet like a child. "I don't love them," he spit. "How can I love them if I hate them?"

For now there was no more to be said. Victor picked up the coats off the table, stepped back into his space, and shut the self-locking wire-mesh door behind him.

"May a dog shit on you!" Bolek yelled through the mesh, then he yanked me into the waiting elevator. "I don't know what it is," he said. "What is happening? Is this place not mine?"

There was no way to make Bolek understand. He had memories of old times, not even all that long ago, when it felt good to give someone more money for a job well done, when some old woman bent over a sewing machine would kiss his fingers for a few more zlotys.

I began bringing my sketchbook to work. The times I got there first, I'd park myself in one of Jacques's or Emile's favorite corners and let my mind spill out its accumulated stopped-up images. I made drawings of them all, portraits of Mlle. Sacha, Jacques, Emile, Yvette, Elsa. As they saw themselves materialize on the paper of my pocket-size pad, they changed their attitude toward me. Their likenesses estranged them from the magician who made them. Half in awe of the shaman, half in disgust as with a classmate who can do *anything* without even trying, they stopped being amused. But I was beginning to feel transformed by this act of drawing. It defused me, calmed me, and entranced me all at once.

Bolek wasn't particularly enchanted when he first saw my

sketchbook on my lap again, even during lunch hour. I felt like a boy caught reading under the covers with a flashlight. "You'll spoil your eyes," Bolek said and pushed fur coats in front of me. "If you must do this, darling, make me a quick sketch of the little mink stole. Quick, darling, with lines that fly. It must look wild and sexy, like fantasy."

I also began drawing upstairs in the factory. I found a seat near the big windows among the row of clothes dummies. I drew what I saw in front of me: workers bent over their benches, cutting up pelts, tacking them to pieces of canvas. Downstairs life consisted of dozing on the rim of a volcano. Here, on the fifth floor, things were more predictable, regulated by Victor and the clock.

Victor came over to see what I was doing. He said nothing but brought over a white coat to put on top of my third-floor suit. At noon the machines stopped. Hannah Goldman came over to look. "What a talented boy," she said. "You learned at school?"

Flora Fein stood behind Hannah. "Did you ask him to eat with us?" she asked Hannah. Hannah shook her head. "So ask," Flora said.

Hannah asked.

"Here?" I said.

"Where else?" Hannah said, "the Russian Tea Room?"

"I didn't bring my lunch," I said.

"So big deal," said Bronka Teitlebaum, a tiny woman who worked at one of the machines, "We'll take up a collection."

Someone cleared one of the long tables and put a cloth over it. The collection of food put before me was astounding. "Enough for an army," I said.

"What army?" Flora said. "You're a growing boy." From their pots and pans they spilled out pirogi and boiled chicken, even kasha. They heated things on a hot plate. They piled it all on real porcelain with wedges of babka on the side. They served tea in glasses.

Victor sat at the head of the table smiling at me. "I speak for all of us," he said. "Welcome, Adam, welcome to the business. We have watched you grow up."

I raised my glass of tea. "I'm trying to learn," I said.

"He's trying to learn," a heavy woman told her friend, who was apparently hard-of-hearing.

"What's to learn?" the friend wanted to know. "It's in his blood."

Someone said to the hard-of-hearing woman, "He's a very good artist."

"He's an artist? You have to be a genius to be an artist," she decided.

Bronka Teitlebaum said to me, "Here you can at least make a living."

"His uncle's an artist, too," the hard-of-hearing woman said.

"A taking-advantage-artist," a little man at the end of the table said in a thick Yiddish accent. He was shushed playfully by everyone.

"So why aren't you in college?" someone asked.

"School's not for me," I said, my mouth full of pirogi.

"What does that mean? You want to toil like a regular worker?"

"So what's wrong with workers?" asked the little man.

"I got kicked out of school," I told them. There was silence. They were embarrassed. "I love to draw, you see, and I was copying the Old Masters—"

"Really? They threw you out for copying?"

"I made nudes."

"Nudes in painting is all right," someone said. "In art it's all right."

"I made them do, well, funny things."

"A little dirty?" Victor asked.

"Yes, like that," I admitted.

"And they kicked you out for that?"

"I sold them to all the boys in school."

"Listen to him, a regular businessman. What a businessman!" Even the little man in back laughed. Everyone slid their plates over a bit, coming closer.

Flora said, "I knew his mother in Warsaw." I looked at her, large and tough like a horse. "That's right," Flora said. "I didn't know her well, but even to know her a little was to love her." Flora took out a handkerchief and dabbed at her eyes. "A wonderful woman," she said, "and how she adored this boy."

A reverent hush settled on our festive meal. "She never took time off from work, *never*, except when he needed her."

"So what are mothers for?" the Yiddish-speaker in back asked.

"He is sick, she takes him to the doctor," Flora went on, disregarding the commentary from the rear. "*She* is sick, nothing. She doesn't care."

I heard someone explaining to someone else, "She perished who knows how."

Stan, the white-haired cutter who also worked for Mandelbaum's in Warsaw, told the story of my mother's coming back home from Paris, where she went regularly for the fashion shows. "The minute she steps off the train," Stan said, "she asks where he is, my son? 'Where?' the chauffeur says. 'In Zopot with the governess. Mr. Mandelbaum sent him there.' Your mother is driven directly to a little airfield," Stan said, rubbing his hands together. "At the time, there were no big airports," he explained, "not in Poland. A little airplane," he said, bringing his hands together so they almost touched, "that's what there was, parked in the grass. She got on it and flew to Zopot just to see you." Stan stopped to look at his hushed audience. Stan had a deep basso voice. "How do I know all this? I used to take coffee with Kleist the chauffeur on Sundays. This young man was in Zopot with that beautiful little Magdalena Kornfeld, plus the two governesses. You and Magdalena were always together, just like brother and sister."

The short man in back growled something in Yiddish. "A Marxist Zionist," Hannah explained.

I said, "I hope you will teach me. Everyone says you are the last of the great craftsmen."

"Not many left," Bronka Teitlebaum agreed. "My mother did this work, and her mother, too."

Stan shook his head sadly. "It's not the same now," he said. "Before, it was like family."

"What family?" the Yiddish-speaking man said. "It's them and it's us."

"If your uncle came up now, he wouldn't like us all together like this," Bronka Teitlebaum said.

"It's not right," I said, "but he can't help himself."

"Never mind," Flora said. "He means well. We know he means well. He's a very nervous man. And look what he has done. It's a miracle."

"But he's accepted the union," I lied.

The man in back moaned.

Hannah said to me, "One day you'll be the boss."

"Me?" I was chewing on a piece of babka. "No, not me."

"What, not you. Of course you. . . ."

"I'm trying this for a while. I don't know yet. . . ."

"You remember my daughter, Malca?" Hannah asked me. "Once you went with her to the Radio City Music Hall. *Mrs. Miniver* it was. You remember? God, I'm embarrassed to tell you this—"

"Tell him already," Flora urged.

"I used to dream you liked Malca." Hannah blushed, covering her face. "That you and she would be married one day, that you would have babies." Hannah laughed. "You know where she is, Malca? Anthropology in Wisconsin. How do you like that? She's going to marry an American."

There was warmth and history upstairs, a feeling of family. Downstairs on the third floor, they were all illegitimate, they were black sheep, the distrusted stepchildren of a jealous, angry father. Up here, separated by rules and wire mesh, there were feelings of a shared past, and in those sweet memories of better times, of things as they should be, lived memories of my mother, mourned and loved. For the first time in years, I had a recurrence of my nightmare.

But the longer I stayed at Prince Casimir Furs, the more I fit into the general craziness. Like Bolek, I ran up to the fifth floor and back, yelling at Victor, pushing Elsa and Yvette. The furs, once objects of my derision, took on the value they had for everyone else. I loved not only the money I took home and spent, but the idea of adding new value, new capital to the business. And then, to cancel it out, I whored with Abe Strawberry and drank myself to distraction.

I learned to play bridge and sometimes went with Bolek to the Dakota to make a foursome with Weinglass and Spektor. Between rubbers, Weinglass swished the brandy around in his glass, stuck his nose into it, and inhaled deeply. He took a small sip. "Francesca is organizing for the union," he said.

"The union? What union?" Bolek wanted to know.

"Any union," Weinglass reported painfully. "What do I know about the middle of America? Furniture, steel, automobiles? It doesn't matter. She gives out pamphlets in the street, she talks, she has no accent."

"She is young," old man Spektor reassured him. "Even you were a socialist once." Spektor was a small, fat, bald man whose guttural English sometimes sounded like pneumatic drills.

"She doesn't take care of herself," Weinglass whined. "She looks terrible."

"Such a pretty girl," Spektor said.

"She doesn't brush her hair," Weinglass said, finishing his brandy, "and the clothes . . ."

"Let her live her own life," I said, holding out my empty snifter in the direction of Spektor's bottle of Courvoisier.

"Yes, you are right," Spektor said. "We have worked hard, Zyga, to raise ourselves in the world, to be where we are. We have earned for our children the right to be what they want to be."

Bolek smiled proudly to himself. This was no longer his problem. He didn't want to push his luck, so instead of saying anything, he gave me a quick, happy glance. Then he leaned over to me and whispered in my ear, "One day we'll even beat them at bridge."

In the taxi on our way home, Bolek could not stop smiling. "You are wonderful in the business beyond any dream," he told me. "How I love to see those rag merchants jealous."

At the Buckingham desk, there was a letter from Maggie. Bolek was pleased to see it. Everything was now adding to his joy. I took it into my room to read. "I am coming, my darling," it said. "I can't wait any longer. I must see you. They won't make any decisions about the movie for at least two weeks. I'll call to let you know exactly when. Don't go away. I am hungry for you."

To add to Bolek's pleasure, he loved the sketches I was

making of his new styles. My hand became much looser and, as is sometimes the case, my ignorance about fashion drawing allowed me to inadvertently set new styles. With brush and ink, I slashed and dripped, the intense blacks like the cut or fall of a coat, while smudges and fine-point quills marked textures, sheens, and lusters. Bolek made sure that Enid saw the drawings, and when she published a few in *Mirabelle*, I began receiving calls asking me to illustrate for other fashion houses. "This is perfect Prince Casimir style," Bolek said. "You have only elegant bones in your body. It is mah-velous." He'd started to imitate some of his customers by removing the *r* from marvelous.

We reserved a session with Mr. Traister one Sunday just for the purpose of translating some technical fur words into English. "Now I want to teach you everything," Bolek said. Using a small, dog-eared Polish-English dictionary that contained very few of the words we needed, the three of us gesticulated and screamed our way through *snaring* and *trapping* and just plain *cudgeling*. We screamed about breeding and mutants, about the difference between *dressed* and *raw*, about who grows pelts, who skins, who hides, about underfur and overhair and vice versa. I went down the elevator with Traister, who had barely survived another Sunday morning at the Buckingham. "I have my own picture of what's happening in our little processing plant next door," I told him.

"I see you are falling in love with the business," he said.

I was walking Traister to the park, where he liked reading his Polish newspaper. "In the dead of night," I said, "they bring in cages full of their pesky little weasels. God knows how they subdue them. All I know is sometimes I find bloody animals turned inside out like gloves in the cold-storage vaults."

"Is this true, Adam?" he asked. "They kill the animals right here on Fifty-seventh Street?"

"I think so."

"Someone should do something," Traister said.

Many strange things were beginning to happen at Prince Casimir Furs. One afternoon the elevator disgorged two plump, cheery people, unannounced and unexpected. The

Minsenbergers exuded a kind of democratic warmth I had seen before with guilt-ridden Germans. They wanted to please, but quietly, without a fuss. "We are nothing, we want nothing," Mr. and Mrs. Minsenberger seemed to say. They handed their coats and hats and newspaper eagerly to Mignon, apologizing for the trouble.

Jacques was suspicious from the moment he saw them. Very few people came through our portals off the street. "Did madame have something special in mind?" Jacques asked, keeping the entrance to the showroom blocked.

"I would be very pleased to see Mr. Casimir," Mr. Minsenberger said.

"He's very busy," Jacques said. "Are you interested in our collection?" Jacques could tell class by a glance from across the street, he had told me. He knew instinctively where the customer lived, how she spent her evenings, where she volunteered her time, whether she played golf or tennis, or traveled beyond Europe. Bolek always said, "She may ask for a white mink, but if she is not a white-mink person, *she cannot have a white mink.*"

Jacques could be rude, but chose not to be. He acted rather like the friendly neighborhood butcher. "Madame is interested in beaver? Perhaps dyed muskrat."

Mr. Minsenberger told Jacques that he and his wife would be honored to see whatever Jacques wished to show them. Jacques asked me to get Elsa, who also understood right away and hardly showed her toothy Teutonic smile. Mrs. Minsenberger squealed with pleasure every time Elsa turned on her heels, opened up the coat she was showing, buttoned up again. They could not say enough about the quality, the workmanship, the style. Mr. Minsenberger got up to thank Elsa warmly for her trouble. "And now," Mr. Minsenberger said, addressing Jacques and me, "would you be kind enough to inform Mr. Casimir that my mission relates to his beautiful business in Warschau."

I went to tell Bolek. "Germans," I said, "bad Germans."

"There are only bad Germans," Bolek said, and followed me into the showroom.

Mr. Minsenberger clicked his heels, expressed his gratitude for the beautiful collection he'd just seen. "It is as wonderful as opera," he said. "But perhaps we can talk in private?" We walked into Bolek's office, leaving Jacques and Elsa in the showroom. "You see, my sir," Mr. Minsenberger said, "I was in Warschau during the occupation. . . ."

Bolek did not lose his composure. He helped them into the chairs and sat in his own, behind the desk. "My nephew, Adam Krinsky," he said. "He will stay here with us." Then, "You—occupied?" he asked.

"I assure you, sir, that my hands are clean. I was a—how do you say it?—a supplier."

"You supplied the occupying forces?" Bolek asked.

"Yes, sir, I did," Mr. Minsenberger admitted. "We are men of the world, Mr. Casimir. It was a matter of my livelihood—no, survival. I was, I am, a businessman."

"You knew my business well then?" Bolek asked.

"I was a silent witness to all that went on there," Mr. Minsenberger said.

"You arrived in September?" Bolek asked.

"The twenty-fourth," Mr. Minsenberger said, "in the morning."

"With the panzers?"

"On their heels," Mr. Minsenberger said.

Mrs. Minsenberger was skimming through *Women's Wear Daily*. She sat sideways on a small chair, unable to hide her large round knees.

Bolek's face was like steel. His expression hardly changed as he questioned and listened. "You supplied—what did you supply?" he asked quietly as his eyes opened wide, wrinkling his forehead.

"Please, I am not on trial here," Mr. Minsenberger said sternly. His jollity disappeared quickly and a stark intensity burned in his little pig eyes. "Not bullets," he said. "Food. I was a sausage dealer. This is not a war crime. But enough. I have come to offer my services." He relaxed and smiled again. "It is a matter of the strictest confidence. I have come to ask if you wish to sue for war reparations."

"You offer money?" Bolek said.

"I witnessed the removal of your entire stock to Berlin. Göring himself was in charge."

"And now you want to help me," Bolek said.

"I am a businessman," Mr. Minsenberger repeated. He stretched his arm, put two meaty fingers on the edge of Bolek's desk, and chuckled cordially.

"And your price?"

"One-half," Mr. Minsenberger said flatly. "I think that is fair. Without me, there is nothing."

"One-half of what?" Bolek asked.

"I think it can run into the millions of dollars," Mr. Minsenberger said.

Bolek closed his eyes. He looked like a death mask. He ran his hand hard over his whole face, then up along his cranium. "Tell us what you saw when you entered my place."

"A beautiful location," Mr. Minsenberger said, "although some of the buildings across the street had been destroyed by bombs. Ah, what a grand boulevard—the trees, the architecture, like Paris. And in your place, furs everywhere. All the lights were on, the only lights in Warschau. Waiting for us on the second floor was a woman. I could see that she was beautiful although very tired. Her eyes were sunken, perhaps afraid. She very kindly offered to serve us. . . ."

Mrs. Minsenberger was standing, looking at the photographs on the walls of the office. I went over to stand by Bolek.

"If I am not mistaken, sir, I believe it was your sister," Mr. Minsenberger said. He had apparently done some research.

"His mother," Bolek said, taking my hand.

"A charming woman," Mr. Minsenberger told us. "May I be so bold as to say you resemble her." My hand squeezed Bolek's. "She was, of course, a little tired, mixed up, with all that was going on. She treated us perhaps too well. She modeled the coats, quoted prices."

"When did you last see her?" Bolek asked.

"The high command took over the salons. An officer escorted her to her rooms. I personally went to visit her some time later, but she was no longer there. I am sorry to say that I don't know what happened." My knees felt weak. "I am sorry to have lost contact with her," Mr. Minsenberger said. "She was a charming woman."

Mrs. Minsenberger had sat down again, smiling, as if she had not heard what was said here. "Do you have credentials?" Bolek asked Minsenberger, who produced them immediately from his inside pocket. Mr. Minsenberger was in fact a deputy commissioner in the Adenauer government. Bolek excused himself to call the German Embassy from Mlle. Sacha's office. In his absence, Mr. Minsenberger turned to me. "The war was terrible for everyone," he said. "Did your mother survive?"

"No," I said. "How did she die?"

"My dear boy," he said "you are asking the wrong person. I don't know these things."

When Bolek returned, apparently satisfied with the Minsenbergers' identity, Mr. Minsenberger stood up and stretched, looked around the office for the first time. "I assure you, Mr. Casimir," he said, "that our case is perfect."

Bolek asked not to be disturbed for the rest of the day. He sat alone in his office for a while, then walked out of the building. When he left, I went into his office and locked the door behind me. I was seized with panic, touched by death in *this* of all places. I wanted to scream. I held my breath. I saw my mother selling bloody carnivorous mammals turned into emblems of wealth to her own killers. This place was stamped with greed and vanity and madness. Was *she* mad? Was it because she lost us, lost *me?*

Like so many times in my life, I thought of my old friend, the chronicler of the world's insanity, Goya. I went to the League to see Grosz, who I knew had special access to the collection of prints at the Metropolitan. Grosz loved seeing me in my business suit. "Here is a smart boy," he announced to a studio full of silent painters. "He is not scratching away at a canvas. He is *making money.*" He wrote a note that opened the necessary doors to the *Caprichos,* the *Disparates,* the *Disasters of War,* Goya's pivotal sets of etchings balancing between sanity and madness, hope and despair. As I sat with these terrifying images of superstition, injustice, stupidity, cruelty, I thought that, like Goya, I, too, was immersing myself in the roots of *my* madness, perhaps even exorcising my own attraction to butchery, vanity, folly. Goya dealt with it first by outraged moralizing, then, understanding that he himself was as capable as any man of involvement in the horror, he simply rendered it, without commentary. Finally, his art became mad. There were no ups or downs, no real sources of light, just painterly values of light and dark, just hideous scenes of creatures preying on each other, the landscape of our time.

Yes, there were ways of chronicling inhumanity. Even scratching through the resin on a zinc plate could convey a world that makes no sense.

9

Bolek and I had started going to the opera together the year we arrived in New York. Opera suited us well. It was the one art form we loved equally. Neither Bolek nor I looked down or up at it. It stood exactly halfway between furs and painting. Over the years, no matter what petty irritation or major explosion, our problems were usually solved, our pain soothed, our anger calmed, at the opera.

Bolek had gone to every opera performed in Warsaw, but I was too young to go with him. My parents and I lived near the opera house, and on opera nights Bolek, in evening clothes, ate with us, then walked over at his leisure. Just before the war, I had begun walking with him as far as the lobby, which was so crowded, so noisy with happy chatter, so bright from the lights of the giant chandeliers, that I always walked home dazed and dreamy. Sometimes, even now, Bolek would sing me an aria from *Traviata* in Polish.

At the Buckingham, we put on our evening clothes to see

Rosenkavalier. We drove over in silence. Deep in thought, Bolek looked out his window in the taxi while I, just as alone, looked out mine. Bolek looked wonderful in his tuxedo, like the Max Beckmann self-portrait, even to the graceful way he held his cigarette, his hand close to his body, his fingers extended like a dolphin's fin.

After the Minsenbergers, the Richard Strauss opera would not have been our choice. Even at the best of times, *Rosenkavalier* was not Bolek's favorite, though he liked its turn-of-the-century sensuality, the opulence of its silver and red and pink. He said it was an exclusive sensuality, meant for Aryans. During our last *Rosenkavalier* a few seasons ago, he said that just as in Southampton, he felt he needed a transit visa.

In the best of times, it took us a while to warm up to German opera. Wagner excluded. We drew the line at Wagner. But take a good Italian opera with plots you could trust, plots you knew would be an apotheosis of the bourgeoisie, harassed and violated by a cruel nobility and a stupid proletariat. Take *Traviata.* There, even before the story began to unfold, often at the very moment the curtain went up on Violetta's lavish drawing room, Bolek was already weeping, in expectation of her terrible end. With Richard Strauss, who Bolek said was only half a Nazi, he usually didn't last till the end of the opera.

Both of us preoccupied, we said nothing as we walked into the Met, found our stairs and our box. Bolek sat pretending to read the program, his glasses slowly sliding down his nose. He looked over the railing to the orchestra below. He loved the packed houses, full of *his* people. He loved the dazzle of the gold and diamonds, the shared conviction that opera was the reward and the atonement for their lives.

We were not more than a few minutes into the overture of *Rosenkavalier* when our week's cares began to peel away. At the end of this week, just being here was enough. We could not keep our delight to ourselves. We looked at each other. He nudged me with his elbow. My hand wandered over to rest on his. As the boy Octavian, pulsating with triumph and bravado, sang his song of love to the worldly Marschallin, we allowed the song to enter our hearts, too.

At intermission we had a glass of champagne at the bar. We bowed to the same people we saw at every performance, but even though at times someone might make a stab at conversation, Bolek invariably cut it short. Opera was ours, exclusively ours. Like boys talking baseball averages, we compared singers, discussed how we would have costumed this or furnished that. Sophie and Enid and even Maggie wanted a part of our opera bond, but this was a bed that only Bolek and I shared.

"This could be anywhere," Bolek said, "these are the same people as in Warsaw or Paris or Leningrad." He took a sip of champagne. "And when they take their coats off, you are certain not to see rags." We walked arm in arm through the crowded bar. "Here," Bolek said, "fur coats will always be in style. Even at the theater these days, you are never sure that everyone has had a bath. At the opera, you need not worry."

During the second act, Bolek became restless. The older he got, the more annoyed he was watching the portly Baron Ochs make a fool of himself while the focus of young Octavian's love shifted from the older Marschallin to the innocent Sophie, a girl his own age. By the third act, when the Marschallin resigned herself to the loss of Octavian, Bolek whispered that he was ready to leave. "We can miss the traffic," he said. But I was not ready. As I watched the sweet flowering of young love, I allowed myself to pine for Maggie for the first time in weeks.

We stayed until the end and waited our turn for a taxi. On the way back to the Buckingham, Bolek examined his face in the driver's rearview mirror. He smoothed the pouches under his eyes by pulling at the flesh. "I am not so young anymore," he said as he opened his mouth to inspect his teeth.

"You look terrific," I said.

"I don't know what it is," Bolek said. "I don't *think* young anymore."

We checked the mail at the desk. There was another letter from Maggie. Her handwriting on the envelope was becoming bigger and bigger, as if California in all its hugeness, the whole Pacific Ocean, had entered her soul. I ripped it open to find that she couldn't come east after all, not now, because, alas, she'd been cast in a movie. My heart sank. Until now I had hoped that her movie career would flop before it started, that she would be back, that we would each work on our art, become successful in New York. Instead, it was to be Magdalena Kornfeld and Jed Seacliff in *The Good and the True*.

Alone, in our tuxedoes, Bolek and I made tea. "Maggie's making a movie," I said. "She's not coming."

Bolek was happily surprised. I suppose that none of us really expected it to happen. "Right after the show, you will go to her for a visit."

"Don't you sometimes think that I should travel, see things?" I said.

"Yes, darling, you will have enough money to go anywhere you like."

"Bolek, do you believe she really tried to sell to them?"

"Who?"

"You know who."

"She hated Germans," Bolek said. "We all hated Germans."

"There is something about this business, Bolek. Anyone could have done it."

"That was just a story," Bolek said. "He told us that story to make himself look better."

We went into our rooms, undressed, each of us leaving a pile of evening clothes by the foot of our beds, and then, wanting more of him tonight, I went back into the living room, where Bolek was placing pillows for himself on the couch. He lit a cigarette, moved a stack of *Vogues* to his side, and sipped the cold tea. I lay down on the carpet, my knees up, staring at the ceiling. "You always wanted to protect me from what happened," I said. "I'm nearly twenty-one, working in your business. I feel old for my age."

Bolek laughed. "You have your whole life ahead of you," he said.

"They died so young, Bolek. I never realized that before." I turned on my side so I could see him. "How old were they?"

Bolek thought for a minute with his eyes closed. "She was thirty-eight."

I sat up and looked at him. "Thirty-eight? You never told me that." I did some quick figuring. "She died in 1943? How do you know that?"

"It's a guess," he said.

"You're not telling me something."

He finished his tea and got up to go to the bathroom. I followed him in. "Did I tell you," he said, "that Madame Schmeck's daughter—what is her name?—is coming in to buy a coat? She told Sacha that you will fit her—"

"What do you know about her death? What are you trying to hide?"

"Nothing," Bolek said. He examined his tired face again in the bathroom mirror, then walked by me, back to the living room.

"Tell me," I said.

He settled himself down again. He looked at me tenderly. "Come here," he said. I got up and sat by him. He took my hand and I saw the struggle going on inside him as he frowned, then tried to speak. "They murdered her in Treblinka," he finally said.

I gasped. "How did you know? How long did you know?"

Bolek was ashen now and breathing hard. "A few years," he said. "I got a letter. I thought that Minsenberger swine would tell you, but he didn't know. I didn't want to tell you. Why should you know these terrible things? It is history. It is over."

I lay down next to him and we shook in each other's arms. For a long time we said nothing, and then Bolek started snoring, a parody of a snore, as if he were chasing a fly from his nose, his whole face shaking it off, then calm again. I got off the couch quietly and went into my room. I opened the window and lay on top of my bed. Nineteen forty-three. Bolek and I were *here*, right here in the hotel, for three years while she was in the ghetto or in Treblinka. While Bolek and I ate lunches at Longchamps, while we watched some inane *Carmen* or *La Bohème*, while he built Prince Casimir Furs and I trudged up that cliff in Riverdale with my book bag stuffed with the lists of English kings and idiotic French proverbs, *my mother was alive.*

I got up to look for sketchbooks from that time. The number

of sketchbooks in my closet was immense. I had to separate the stacks into smaller stacks just to be able to pull the early ones out of there. The pressure of the piles had even transferred some of the pencil drawings to the back of the sheet of paper directly above. I saw Maggie again, an angelic Maggie like a Botticelli—and Bolek, bold, pugnacious, my hero. I found the detailed airplanes, the Spitfires, the P-38s, the Messerschmidts plummeting with tails of fire and smoke. I found the tanks I had remembered, big as houses, their gun barrels coming off the page into my space. And then the ranks of soldiers, loaded with firearms and ammunition, marching in formation, page after page of marching soldiers, marching left, marching right, marching straight toward me, always as a unit, an entity, a mindless mass, unthinking and unstoppable. They continued from sketchbook to sketchbook. They were everywhere.

I went back into the living room to wake Bolek. "Is Treblinka still there?" I asked him.

"I don't know. I think they destroyed it."

"I want to go there."

"Go to sleep," Bolek said.

They emptied the ghetto into Treblinka, not far from Warsaw. I couldn't even picture my mother in the ghetto. Marysia Krinsky, née Mandelbaum, tall, beautiful, strands of perfect pearls always around her neck, bright red lipstick, a rich olive complexion. In the ghetto? Climbing over bodies in the gas chambers? Bones in a mass grave.

I had missed the last fashion show, but there was no way to miss this one. We reserved the Pierre ballroom, we hired a new publicity man. But as show time approached, Bolek became unbearable to be with. Something was wrong with everything. They weren't working fast enough upstairs. "Sabotage!" Bolek screamed at everyone, even Whitney Wetherbee, the publicity man, who became the brunt of much of Bolek's rage. When it came time to arrange for music, Bolek yelled at Wetherbee about that. "You—you—you pederast!" he screamed at him, a very nice pederast with impeccable taste. "I will not have *your* kind of music." No one knew what Mr. Wetherbee's kind of music was. But he was smart enough to begin conducting as much of the preshow business as possible from his Madison Avenue office. Bolek was convinced that Mr. Wetherbee's idea of food was hot dogs with sauerkraut. It made no difference what I said. "He is also an anti-Semite!" Bolek yelled. "No one will come from the press! No one will come from anywhere!"

The September show in the Pierre ballroom was gorgeous. Even I was impressed. The only thing lacking from this *Aida* was elephants. *Everyone* was there, so many people in fact that they spilled into adjoining rooms. Claudette Colbert, who announced the show, was heard via loudspeaker in the smaller ballroom where the models made a short appearance on their way backstage to change. Elsa and Yvette were joined by twenty of the tallest and thinnest girls in New York. In their very brief behind-the-scenes turnaround time, they were served on the run by an army of Polish seamstresses and Mlle. Sacha, who stuffed them into appropriate hats and gloves, buttoned them into suits and blouses, and sent them out again in new coats.

I was backstage for the first few minutes, but the frantic activity left no room for anyone who didn't have a specific job. I went out into the ballroom, where, at a table way in back, I found Sophie with a man I'd never seen before, and Kor with Lala. It was hard to believe that Kor had shown up. When I had helped stuff invitations into envelopes, I almost hadn't mailed Kor's, not wanting him to see me like this. Then I sent it, feeling sure he wouldn't come. But here he was, looking a bit disgruntled and standing out like a sore thumb in his cape and spats.

Sophie, who didn't like doing it, had taken the afternoon off. She had gotten a little fatter, but she had a way of making her excess flesh add to her allure. Her full, rosy face could not stop smiling, as if this spectacle were also hers. She introduced me to her companion, a Count Bruno Brunini. "Adam will always be my first love," she told him. "How handsome you look, darling," she said to me as I crouched between her and the Count. "You should never get out of those clothes."

"Your daughter's broken my heart again," I said.

Kor got up to stretch but was too big to stand anywhere in this place. He sat down again, fiddling with a new cigarette holder.

Perhaps a hundred tables had been crammed into the ballroom, each with a powder-blue tablecloth, matching napkins, and a silver dessert setting. Gorgeous French pastries were wheeled around by waiters in blue, black, and white while waitresses filled demitasse cups with espresso.

"She's in a movie, Adam," Sophie said. "Has she told you?"

"Yes, some ridiculous thing . . ."

Sophie scowled. "With Jed Seacliff, Adam. Directed by Hal Wallis. That's not bad." But I had just a small fraction of Sophie's attention. Her eyes were glued to the stage and runway. She gasped as wantonly opulent coats appeared in shades of blue, tones of silver, and, rarest of the rare, pure white. Claudette Colbert's voice blessed the lot with irresistible names: Silver Blue and Royal Pastel and, as the swing band played "A String of Pearls," Starlight Royal Sapphire.

"What in God's name is Kor doing here?" I asked. "He hates this stuff."

"With Maggie gone," Sophie whispered, "I see more of him than ever before." Then Sophie's eyes got big again as a string of models with broadtail coats and jackets in blue and black and white glided by in a beautiful visual counterpoint. Sophie took a sip of Cognac. "Oh, God, I miss Maggie so," Sophie said. "I'm going out there again in two weeks. Come with me, Adam."

Kor, whom I'd been avoiding, leaned over. "The marvelous and the ridiculous are opposite sides of the same coin," he said. He didn't look good. His face was beginning to sag and a couple of ugly warts had sprouted on his cheek.

"What about immoral?" I said. "Just plain wrong."

"That's true, but it doesn't amount to much," Kor said.

"But every detail is perfect," I said. "Bolek's the best in the business."

"You know," Kor said, "Bolek *is* an artist. Imagine what he could have done if he had read or thought anything."

"Did *you* design anything?" Sophie asked me. "Bolek says you have been amazing." She looked around. "Where is he, Adam?"

"I'd better look."

I found Bolek pacing and smoking in the corridor. "It's magnificent," I told him. He put his arms around me and kissed me. I pulled him into the ballroom and as soon as he was seen, the customers started applauding, applause that swept through the whole room within moments, ending up in a standing ovation.

He had choreographed two separate finales, one for daytime coats, the other for evening wear, "furs for kings and queens." Each of the two endings was a well-planned coda, beginning with the pianissimo of baby seals, leading to the clash of cymbals, the blare of horns, as all the models spilled out wearing sable, ermine, and chinchilla. The music was not Toscanini, not even the Warsaw Philharmonic, but a nifty swing band that produced the mood Bolek wanted, carefree and gay. The ovation at the end was thunderous. Bolek had done it again.

The phrase common to all the reviews in the magazines and the dailies was "Nothing like it has ever been seen before." It was "lavish," it was "regal." With me at his side, Bolek gave interviews. His English was "charming." All the interviewers, to a woman, lost their hearts to "this thrilling man."

Weinglass was pleased but complained to me about the money. Why two endings? Why two ballrooms? Why *Cognac*? He took some solace when I told him I would probably be going to Europe soon. "Enough business?" he asked.

"Who knows?" I said. "Just a vacation."

"You can think about that when you are there, darling," he said. Probably because of his troublesome Bolshevik daughter, Francesca, Weinglass could hardly bear it when Bolek was having an easy time with me. He was jealous of whatever little success I'd had in the world. If I did well at Prince Casimir Furs, then he'd be glad to see me in Paris. I think that above all he wanted me to pursue my artist's dreams, for who but an antisocial genius ever succeeds at *that*? "Real artists are as rare as a whore in the rain," Spektor had growled during one of our bridge games. Weinglass offered me money for my European journey. "Take it, take it," he said. "What do I need it for?"

"I have all I need," I told him.

"Is your uncle paying?"

"I've earned the money."

"Yes, but you need a lot. Paris, you know," he said, winking. "If you need *anything*, you must promise to write to me." He stroked my cheek as he clamped his jaws together. "If anything at all goes wrong, you must let me know, anytime, day or night."

Not long after the show, Bolek heard from Minsenberger. "The money—and what money!—is nearly in the pocket, my sir," Minsenberger told Bolek on the phone from Bonn. And this wasn't all. Everything seemed to be happening at once. A group of businessmen from California, Mike Craig among them, were negotiating with Bolek and Weinglass for the re-capitalization of Prince Casimir Furs and its expansion into perfumes, then into elegant ready-to-wear clothes. I thought Bolek would burst with joy. Weinglass, as always, said he preferred things the way they were. He was getting a neat return on his investment without taking any further risks. "Why perfumes?" he whined. "Why not stay with furs, which is in our blood?"

As Sophie, Bolek, and I walked to the Russian Tea Room to celebrate Bolek's departure for California the next morning, I said, "I should find myself a place to live where I can also paint."

"For me, darling," Bolek said, "I would prefer if paintings these days were more polished. Perhaps this is the new way. Painters are lazy. They don't bother to *finish* paintings any-more like they used to." These days Bolek felt competent to talk about everything. "In fashion," he went on, "to suggest is perfect. Fashion moves like the wind, like clouds. Painting is for always, darling, and must be a monument that never fades."

We crossed Fifty-seventh Street in the middle of the block. "I should go to Paris to see some monuments," I said.

Bolek smiled and flared the handkerchief in his breast

pocket. "I wouldn't say that Paris is precisely *dead,*" he declared. "In fashion it is like birds in the spring. But in painting . . ."

Inside the revolving doors of the Russian Tea Room, we were greeted, as always, by Constantine, the maître d'. Spotting us as we were checking our coats, he all but ran the length of the bar to kiss Sophie's hand, shake Bolek's, then mine. We followed the beaming Constantine to our table. *"Voilà,"* Constantine said as he pulled out Sophie's chair, then Bolek's, commanding the Tatar waiter with his free hand to bring us snifters of vodka and plates of herring. *"Vite, vite,"* he ordered, *"c'est pour le Prince Casimir."*

Bolek's face wrinkled into a wide, satisfied grin. A tray of herrings—creamed, marinated, smoked—arrived with the vodka. We were immersed in plenty. We were all smiling. It was the beginning of the kind of evening Bolek loved to provide, the kind of evening he wanted me to be addicted to.

And I was fast approaching this addiction. This Old World restaurant had always intoxicated me. Its black bread and sweet butter, its aromatic vodka and côtelette Piarski nourished my body, anesthetized my mind. It was a numbing luxury. Even if an army of revolutionary troops had marched down Fifty-seventh Street singing the "Internationale" and shouting slogans, it would not have been heard here, over the hum of conviviality inside the Russian Tea Room.

"Have you ever looked at these paintings, Adam?" Sophie asked, flushed with good feelings.

The paintings crowding one another on every wall were awful, meaningless, and I told her so.

"This is not a museum," Bolek reminded us.

"Still," Sophie said, "they are undistinguished. But taken all together, they do add class."

Bolek agreed. "They will have their day again," he predicted, "just like padded shoulders."

"Bruno thought you were charming," Sophie said to me. "His family once owned half of Italy. Now he must work. Europe has lost something, don't you think?"

"The world can do without them," Bolek said, meaning Count Bruno and the whole rotten aristocracy.

"But he works for a tractor company now," Sophie reported.

"Everyone must expand, not like before," Bolek said. "This is how business is done in America. You cannot stand still, because if you stand still, everyone else will run past you. . . ."

Sophie listened intently to this lesson in economics. "Poor Bruno," she said.

"Yes, in Europe we once could make our little corner more and more perfect. Here there is no time. Here we must build our empire."

"So you will soon be an emperor," I said. Balenciaga had come into the showroom soon after the show and said to Bolek in his singsong French that Bolek would be the Napoleon of furs. Bolek, who often stood like Napoleon anyway, with his hand inside his jacket, bowed like an emperor. I realized I was beginning to hate the Christian Diors and Balenciagas and the rest. I'd had it with all those funny gentlemen who held my hand too long, who made me feel clumsy and crude. Bolek, who taunted "the little pederasts" in their absence, clung to the Balenciagas like a wet leaf to a tree trunk. In fact, Bolek's attitude became decidedly effeminate when the handsome Spaniard waltzed into Prince Casimir's showroom with his favorite boy. As Elsa and Yvette glided silently back and forth wrapped in animal skins, Balenciaga, Bolek, and the boy played as if they were on the beach at Formentor.

Constantine kept supplying vodka. Each thin glass of it was buried in a silver bucket of chipped ice. I drank and I ate, but there was always more. Constantine smiled at me with pleasure as he replaced the basket of bread with a fresh one, as he had the waiter bring still more herring for me.

"I have been thinking about names," Bolek said. "The perfume, of course, must be Casimir, but the aftershave, what do you think?" Before we had time to consider, Bolek said, "Adam."

"Adam?"

"Yes, my darlings, is that not a beautiful name for a man's cologne? Adam, the first man. Adam, *my* Adam. Adam, what every man wants to be, smelling like flowers for Eve."

Sophie thought it was brilliant. She kissed Bolek, then took out her compact to fix her face. She dabbed with her powder puff at the soft expanse of lovely flesh above her low-cut dress. We were all beginning to sweat.

"I think I must go away for a while," I said.

"You have deserved a good vacation," Bolek said. "Come with me to California tomorrow. Magdalena will refresh you."

"I don't think so. Maggie's busy now."

"No, no," Bolek said. "Chwast will take us to the movie studio. And she doesn't make a movie all night."

"Mr. Chwast, darling," Sophie reminded him, an important point among us all, "is now Mr. Craig. You mustn't forget that. And Magdalena, too. They want to change her name—"

"Oh, no," I moaned.

"Maggie Coe," Sophie said as slowly as she could say those three syllables.

I took a large swig of my vodka. Soon there would be nothing left of our names, I thought. Mandelbaum to Casimir, for who would buy perfume named Mandelbaum? Rytek Kornfeld to Kor. And now this, as if Maggie were some daffy Highland lass dancing on the heather.

"Maggie doesn't mind the name. After all, they change them even when they don't sound Jewish. But they don't want her to say that she is Jewish—"

"My God, what do they want her to be?"

"Nothing, as long as she's not Jewish," Sophie said.

"Sometimes that's important," Bolek said. "What does it matter?"

"It matters," I said, hitting the table with my fist. "She shouldn't do it. It's wrong—"

"They are telling her that it is the last barrier between her and stardom." The party at the next table, as Russian as we were Polish, began to take notice of us. Just as Bolek's accent was hard-edged, so the accents of our neighbors were aqueous and slippery, dipped in sour cream. The tempo of their good cheer seemed to slow as the volume at our table rose.

"Do you sometimes get the impression that there is something wrong with all our lives?" I asked.

"What do you mean, darling?" Sophie asked as Bolek looked through the menu.

"That there's something immoral about being what you're not. It's a masquerade. You make fur coats, they buy fur coats, all to cover what they are. . . ."

Bolek looked up. "What?" he asked. "What are you saying?"

"I don't know. . . ."

"Don't be naïve," Bolek said. "That is the way of the world."

"And now," I went on, "there is the problem of the Germans."

"What problem?" Sophie asked.

"The money," I said, "the German money."

"This is not a problem," Bolek said. "We take money from them. They owe us something. Lives for money is not a fair trade, but it is better than nothing."

"They're not paying for lives, Bolek. They're paying for the furs they stole." Bolek and Sophie looked at each other. "They want you to be grateful."

"I will not be grateful," Bolek said, and hit the floor hard with both his feet, getting the attention of our Russian neighbors again. They seemed more curious than disapproving.

"They're getting off cheap, Bolek. You're making it easy for them. You're buying their guilt."

"Adam, Adam, this is nothing," Bolek said. "I am leaving early in the morning. Let us enjoy this evening."

"It's all dirty, Bolek. Any of us might have tried to sell coats to the Nazis. It makes me sick."

"Who sold coats?" Sophie asked. "What is going on?"

Bolek told her Minsenberger's story, clucking his tongue, dismissing it as nonsense.

"Why didn't she come with us, Bolek?" I asked.

"She was a patriot," Bolek said.

"Bolek, why?"

"She thought we'd be right back. This is true. No one thought that it was real war."

"Of course they did. Kor and Sophie did. Many did."

"Well, our family is stubborn. She was going to look after the business until we came back—"

"And you let her?"

"Adam," Sophie said, "it was war. Everybody was crazy."

"Yes, crazy," Bolek said. "Can you believe it? None of us wanted to leave. Suddenly everyone wants to stay in that filthy place, that rotten slice of mud—"

"I'm leaving. I'm going to Poland."

"Poland?" Bolek said, dropping his spoon in the borscht.

"To feel it, to know the horror that made us, to know where we come from—"

"What you come from is *dead*," Bolek said. "Do you understand now? Nothing is left that belongs to you. They'll kill you. They know your name. Do you think they have stopped killing Jews? They get drunk and they kill."

"I have to find out for myself."

He slapped his forehead repeatedly with increasing force. "Just like your father," Bolek said. "You want to go back to be slaughtered just like your father."

"I just can't stand it anymore, none of it." I wanted to stop, to leave, to take a walk, but I couldn't stop. I yelled into Bolek's face, "I hate that filthy business!"

He began to shake. "What filthy business? I am a robber? I have wasted my life?"

"It's all garbage."

"I don't make beautiful things? I don't make art?"

"That isn't art," I said from between clenched teeth. "You think everyone makes art. *You make coats! I make art!*"

Our neighbors now tried to move their chairs away from us, but there was no room. The concert next door at Carnegie Hall must have finished, for new people arrived. Someone was humming a Rachmaninoff prelude as he passed by our table. Bolek and I behaved as if we were all alone. Sophie was looking desperately around the room.

"I change the way furs look. I give them new color. This is not art? Color is not art?"

"Everything you do is easy," I said. "If it's easy, it's fashion. It it's hard, it's art."

"Who else has thought of pearl gray inside a natural mink, knit sleeves with nutria bolero? Who else had the eye to match sable skins?"

I couldn't bear yelling at him, but I couldn't help myself. Something had snapped and I couldn't stop. "I'm leaving you!" I yelled.

"I pulled you out of the ovens," Bolek cried. "I have some rights—"

"So, you want to talk about that again—"

"Without me, you would be smoke!" Bolek yelled.

"It's an accident that you came. You wanted to stay just like they stayed."

"You throw that in my face? You are like my son, always like my son—"

I was totally out of control. "They stayed to protect their fucking furs!"

"Adam, stop, I beg you," Sophie said.

Bolek shouted, "That was war! What does he know about war?"

"I know plenty. More than I want to know."

"He is dreaming again."

"Why wasn't she in our car?"

"I told you. She didn't want to come."

"She wanted to go to the ovens," I said. Then, in bad Polish, I screamed, "May a herd of wild dogs shit on you and your furs!"

Sophie whispered calming words in Bolek's ear. The Russians at the next table were silent. Half of the Russian Tea Room had turned toward us. Constantine flew over to our table and stood in front of us, protecting us, protecting the rest of his customers from us. After a moment's lull, though, the room, provoked by us, by vodka, by herring, by God only knows what else, erupted with its own battles. It was nightmarish, like a monkey house, an East European monkey house.

For good measure I said, "You are a servant to the rich, a valet, a whore! *You are a tailor!*" For a moment I thought Bolek was going to have a heart attack. When I saw that he wasn't, I pushed the table away from me, knocking over our glasses. I ran out.

I ran down Fifty-seventh Street to the hotel. Shaking, I

waited for the elevator man, who was busy at the front desk. I got in, slammed the heavy doors shut, and took myself up to the twelfth floor. I tore off my sweaty shirt and suit. I lay down naked on my bed. She could have stayed until the end. She might have fought with the Jewish resistance. She might even have escaped. Who wrote that letter to Bolek? It could have been wrong. And what about my father? If he wasn't shot by angry Poles, did he go back to Warsaw? Did he find her? Did they die together? Are they alive together? Did they love each other? Would I ever know anything for sure?

I opened the window wide, then lay back down as a cold wind swept over me, drying my sweat. Was she alive while I was listening to Jack Benny, while I was singing "Waltzing Matilda" during Wednesday-morning assembly, while I was jerking off in this little Fifty-seventh Street bathroom?

I dialed Maggie's number in California. After a few rings, a man answered.

"I want Maggie," I said.

"She's not here," he said.

"What do you mean? Where is she?"

"Who's this?" the man said. I recognized the voice from somewhere.

"Krinsky," I said.

"Krinsky?" he said. "What Krinsky?"

"What Krinsky? *The only Krinsky left!*"

"You want to leave a message?" the man asked.

I left a number for her to call, then put on khakis, T-shirt, and windbreaker. I found my box of paints and supplies and went out into the hall. The elevator man was banging on the elevator doors downstairs. When I brought his elevator back to the lobby, I had to push my way by him to get out into the street. I dodged the fast-moving traffic on Sixth Avenue and ran down the block to Prince Casimir Furs.

I ducked into the dark building like a thief. Fuck their furs, I thought as I unlocked the front door and carefully turned off the alarm. Fuck everyone's furs, fuck those who buy them and sell them, cut and clean them. Fuck the furriers of Leipzig, the auctioneers of Leningrad, the toilers on Seventh Avenue. I skipped up the back stairs to the third floor and remembered the alarm up there. "I'll stay with the furs," my mother said. "Yes, you stay with the furs," they all said. "Come back when the war is over," my mother said. "Goodbye," we said. "Goodbye."

I let myself into the corridor behind one of the showrooms. It was always quiet on the third floor. It was eerie not to have Mignon or Mlle. Sacha pop out of one of the back rooms. I drew the drapes and pushed the couches up against the windows. I turned on all the lights. I think I had dreamed of this moment, for the strangeness seemed familiar.

Opposite the elevators, I studied the photograph of Pope Pius XII. He was being helped into an ermine robe Bolek had made for him, his dour old face looked almost pleased. I walked back through the offices, my heart pounding.

Soft leather-bound appointment books and oversized albums with pictures of the most glamorous of their customers sat on the pretty Empire writing desks and secretaries. Mlle. Sacha's little office had a small refrigerator, the size of ours at the Buckingham. Inside were unopened jars of Iranian caviar and a few lemons. Above it was a cabinet with sliding glass doors where the crystal was stored, together with silver and ivory toothpicks, tiny forks, knives, and spoons.

I looked into the room where canvas patterns lay on wide shelves before they were taken to the factory. There were two mannequin dummies and some milliner's heads that made me think of Kor's early work from Paris.

Bolek's office was the only one with vestiges of disorder. I sat and looked. The surfaces gleamed, the scent of the white narcissus on a cabinet with fashion magazines was intoxicating, the silver Coty Award he had won the year before was so polished that it blinded me. Large framed photographs of Greta Garbo and Claudette Colbert hung opposite his English desk. I opened his desk drawers. Like his life, the deepest recesses were stuffed with papers and trinkets, thank-you letters from old sailors' homes, actors' funds, unwed mothers, Jewish agencies. The bottoms of his drawers were strewn with cuff links, emery boards, scratched pairs of eyeglasses with missing earpieces, open packets of headache powder. There were letters from Poland and Germany. Buried in there somewhere must have been *something* about my mother's journey, about the journeys of the uncles, aunts, grandparents, and cousins who stayed behind, sent to Bolek by some survivor of the ghetto and written in a Polish too rich and complex for me to understand.

I ran up the back stairs to the factory, where I grabbed the equipment I needed: hammer, stapler, scissors, pliers, pins, nails, rolls of canvas. My arms were loaded coming back down. I dropped a box of shiny silver pins all over the back stairs. I dragged in the two mannequins and the milliner's heads. I stood the dummies up against one wall of the big showroom and pulled one of the couches into the center, facing them. My ears began to buzz and painful tremors shot up and down my arms and legs. Just as I had once experienced the unconscious appearance of the *Third of May* in one of my early sketchbooks, so now, in my mind's eye, Goya's *Family of Charles IV* began to take shape. Goya's large group portrait of the Spanish royal family—empty faces staring dumbly into space—dissolved, and *my* group began to take shape. The figure on the right would have to be Bolek himself, the other mannequin Pius XII.

Bolek assumed a Napoleonic stance, which had always suited him best. On the racks outside his office, I found a nutria bolero with knit sleeves, one of several they had manufactured after the fashion show, and I slipped it on him. Not to be outdone by the foppish King Charles, I cut a wide band of canvas, which I painted with stripes of red, white, and blue, and placed it diagonally across Bolek's chest. The fur looked dull and lifeless. It occurred to me that I could fix that. The jacket *yearned* to be painted. I mixed my pigments with oil and turpentine and jabbed the paint into the thick fur. The improvement was immediate. I searched the racks for more, for furs fit for my Pope. I found a full-length ermine in the back of the cold-storage vault and draped it on the shoulders of the Bishop of Rome. It, too, begged for decoration and, happily, its shorter hairs made painting a pleasure. Around the fur's handsome black markings, I scumbled in areas of cadmium red and orange and yellow.

The way they stood, Bolek and the Pope framed a wall that itself bristled with painterly possibilities. But I found the illustrious pair too much like the lions on either side of the entrance to the Forty-second Street library, too symmetrical, too static. I moved them around, pulling them out into the salon, then back against the wall again. When Bolek slipped out of my hands and lay sprawled on the thick carpet near the Pope, he seemed to place himself. This Pope, who had been careful during the war to stay on the good side of Adolf Hitler, was now waiting patiently as Boleslaw Mandelbaum sewed the bottom buttons on his ermine.

In the bathroom, hidden in a janitor's closet, I found a ladder. I brought it out and began racing up and down it like Goya in the Church of San Antonio de la Florida, dabbing, dripping, splashing the wall with paint. I blocked out more figures. On the wall behind Bolek and the Pope, I painted the Duchess of Windsor, who, I had always thought, bore a striking resemblance to Goya's insipid Bourbon queen. The Minsenbergers stood by her side, swinish and self-satisfied. I painted Greta Garbo and Claudette Colbert as best I could, and then Zyga Weinglass. If Bolek could ever see this construction with any sort of equanimity, he would especially appreciate my little stodgy Weinglass with his flat pomaded head, his great hooknose, his rheumy eyes, dwarf and jester both, lackey to the great and near-great.

I used four fur coats in all. I cut up a three-quarter-length mink and nailed its parts to the wall for my movie queens. Slices of Persian lamb made hair, accessories, and background. I added canvas patterns painted in bright colors, and stripes of interior drapes cut into heraldic banners. Then, as in the Goya and the Valázquez before it, I painted a self-portrait standing stage left in front of an easel, so that no one would mistake the identity of the artist. Well after midnight, the phone in Bolek's office rang.

"Maggie, Maggie, I was in such pain I thought I'd die."

"What is it, Adam, tell me."

I told her about Treblinka, about the Minsenbergers, about wrapping some bodies in fur while others were climbing over one another in the gas chamber. The words spilled out in a torrent.

"Oh, my Adam, I've been thinking of you so much," Maggie said, "and dreaming about your mother."

"I know, I know."

"Can you come out here?"

"I don't know."

"Where are you now?" Maggie asked.

"You're not going to believe this."

"Tell me."

"I'm painting."

"Why shouldn't I believe it?"

"At Prince Casimir's . . ."

"Prince Casimir's?"

"I've painted up the showroom and the furs . . ."

"Adam—"

"It's not easy," I said.

"Adam, are you all right?"

"Broadtail's the best, Maggie. You can still see the moiré pattern under the paint—"

"Adam—"

"I don't understand it, Maggie. It's a bad business—"

"Adam, I'm scared. Let me call mother—"

"No."

"You need someone. What about my father?"

"I'm okay," I said.

"Don't blame Bolek," Maggie said. "It's just the way things are."

"I know."

"You forget things like that out here," Maggie said.

"I've got to go back there to see it, the ghetto, Treblinka . . ."

"There's nothing left."

"Just the place, the ground where it was," I said. "Do you think that will settle it?"

"Yes," Maggie said. "I want to go with you."

"Yes, Maggie, that's what I want."

"When this movie's done," Maggie said. "Is that all right?"

"I don't know. I think I've got to go now. At least get out of here now. I don't think I can come back here. This is it for Bolek and me."

"He's coming to California tomorrow," Maggie said.

"Yes."

"I'll talk to him," Maggie said.

"What about?"

"I'll think of something," Maggie said.

"He won't know about this," I said. "No one will be here tomorrow. It's Sunday."

"Okay, I won't mention it," Maggie said.

"Maggie, I think I've stumbled into something. I love using the fur, the mannequins, all the junk—"

"It sounds weird and interesting," Maggie said.

"More than that. It's *right*. It's not like the cubist stuff. If I had time, I'd stay here until I'd used everything in this place—"

"No more business for you," Maggie said.

"No, never."

"You'll earn money other ways."

"Yes," I said. "I haven't even asked you how you are."

"Well, I'm making a movie—"

"Maggie Coe," I said.

"Yes. Adam—"

"I love Magdalena Kornfeld," I said. "Who answered your phone before?"

"You know who it was?"

"No."

"Jed Seacliff."

"Really? I knew the voice. Jed Seacliff . . ."

"What a lovely man," Maggie said. "He's as gentle and funny as he is in his movies."

"He's about your father's age?"

"About," Maggie said.

"Is he still there now?"

"No."

"Well," I said, "what's it like making a movie?"

"Everybody's terrific to me. They want me to succeed. I'm getting a lot of help."

"Maggie, I've got to finish this."

"Are you sure you have to?"

"I'm sure."

"I love you, Adam Krinsky," Maggie said.

I went back to work. All the rough layout was finished and I began on details. Everybody was beginning to look the way they were supposed to. They gave me enormous pleasure.

The silver carpet under me was soaked with paint, as were the couches and some of the heavy drapes. I packed up my remaining supplies and let myself out of the building. It was already morning, but there were only a few people on the street and practically no cars. I found an open drugstore off Sixth Avenue. I had coffee and a Danish. My eyes hurt. I tried to figure out how much damage I had done in dollars and cents. Twenty-five thousand? Fifty? I should know, I told myself. What had I been doing for a whole year?

I walked downtown with my box of paints. The city streets began humming. People were going up the stairs to St. Patrick's. I could hear the organ inside playing a Bach chorale. Tired and grimy, I found myself in Gramercy Park, on Kor's doorstep.

"I've been painting," I said.

"I can see that. You look awful."

"I locked myself out of the hotel."

"You did?" He didn't believe me. "Probably any other Sunday morning you would not have found me here," Kor said, "but this weekend Lala is visiting her family in Ohio." He sliced some fruit into a bowl. He put out some bran and milk.

"I'm leaving the fur business," I told him.

"Of course you are," Kor said.

"I'm going to Europe."

"I'll give you names of people," Kor said.

I wanted to tell him a lot more, but I couldn't. I felt that I had to be quiet. Kor offered me his bed. It took me a couple of hours to fall asleep.

* * *

In the late afternoon, with Bolek already in Los Angeles, I went to the Buckingham to pack a bag, then to the West Side piers to look for a boat. The *Queen Mary* was docked, but a ship's officer said they'd been booked for months. Farther downtown, I found a Norwegian freighter with an empty bunk, bound for Liverpool in two days. The mate didn't mind if I slept on board while the ship was docked. On Monday I withdrew the money I'd put away in the bank. It was enough for the passage plus a few hundred dollars. I had worked one year and spent it all on presents and booze, nights in expensive hotel rooms, clothes I never wanted to wear again.

When, two days later, we finally steamed out of New York Harbor and the breathtaking silhouette of the city had receded behind the waves, I began to feel giddy and light, as if chunks of new spirit were entering my body with each gulp of sea air, each clean, fresh breath.

10

Once I was curled up in my cramped bunk on the *King Haakon VII*, I slept for nearly two days. When I finally found my way to the captain's table for dinner, I got an unexpected reception. Captain Rasmussen came to the door to greet me. He seemed glad to have me at his table, eager to find out whom he was carrying across the ocean.

Lovely daisies in polished silver vases were set on the stiff white tablecloths. In his clipped Norwegian accent, Captain Rasmussen told me that he had picked them himself in New Jersey. Gaslit sconces illuminated the shiny wood-paneled dining quarters, which creaked pleasantly with the ship's movement.

Though no competition for the Russian Tea Room, there was plenty to eat and drink. With the herring, there was vodka, with the overcooked Bourguignon, a nice red wine, with the block of smelly cheeses, a rich white, and after we had eaten all there was to eat, the white-haired captain sent a sailor to bring some of his choice cognac, which he kept in his quarters.

Captain Rasmussen came from a family of herring merchants, and was very interested to find parallels with my back-ground in mink. "Minks and herrings," he reflected, "the very bottom of the barrel."

"For my uncle, minks sit at God's right hand," I said.

"And in Bergen, lad, my great-grandfather, who owned all the herrings in the North Sea, called the bony little thing a heavenly fish."

I told him a little about the destruction I had visited upon my mink-crazed family. Captain Rasmussen was only slightly amused, probably a little afraid about the sanity of his cargo. "Your whole family is in New York then?" he asked.

I told him that my parents were dead. I said it with a finality I hadn't heard in my voice before.

"You are alone then?" Captain Rasmussen asked.

"Now I am. I've been living with my uncle."

"An uncle, eh? Must be a good uncle, lad, to take on a son," he said. "We have seen the death of families in our time."

I felt free to draw again, stretching my fingers from their long sleep, opening my eyes as if for the first time. During our crossing, groups of sailors looked over my shoulder silently as I drew everything in sight. My greatest pleasure was at the stern, mesmerized by the wake, drawing its bubbly green oxides, metallic blues, seething caustic whites. It spoke to me and teased me, this fulminating window into buried secrets. It seemed to clear my mind of its accumulated debris.

Sometimes Captain Rasmussen joined me at the stern of his ship. "This is also my favorite place," he said. "The sea is the source of all our visions. You will find it all here."

"I have always been afraid of standing still," I told him. "I've never slept well until now, on this ship."

Memories of the crossing to America on the *Lisboa* in 1940 began coming back, memories of Bolek and me becoming close, the new father and the new son. As periscopes pursued us halfway across the Atlantic, I got over the shyness I had felt with this hero uncle, this suave, opera-going impresario, my mother's perfect brother, all I had left in the world. On that crossing, our skins learned to accept the other's touch. Slowly our lips gave and our cheeks took those new kisses, this new bond of love. During the last two nights before Ellis Island,

Bolek took me and my nightmares into bed with him, where he held me tenderly the whole night long.

In our Norwegian freighter, hauling corn to England, I dozed on the aft deck, snuggled among the ropes and hawsers, lulled by the rolling motion and the hum of engines below. Time's only function was to cover up our tracks, and I reached back into forgotten memories, past the *Lisboa*, back into our frantic exit, the huge Bulgars gaping at us from the side of the rutted roads as they ate their hunks of yellow bread, the gypsies who hounded us as long as our Packard functioned, hanging on to it, singing, begging, clinging like barnacles to the hull of a ship. I remembered the great pile of rifles in the dried-up riverbed under the bridge that connected Poland to Rumania. I had seen the Polish soldiers throw them over the side as they walked out of Poland. There were memories frozen by time into unyielding images, monoliths that would not budge: my father's curly hair disappearing among the cars, the country house shattering with who knows who inside, my mother running out of the apartment for the last time. I remembered a monument of my childhood, a portrait of my mother, a full-length portrait that hung in our great tiled vestibule in Warsaw. It was sketchy, impressionistic, suggestive. It took my mother's place. I remembered the artist's brushstrokes, clearly visible, and some of his brush hairs left under the varnish, one under my mother's ear, another on her ring finger. These marks of the artist's passage added to my awe before this icon, this mother who breathed for me, the mother who was always there.

One evening after dinner, as he poured out two glasses of his good cognac, Captain Rasmussen asked me if I was a Lutheran. "We have some things in common," he said, "maybe this as well."

"No," I said.

"No? What does that mean, no? If you are not a Lutheran, you are surely something—"

"A painter," I said.

Captain Rasmussen laughed. "Yes, of course," he said, "you are that first, but have you no faith?"

"I'm Jewish," I told him.

"You are a Jew? I would not have guessed that. How splendid! What a precious cargo you are then." It seemed to me too warm a reception until he told me that he was in the business of saving Jews during the war, his being one of the boats that made refugee runs to Palestine. "I would do anything for the Jewish people," Captain Rasmussen said. "They have suffered like no one else, and now they are making a garden out of the desert." This time he asked for his cigars to be brought and we both lit up. "So when did your family leave Poland?" he asked.

"Nineteen thirty-nine."

"Nineteen thirty-nine? Before it all started?"

"During," I said. "It took us a long time to get to America."

"And your parents stayed behind?"

"Yes."

With our long Havana cigars dangling from our mouths, we went out to walk the decks as the *King Haakon VII* rolled gently under the starry sky.

"I want to go back to Poland now, to see what was left behind."

"You won't find anything," Captain Rasmussen said.

"Just a stone of a building, a tree in a park," I said. "That would be enough. And I must see the remains of Treblinka."

"I have many Polish-Jewish friends," Captain Rasmussen informed me. "I know that there is nothing left. Not one stone of the ghetto, not one building at Treblinka."

"Well, then, it will have to be enough just to stand in the place where things once were."

"No, lad, don't go."

"Don't go? Why?"

"You will not be welcome. They will probably recognize your name. They are not kind to Jews."

"You mean Kielce. Kielce happened years ago," I said.

"Kielce was not alone, not the first and not the last. Killing Jews is a national characteristic. There was Kielce, Radom, Poznan, Lublin . . ."

"After the war?"

"After the war," he said. "But even this doesn't mean that all

Poles are murderers. Far from it. They are also some of the bravest, most decent people in the world. They have a true European culture—"

"So do the Germans," I said.

"Yes, it is confusing, very difficult to understand it all."

I would have to make this decision later, when I found out more about the present state of Poland. But I felt whole. The decision I would make would be my decision. I was alone but in charge, responsible for my own life. I could almost feel my chest swelling with the feeling that these would be my choices just as these were my memories. Everything that happened to me did so because of me. Accident, coincidence, war itself, all receded into the status of the rotation of the earth and the blue eyes I had inherited from my mother. All this was woven into the great empty canvas that was there for me to see. I had stored the memories, it was the material of my life. I was determining my own future, I was closing doors behind me.

I seemed to be good at picking up uncles everywhere. The moment I stepped on one, I had my nose smelling out others. I became very fond of Captain Rasmussen and promised to keep in touch with him via his Bergen home, his family of herring merchants. Before we docked at Liverpool, I made some portrait sketches of his chiseled face with its prematurely white hair. Strictly speaking, it was my first European work.

I took a train to London, where I made a whirlwind tour of the National Gallery, seeking out the few Goyas and Bronzino's *Allegory of Passion,* which had once looked to me exactly like Carla. I already missed Carla and Paul. I saw Maggie everywhere: in the middle of Trafalgar Square, in the bookstores on Charing Cross Road, turning a corner off Shaftesbury Avenue. I stayed two nights in a Knightsbridge bed-sitter and then, anxious to be on the Continent itself, connected to that bloodied soil, I left Victoria Station for Dover and from there crossed the Channel to Calais.

I burst into the streets of Paris from the steamy Gare St. Lazare. With my duffel bag on my shoulder and my carton of paints under one arm, I headed toward the Seine. New York made these streets look quaint and small. I smelled Warsaw in the low gray buildings with mansard roofs, the bright colors of the markets and shops. I was now part of this great European muddle again, this quarrelsome little continent that gave birth to both Treblinka and Goya. My mother and Bolek had walked on these sidewalks, Kor had lived here, and even Maggie, little Maggie, with a bright red ribbon in her hair and sucking on her teddy bear, had been shuttled through this Paris on her way to America.

As I raced through the streets, I thought of the painters, my predecessors, who had done just this before me. Picasso from Spain, Chagall from his little Russian village, Soutine from Lithuania. The closer I came to the river, the more exclusively I saw this city as a canvas in the hands of artists, the Paris of Manet, Seurat, Delaunay, the Paris of pointillist panoramas, cubist configurations, the Paris of the rayonnists, the futurists, the impressionists, the surrealists, the Paris that had been home to Kor.

As soon as I saw the Seine, I found the Louvre. I ran inside the museum as if I were catching a train. I skipped upstairs two steps at a time, and found the Goyas, the Delacroix, the Géricaults.

Before long, a guard approached and pointed to the baggage I was carrying. He clucked and shook his head. It struck me that my French was nearly nonexistent in spite of Mr. Barry's classes of idioms and proverbs. The guard began to jabber at me, his finger poking at my chest. I pointed cheerfully to the wonderfully busy walls all around us, smiling, trying to demonstrate my happiness at being here. But he would have none of it. He talked and talked, threw up his hands in disgust. "*Sortez, monsieur, sortez,*" he commanded, giving me a push from behind.

And then I shouted the cruelest words I knew in his language, the names of the French painters I despised. "Fragonard!" I cried, pointing at the stunned guard. "Bouguereau! Bonvin!" But it was *his* museum, not mine. I left the Louvre, having introduced myself to some of its marvels, and went out into the Tuileries.

I sat down in a garden chair near the Petit Carousel. Children played demurely in the wide dirt paths, while nannies faced their prams toward the sinking afternoon sun. I could see the tall column in the middle of the Place de la Concorde, and beyond it the hazy outline of the Arc de Triomphe. I started across a bridge to the Left Bank and in the middle I stopped to look at the round pink disk of the setting sun. I was on *my* continent, the landmass of Europe. I crossed to the other side of the bridge to look east. I realized that I could walk past Notre Dame, through les Halles and the Marais, and eventually end up in Warsaw and then Treblinka.

I took a room in a small hotel near the junction of the boulevard Raspail and Montparnasse. I was on my own in a dingy fourth-floor walk-up, a bare bulb hanging from the yellow ceiling and another on an imitation candle fixture nailed carelessly to the wall. If not for the euphoria of endless new possibilities before me and my lifelong attachment to hotels, this little smelly room, which caught the stench from the three floors below it, would have had to be considered totally depressing. To the surprise of the concierge who sat at the reception desk crowded between the front door and the dark staircase, I passed her daily with a cheerful smile on my face, a smile she never returned.

I bought a couple of old prints of eighteenth-century Paris, some flowers from an old blind woman in a stall on the boulevard. I left my room early most mornings, walking all over the city, spending hours in the Louvre, the Orangerie, the Jeu des Paumes, the desolate Moderne with its stiff little abstractions, its humorless geometric imports. I sat in cafés, smiling out into Paris. I loved the whole world.

As my small canvases began to pile up, my room became too crowded to continue working in. I looked through Kor's list of artists and teachers and decided to try the studio of André Lhote, beside whose name Kor had written "neocubist, nothing remarkable to look at, but a known and respected teacher."

Lhote's teaching studio was in a drab working-class section of the city, in a small building to which many remodelings had been added, a room jutting out here, another there, so that finding the door to the studio was like finding one's way through a dark labyrinth.

Inside, it was essential to have one's easel near the single window even though the glass had become caked with pigeon droppings and soot, creeping higher and higher like a live fungus. In spite of the darkness, students kept coming, and once there, they, we, were somehow able to distinguish colors in this murky obscurity where neither the finest photoelectric cells of a German camera nor the cones of the human eye could realistically be expected to function.

Mischa Poliakoff, Lhote's *chef d'atelier*, settled me into a black corner. "You start here, *mon ami*. We shall see how far you get."

An American woman, an arm's length from me, explained Lhote's meritocracy. "The window," she said, "is occupied by the loudmouths." I looked in their direction and saw only silhouettes. "Ex-GIs," she added. "Poliakoff says it is an earned position, but wait until you see what those schmucks are doing. They muscled their way in."

I went over to the window to see. Each of the ex-GIs was making a kind of neocubist rendition of little French boats sporting the tricolor and bobbing merrily in a cerulean sea. "Is that how Lhote paints?" I asked my neighbor when I returned.

"Who knows how he paints? He's too old to paint."

"Why are you here then?"

"Where else?" she asked. "It's the Beaux-Arts or here. They copy Roman ornaments, we activate pictorial space. Big deal. What's the difference?" She continued to work on her canvas, whose rectangular shape I could just barely make out.

"Is he a good teacher?"

"He comes in once a week," she said. "The strangest things turn out to be good." She talked fast, never stopping her nervous brushwork. "He says the only difference between him and Picasso is that he's never painted guitars or tobacco packets. Take my word for it," she said, "there are other differences."

"What about Poliakoff?"

"Now there's a man of our time," she said. "When he's not here, he's over at the Louvre painting ears."

"Ears?"

"Ever read Krafft-Ebing?" she asked. "Poliakoff's got an ear fetish. He comes back here with sketchbooks full of Rubens ears, Poussin ears, Ingres ears. Ears to Poliakoff are like apples to Cézanne."

"What about all those little GI boats?" I asked.

"Boats? Don't say boats to them. They're cylinders, truncated cones, sections of spheres. You call them boats and they'll give you an earful of cubist theory. They know Gleizes and Metzinger by heart."

I set a canvas on my easel. "They seem happy, those bubbly little cubes—"

"*Bubbly*," she said. "They're solving *pictorial* problems. Bubbly!"

On the ceiling above us hung a bare fixture with no light bulb. My neighbor, Jeannie, had resisted the temptation to put one in so that she might develop her "inner eye." I agreed that painting in the dark might be fun. What better ambience to try some "gestural" work like Abe Strawberry. I stretched a few more canvases and for a week I swung my arm, snapped my wrist, scribbled randomly, and lunged.

I also found a large, unused loft space farther up the boulevard Raspail in a beautiful mansion called the American Club. There, almost always alone with a large, clear skylight above me, I glued, wired, and stapled the Parisian junk I was beginning to collect. As groups of American college girls on their junior year abroad sat primly around a fireplace sipping tea and chatting decorously, I tried to sneak up the grand staircase, hauling broken cobblestones, partly defoliated straw brooms, the few bits of garbage I could find in the finely picked-over Paris trash. Up there in the luxurious light, in splendid solitude and with room enough for two of Lhote's studios, I assembled my "conglomerates." The more I had seen of American abstraction—the marvels of Motherwell and Kline, de Kooning and Pollock—the more I had felt that there was no room there for me, that I needed to find other ways of expression. The night at Bolek's provided a route that seemed almost exalted and certainly right. Using junk plus action painting plus photographs, posters, maps, all mixed in with my precise, delicate drawing, I created objects of great ambiguity and sometimes enormous fun.

At the American Club I merged, at Lhote's I tried to glorify the painting as event. Speak of action, this was untrammeled action; speak of Kor's kind of automatism, this was created in the dark, without recourse to judgment or taste. An unmistakable aesthetic direction was emerging from the back of Lhote's studio, which Jeannie called "obscurism."

When she painted in the light, Jeannie Hebert's work tried to be hard-edged. It softened considerably in our dark corner, giving it the life that wasn't always there otherwise. She was married to an embassy official, "probably a goddam spy, my Thin Man," she said. "Why do you think I spend all day at Lhote's? It's either this or shopping with the embassy wives." We began having a glass of wine together at the Select. "I've got zero ambition," she told me. "No great talent, either."

Jeannie was wiry—more than that, she was braided like a cable, firm and tough. She unraveled only at the top, above her tightly wound body, in the area of her pretty head and its hectic, crackling contents. She had a painting costume, which she left on a hook at Lhote's. "What can I tell you? I'm superstitious. I wore it when I won first prize in goddam Plattsburg." It was a threadbare, dusty Persian lamb jacket over which she wore a pink apron with ruffles on the shoulders. Outside the studio, though, she was very chic. She covered herself with finely tailored suits, stockings, and heels. She moved stiffly, boyishly. All her sexiness was concentrated in her eyes and mouth. "I wear this shit," she said, showing me the Balmain label, "in case the Thin Man calls from the embassy and wants me to wave to orphans on Washington's goddam birthday."

When I told Jeannie about my night at Prince Casimir Furs, her eyes lit up. She offered me her Persian lamb. "Go on, take it," she said. "What do I need it for?"

"How can you paint without it?" I said. "I can get more anytime I need it."

"Okay, *hombre*, whatever you say."

"Could you do something for me at the embassy?" I asked.

Jeannie loosened up after two glasses of wine. "Anything," she said, already slurring her words. "Naval movements in the

Med? Lists of multinational corporations? You name it."

"It's about my uncle, in case he's looking for me. . . ."

"I'll snoop around, *hombre,*" Jeannie said. "Not to worry."

Missing Bolek, yet unable still to make the first move, I got myself a single ticket to the opera. I saw *Traviata* and cried from beginning to end. All his people were there, just as he had once said, nearly indistinguishable from opera house to opera house.

Lhote didn't show up in his studio for two months. "Influenza," Poliakoff reported gravely. Wanting to be ready for him when he recovered, with Jeannie's help I transported some of my heavier conglomerates from the American Club. Among them were reconstituted crates picked up at Les Halles and filled, in the dead of night, with dirt from the Bois de Boulogne. When Lhote finally appeared to give critiques, he looked very pale and shaky. I had several canvases and conglomerates that I was anxious to show him. Poliakoff had set up a folding chair in front of an easel on which, one by one, we placed our work for Lhote to see. Poliakoff had gone around with a large wooden palette, asking for contributions of blobs of pigment from each of us. Then, in turn, Poliakoff announced the painters. I was the last to arrive in the studio and thus the last to be seen by the master. When my turn did come, Poliakoff grinned sheepishly, as if he had been waiting for this moment. He crossed his arms on his chest and waited.

Lhote's face, like an animal's, showed little expression. "*Qu'est-ce que c'est, ce cochonnerie?*" he growled. He was a small man, stooped with age. "So this is the new American," he said. "You are cowboy, monsieur?" He put his paintbrush down and rubbed his eyes wearily. He was obviously a man who had seen it all, and was running out of the steam necessary to deal with it one more time. "What is this?" he asked. "Why do you people *insist?* You are like children at the gates of heaven." He trembled like an old wet dog. "*En France,*" he said, "we have the habit of—how you say it, Poliakoff?— *emmailloter . . .*"

"*Emmailloter,*" Poliakoff repeated, his brow furrowed, searching for the English equivalent. The word passed through the anxious polyglot crowd, its fluid tones like waves on a swelling sea. *"Emmailloter, emmailloter."* Finally, from the back, Jeannie yelled, "Swaddle. To swaddle, maître." Poliakoff yelled "swaddle" into Lhote's ear.

"Swaddle," Lhote said with difficulty. "Swaddle." He cleared his throat. *"En France,* monsieur, we *swaddle* our infants. Some say it is barbaric, our custom to swaddle, but we have all been swaddle. Monsieur Cézanne had been swaddle and Monsieur Braque. Before them, Monsieur David has swaddle and Monsieur Poussin." He paused, looking at his audience. "About Monsieur Monet I am not so sure." Everyone laughed.

"This to swaddle," Lhote went on, "is intended to inhibit animal tendencies. We are a race of philosophers. We do not scratch on canvas with our feet." The group of students pressed closer. "As *artistes,* we transfer images from life to pictorial space. This must be the only abstraction!"

As he spoke, Lhote slipped a palette knife under a torn white sneaker I had glued to the canvas. He strained to pry it loose. The sneaker popped off, then the T-shirt tore, leaving shreds of cloth and rubber on the canvas board. Lhote took up a brush and illustrated his talk with a neocubist nude that he absentmindedly re-created.

"The *charactéristiques humaines,"* he said slowly, are an essential point of support for the *artiste."* His voice grew faint. "It is necessary to——justify—the sensibility in a material order which conforms to the natural order of things—"

"Monsieur Lhote," I interrupted. *"Maître.* Although I have never been swaddled, I am a European, one who looks to history with humility and awe. Still, *Monsieur Maître,* there are times when one must stick a finger up the rectum of art."

Lhote was no pushover. He was angry, trembling. "The sublime is fragile," he said confidentially to Poliakoff. "Rome could not support the *barbares—"*

"Maître," I interrupted loudly, "some discover by affirming, others by negating. In these times, there is nothing as dangerous as the true believer."

Lhote blinked. He looked up toward the single yellow light

bulb. He fished in his pocket and found his little penknife, with which he undoubtedly peeled his apples, and he stabbed my canvas with such force that Poliakoff backed off. Lhote was breathing hard. "Thank God I am a Frenchman," he said, and coughed. "I *belong,* you *barbare.* I belong to the glorious tradition—"

"Your countryman, Marcel Duchamp, said that in art it is every man for himself, as in a shipwreck."

Poliakoff helped Lhote out of the creaky little chair and walked him over to the coatrack. He put Lhote's hat on his head and accompanied the master to the street. As soon as the door had closed behind them, Jeannie flew into my arms. "A great performance," she said, and pressed her lips to mine.

I think I would have left Lhote's studio after that, but an interesting social situation kept me there. Having slipped into the role of Lhote's bad boy, I became a thoroughly exposed item, everyone's bad boy. Everyone talked to me differently now, some carefully, as in the presence of genius, but most with wanton disrespect. GI Walt, short and solid, would creep into my corner and laugh, *guffaw,* at what he saw on my easel. Sometimes GI Hank would stand between Jeannie and me, just telling bad jokes or mouthing obscenities.

"They think I'm shit," I told Jeannie.

"Just the opposite," she said. "You make them feel like the dried-up schmucks they are."

I even received a visit from Number One, GI Buddy Holbein from Nebraska. "You're okay, Krinsky," he said. "You've got spunk, you're not stupid. Why do you glue all that shit? Collage is a delicate business. This stuff's like fucking barnacles."

"Better safe right here on my canvas than out there in the streets," I said.

"Hey, don't fuck with me, fella," Buddy Holbein said. "What is he, nuts? You crazy, Krinsky?"

I *loved* being nuts. I'd been thinking a lot about another nut, the painter Chaim Soutine. He was driven insane by the Lithuanian Jews who saw him only as the demon making graven images, and by the Lithuanian cossacks who hated his

Jewish ass. He *walked* all the way to Paris from Lithuania. And his images—oh, his images!—they were the primal, guileless smudges of a mad innocent, as far as you can get from the world of Bolek, Enid, Lhote, and Buddy Holbein.

I ran down to the street, found a butcher shop, and bought two of the mangiest chickens I could find. I hung my scrawny chickens, as Soutine had hung his turkeys, on a nail in the wall. I screwed a light bulb into the socket above me, and I painted until Poliakoff kicked us all out late in the afternoon. The next morning, my birds smelled pretty bad. I had to fight to keep them until I finished. Everyone hated me that day. Even Jeannie left early. But Buddy Holbein continued to be interested. He wanted to talk.

"Why are you doing this, Krinsky?" he asked. "You don't have to paint rotten fucking chickens."

"For Picasso," I said, "it was a case of first eating the thing and then painting it."

"What the fuck are you talking about?"

"For Matisse, the food he painted had little to do with the food he ate."

"You are fucking insane," Buddy said.

"For me, the painting *is* the meal. I'm going to eat these fucking chickens."

I decided that, for a while anyway, I had had enough. "Take a week off with me, Jeannie," I urged. "We'll spend it in museums."

"Nah, I gotta paint," she said. But late the next day, after I had come back to the hotel from a long afternoon with the Messieurs Delacroix and Géricault, Jeannie was waiting for me in my room. "I told the concierge I was your sister. Jesus Christ, anyone can get into your room."

Jeannie had cleared off a little chair and sat smoking. The ashtray in her lap was full of half-smoked cigarettes.

"Today it was the Romantics," I said. "Tomorrow it's Goya day at the Bibliothèque Nationale."

"I'm going with you," Jeannie said. "Not only that but I want to buy one of those conglomerates, Krinsky."

"Yeah? Really?"

"Do you want to sell them?"

"Sure," I said. "How about a drink at the Select right now?"

"I brought a bottle of wine," Jeannie said, her green eyes sparkling, *lambent* eyes, pools of warm liquid. Sophie called Maggie's eyes "lambent," though I don't know where she found the word.

"I don't even have a glass," I said.

"We can drink out of the bottle," Jeannie said. "But don't get me wrong, *hombre,* we don't have to drink it now."

"I want to. Don't you?"

She took a Swiss Army knife out of her pocketbook and started to uncork the bottle. "Let me," I said, and as our hands touched in the clumsy exchange, we pulled back as if we had touched fire, and the bottle dropped, still corked but shaken. The moment she finished saying "Can I see your drawings?" Jeannie began to laugh so hard she had to wipe the tears from her eyes.

I brought over a couple of sketchbooks, sketches from the *King Haakon VII,* from the Luxembourg gardens, some copies of the Goyas in the Louvre, and some of Maggie from memory. Jeannie took a long sip of wine from the bottle, then passed it to me. She leafed through the sketchbooks silently, then looked curiously at me. "I wouldn't have expected *this* from the guy who puts dirt in boxes," she said. "You selling these? How much do you want for the drawings?"

"I don't know. Let me make some of you." I sat on a corner of my bed to make a sketch of her. Her knees knocked against each other, her shoes were turned inward. She looked like a lovely little girl. "Nobody has ever seen me like this," she said when I handed her the sketch. "Jesus, Krinsky, you think I'm cute."

"It's not cute," I said, "it's sexy."

"Sexy?" she said. "You mean it?"

I knelt by her and took the sketchbook from her hands. I put my arms around her legs. Jeannie ran her fingers through my hair. She leaned back and took a deep breath. "More wine," she said. We each drank and then I pulled her up and onto my bed with its musty chenille cover. Cradled in the hollow of my pitted mattress, Jeannie couldn't move. "You know what, *hombre?*" she said. "I'm scared." I ran my hands over her body, but neither of us was really inspired. "You're sweet, Krinsky, and you do turn me on, but let's have another belt of wine." We finished the bottle and went to Lipp's for supper. I stuffed myself with *choucroute* and Alsatian beer, but Jeannie wasn't hungry. She finished off a half-bottle of cognac, though, and wanted to go back to the hotel. "Let's try again," she said, slurring her words.

"Where's your husband?"

"The Thin Man's gone. He never tells me where—probably stirring up trouble in the goddam Balkans again." Jeannie took my hand. Back in the hotel, she fell asleep in her underwear, snoring lightly until morning.

At breakfast on the terrace of the Dome, Jeannie said she was embarrassed.

"Why?"

"You know, Krinsky," Jeannie said. "I got drunk, I was frigid, I snored. . . ."

"Oh, well," I said, "and what about me? I wasn't exactly suave and sophisticated."

"Oh, Krinsky," she said, reaching across the table to fish my hand off my lap and kissing it. "You're terrific. You've got so much going on inside that I feel I'll catch fire just touching you." A waiter brought us a basket of croissants and coffee. "Besides, I'm a married woman."

"I know. I couldn't get that out of my mind."

"It's not that I think the Thin Man would even care. I don't know, he probably has something going on the side, some rosy-cheeked Yugoslav. It's me, not him. It's goddam Plattsburg, that's what it is." Jeannie looked around the terrace nervously. For days she had felt that we were being watched. "What about you? Don't you have some little sweetie stashed away somewhere?"

"She's not exactly stashed away. She's making a movie."

"The plot thickens," Jeannie said, gulping down her second cup of black coffee.

"She and I have been more or less together since we were babies."

"Babies?"

"I don't know what it means. We're always separating and coming back. Right now she's in Hollywood, making a movie with Jed Seacliff."

"Jed Seacliff? Mother of God! What's her name?"

"Maggie—Magdalena—Maggie Coe . . ."

"Never heard of her," Jeannie said. She seemed a little relieved.

We left the Dome and walked down the boulevard Raspail toward the Seine. I stopped in a little printshop and bought some fifty-year-old postcards, a map of Alsace-Lorraine, a drawing of a girl lifting her skirts toward a gentleman in a high hat.

"Maggie wants the whole thing, Jeannie. Marriage, babies, a house in the country . . ."

"What's wrong with that?" Jeannie asked.

"It scares me."

"Why, *hombre*? Artists have families. Look at Picasso. Look at Dumas *père* and Dumas *fils*, for Christ's sake."

"It's not only that," I said. "There's something *stupid* about families—"

"Stupid? It's how we mortals live together, how we keep each other from dying of loneliness, keep each other comfy and dry. Babies keep the whole thing going—"

"I know, I know. I can't explain it. When you're alone, you breeze through things, you push your way through borders. Do you know what I'm saying? You don't have a caravan of grandmothers and kids and dogs—"

"Most people don't have to worry about borders."

"That's changed. I don't believe that. But even if you stay put, you begin collecting things, like bicycles and furniture and rosebushes. You're tied. You can't leave it. Then the others come, they find you sitting there all comfy, and they blow the shit out of it."

"Poor Krinsky," Jeannie said. "You've been traumatized. We don't think like that in the U. S. of A. We can fix that. We can fix anything. We can have it fixed."

"I don't want it fixed," I said. "It's my edge, being a little nuts. It's all that makes me different. It's painful, but it's me."

"So you've kissed your Maggie goodbye," Jeannie said.

"Oh, God, I don't know. . . ." We had crossed the Pont Neuf and walked up the Champs-Elysées toward the Etoile.

"How much do you want for the drawings?" Jeannie asked.

"You really want to buy drawings?"

"If I can afford them."

"How about five thousand francs?"

"You sure?"

"Sure." I walked Jeannie to her place on the avenue Kléber, where her concierge was sweeping the sidewalk in front of the huge wooden door. The concierge began talking to herself, shaking her head. Jeannie insisted on giving me ten thousand francs on account. She wanted to pick out several drawings. She said that she would spread the word at the embassy. "I'll tell them it's a great investment," Jeannie said. "They'll line up to get a shot at it."

I took a few days off by myself. Everyone was heading down the Loire Valley, making their way through the châteaux, or down to the Mediterranean to soak up the sun, but I went to poke around France's eastern border, on the edge of Germany. Like sticking my tongue into a tooth abscess, I walked around in the mud, in cemeteries, in the drab cold cities of the Northeast. I spoke to no one. I bought junk and wrote to Maggie every day. My letters to her were changing. Once I had illustrated them in the margins, but now I wrote in the margins, the drawings having taken over the main space. I began gluing things to the letters so that the clerk at the Chalons post office told me I was mailing a package and would have to take the damn thing through customs.

Having teased myself by looking across the border into Germany, I came back to Paris ready to work. But on the day of my return, I received a cable from Sophie telling me that she had arranged to change planes at Orly in order to spend a couple of hours with me on her way to Rome.

Paris felt more like home with Sophie's visit. She looked beautiful, round and plump, waiting for me in a dark lounge of the airport. "Did Maggie tell you how to get hold of me?" I asked.

"Maggie? No. We all know where you are."

"You do? How do you know?"

"Oh, darling," Sophie said as to a child. "Bolek gave someone the job, the *directrice* at Balmain, I think. We know where you are working, who you are going out with, where you are eating—"

"I don't believe this."

"You are a naughty boy with the wife of a secret agent, I hear—"

"Sophie—"

"But I really wanted to talk to you about Maggie. That's why I cabled," Sophie said over a bottle of very good champagne. "I am worried and I believe *you* have cause for worry. I don't like what is happening. Maggie seems infatuated with Jed Seacliff."

"Good God, that's ridiculous," I said. "He's a relic."

"Well, not exactly that bad, Adam," Sophie said, "but he certainly is more than twice her age."

"Older than Kor," I said.

"But worse than that, darling. Jed Seacliff is absolutely head over heels in love with her."

"I can't believe it, Sophie. It's wrong."

"He's making it difficult for her to refuse. . . ."

"Refuse what?"

"Refuse marriage."

"Oh, Sophie! I shouldn't have left."

"I don't know if that made a difference," Sophie said.

"What do you mean?"

"It's Jed. How could anyone resist that charming man?" Sophie said. "He has the best of the American spirit, that gentle man, so kind, so handsome." Sophie took out her compact and straightened her feathery hat. "He absolutely *craves* having a family," she added.

I just couldn't get myself to believe it. When Sophie left to board her plane, I hung around the airport, severely tempted to fly to Los Angeles, but I neither had the money nor knew what I would do once I arrived there. I tried to call Maggie from the hotel, but a maid answered and the connection was so bad that

I understood nothing. I wrote Maggie another letter that night, this time without illustrations. I pleaded my case as the person who knew her best, as her true soul mate, as the proper eventual father of her children. But even as I wrote, even as I felt a new loneliness worse than any I had ever known, I realized that my promises were a little empty, that as much as I loved Maggie, I wasn't ready for all those things that Jed Seacliff apparently wanted with such passion.

Everyone seemed to be converging on Paris, for two days later I got a telephone call from Paul.

"You are one son of a bitch, Krinsky" was the first thing he said. "Some friend. You call no one. We don't know where you are, if you're alive or dead—"

"I've been writing you a long letter."

"Not good enough," Paul said. "You're no damn good."

"Kaitz, I've missed you," I said. "How's Carla?"

"She's fine, too busy to come now. I flew over with her aunt and uncle. They want to see you too."

"To see *me*? Why?"

"They'll tell you when they get back from Switzerland."

"How's Bolek? Have you seen Bolek?"

"He's fine," Paul said, "but listen, Krinsky, I can't talk right now. I have to do some business for my father."

"Nothing distasteful, I hope."

"Very funny," Paul said. "I've got things to do tomorrow, too, but we can get together, okay? It's in the country. Come with me. We've got a lot to talk about."

In the morning, Paul picked me up in a rented limousine. He looked very dapper in a light gray suit. The handkerchief in his breast pocket matched his deep blue tie. As we sped out of the city, we could hardly stop smiling at each other. He told me a little about his business in Jouy-en-Josas with an ex-judge, an old associate of Lou's. Something about Las Vegas and the south of France. I could hardly wait to ask him about *my* business, my *Family of Prince Casimir.* "What do you know about the little gift I left behind for Bolek?"

I could see that Paul knew plenty, for his eyes lit up with

anticipation. "Later, later," he said, sounding like Lou. But even though he tried to talk about Carla, about Lou, about *anything*, he was too impatient not to spill the beans. "The thing you left behind in the showroom caused a real sensation," he told me.

"A sensation? Go on, go on. . . ."

"This guy we're going to see used to own property in Nice," Paul said, and I leaned across the plush gray seats to tickle him under his arms. "Okay, okay, Krinsky," he said as the long car entered elegant domesticated landscapes that reminded me a little of Southampton. "Your thing wasn't discovered until early Monday morning by the man who vacuumed the place. He didn't know what to make of it, so he cleaned up around it, messing up even more, not knowing the drips on the carpet were still wet."

"I wasn't too careful," I admitted.

We turned into the grand circular driveway lined with poplars and tall bushes just beginning to leaf. Two servants came out to lead us inside a great baronial estate where Maître Pandolfini, a fat old man, rocked on a long chaise hooked to a metal frame. The house was eclectic in style, its heavy Tudor beams hanging ominously over a neat Dutch interior of Delft tiles and homey bric-a-brac. "I don't see your father a long time," the maître said to Paul. "He's doing real good business out there in the West."

"Real good," Paul said.

A long table from some medieval castle was laden with cakes and tarts, fruits and cheeses. Coffee and tea were wheeled in by servants, poured into cups by others. Maître Pandolfini ate the cakes as if they were heart medicine, gulping them down, then holding his plate out for more. His eyes teared with satisfaction. He pointed out his favorites to us, nodding approval as Paul and I took two tall, fluffy *mille feuilles*. After our host finished a glass of seltzer and a cup of coffee, he tugged at Paul's sleeve and whispered things into his ear. "Business," Paul told me. I heard mention of restaurants and casinos, in Nice, in Cannes, in St. Tropez. Forgetting to whisper, they discussed apartment buildings they were helping to finance on the periphery of Paris.

"Lou's got his hand in everything," I said to Paul.

"He's driven," Paul said. "Typical Jewish behavior. From the pushcart to the palace."

We went for a walk in the formal, beautifully tended gardens. Maître Pandolfini walked slowly and sometimes prodded Paul in the back with the rubber tip of his cane. This made him laugh, and laughter forced him to stop and rest. He sat down on one of the benches placed every few yards on the narrow path and urged us to pick some flowers from a hothouse at the bottom of the garden, below the last terrace. Inside the inferno of the hothouse, among the gorgeous flowers, we stood facing each other and I listened eagerly as Paul went on with his story.

"After the janitor, Mlle. Sacha came in and fainted dead away. When Jacques came off the elevator, she was out cold next to the dummy of Bolek, who was himself prone at the feet of the Pope." Paul slapped my back playfully. "Jesus, Krinsky," he said, "I've laughed my ass off about this thing. In the middle of goddam class, I'd start laughing. They thought *I* was nuts."

We came out of the hothouse with flowers. We stuck a carnation in the lapel of Maître Pandolfini's safari jacket, one in Paul's suit, one in a buttonhole of my open shirt. Bumblebees shot back and forth from bloom to bloom. We walked on, leaving our host behind again.

"Jacques said he couldn't tell who was real and who wasn't," Paul said. "When they revived Sacha, she called Bolek at the Beverly Hills Hotel. He was in the pool with Mike Craig and a few other businessmen. After he took Sacha's call, he looked as if he was going to faint, so Mike Craig called a cardiologist. Even though Bolek was turning blue, the EKG was fine, and by the time Maggie came over, Bolek was drinking tea."

"Poor Bolek," I said. "All the pain I've caused him." Maître Pandolfini was nearly out of sight. A young woman in a nurse's costume had caught up with him and was fanning him with a copy of *Humanité*. We stopped to wait for them.

"I have it, I have it!" Maître Pandolfini said in his thick Marseillaise accent. "Alouette," he said, confusing us. He poked Paul with his cane. "Our new hotel. Alouette, do you see it?"

"I'll tell my father," Paul said. "What is it in English?"

The pretty nurse knew. "Skylark," she said in a lovely sing-song.

"A perfect name for the hotel," Paul said.

"Telegraph immediately," Maître Pandolfini commanded. "Go now to the post office."

We took the waiting limousine to the Jouy-en-Josas post office and sent the cable to Lou. On the way back, Paul continued the saga of *The Family of Prince Casimir*.

"Maggie called Enid Swope at *Mirabelle*, and Enid, really using her head, sent a photographer up to the showroom before Sacha had time to destroy the thing—which, by the way, she was trying to do even while the poor man was shooting."

"I can't believe all this, Paul. I just can't believe it."

"Just wait. A couple of days later, Draga Baku went up there to look at a coat. She already owned one Casimir mink, did you know that? Well, when she saw that the main showroom was roped off, she asked Yvette what was going on. Yvette told Draga everything, including about Enid and the photographer. Draga raced out of there, straight to Enid's office."

The maître's nurse came out to the car to tell us that he was taking his afternoon nap and expected to see us when he awoke. Paul told her that we had to go and that he would return by himself in a day or two. My head was spinning, my ears were buzzing. "Anyway, Krinsky," Paul said as we moved slowly through the French countryside back to Paris, "Draga brought the pictures home for Timor. They called Carla and me, and the four of us sat down together to decide what to do next."

"What did you decide?"

"They should tell you, Adam. They want to tell you—"

"Tell me," I begged.

"They'll be back here in a week."

"I can't wait a week."

"Swear you'll act surprised when they tell you."

"I swear."

"They want to give you a show."

"On the basis of *that*?"

"What else?" Paul said. "It is pretty fucking amazing, your piece."

When the Bakus came back to Paris and I told them that Jeannie had bought one of the conglomerates and embassy people had nearly decimated my sketchbooks, they didn't take the news lightly. "We are your dealers now, Adam, and we don't want you to sell anything to anyone, not yet. And that *assemblage* you left at your uncle's, Adam, is precisely what we have been looking for."

"You, darling," Draga said, " are our *enfant terrible.*"

I had forgotten how small, how white, how impish they both were. To the Bakus, the whole world was part circus, part *opera buffa*, part flea market. "Do you have those photographs?" I asked.

"Of course we do," Timor Baku said, and picked the lot of them out of his briefcase. They were shot from all angles. There were details and panoramic views. I was transported back to that long, hard night and the luxurious pleasure of sustained criminal activity. "The gallery space is fantastic," Timor said, "but we cannot possess it for nearly a year. We want your show, our first in America, a year from autumn."

"What a remarkable coincidence," Draga said, "that Carla is writing a marvelous, original piece on Marcel Duchamp."

"She's going to be very involved with the gallery," Timor said.

"Where is the gallery?" I finally thought to ask.

"Where else but Fifty-seventh Street?"

The three of us went to the American Club, to Lhote's, to my hotel room, so the Bakus could see everything I'd been doing. They loved the conglomerates, the boxes, the placing of my junk and my drawing, the newspaper clippings, the old maps and prints. They said that action painting had never looked so good to them. "We love the eclecticism, the profanity, the delicious blasphemy," Draga said as we sat in a café afterward.

"There are other images that are equally important to me," I said.

"Anything," Draga proclaimed.

"Images of loss and of death," I said.

"Adam, dear Adam," they chorused, "death is for later." Timor smiled and ordered another bottle of wine. "You are young, we are young, America is young. Death does not exist." When the wine arrived, he poured each of us another glass. "To the death of death," he toasted. "We shall wake up America. To our maiden voyage."

When Paul and the Bakus left, I wrote a long letter to Bolek, trying to make him understand what I had done, why I had exploded at his expense, and how, miraculously, something extraordinary would come out of it for me. I told him how sorry I was to have hurt him. I told him that I loved him more than anyone on earth. A couple of weeks later, I received a package from Bolek. Beautifully wrapped in tissue paper, in a silver Prince Casimir box, lay a large beret made of soft, brown nutria, and two oversize, marvelously crafted paintbrushes with sable tips. Proud and happy, I brought them over to show to Jeannie. "The whole goddam family's nuts," she concluded.

I was beginning to find out that no matter where you were, everybody passed through there to see you sooner or later. Paris wasn't exactly the South Pacific, but I knew that had I stayed longer, pals from camp, the League, the Cedar Bar would have showed up as well. A messenger arrived at my little Hotel Beau Rivage, nestled in the streets and alleys behind the Dome, from the Hotel Plaza-Athenée, in the forefront of Parisian splendor on the avenue Matignon. It wasn't the season for fashion shows, yet Bolek was in Paris.

He waited for me in his suite, standing by the windows, one hand inside his jacket pocket, the other on the sill, as if he were posing for a photograph. I was nervous and excited about seeing him. He was the wronged party and I the transgressor, coming into his space to sign the surrender documents. I walked to him humbly. I put my arms around him and hugged him hard. Before we had time to say anything, a woman came out of the bedroom. She stopped, leaned back against the wall to admire us. Her frilly blouse was buttoned right up under her chin, and her sober English suit lay perfectly on her long body. Bolek turned to her. "I present to you a bandit, a regular fur killer," Bolek said, and then to me, with tenderness in his voice, "Mademoiselle Suzi, my dear friend."

Suzi took my hands. Her look implored me to be her ally, her friend. "We must order drinks, don't you think so?" she said with a German accent. Inside her thin lips, her sexy rabbit teeth pushed forward into a pout.

Bolek was smiling proudly, looking from the one to the other of us. Suzi was not much older than I. Even though Bolek and I seemed to have survived the severe test I had inflicted on us, he may have been fortifying himself with a daughter, at least someone who could have passed as his daughter. He wanted me to like her, and she seemed ready to do anything to ingratiate herself with me. "Please be so kind as to sit here," she said to me, brushing off a place on the white couch. "You will be most comfortable."

"Well," I said, "what are you both doing in Paris?"

Before Bolek had a chance to answer, Suzi said, "It is a little vacation and a chance for me to meet you."

"Yes, that's wonderful," I said, "a lovely time in Paris, all the trees in bloom."

"We will also watch our new publicity," Bolek explained. "Mademoiselle Suzi and I brought furs to photograph. We have some left, you know," he told me, "for which we are grateful."

"We must forget the past," Suzi said.

"Where is your girlfriend?" Bolek asked me. "We can invite her to eat with us."

"What girlfriend?"

"The wife of the spy," Bolek said.

"She's not a girlfriend, just a friend," I said.

He turned to Suzi. "They talk about him already like a big shot. Art people are talking." He looked over to me. "You have Zizi to thank," he said.

"Yes, I know."

"Sacha is ready to kill you," Bolek said, "and so is Yvette."

"And you?" I asked.

"Victor cried when he saw the coats. He took the ermine home with him and now it looks like new. He cleaned it hair by hair. The others are *schmatas.* I put them in the Frigidaire—"

"You did?"

"When he is a *real* big shot," Bolek said to Suzi, "someone will want to buy those coats."

We went walking along the Seine, Bolek in the middle between Suzi and me. He seemed immensely happy, breathing in the wind that blew gently up the river, smiling at Suzi and me, pointing to the Eiffel Tower on the other side, to birds fighting in the trees along the quay, to the imposing Grand Palais. Suzi began swinging her leather handbag, finally more relaxed herself.

We ate at the hotel, and then, as I was about to leave them for the night, Bolek asked if I would meet him the next day at the Louvre. "Of course," I said. "But tomorrow is Tuesday," I remembered, "all the museums are closed."

"No, no, darling," Bolek said, "it is open, believe me. Meet us at ten in the Médici Gallery."

I had never suspected that I would have to mention Bolek's name plus the name of Prince Casimir Furs to be allowed into the goddam Louvre, but that was precisely what I had to do. The entrance was barred to everyone but those associated with Bolek's organization. The Médici Gallery, where some twenty huge Rubens paintings celebrated Marie de Médici's ascendance to the French throne, was teeming with photographers, directors, models, everyone scribbling in notebooks, yelling directions, arguing about the eerie lights, which added heat and glare to the turmoil. A rack of furs was set up outside the gallery and carefully watched by uniformed police.

Bolek spotted me and came over, indicating with a sweep of his hand everything before us. "You see, darling, I am in the Louvre first," he said. "It was not easy to make it before you, but *voilà*, it is me! Now stand by the wall, darling, so they can take their pictures."

They photographed ermine and chinchilla with the great Rubens panoply of flesh and material in the background, then they moved down to the Egyptians. Mme. Clothilde, Count Kaczka's *Vogue* friend, seemed to be directing traffic. On her forearm, a honey-colored kinkajou swung by its long prehensile tail. Mme. Clothilde pierced the sacred Louvre air with her coloratura voice, indicating the poses she wanted from the models, contorting them into weird and awkward positions. The models quibbled, pushed, and shouted. The photographers and their assistants had taken off their shirts in the intense heat, then kept walking off the job, protesting the conditions and the general chaos, only to be cajoled back by people from the agency, whose day was spent making peace, running out for food and drink, patching prickly relationships.

"Clothilde is amazing," Suzi told me. "Only she knows how to make anything happen in this country. It is very different where I come from."

Mme. Clothilde came over to us, her kinkajou's tail wrapped around her neck. "Ah, don't listen to a word she says. Everything works because of your fabulous uncle."

I watched most of the day as they photographed next to the *Venus de Milo.* I suggested Uccello's *Battle of San Romano,* which they were delighted to try. Bolek asked if there were Goyas in the Louvre, and when I told him, he had the entire crew move upstairs again to a lovely portrait from the middle period and a small still life of a slab of salmon. At the end of the day, they shot outside, in the majestic Court Carrée and among the Maillol sculptures in the formal gardens.

Yes, Bolek had made it to the Louvre first, and as I watched the furs and fur people mingle with France's treasures, I found myself thinking about the parallels of fashion and art, each depending on the mood of the times, each with its outrageous cast of characters, plunging into the thick of things in order to *épater* the bourgeois. What was the difference between Bolek, Clothilde, and the Bakus? Had old, elegant Rubens been a spectator at today's goings-on, with sexy young Hélène de Froment on his arm, he would have felt right at home. Eternal youth, pink soft flesh, yards of ermine, silk, and lace, the death of death, would have suited them all.

Soon after Bolek left Paris, I was ready to leave myself. The Bakus arranged for carpenters to come to the American Club, where I had collected my year's work. They crated every last piece, plus all the unused junk. An agent pushed it all through customs and, sealed with globs of red wax, had it shipped back to America.

11

*B*olek was now the master of an empire. His personal fortune was soon to be even further enhanced by big money from Germany. He was in love with Suzi. Life was bestowing gifts upon him with reckless abandon.

The new financial powers of Prince Casimir Furs were imposing a managerial hierarchy on the growing business. Among many changes, they wanted Bolek out of his office. "Listen to me, Bolek," Dick Connally from Santa Barbara said, "this is no longer a mom-and-pop candy store." They wanted to integrate the operation of all the divisions, they wanted to lease several floors of a building on Park Avenue, they wanted *efficiency*.

But Bolek wouldn't move out of the office he had occupied since 1940. He needed the contact with his customers, the touch and smell of his furs. "I am surrounded by these money machines," Bolek complained. "It is the Waffen SS."

Suzi comforted him. "You can do anything you set your mind to," she told Bolek.

"They want only numbers," Bolek said. "I am no good with numbers. I can only make the dance."

The perfume "Casimir" was a great success, as was "Adam," the aftershave. Quickly they manufactured another, "L'Animal," with leopard spots sandblasted on the bottle and a screw top shaped like a cat's head. "It is not metal," Bolek screamed at John Hegel from Denver, who managed the production of the new scents. "It is papier-mâché!"

John Hegel's laugh was decidedly patronizing. "It's plastic, Bolek," he said. "You can't hold back progress."

"Who are these people?" Bolek said to me on one of our rare evenings together. "What have I done?"

"Maybe you can rest a little now," I said. "Let them run the business."

"All my life I want only to make beautiful things. These idiots know only plus and minus."

"You're an artist, Bolek," I told him. "They are insects."

Since I'd come back from Paris, I'd been living in Kor's vacated Gramercy Park rooms and painting in Abe Strawberry's abandoned loft. "I want you to have it," Kor said. "I cannot tell you how very pleased I was when you came to me to sleep after your *Walpurgisnacht*." As for Abe Strawberry, he was living with an older woman, a patroness of the arts, on upper Fifth Avenue. Her husband had died and her children were away at college. There was plenty of space for painting.

Suzi took my place at the Buckingham, though she used my room only for her clothes. She hated living in a hotel. "I am not that kind of girl," she pouted. Delighted to have her young flesh next to him nightly, Bolek agreed to move and the next day Suzi found a light, airy apartment on Sutton Place. The move from the Buckingham wasn't easy. My sketchbooks alone weighed a ton and, to my surprise, Bolek asked if he could keep them. "I will keep them for you, darling," he said. "I like looking into them once in a while." As much as we had both denied it over the years, the Buckingham was home, and moving from it was painful. Bolek threw out piles of what he considered to be old clothes and the hotel carted off buckets full of fashion magazines. But my report cards and other relics like my baseball mitt, Bolek wanted to take with him to Sutton Place.

"This was my only home," I said.

"You lived nearly ten years in Warsaw," Bolek reminded me.

"Not with you," I said.

Bolek's eyes were moist. He hugged me. "The hotel was for another life," he said. "Everything is different now."

"You'll be happy in the new place," I said, "but it's so big. . . ."

"Suzi will be there, too," Bolek said.

"Always?"

"She is a wonderful girl," Bolek assured me.

The building was new and elegant; its balconies looked over the East River. Suzi began decorating. "Don't bother with anything, schatzie," she told Bolek. "Leave the color of the curtains to me. You have enough to think about." She did everything. She bought Scandinavian walnut furniture, she bought squared-off couches covered with nubby wools, and chairs to match. Everything was simple, unornamented, and grand, a little like Albert Speer's Nuremberg.

The Bakus sent a cleaning brigade down to my studio on the Bowery. They also sent a couple of carpenters, who built me long tables on which to lay out the materials for my con-glomerates. Together with my crates of junk from Paris, I would never want for garbage.

The many new pieces were beginning to take shape. The theme emerging from them was that of the family, which I now saw alternately as a fighting unit or a gathering of slugs under a rock, sometimes equipped to defend its turf, at other times mobilized for action, looking for *lebensraum*. The family of the peaceable kingdom was not a part of it. I endowed the family with all my rage. It had become a lot more volatile than Kor's friendly admonition that "a pram in the hall is the enemy of art."

Paul and Carla liked the work in progress, though they didn't agree with its sentiment. "When you're in love," Paul said, "you want to make a family, to have babies." He and Carla had moved into a nice little apartment not far from Columbia.

"Sociology 101," I said, as the radiators banged and hissed in their place. Even in my T-shirt, I was always too hot in New York.

"You're making a big mistake with Maggie," Paul warned.

"What do you want me to do?"

"You could start thinking about *her*," Carla said. "You could go out there, you could tell her how much you love her. You could propose marriage. . . ."

"I'm not about to get married," I stated flatly.

"Maybe he really doesn't care," Paul said.

"She's no goddam Penelope who's going to wait forever," Carla warned.

"I'm not worried," I said, and resolved that I would call Maggie as soon as I got home. I got up to look at their books, which now included French and Italian monographs on surrealism and Dada, on Duchamp and Tzara and the others. Carla's paper on Marcel Duchamp was terrific. I was drawn to the *enterprise* of art as a statement about art, especially since the pursuit of beauty seemed to be everyone else's preoccupation, from Bolek's easy appreciation of the easy to Abe Strawberry's tasty eruptions. "The artist's signing and exhibiting a manufactured or found object brings that object into relation with the paintings of madonnas," Carla had written about Duchamp's signing and exhibiting his snow shovel. Carla, Paul, and I talked until late at night about art as formal adulteration, about the aesthetics of actual objects on painted surfaces, about impossible combinations. Together with the Bakus, we were a bastion of the new Dada.

Some days I painted and stuck things together around the clock, and then, unable to sleep for more than a couple of hours, I was up again, working with my emblems of ambiguity. Putting together elements that were apparently alien to one another seemed to set *them* on fire and my imagination with them. Like Kor's emblems of Enlightenment Europe set within a tangle of natural forms, my placements felt like my personal heritage, inherited from Kor, from the old Grosz, from the Goya etchings, and even in a strange way from the displaced Bolek. They all delighted in ambiguity and irony—the opposite, I thought, of the straightforwardness, the immediate appeal, the brutal honesty of American painting.

I called Maggie over and over. Strange voices answered, but never Maggie. Nor did she return my calls. I felt half-crazed with regret and jealousy. Kor, quite out of character, urged me to go out to California to stake out my claim. Sophie, Paul, and Carla did the same. I have tried often since then to imagine how Maggie was able to do what she did. Everyone said that it was my fault, that I was too self-absorbed to listen or to care.

Maggie's letters had become scarce and cool. She wrote a lot about Jed Seacliff, about how professional he was, how skilled, how unspoiled by the world's adulation. When she called to tell me, I still didn't believe it. "You can't do this," I insisted. "We are bound to each other forever. *I* want to marry you."

"It's too late, Adam," she said. "I'm sorry."

She asked me to come out to L.A. for the wedding, but I could scarcely move, much less fly across the continent. The deck had been stacked, the competition unfair. What would I have done had Barbara Stanwyck proposed marriage to me? How could I compete with America's heartthrob?

My work collapsed, lost its magic. The magician's sleeve was torn open, the rabbit exposed, blinking in the bright daylight.

Kor and Sophie went out for the wedding, which took place on Jed Seacliff's yacht. Paul and Carla nursed me. The Bakus, white with fear that I would refuse to paint or would simply die, came down often to tell jokes. I met Kor at the airport when he returned from the West Coast. "How can a young woman not be seduced by this matinee idol? You didn't take the competition seriously, Adam. You were foolish. Jed Seacliff is a charming man. How could she have refused him? He adores her, he worships the ground she walks on. He wants to have a family."

We took a bus downtown, where Kor wanted to see my work. "How old is he?" I asked.

"Ah, you are hoping he will die soon," Kor ascertained. "Well, *mon cher,* he and I are probably the same age."

"I didn't mean that," I said without much conviction. Kor took a copy of *Le Figaro* from his pocket and read.

At Abe's, Kor walked slowly around, looking carefully, in

silence. He hadn't seen anything of mine since the photographs of *The Family of Prince Casimir.* "Adam, Adam," he finally said. "I am touched by this." He dabbed at his eyes with his enormous handkerchief. "It is alive and well in your hands," he said. "It is full of tensions, it explodes with ambiguity, darling."

I hadn't realized how I craved Kor's good opinion of my work, how perhaps I had gone in this direction to search out *his* approval, and now that it came, I felt blessed by the benediction of this giant. He saw nothing finished, only suggestions of what was to come, but the direction was enough for him, enough for me, too. The very pram he had talked about was there, stuffed with trumpets, tubas, and an old French horn. Paul had brought me a life-size pink and blue and yellow madonna from an Italian street fair. She stood in a corner of the loft with an expression of sticky rapture, awaiting her new wardrobe, which would include whatever fur I could afford at the Ritz Thrift Shop. I had begun my own version of Manet's *Olympia.* In his version, the nude, as wildly profane as Goya's Maja, lies facing the viewer directly, propped up by pillows and attended by a black mammy. My translation, renamed *Olympia's Family,* had a different perspective. I viewed her from the back of the room in which she poses. There, her family, a group of stolid French farmers, sits playing cards, waiting to take her home after Manet pays her for modeling. I hoarded parts of billboards, signs from store windows, neon tubing that spelled Vacancy and Breakfast 7–9.

Sophie called me with condolences, advice, and gossip. "Do you know that he was married three times?" she asked, a little dismayed.

"Let's hope this isn't his last," I said.

"He's always had an alcohol problem, but he hasn't touched the poison since Magdalena."

"Too bad."

"Be nice, Adam," Sophie said. "It's your own fault. Did you know he was a diabetic?"

"Jesus Christ, Sophie, don't tell me all this movie-magazine shit."

But I was hurting and went up to have supper with her. It was the first time I'd been up to Eighty-fourth Street since Maggie left. I went straight to Maggie's room. The bed was still covered with the dull green cover of the Maja's couch, though its edges were now bordered with a wide ribbon of lace. The pillows were crimson and mustard corduroy. In the back of the closet, I found the two Maja canvases, and as I invaded the closet's secret corners, I began to breathe Maggie's smells—the faint lilac perfume she sometimes used, the locked-in musk of her pores. I took up a leather loafer and stuck my nose inside it, and then I inhaled a nightgown, a wool suit, a red beret. I sat down behind the hanging dresses and cried.

Sophie called from down the hall. "Stop torturing yourself, darling. Come, have a piece of cake. I'm sure that you're not eating anything down there in Hieronymus Bosch country."

We sat down at the table where I had grown up. I nibbled at my piece of babka and felt sick. I went down the hall to the bathroom, Maggie's bathroom, to throw up. With my head hanging over the toilet, I thought I heard water splashing over Maggie's long, lithe body. "Oh, Maggie," I cried, "how could you do this to me?" I straightened up and started to pick through the remnants of her past—her lipsticks, hairpins, the zinc ointment, the half-used box of Tampax.

I helped Sophie make a meat loaf. I had gotten too thin, not having eaten properly for weeks. I could no longer count on a good weekly meal with Bolek. "About his diabetes, Sophie . . ."

"What diabetes?"

"I'm speaking of your son-in-law."

"That sounds so silly," Sophie said. "I'm younger than he is, you know."

"Doesn't that *horrify* you?"

"Adam, darling. This isn't like marrying *any* older man. This is like marrying *America*."

"Is the diabetes serious?"

"He's had it all his life. He has to be careful." Sophie piled food on my plate. "Bruno is coming next week," she said, and instinctively felt the contour of her dark blond curls. "He's an angel, Adam. We're going to spend the summer together in Tuscany."

"Giving up your job?"

"Leave of absence, darling," Sophie said. "Bruno also has a villa in Rome. . . ." My thoughts were elsewhere. "Poor darling," Sophie said, collecting the dishes. "Everyone heals sooner or later. It's important that you go on preparing for your exhibition."

"I'm thinking about Bolek."

"He seems happy with his Suzi," Sophie said amid the clatter of dishes lowered into the sink.

I followed her into the kitchen with the empty wine bottle and glasses. "He's tired all the time, the business has gotten away from him, and Suzi—I don't know, I just don't like her."

"She seems decent enough," Sophie said, "and so helpful . . ."

"She's too young, like Maggie." I began drying dishes.

"Those things don't matter anymore," Sophie said. "Bruno's younger than I am."

"There's something bloodthirsty about Suzi. . . ."

"My goodness," Sophie said.

I thought my comment pleased her, though I wasn't sure. "Efficient's more like it," I said.

"She'll make things easier for Bolek."

We sat down again with coffee. "Does any of this hurt you?" I asked.

Sophie thought about it for a minute. "We have been a long time together, Bolek and I," she said. "But it was never going anywhere." She leaned forward and stuck her chin in her hand. "It was *en famille*, Adam, so comfortable . . ." She picked crumbs off the tablecloth with her index finger, then sucked them off. "He is a man who truly loves women. I adored giving him something to love." She reached across and ran her fingers through my hair. "Do you love women, darling?"

I looked at wonderful, soft Sophie and smiled. How could anyone not love women in her presence? She had just taken off the apron she'd been wearing all evening. As usual, her blouse had several of the top buttons unbuttoned. I looked at the lush landscape of her chest. "Sophie," I said, "I've always loved the way you look, the way you smell. I've spent many nights of my life dreaming about you, about your breasts . . ."

For an instant she looked like a lover, as if she were considering fulfilling my fantasies of childhood. In that instant, all the blood in my body choked my throat. Then it all passed. Sophie got up, straightened her skirt, put her hand up almost defensively to the cleavage between her breasts. "Ah, my darling, it's as I've always told you. If only you had been a little older . . ."

It was time to leave. In the hall, I put my arms around her and felt the fullness of her breasts against me. "How could Maggie have been anything but wonderful?" I said.

Sophie kissed both my cheeks, my nose, then my mouth. "My sweet, precious Adam," she said.

Next day, I went up to the Bakus' new gallery, between Madison and Park. Tarpaulins covered the floors in every room. Men were installing indirect lighting and nailing high moldings just below the ceilings. Timor Baku, in shirt sleeves, was studying carpet swatches. "Which of these?" he asked me the moment he saw me. Each of his four semifinal choices was another shade of unobtrusive, corporate gray. I chose one and Timor put the rest away, pleased to have done with it. What the place lacked in Old World charm, it picked up in drab anonymity—the clean, new, international style of mercantilism, of bureaucratic sameness, a neutral background that was to be *my* responsibility to invigorate. This job had always been Bolek's, his very philosophy of interiors, whose elegance, he thought, should be so silent as to offer up the ideal background for genius.

"Why aren't you working?" Timor asked, then, slapping his knees, he giggled happily. "Isn't this place perfect?" he asked.

He hooked his arm through mine and walked me around again, introducing me to the men on the ladders, the foreman, the building superintendent. "I need your help with a new piece," I told him.

"*Zut!*" he hooted. "We are in business together, *mon ami*, we are partners. Anything, anything."

"I need some full-length dummies, with feet," I said.

He took a deep breath and looked astounded. "Coincidence stays with me like fleas on a dog," he said. "Dummies, you say? I can have my choice of mannequins from the Museum of Natural History, where they are building new exhibitions." He told me of his friend, the Rumanian anthropologist, who that very day had asked him . . . "I can get you used cavemen," Timor said grandly.

"Cavemen will be perfect," I said. "I'd like one male, one female."

"No problem, *jeune homme*," Timor said. "Do you need snakes or okapis? Do you need a piece of the Great Coral Reef? We shall go have a look at what they are throwing away."

When Timor was called away to supervise the installation of the great reception desk, I walked through the place again, the two big rooms and the two smaller ones that I was to fill. I began to picture this Baku whiteness and grayness alive with my color, a blank stage waiting for the actors.

I got up my courage to stop in at Prince Casimir Furs, where I hadn't been since the great destruction. My heart pounded wildly in my rib cage as I first saw Mignon. Her lower lip slackened. She stared as if I were an escaped convict. I bowed to her, ready now to take on the rest. One by one, they appeared, Jacques winking mischievously but guardedly, as at a dangerous child. Elsa came out to stare at me. Yvette was too embarrassed to leave her cubicle. Sacha didn't even nod.

Bolek was in his office, half asleep sitting up, just back from a long luncheon with some of his new associates. He opened his eyes, pulled his glasses back up on his nose. "Aha," he said, "he is back." He winced as if in pain, then reached into his drawer for aspirin.

"What's the matter?" I asked. "What hurts?"

"A little here, a little there," he said. "A little in front, a little in back."

"Have you been to a doctor?"

"What doctor? They know nothing," Bolek said.

"Let's go see Dr. Heller together," I said.

"Another time."

"Let me call him."

"All right, all right," Bolek said. "Call him tomorrow, not now." He shook off whatever pain was bothering him, got up and stretched. "So why such a big shot like you in this place?" he asked.

"I wanted to see you, that's all."

"That's all? What else?"

"I thought you might have an extra fur or bits of fur you don't need. . . ."

Bolek sat down again and howled with laughter. He called for Mlle. Sacha, who came in reluctantly. "He is back, Sacha, can you believe it? Do you know what he wants?"

"Money?" she said. "Hostages?"

"Furs," Bolek said, "just furs."

Mlle. Sacha shot me a dart of a glance, then turned away. "He needs more furs," she said.

"Of course," Bolek said with a flourish of one hand. "What else?"

"Perhaps some beaver," Mlle. Sacha suggested. She had obviously never negotiated with madmen before.

"Will beaver do?" Bolek asked me.

"I do need one ermine," I said, smiling at Bolek. Sacha gasped. "But whatever you can spare will have to do."

They looked at each other, considering their options. Should she agree to give? Should she call the police? She must do something before this maniac no longer asks but *takes*, before he loses his patience and *destroys*.

Bolek was enjoying the game as much as I was. "Show him what we have, darling," he said to Sacha, who fled Bolek's office, saying that Yvette would wait on me.

Bolek chose some serviceable scraps, some ermine tails, some felted beaver, some badly finished mink. He offered me cash to buy the ermine I needed at the Ritz Thrift Shop, but I had *some* pride and bought a ratty ermine imitation myself.

Bolek went to see Dr. Heller the next day. Apparently the doctor wasn't pleased with what he saw. He examined him and insisted on all kinds of laboratory tests. He also insisted that Bolek go lie in the sun for a week, and to my surprise, Bolek and Suzi flew to Palm Springs right away.

My cave couple was delivered to Abe's Bowery loft and I began work on them seeing them as a slouchy version of Van Eyck's *Arnolfini Marriage*. In the course of the next month, Timor sent odds and ends from the garbage pails of the Museum of Natural History, whose exhibitions were being updated through the use of new materials, new techniques of display, and new thoughts on ancient environments. The walls of Abe's loft were now very white and small groups of figures wrapped in fur, together with paintings on canvas and a combination of both, created a kind of Dada Madame Tussaud's atmosphere. I buried myself in the work and in the music that accompanied it on the little portable record player I had bought.

The results of Bolek's lab tests were frightening. He had prostate cancer and they wanted to operate immediately. Suzi knew something had been wrong in Palm Springs. She'd described him as listless, but I was sure that it was her fault. He was well until she appeared on the scene.

"I don't know what they are cutting out," Bolek said as we walked slowly along the river, a few days before surgery. From my own scant understanding of human anatomy, I explained the best I could. "I will have sex after?" he wanted to know.

"Of course," I said, wondering myself.

"Why of course? They cut through here." He pointed to his penis. "They are taking what makes sex."

"You won't be able to have babies, Bolek, but you'll be as manly as ever."

"Suzi wasn't happy," he confided.

"That's her problem," I snapped.

"Don't talk like that," Bolek said. "She deserves the best."

"You are the best," I assured him.

"Sophie says Magdalena is coming to New York."

"She is? When?"

"I don't know when," Bolek said. "It is for publicity."

It turned out that Maggie and her husband were supposed to make a grand entrance to the city with her husband to plug *The Good and the True*, which the studios were already calling the greatest drama since *30 Seconds over Tokyo*. The visit was still some months away, but I was dismayed. I wasn't sure what I was supposed to do while Maggie occupied the city. I prepared for the invasion early by stocking up on records of Mahler symphonies and Richard Strauss tone poems that would blast within my several thousand square feet in an accompaniment of studied mirth and ironic ambiguity.

Even during the awful days of Bolek's surgery and his relatively slow recovery in New York Hospital, a day didn't go by when I didn't revise my plans for dealing with Maggie's presence in the city. I would lock the doors, I would take the week off, explore New Jersey, move in with Paul and Carla.

I spent days at New York Hospital, as did Suzi. We shared a little solarium at the end of Bolek's floor, as she embroidered pillowcases and riffled through fashion magazines. "The Germans say," she told me, "that the devil finds work for those who are lazy bums." When we were not in the solarium, we sat at the foot of Bolek's bed while he gathered strength. Dr. Heller was more than satisfied, he was jubilant. "That's it, there is no more," he said, slapping his palms together like cymbals. "You will lead your normal life again."

And normal it more or less was again. The first time Bolek and Suzi had sex—both of them watching his penis intently, he and she both told me later, rejoicing to see it make its painful arc to stiffness—they not only made love, they decided to get married. It was not until after they exchanged vows in the living room of the Sutton Place apartment, with a handful of friends looking on, that Suzi began complaining to *me* that now it was "just in and out." I asked her not to tell me things like that. "Nothing comes out of him," she sobbed. "I am such a young woman still."

The week before Maggie was to arrive, amid the fanfare reserved for legends in the making, Gus the bartender at the Cedar Bar read me an Earl Wilson column that verbalized America's adoration for legend material. "It is said," wrote Earl, "that a beauty such as Maggie Coe, a natural beauty, a real American beauty, has not been seen in Hollywood since the Ice Age."

"Some American beauty," I told Gus. "A Polish Jew like me."

"This is a melting pot," Gus retorted. "We're all Americans now."

At Sophie and Kor's insistence, I went with them to Grand Central to meet the train that carried the celebrated duo east. By the time we arrived, the crowd at the gate was so enormous that we had to request a police escort to force our way through and down the stairs to the platform. I chose to stay in the middle of the staircase, where I had a view of the train but didn't have my nose rubbed in America's perfect couple. Maggie had been hailed by Hedda Hopper as the new Greta Garbo, mysterious and unfathomable, stirring people up, causing the creation of fan clubs, their only icons thus far the few publicity photographs that Warner Brothers had issued. Earl Wilson had reported in another column that Jed Seacliff called Maggie "pun-kin," and now the press corps and the fans were pressing close to the incoming train chanting, "Give us the look, pun-kin, pun-kin. . . ."

My heart pounded. Finally I caught a glimpse of her. She was smiling, waving, blowing kisses to the crowd as a uniformed escort tried to make room for pictures to be taken. "Pun-kin, pun-kin," the crowd cheered. Maggie almost didn't look like Maggie, but I couldn't put my finger on why. I craned my neck to find Jed Seacliff. I asked my neighbors on the stairs if they knew where he was, but no one did. Maggie embraced Sophie, then Kor. I decided that I had had enough. I pushed my way back up the stairs and took a bus downtown to the Cedar Bar.

I had Gus all to myself except for "As the World Turns" on the radio. I finished my first beer, then he came over. "You look sick," he said. "Did she come?"

"She's here, all right," I reported.

Gus leaned over the bar and propped his big bald head on his elbows. "Same girl?" he asked.

"I hardly recognized her."

Gus pressed me another draft. "Well, you know," he explained, "they have to change the way you look out there so you'll look just right for the cameras."

"They did their magic on her," I said.

"Did you know that you can get the most beautiful girl in the world, you take a picture of her and she turns to shit?"

"You really know about these things," I said.

"Conversely," he said, "a dog can become a real dish."

If there had been window shades in Abe's loft, I would have pulled them down and painted by artificial light. Because there were none, I insulated myself with my Mahler, with one symphony after another. I turned the volume up so loud that nothing could distract me, not the downstairs door, not the ring of the phone. Mahler turned out to be the perfect choice. The majestic themes constantly undermined by the carefree strains of street bands, the swift changes of mood, the heart-rending tunes cracked wide open by the pounding blows of hammers, gave substance to my own ambivalence about Maggie. In the back of my mind, I still entertained the notion that she would always be mine, and with equal conviction I understood that she was lost to me forever. My body alternately pined for her, then shook with rage and self-recrimination at the emptiness I'd helped engineer.

The telephone must have rung—the doorbell, too—though its unpleasant sound was absorbed by Mahler's torrential orchestration. Not until I needed a pack of cigarettes did I find a note pushed under the downstairs door. On Warner Brothers stationery, Maggie's loopy handwriting invited me to the St. Regis to see her. "Please," written twice, was underlined with a red pen.

I called her that evening. It wasn't easy to get through, and even when I was finally connected to her room, I could hear the racket inside. "I thought you'd never call," Maggie whispered into the phone from her bedroom. "I've saved later this evening for you."

"That's nice, but I have to work."

"Adam, it's *me*," Maggie said. "We looked all over for you at the train—"

"What time do you want me?"

"It's bedlam here," she said. "I'll have everyone out by nine."

"How about another day?" I could hardly believe how cool my self-righteousness could make me sound.

"Tonight," Maggie insisted, and that was that.

"What about him? Is this the night we meet?"

"Jed's not here," Maggie said. "He's coming just for the opening."

Thinking about the St. Regis, I realized how dirty, how badly dressed, had badly fed I was. I hadn't been at Kor's to sleep for weeks. I hadn't taken a shower since Sutton Place a week before, and my last regular meal was there as well. I looked into the little tin mirror from Abe's bootcamp days that he'd left near the toilet. I needed a shave. I hadn't slept well since the *King Haakon VII*. Tough shit, I thought. This is how I am, this is how Maggie gets me.

At the St. Regis, the desk clerk stopped me in my tracks. He wouldn't even call Maggie's suite to announce me. "May cholera take you," I told him in Polish, and jostled my way into the street again. I called Maggie from a pay phone. "They won't let me in," I said.

She didn't believe me. "Please come, Adam," she said.

"You'll have to meet me downstairs," I said. "I'll be with the doorman."

Maggie appeared in sunglasses and a wide-brimmed hat turned down over her face. No one could have known who she was. I certainly didn't.

"You look terrible," Maggie said as we weaved our way through the fancy luggage in the lobby. "What happened to you?"

We stood as inconspicuously as spies in a corner of the elevator. "It's the real me," I said under my breath. "No cover-ups."

We couldn't even wait to get off the elevator to snarl. "Some people's business *requires* cover-ups," she said. "Appearance is to the movies as growling is to the artist."

"Is this the Marxist I used to know?" I asked our fellow passengers.

On the top floor, I followed Maggie down the dimly lit hall. "Don't be hard on me," Maggie said as she took off her hat and glasses. "Just look what's happened." Maggie's eyes were round and black with mascara. "We knew we were going to make it, Adam, but isn't this ridiculous?" As she shook out her hair, the heavy locks bounced without losing their shape, like the limbs of an olive tree. The only person in the room with us was a hotel maid who was changing the water in the flower vases, *all* the flower vases.

"It's happened to you," I said. "Just to you."

"You're having a show," Maggie said.

"What is that compared with being the perfect American couple, beauty and the beast, the innocent and the needy?"

"Why are you being such a shit? What should I have done?"

I took her by the shoulders and held her at arm's length. "I would have married you if you wanted," I said.

"You don't care about me," Maggie said. "You're in love with some romantic idea of me, some goddam Tristan and Isolde. You're as German as the Germans." Maggie bared her newly capped teeth. "You are a ruthless son of a bitch." She backed off to the mantelpiece, where she took a cigarette from a leather box and lit it. "You only care about yourself. When you need me, you take me. When you don't, you let me go." She went into the bedroom. I sat down on the couch. The maid stared at me icily. I hadn't only dared to yell at Miss America, I was sullying the hotel's furniture with my ass. "You don't even know what a prick you are," Maggie shouted in to us. The maid nodded in agreement. "Marriage isn't all I wanted. I wanted children and so does Jed. You always hated the whole idea of family."

"I still do," I said.

"Jed can afford to be tender. He isn't afraid to love. He'll be a real father."

"If you needed a father figure, I could have lent you one of mine. I'm a connoisseur of father figures. I've got Bolek and Kor and Grosz, even Lou Kaitz wants to be my father."

"That's not what I was looking for."

"Why not? You've never had a father either. What bothers me about your new daddy is that he also sticks it inside you—"

"Adam!"

"Doesn't he?" The maid stood by the door for a moment waiting for an answer, but Maggie didn't say anything. The maid slammed the door to the suite and left us. Maggie came out, having changed into a skirt and sweater. "Can't we get out of here?" I asked.

"When the lobby empties out," Maggie said.

"I need a drink," I said, and Maggie ordered drinks. When the waiter came, he asked for her autograph. "Damn you," I said to her under my breath.

When we finally escaped through the lobby, I steered us away from the hotel, across Fifth Avenue, headed toward Sixth. From early on, unprepossessing Sixth was my avenue. I felt comfortable there. Fifth was definitely Bolek's. On Sixth Avenue, everything changed. It was as if the last two years hadn't happened, as if we were walking through the park after Maggie had posed for me as the great Maja. I was embarrassed for the things I'd just said. I ached for the glow of her pink lipstick under her white angora sweater, I ached for the time when nothing had been decided. "I'm sorry," I said, taking Maggie's arm. "I'm so very sorry." I could feel Maggie relax the tension in her elbow. "I'm more angry with myself than anything else," I said. "Where is Jed?"

"He's finishing another movie. He'll be here for the opening. He wants to meet you."

The streets were fairly empty. Otherwise we could not have walked unmolested. Maggie's photograph was in every edition of every newspaper. People seemed to long for a new idol and it looked as if Maggie was going to be it. We looked into the dark windows of the Buckingham drugstore. We walked into the park and sat on a bench while all the lights of New York shone brightly for us. For a long time, we said nothing. Maggie put her head on my shoulder. I turned my face to her and smelled the perfume in her hair. I so wanted to burrow through those heavy locks to smell Maggie underneath. But I held back. "Is the movie good?" I asked.

"It's a hackneyed story, but it's pretty good," Maggie said. She was tired and spoke quietly.

"Was it hard work?"

"A lot of waiting around, a lot of time doing nothing. Not really hard work. Nervous work. I was terrified."

"What will you do next?"

She sat up. "It depends on what happens to this one," Maggie said. "Will you come to the opening?"

"I don't know."

"Come, Adam. It's *my* first premiere. You have to come."

I walked Maggie back to the St. Regis. Publicity had lined up another full day of interviews. Under the bright awning of the hotel, we shook hands goodnight, and I walked down to Gramercy Park to Kor's.

The next day, the persistent honking of a car below Abe's loft finally got my attention. The *Resurrection* Symphony had effectively absorbed the telephone. I looked down to see a frantic Sophie yelling up at me while the chauffeur of a long black limousine pounded on the downstairs door. The winos had spotted them from as far away as Astor Place, and I saw them coming from all directions like piranhas toward a wounded crocodile. They ran from doorways and side streets, clutching their paper bags, their coattails flying. I skipped down the stairs to pull Sophie and the beleaguered chauffeur inside.

Sophie was in tears. Matters had taken a strange twist. Jed Seacliff, expected that day, would not come. He was stricken by some sort of diabetic attack, conscious but in serious trouble in a Beverly Hills hospital. "Magdalena is beside herself," Sophie said. "Will you be her escort? Do you have the proper clothes? Oh, darling, what a shock this is. . . ."

I agreed to everything. We had the limousine at our disposal. We ran around the city. We rented a tuxedo. We picked up Sophie's ball gown from the seamstress. We made sure that Kor would pull no surprises by appearing in a bathrobe or worse, an act not beyond him. And on top of it all, Sophie herself was hounded by interviewers. We had lunch with the *Woman's Home Companion*, tea with *Look*.

"How bad is he?" I asked on the way from dry cleaner to manicurist.

"He was unconscious when they brought him to the hospital."

"Sugar fit?"

"He binged, darling. His comrades threw him a goodbye party."

"But it'll all go away, won't it?"

"Magdalena says his kidneys are involved, even worse. . . ."

That night at the Cedar Bar, Gus shoved a *Daily News* under my nose. He stood back with his big arms crossed as I read the Earl Wilson column.

Jed Seacliff, a legend in his own time, ran into a buzz saw as he prepared to join his beautiful wife, Maggie Coe, for the world premiere of their new movie, *The Good and the True*. The name of the buzz saw is diabetes. This brave man, a great American in anyone's book, has turned things around for himself, he has licked all his demons, and he has grabbed on to life again in the person of lovely Maggie. The hospital's not going to keep him long. Jed says he'll fight this thing until it cries uncle. We've seen him do it before. We know he can do it again. We love you, Jed, we love your new movie, and we're head over heels in love with your gorgeous bride.

"Jesus Christ," I said.

"He did it in *Yankee Doodle*," Gus said. "And he did it in *The Star Spangled Banner*."

"And so?"

Gus wiped a tear from his eye. "So he's gonna beat the shit out of this one, too."

The night of the opening of *The Good and the True*, I saw more limousines than I had ever seen before, including Bolek's shows. Practically everyone I knew was there. Bolek and Suzi, Sophie, Kor and Lala, Paul and Carla, Enid Swope with a new beau, bunches of Maggie's Tamarack friends, friends from the Drama Institute, from the Seventh Avenue lofts where she had modeled. Even old Count Kaczka stumbled out of his beige Cadillac with his infirm countess, a shaky lady named Veronica.

Crowds of the curious and the avid milled about behind barriers across the street from the Paramount. Cops on horseback pranced up and down Broadway. Though not allowed within touching distance, everyone had a view of the floodlit movie house, the lines of limousines and their passengers, the gigantic hundred-foot cutout of Maggie bent backward in Jed Seacliff's arms that dominated the avenue.

Maggie looked unbelievable. I felt like a doorman next to her. She had washed the stiffness from her hair so it was full and fuzzy. She wore a long royal-blue strapless gown whose every tuck and fold accented her wide hips, her perfect breasts. She wore long white gloves, and tiers of diamonds on her bare neck and chest. Her head was crowned with a diamond-studded tiara. Bolek had himself placed a dramatic ermine cape on her shoulders. The combination of the young, wholesome Maggie with the wildly sophisticated costume was dazzling. When she got out of our car and stood for a moment like a goddess under the marquee, a spontaneous gasp greeted her, and then the roar. Amid the blinding crackle of flashbulbs, Maggie walked out to the median line in the middle of Broadway, faced her fans, curtsied, and blew kisses up and down the avenue.

"You're a real trooper already," I told her. "That was a wonderful thing to do."

None of it was easy for Maggie. Even as we had driven to the Paramount, I'd tried to keep her mind off her misery by suggesting a deal for her ermine, which I said I needed more than she did. But Maggie worried and felt disloyal. "I should have gone back yesterday," she said. "This is no good without him."

Aside from Maggie's performance, the movie was pretty bad. She was magical, as thrilling as Sylvana Mangano in the rice fields, Anna Magnani in the shadows of Rome's tenements, except that Maggie was funny, an irrepressible comedienne aware of the melodrama that surrounded her. The story could have been made up by us when we were very young and the plots of our lives became the starting point of wild romantic war tales. Maggie was the street-smart Balkan demimondaine turned fearless partisan, moving up and down the craggy slopes like a goat, streaking across the fallow fields like an antelope, pouncing on traitors like a snow leopard. She seemed to me, and to Kor, who *hated* the movie—"all except for Magdalena of course"—to play the part with a marvelously self-reflective intelligence, always looking in on itself, a quality that has kept this mountain operetta playing forever in thousands of little college towns throughout the country, to self-renewing groups of passionately devoted fans.

Even without Jed to guide her, Maggie behaved from beginning to end like a sensitive and practiced celebrity. The glittering house at the Paramount gave her ovation after ovation. Bolek screamed "Bravo!" until he was hoarse and could not speak, Sophie and Kor cried, Maggie's friends shrieked with delight. Maggie kept thanking me for being with her, presenting me as her oldest and dearest friend, gracious enough to come to her rescue. She held on to me as to a lifeline while people pressed all around her after the showing, loving her, wanting to touch her.

When it was over, Maggie and I managed to escape alone. We drove to Eighty-fourth Street, where she spent an hour on the phone with Jed, with the doctors, the nurses who watched over him. Finally satisfied there was nothing more to do, we walked out into the park, our playground that connected Eighty-fourth Street to the Buckingham.

"I guess he's all right for the moment anyway," Maggie said.

"Has this ever happened before?"

"I don't know. There's a lot about his life I still don't know. The doctor said his eyes are affected."

"Why his eyes?"

"I don't know," Maggie said. "Let's try to forget all of that until tomorrow. I should have changed out of this dress."

I was glad she hadn't. I liked being the storybook couple for a night, privileged royalty dogged by sadness and uncertainty, out for an incomparable night. We took a taxi to the hansom cabs on Central Park South. The driver wrapped us in blankets and we entered the park again.

"What did you really think?" Maggie asked, snuggling up to me.

I breathed in the musty smell of the blanket, the manure, the whiskey that wafted back to us from our driver's breath. "I think you were remarkable, sexy, funny, really touching, full of spirit and energy."

Maggie lifted her face toward me. "You really mean that?"

"You are a first-rate actress," I said, moved by my own words as well as Maggie's performance.

She sighed and laid her head on my chest. "I don't even know how your work is going," Maggie said. We were somewhat behind the zoo. "I know nothing about the Bakus or their gallery."

"I'm kind of terrified. I have less than six months to go."

"I want to see your work," Maggie said.

"I want you to."

"When can I?"

"Now."

We took the carriage all the way to the Bowery. "Soon everyone will know your work," Maggie said.

"It's not the same. Even if people like it, it's only painting."

"Don't be silly, Adam. My kind of fame is worth money. It's just entertainment. Yours is forever."

I thought of all the boys the world over, and the toothless old men with glossy pictures of Maggie in their grubby hands, gloating, their eyes half-closed, breathing hard, raising a sweat. "People are going to name their kids after you," I said. "The stalls in Grand Central will be packed with bums jerking off over you."

"It goes with the job," Maggie said in a muffled, sleepy voice.

"I don't like it."

"What about the art disciples, the eager students?"

"Not to worry. Nothing sleazy enough there."

Maggie squeezed me. "They're the loose ones. No morals," she said.

Bundled up in back, with just our noses peeking out of the blankets, it was as close as either of us had been to Warsaw in all these years. It was like going home from Bolek's apartment on the Vistula, the little horse bells ringing, the drivers greeting one another in the winter night. "Remember going home from the park in a *dorozhka?*" I asked.

"Yes. And I remember being in Lazienki Park with you. I

was eating an ice cream on a stick, the ice cream inside a tube of striped cardboard. And you didn't have one because you had done something bad. . . ."

"I remember," I said. "I remember what I did. Don't you?"

"No."

"I looked up your dress."

"No!" Maggie said. She sat up and kissed my nose. "You were always filthy."

"It wasn't the only time I looked up your dress. Why can't you remember? It meant *nothing* to you."

"I didn't even know what I owned down there," Maggie said.

"It was at a party at my house. You and I were playing in my room—"

"Oh, Jesus, here we go," Maggie said. "I'm not going to listen to this filth." She covered herself with the blankets again, her face on my chest.

"You're the one who did it."

"I'm not listening," Maggie said.

"You took off your panties and showed me everything."

"You're lying," Maggie said.

"You made me touch it."

"Adam—"

"I loved it," I said.

"I'm sure I didn't," Maggie said.

"You told on me."

"Somebody had to put an end to your career," Maggie said, and kissed my nose again.

"That one cost me more than an ice cream," I said.

"What did they do to child molesters then?"

"They wouldn't let me see you. I wasn't allowed to go to your birthday party."

"It was a great party," Maggie said. "Magicians, clowns, dancing bears, pony rides . . ."

The rest of the way we dreamed. The hooves of our horse echoed off the bleak, empty Bowery. Maggie and I climbed the stairs to Abe's place, where I made us tea and poured two glasses of cognac. Maggie went around the walls looking at the work in progress, holding the cognac with both hands. I went to the windows and stared at the empty street. I heard Maggie put her glass down and then felt her hands slowly come around me, clasping me to her. "My father told me what to expect," she said, "but nothing could have prepared me for this."

"You hate it," I said.

"Speak of magic, Adam, this is either magic or a dream. It changes as you look, as you think. It's a story, interrupted by unexpected guests, by laughter, by shrieks of rage, by non sequiturs. These photographs are horrible, the tubas insane, *Olympia* a howl, as Bolek used to say. And you left the door open, open for me, for everyone to spin their own tales. I've never seen anything like it."

"Maggie—"

"Where does this come from? My God, do I really know you?"

"You know me."

Maggie laughed. "The little beaver family," she said, "and the block of—what is it?—cans of corn?"

"*The Family Unit*, it's called. And by the way," I said, pointing to my *Arnolfini* couple, "that's a wedding present."

"Oh, Adam, I love them, and Jed is going to love them, too," Maggie said, putting her arms round me and breathing her hot, hot breath into my chest.

"How can I watch you leave tomorrow? What am I going to do?"

Maggie held on to me, then began to cry, wetting my rented white dress shirt right through. I kissed her hair gently, carefully, holding back. I knew that her tears were mostly for Jed, though maybe a little for me. I walked her over to one of the folding chairs. I refilled our glasses of cognac. I spoke to fill the silence. "Your father was touched by this stuff and he touched me. Carla is great because she puts it into historical perspective. Paul enjoys it, which I love. My friend Strawberry's threatened by it."

It felt as if we were children again and I had to amuse her. On rainy days when the governesses wouldn't go to the park. I had to invent stories to tell Maggie, to keep her from going home to play with her dolls. I had to keep talking to prevent her from lying in bed alone at the St. Regis. I began speaking

Polish to her, and Maggie spoke Polish back to me. I knew more of the language than she did, for she never spoke it with Sophie or Kor. We sang a stanza of the Polish national anthem, with the slouchy Arnolfinis/Seacliffs behind us, with Maggie's diamonds sparkling under the fluorescent painting lights, with her ermine held high above her head like a triumphant banner in the midst of battle. Like lunatics, we sang the lyrics— "March, march, Dombrowski!"—as if it had been *our song*, our crazy lullaby.

"I have to lie down," Maggie said suddenly, looking totally exhausted. "Don't stop talking. Sing to me, talk me to sleep."

I fluffed up the pillows and pulled back the blankets, but Maggie didn't want to get under the covers. She took off her diamonds, she loosened her royal-blue dress, which came right down to her ankles. I slipped off her golden shoes and rubbed her feet. Maggie put her arms up, an invitation for a goodnight kiss. I knelt beside her and lightly kissed her lips, then, as she was already half asleep, my fingers traced her heavy eyebrows, her cheeks, her parted lips.

I poured myself another cognac and pulled a chair up to the card table, from which I could see beautiful sleeping Maggie. On the screen, this face, this long graceful body, became someone else, a glossy version, magnified under water, not quite real. Seen through a lens, through mirrors, stuck on to celluloid, she became their version of beauty, a body disembodied, a faceless face, without an aura, without fragrance, without the imperfections that humanized Maggie's beauty. I got a sketchbook and began exploring her again, intruding, possessing the too-long neck, the nose with an almost imperceptible veer off axis. I made one drawing, then another, and a third. In her sleep, Maggie turned as if she were setting the poses, as if she were aware that she was being created by me. And then she opened her eyes and looked at me. Her lips hardly parted as she tried to say something. I stopped drawing and listened. Her voice found barely enough breath to be heard. But it was heard. "Hold me, Adam," she said.

As in a dream, noiselessly, I lay down next to her, my arms slowly bringing her close, my hands keeping her there. I inhaled her breath as if I'd been away from the earth's sweet atmosphere all these years. *This* was my air, this my native habitat. I held her as she moved in and out of sleep, murmuring something incomprehensible, then breathing evenly again. Her hand stetched out in sleep, then came back around me. Our bodies curled and touched everywhere, from cheek to toe. My eyes wouldn't close. I wanted to remember every bit of smooth, warm skin, every curve, every patch of elbow and knee. I took off her bra, her panties, and I pulled her to me again, my hands unable to stop themselves from clutching, memorizing all the dips, the slopes, plunging into downy crevices, claiming her more recklessly now, nearly out of control. I sat up to look at her, then began exploring with my lips. My mouth found her breasts, her nipples, her belly. I began to cry softly, aware how soon she would leave, wanting my tears to fill her belly button like a tiny puddle of champagne. I spread her legs gently and burrowed my face into the hot wetness, drinking her like wine, pulling her into my mouth, surrounded by her, unaware of anything but her. From miles away where her face was I heard her low keening sound, the steady moan I hadn't heard for so long. I ached to be near that, too. I slid up Maggie's body and we drank greedily from each other's mouth, and then I was inside her, our hips moving slowly, languorously, making circles. We began to move faster, impatiently teasing the very cores from deep inside, our joy building until nothing remained but the torrent I was pouring into her, wave after wave of imprisoned desire.

We slept until the first rays of the sun found the bed. When our eyes opened, they were filled with love and grief and longing. There was too much to say, so we said nothing.

Maggie put on her clothes and I ran down to find a taxi. Wrapped in my raincoat, she got in and, still not speaking, we drove to Eighty-fourth Street, where she found some old clothes to wear. Sophie, not quite awake, was puzzled. "You were a great star last night, my darling Maggie," she said. We stuffed Maggie's gown and jewels and the ermine into paper bags and drove to the St. Regis. Fighting to contain my tears, I helped her out into the street. And then I let her go.

A few hours later, Maggie flew to Los Angeles.

12

*T*he Baku Gallery was nearly ready. Right on Fifty-seventh Street, the upkeep must have been fabulous, but Timor and Draga decided to engage only in what they called "little barter" until my show opened early in October. Selling an occasional Magritte must have at least paid the rent, while swapping a faded Modigliani for a cryptic Duchamp box set the tone for things to come.

"What can your uncle do to help?" Draga asked me. "Would he make a statement—no, a complaint, to the press about his furs after you had your way with them?"

"I don't want to use him," I said.

"Don't be naïve, Adam," Timor said. "This is a business like any other. We need all the help we can get." He turned to his wife. "We could use some of Mr. Casimir's models as well. And what about Maggie Coe? *Cara mia*," he cried as he threw up his arms, "that would bring them in from the Bronx!"

I didn't want any part of this. If this business was like any other, then I didn't want to know about it. For me, art and money didn't mix. I wasn't entirely naïve and needed no reminders of the kinship of fashion with art. But deep inside I believed that serious art was rewarded only in heaven, that the only rich artist was a dead artist.

The Bakus were beginning to be quoted in the art press and the popular press as well. Most of what they said they positioned carefully in the crackling middle ground between the ambiguous and the outrageous. "What is art?" Timor was asked by Inez Robb of the International News Service.

"Art is shit," Timor was quoted as saying, though the two middle letters were dashes in the text.

"Are you seriously saying that art is s--t?" asked Miss Robb.

"Do you mean to tell me it isn't?" an unbelieving Timor Baku was supposed to have replied.

"And that," Inez Robb concluded, "is what is happening to the flowering New York art scene."

I went to see Kor at Lala's Park Avenue apartment. "I don't know what to make of any of this," I told him.

"It is *their* business, *chéri*," Kor said. "Don't concern yourself with it."

"Art must stand alone," I proclaimed, "without publicity. Can you imagine staging some stunt to drum up trade?"

Kor was licking envelopes as we spoke, linen envelopes with paisley linings, each addressed in his ornate script to friends overseas. "On the other hand," Kor said, "an artist must live." He took a bottle of white wine out of the fridge and poured out two glasses. "We need sponsors, Adam, we need support."

"But the risks . . ."

"Yes, yes," Kor said. "Let all that happen somewhere else. In the background we need our Boleks, our Lalas, our Guggenheims, our Bakus. Even in this country, where art has always been suspect, the legend of the starving artist has made art tolerable to the burgers. But it is fast disappearing. Artists will pop up everywhere to satisfy the market. The market will cry out for new commodities. Do you understand, *chéri*? Like soybeans, like antique furniture, like bouillabaisse. But also something else." He stood up and pounded his chest like a gorilla. "These people are starved for feeling, *any* feeling. In this country, they kill to feel something." He sipped his wine delicately. "They need their melodrama like soup, and that, too, the artist will supply." He got up to look for his cigarette holder. "They will have their soup, but what to eat with the soup? For there is no bread in America! I cannot live without bread." He licked another envelope shut. "I am writing my friends everywhere, even in Germany," he said. "I need my old friends, I need bread."

"You will see, there will be bread," I said. "You belong here now. You have friends here, you have Maggie and Sophie and Lala and me. . . ."

"I know, I know," Kor said, "but *belong*? I don't belong. I will die from not belonging. I was always a tourist here. Look how long I tried to become a citizen. They don't want me. They call me a premature antifascist."

"Something is stirring here. There's hope—"

"Hope?" he said, smacking his forehead. "This 'un-American' business is hope? It is barbarism."

"We should visit Poland," I suggested.

"Poland?" He looked at me as if I could not possibly say the right thing on this day. "It's the same thing only worse. Over there we are un-Polish. We are Zionists and Bolsheviks. Here we are *dupes*, there we are dead Jews."

Lala came in, carrying Bloomingdale's shopping bags. "Kor and I will take a trip around the world," she told me.

"A wonderful idea," I said.

"He misses his old friends, don't you, darling? And we'll spend some time with Maggie."

"Jed is a little better," Kor said.

"I know."

"It stopped with one eye," Kor said. "Thank God. That's not so bad, but then again, who knows?"

I talked to Maggie often. I even talked with Jed Seacliff, whose generosity made me feel guilty. Still, I couldn't stop telling Maggie that I adored her.

Two months before my opening, Maggie sent a shock wave over the coast-to-coast telephone cable. "I'm pregnant," she said.

I said nothing for an instant, and then, "How pregnant? It's mine!"

"I don't know," Maggie said.

"I know. Three months? Four months? It must be mine. I knew it then—"

"Adam, I love you both so much," Maggie said.

I celebrated with Paul and Carla, who were uneasy commemorating the deed. "You just don't know," Carla said as I popped the champagne cork.

"If it's got diabetes, it's his," I acknowledged, but I was sure that Maggie was making our love child and that someday I would take my place as its father.

I called Maggie more and more often. Sometimes I talked with Jed, about movies, about art, about life and its surprises. He was cordial and easy to talk to. Then, like a maniac, I questioned Maggie about her health, about her diet, her weight.

"Both of you have to stop this," she said. "I am very well. I live among people who worship health. I will take care of myself, Adam, I really will."

Now that Bolek seemed to be all mended, that some possibility of a life with Maggie, or Maggie *and* Jed, was emerging almost on the very eve of my show, I became racked with doubt. "The stuff's all cheap and unearned," I said to Paul and Carla, whose place was a haven for me.

"Don't be ridiculous," Carla said. "It's the freshest work around."

"Strawberry was right," I moaned. "You don't tell stories on canvas. Canvas is for paint only."

"Just think what you're doing to people," Paul said. "You are going to make them *see* differently, *think* differently. . . ."

"They'll hate it, they'll run," I said, drowning myself in the vodka I brought.

"What key is your stuff in?" Carla asked.

"C-sharp minor," I said without hesitation.

"Now you're talking," Paul said.

"You know, Charlie Parker was no fool," I said.

"You're damn right he wasn't."

"I've become more of an architect, too," I said. "My old stuff was sentimental, like improvisation. Maybe you're right, maybe this stuff's more than that."

"C-sharp minor's pretty complicated," Paul said.

"It ain't the national anthem," I said, momentarily cheered up.

"Look at it this way," Carla said. "If art is just a hunk of nature, who needs art? If it's just an exploration of *angst* or nostalgia for purer times, then fuck it."

As my opening approached, and even as I saw the stuff disappear into crates, then into the backs of trucks, I went around the empty studio punching walls, then sitting like a catatonic on the floor in a corner. I dreamed that my show took place in the silvery salons of Prince Casimir Furs, and that my audience was Bolek's audience, foremost among them the Duke and Duchess of Windsor. They sat in butterfly chairs, and as models holding my work paraded in front of them, the near-royal couple fell fast asleep.

In fact, things turned out quite differently, and the Duke and Duchess were about the only people who weren't there.

On the afternoon of the show, I went to an old Jed Seacliff movie, the nearly forgotten *Joe Pinto Story*, about the great Dodger infielder who succumbed to an inherited heart disease. The near-hysterical daytime audience, including me—ready to cry for any cause—howled with grief as Joe Pinto collapsed between first and second base. Even in this tearjerker, with Jed not at his best, he was so upright, so entirely sympathetic, that entrusting him with the love of one's life wasn't as humiliating as it might have been. Then I went to Sutton Place to change. I put on one of my old Prince Casimir suits, which Bolek had stored in the back of a walk-in closet. Suzi begged me to sit on a hall chair before leaving. "My mother always made us sit before a long journey," she explained. I walked over to the gallery, which, except for the Bakus and some uniformed waiters, was empty.

It didn't stay empty long. Even though the Bakus had been advertising the show for a couple of weeks, I was astounded by the response. Before the sun had fully set, people were elbow to elbow in every room, their bodies obscuring everything that hung or stood beside the walls. Kor brought the Surrealists, including Dali. George Grosz arrived with his wife. Abe Strawberry brought his lovely patroness of the arts and a handful of Abstract Expressionists. Among their ranks, only the Old World de Kooning wore a tie and jacket, though his jacket was threadbare and white. "Doesn't he know that it's nearly winter?" Bolek asked. Count Bruno came with Sophie. Enid's fiancé, a curator at the Metropolitan, arrived with Enid. The Weinglasses brought Francesca, who had reconsidered her radicalism and was studying pastoral counseling in Chicago.

Bolek went around from piece to piece, smiling proudly. He touched them all, rightfully feeling a sense of ownership, having contributed so much to their birth. He greeted people as if they had come to *his* house, *his* party. He constantly surveyed and reappraised the crowd, pleased with their number, with their animated talk, with the atmosphere of discovery. He boasted to George Grosz that his nephew's breakthrough came in the salons of Prince Casimir Furs, "with the help of your brilliant teaching, maestro."

"Ach," Grosz said, "my help was nothing next to yours. To paint, you need capital, and you have provided both money and merchandise." They looked like a couple of Swiss bankers chatting in their Zürich boardroom.

"I continue to love your painting, which now hangs in Sutton Place," Bolek said.

"It is well placed and therefore my pleasure, sir," Grosz said, bowing.

When Suzi joined them, shaking hands energetically with her countryman, Grosz and Suzi together looked as if they had come off the pages of *Ecce Homo,* Grosz's great portfolio, the leering old burger looking up to the luscious Rhine maiden. I found them a little frightening.

But this was the Bolek I loved, Bolek the proud father, Bolek the bountiful, Bolek the grand. Timor Baku, whose antics were more cerebral than lavish, recognized Bolek's heartfelt largesse and took pleasure in allowing my uncle to greet people as they came off the elevator, then escorted them to the table laden with hors d'oeuvres and liquor.

Sophie came up behind me. "Let me feast my eyes upon you," she said, flushed with excitement. Her pearls dipped lusciously into the depression between her breasts. "If only Maggie could have come, darling, everything would have been perfect."

"This is no time for her to travel," I said.

"I'm glad you're so understanding," Sophie said, squeezing my hand.

Count Bruno, silver-haired, tan, and athletic, had eyes only for Sophie, and when Dali dropped at her feet and threw his arms around her knees, I thought the end of the celebration had come. But Bruno surprised us all, smiling grandiloquently. Only when Dali's face approached Sophie's seductive bosom did Bruno gently pull his lady out of harm's way.

I walked around the rooms with Carla. It wasn't easy to see the walls, but the glimpses I caught pleased me. We watched the Weinglasses approach the *Arnolfinis.* Carla held her breath. It was an extraordinary union of art and life. Zyga and Basia Weinglass—in stature, abundance, and paranoia—*were* my version of the Arnolfinis. But they didn't see it that way. They laughed, smacking their lips with pleasure. Family, to the Weinglasses—and to everyone else here—was an uncontested entity, as unchallenged, as sacred, as houses and cars and dogs. The Weinglasses chortled knowingly. "I could have glorified cannibalism and they would have smiled," I said to Carla.

The din became overpowering. My ears buzzed. I worried about the jostling and pushing. The more the gallery jumped, the less the paintings mattered. I didn't know if the festivities celebrated the reemergence of the playful, the contradictory in art, or if the mix of society and artists in the same cauldron boiled up a license for carousal. By early evening, the theme of family was completely overshadowed by drunken cheer.

When Paul and Lou Kaitz stepped off the elevator, the crowd parted, clearing a path directly to me. Lou Kaitz knew more people than I'd imagined. Everyone here shared with him a belief in the game of producing wealth, producing objects of value.

Lou Kaitz looked cleaner than anyone else. His complexion remained without blemish, his nails and hair impeccable, the affable glow of his hazel eyes as comforting and innocent as a child's. By now, everyone else looked as if they had spent the night in their clothes.

"We are seeing history in the making," Lou said as he let go of my hands.

Paul said, "I remember the days when owning a Krinsky was an urgent, passionate need."

"Without redeeming social value," I added.

"Never again will anyone jerk off over Krinsky's version of a Botticelli Venus," Paul said, and Lou howled.

"All right, boys," Lou said, "it's time for business," and left us to ask Timor Baku what there was left to buy.

Little red dots began appearing next to the paintings, and as they did, strangers looked at me with the awe reserved for the rich. The Weinglasses seemed overwhelmed by what was happening. At one point, there was a line of people trying to negotiate with the Bakus. Elated, Bolek said, "You know, darling, I think maybe I'm in the wrong business."

An enormous Chinese vase, filled with a rain forest of lush flowers, was carried off the elevator by two men in white. Word went around that it was from Maggie Coe. Draga, who realized that another object could not withstand the crush of the crowd, had them put it into her office. My friend Jeannie Hebert, who was still in Paris, sent a lemon tree in a big wooden bucket. Inside an envelope, together with her wishes, was a snip of her Persian lamb.

I had one eye on Willem de Kooning, whose work I loved above all the other Abstract Expressionists. He kept pretty much to himself, and went around studiously from piece to piece, pushing his way through the groups that blocked access to the work. Before he left, he came to me, took my hand, and said, "We must drink together and talk." He left early, escorted to the elevator by Yvette, who had also kept to herself until de Kooning found her. Abe Strawberry was alternately amused, excited, and furious with what he saw. "You motherfucker," he whispered in my ear. "Nothing I told you mattered."

"Not true," I tried to assure him. "You opened my eyes to all sorts of new things."

"What things, you devil?"

"That it's okay to leave a mess. That 'finished' and 'polished' are bourgeois ideas, like the crap about cleanliness and godliness. You taught me to go ahead and do what you *have* to do." Abe looked pleased.

Kor and Grosz kept bumping into each other over the course of the evening. "What happened to you, George?" Kor asked Grosz. "Once you were a good dialectician. Just look at you now. . . ."

"Listen to the man who calls me a sellout," Grosz said. "One foot in the party, one foot out. A little dream work, a little *frottage,* a little undecipherable shit."

Dali wouldn't even speak to Grosz. He wandered between Sophie and Suzi and Carla until he tired of them all. He was drawn inexorably to Lou Kaitz, with whom, in low tones, he discussed business. "I want to tell you, monsieur," Dali said to me as Lou beamed, "that Dali delights in your *assemblages.*" He whispered in my ear, "But don't put us poor Surrealists out of business."

The Bakus were thrilled. I think the show surpassed their expectations. Whenever either of them had the opportunity, they found me, stood by my side, and smiled. "There is practically nothing left for the museum people," Timor said. "Mr. Kaitz bought practically every freestanding piece." He looked up at me and grinned. "I did manage to save a couple of major pieces for myself. I shall pay full prices. You are a rich man, Adam."

During the first week, Alfred Barr of the Museum of Modern Art came and stayed two hours. Then he complained to Timor that everything was sold. "I managed to save you a few wonderful pieces," Timor told him, and Alfred Barr put two pieces aside for the museum's collection. Fearing the reaction of the museum's board, though, he told Timor that he would ask his friend Lou Kaitz to buy them and donate them to the museum.

In the middle of the week, I overheard two painters I recognized from the Cedar Bar. "If this is painting," one said, "then I'm going into real estate." Someone else had scrawled "fuck you" on my *Olympia* and it took a full day to repair the damage.

Still, the exhibit was a sensation. The press—editors of feature pages, "women's pages," life-style pages—asked about my life, about how I had come up with such fascinating, provocative ideas. My patience waned quickly. I became callous and unkind. I sat at Lindy's with Deedee Field, a dropout from the University of Oklahoma at Norman and now a very cute assistant editor of *Life*.

"Why the family?" Deedee asked. "Don't you think we should hang on to some traditional values?" She smiled coquettishly.

"Family's okay," I said. "I didn't really mean it."

"Stop pulling my leg," Deedee said. "I know it's sexy to go after sacred cows."

My mouth was full and I washed it down with a glass of wine. "Yes," I said, leering openly at blond, cherubic Deedee. I took the pencil from her hand. "Perhaps you and I . . ."

"You mean couple?" Deedee asked in her best southwestern drawl. "Are you proposing coupling?"

"Just recreationally," I assured her.

"You Europeans," Deedee said with a new intimacy. "You simply reek of corruption."

"Happily, I find Americans equally corrupt," I said.

"Not really corrupt," Deedee said, "but corruptible."

Deedee and I continued the interview the next evening in a little Hungarian restaurant on the East Side. "Tell me," she said in her Oklahoma whine, "do you worship art?"

"Of course I do."

"Sometimes it seems so unavailable," Deedee complained.

"Nonsense."

"I simply *love* your work, Adam, but why are there such— sloppy places?"

Our knees touched under the table. "I care only for the main impact, Deedee," I said, staring into her eyes. "I don't worry about details."

"I'd always thought that art was totally serious," Deedee said.

"It is, Deedee, it's deadly serious."

"But your work makes me smile."

"Shame on you, Deedee," I said. "If I can't trust you, who can I trust?"

Deedee's article was illustrated with a few reproductions. "Adam Krinsky," she wrote, "is an imposing, wiry man who finds it almost impossible to sit still for any length of time. 'I get bored easily,' he says. But the boredom has paid off handsomely. To keep himself interested, he has never stopped experimenting, and his paintings, collages, and freestanding figures have managed to arouse the admiration of fellow artists and the excitement of the public at large."

"The latest darling of the art world," the *Time* reviewer wrote, "is Adam Krinsky, whose new works are beautifully displayed at the Baku Gallery's maiden exhibition. They command up to $5,000 apiece and look like they're being bought up by major museums. The theme of the show is *The Family*, which Krinsky manages to portray in a stunning array of guises, including a solid block of marble entitled *The Family Unit 3* and a grouping of some dozen stuffed beavers munching on a twig and dressed in little fitted beaver coats. There are times when Adam Krinsky seems to be more whimsical than profound, but this work can't ever be called boring. Asked about his most important influences, Krinsky named R. Z. Kor, George Grosz, Francisco Goya, and Charlie Parker. It is impossible not to enjoy this work."

And in *Art News:* "Such public demand for such private images is one of the art boom's most fascinating phenomena. The art public, especially the rich, are starved for subjective experience. They buy this work to share in Krinsky's protest against a cellophane-wrapped world."

I could not escape the effects of my celebrity in the hermetic little art world. Strangers accosted me to talk about mainland China, about the Hudson River school of painting, about the kind of eggs I liked for breakfast. They wanted to talk about anything, to be instructed in everything, they wanted to get laid. And money. I was getting rich on my labors. I loved spending the money, I despised wanting, *needing* more. I was getting calls from brokers and accountants whose tone of voice said: Now you are a grown-up, it is time to give up your charming but stupid naïveté.

The more I was treated like a star, an original, the less original I felt and the harder it was to think about painting again. Every attempt to continue drained my head of ideas. I had never known of any artist who had one moment of glory and nothing more, but that was precisely what I feared was happening to me. And all those themes of my life that I had always thought to be crucial, the Goya themes of war and death and destruction, were still unexpressed. Somewhere at my core, the quiet pool of my history was beginning to seethe. My belly ached and I had a hard time eating. I never was much good at expressing what Goya had been able to express with such superhuman force, such magnificent abandon. My losses, my war, my knowledge and memory of death remained on the level of melodrama. I needed to plunge again, to find my way back to this center.

In an interview with the *Times* just before Kor and Lala were to leave on their round-the-world junket, he told the reporter that he didn't know if he was ever coming back to America. After their departure, articles began to appear discussing the loss of the best of the exiles. "Artists like R. Z. Kor are leaving without ever having been properly appreciated or truly thanked for the services they have rendered to the cultural life of this country. Now a center for the arts, America is forgetting her debt to people like Ernst, Dali, Kor, Brecht, Adorno, and Breton. Would any of this flowering have happened if not for these émigrés who enriched and revitalized every aspect of American culture?"

Together with the departed artists, this small flurry of articles was quickly forgotten, except for some of the authors who were subsequently examined by the House Un-American Activities Committee and then could no longer find work.

I flew out to California to visit Maggie. I paced in the aisle of the Constellation, picturing my meeting with Jed Seacliff.

How much did he know? How much did it matter if he knew? I wavered between an image of the enemy and the sharer of what I loved most in the world. As I stepped off the plane, I felt ready to offer my friendship.

All the reports were true. Jed was entirely lovable, gracious and warm. His thick glasses, his dyed hair now growing back to its natural white, the deep furrows on his suntanned neck and forehead made me feel a little like a child, while Maggie's position seemed to fluctuate between child to one, mother to the other, and lover to both. I'm sure Jed saw me exactly as I was and accepted me as such, a part of his family, a brother, a rival, a partner in Maggie's past, a passionate observer of her present, and—I'm certain he knew it—the lover and companion of her future. But as generous a spirit as he truly was, I felt uncomfortable. Neither Maggie nor I was willing or able to sneak around behind Jed's back. The only indiscretion I allowed myself was to spend as much time as possible with my head resting gently on Maggie's swelling belly, listening to the quickening life inside it. Maggie glowed with contentment. Only Warner Brothers was furious that their new star waddled like a duck.

Midwinter, a baby girl was born to the three of us. Jed and Maggie named her Maria, my mother's name. Sophie went out to Brentwood just before the birth and stayed a week. When she came back, she said that Maria Seacliff reminded her of my mother. "It's rather uncanny, darling," Sophie told me.

In early spring I went to see Sophie just before she was to sail to Italy to join Bruno for a couple of months. She had been planning this trip for a long time. She had booked passage on the *Cristoforo Colombo*. "The Michelangelo *Pietà* goes back to Rome on this crossing," she told me. "I have arranged to have the adjoining stateroom. This time I shall present myself to my Bruno in the company of true magnificence. It will help him think of me as enduring, eternal."

I took her to the pier, where we both watched the *Pietà* in its gigantic crate being lifted high above the beautiful white ship and then lowered slowly, carefully, into its hold.

Bolek and Suzi came with a basket of fruit. "Promise me

you'll paint," Sophie said as the great stacks bellowed a warning for all visitors to leave the ship.

"Of course I will," I said. "What else would I do?"

"He is banned from the fur business," Bolek promised.

"Remember, darling, the world awaits your new work. It trembles with anticipation." Sophie hugged me.

I stayed at the pier alone for a long time watching the *Cristoforo Colombo* disappear. Years ago we had all converged on this little island, and now, like leaves in the wind, we were off in all directions.

13

Bolek had never seen my Vermont house, which is in a remote part of the state called the Northeast Kingdom.

"You say this is in America?" Bolek had asked when I first bought it a year ago.

"Of course it's in America," I said.

"There is a king?"

"It's just a name, Bolek," I told him.

"Better look out for cossacks," he said.

The Northeast Kingdom has entered my dreams as cossack country, the vast flat land below Lithuania with its scrubby pines, tiny backward villages, thatched-roof houses, and miracles.

Bolek's voice on the phone pierced my exile.

"It is nothing to worry about," he began, consoling me even before I had reason to be upset. "The doctor wants me to rest."

"Are you in bed?"

"Where else can I rest? I am in bed, but not for long," Bolek said. "When do I see you, darling? Will you ever leave your country paradise?" He laughed. The joke—he never seemed to tire of it—was that a few miles from my house was a town called Eden. Have I found my Eve? Have I met the serpent? What about God? In fact, once he was convinced that the Northeast Kingdom was not a part of the Holy Russian Empire, he loved the idea of my being there. "I told you America is a paradise," he said.

"When do you want to see me?" I asked, knowing that the answer determined the gravity of his condition.

"Now."

Early the next morning, I left my lovely house, half in a grove of tall cedars, half facing a ten-acre meadow hayed by my neighbor, Wendell Anderson. Wendell flagged me down as I drove slowly over the early spring potholes. I told him where I was going and he assured me that he would look after everything, as if there were things to look after. No one ever traveled on our dirt road except those of us who lived there.

It was a bright, balmy morning. Even the north country was in bud and flocks of starlings chirped along Airport Road.

On the first plane out, I sat next to an attractive young woman named Nancy. She was wearing a short skirt whose hem lay halfway up her hefty thighs. I felt a little irritated with myself for always choosing to be distracted by the Nancys, for always being aware of—no, on the lookout for—female flesh. I wondered if anything *ever* would be solemn enough to negate this obsessive voyeurism. Nancy twisted her finger around a chain that hung from her neck. She looked to be about twenty.

"Are you a student at the university?" I asked.

Nancy said she was, as her fingertips, like feathers, now moved along her stockinged thighs.

"What are you studying?"

"Art," she said.

"Yes? Why here?"

"Why not?" Nancy asked, her eyes busy taking the measure of the rolling green hills below us.

"It's not their best department," I said.

"No?" She examined me more carefully. "You look familiar.

Have I seen you around school? You're a history teacher," she announced.

"Why a history teacher?"

"A legislator? It's the corduroys and the turtleneck. I'll bet you write . . ."

"Yes. Yes, I do."

". . . and paint."

"You're remarkable," I said.

"The Vermont hills are full of people who write and paint," Nancy said.

"Yes, that's true."

"It doesn't matter what people *do*," Nancy said. "What counts is who they *are*." She laid the palm of her hand flat on her heart. "You look *so* familiar."

"And you, what about you?" I asked. As usual I'd already lost interest, yet I couldn't help asking.

Nancy looked into my eyes. It was her turn to get hooked. "I'm a sculptor," she said. I could picture her full, stocky body at work with chisels and hammers. "I feel a religious affinity with natural forms," Nancy said. She was from New Mexico and looked to the Pueblo Indians as her spiritual guardians. I felt myself beginning to nod off, yet I had asked for this. I forced myself to sit up and listen. Suddenly she stopped talking. I looked up to see her staring at me. Then her mouth opened wide, her eyes dilated, her hand flew to her lips. "Oh, my God," she cried, "you're Adam Krinsky!" I was surprised to be identified by a stranger. I blushed. Nancy looked limp, childlike. "I know your work. I've seen your shows. I can't believe this." Maggie would now be recognized in Pakistan and Mongolia. In spite of my protestations to the contrary, I was enjoying being plucked from anonymity on our twin-engine Yellow Bird over Vermont. "I've seen both your shows at the Baku," Nancy continued. "I've seen you at Abe Strawberry's opening. I've seen you on television. I loved your talk on Jews in art."

"Thank you."

"What are you doing *here*?" she asked.

"I live here, but kind of quietly."

"Oh, God, I feel so dumb," Nancy said.

We shared a cab into the city. Nancy's body was turned toward me, one bare knee up on the torn leather seat. "Can I see you again?" she asked.

"I'm kind of in hiding," I told her. "Why don't you give me your number and I'll call you." I furnished a slip of paper on which Nancy wrote her phone number, then the word *please* underlined twice. As we hurtled onto the Fifty-ninth Street bridge, Nancy's fingers touched my corduroys. "No one will believe this," she said.

I got out on Second Avenue just off the bridge and walked to Bolek's. Rose, in uniform, opened the door for me and a day nurse named Emma followed me into his room. Bolek was sleeping peacefully in spite of the bright river light pouring in through open windows. The curtains in his blue and gold bedroom snapped softly in the fresh breeze. The two Goya prints from the *Disasters of War* that I had bought for him in London hung on a long wall opposite the windows. They were our most prized possessions, these two, reminding us of *our* past. A gold Renaissance candelabrum with two portrait heads struck into its base stood on a long mantel, together with less imposing bric-a-brac. Over Bolek's bed hung a delicate Modigliani painting he had bought from the Bakus. He said the sitter, a tall Twenties kind of woman in a red sheath dress, reminded him of my mother. The Grosz painting now hung in a corner of the living room.

I listened to Bolek's breathing. His face was pale and newly shaved, giving it a bluish cast. Miss Emma must have rubbed too much cream into his skin, for it shone like a varnished mask. I took out my handkerchief to gently wipe his face. He opened his eyes.

"I don't see you how long?" he said as he licked his dry lips. "I never see you. I have some pain, darling."

"I know."

"For what is money? It is nothing."

Rose brought in a tray with compote, tea, two round matzohs. She helped him sit up to eat, then fluffed the three down pillows behind him.

"What a business," Bolek said, lifting a spoonful of cooked fruit to his mouth.

"When did you see Dr. Heller?"

"When? He comes all the time."

"Why all the time?" I asked.

"I don't know why all the time. Probaby *she* asks him." Rose poured me a glass of tea with lemon. "Adam," Bolek said, gesturing with his hand for me to come closer. "I think she wants me to die."

"What are you talking about?"

Bolek pushed the tray down to his knees and lay back on the pillows. He didn't want to bicker about anything. He looked out the window. "If you don't know," he said in almost a whisper, "then we won't talk about it."

Of course I knew, and though I'd never said the words, I'd certainly thought them. Suzi had stopped being the protective, deferential wife some time ago. Like Bolek, I now found her impatient.

"Suzi isn't like that," I said without conviction.

Bolek turned to me for a moment, then back to the windows again. His movement intended to tell me that he couldn't be bothered with the little dishonesties of conversation. Either we stuck to the point or he wasn't interested.

"She has real qualities," I persisted. Bolek wiped his mouth and asked me to take the tray away. "Why did you marry her?" I asked as I set the tray on top of his dresser.

"Come back here," he said. "Sit next to me." He took my hand. His hand was cold. "Just look at her. She is beautiful, she is elegant, she is young. What else could I do?"

"You could have had any beautiful young woman you wanted. You didn't have to marry Suzi."

Bolek was remembering other times. "Sophie," he said, and smiled lovingly. "Sophie was plump, like a big red apple, soft like a seal coat. I wanted her near me all the time. But there was more to my Sophie. There was a wild Russian sable in her, too, something extra and rare. You know what it was? It was Mr. R. Z. Kor in the picture."

"Sophie is a prize. She has something for everyone," I said.

"This is a secret," Bolek said. "There is Russian sable in Suzi, too. Do you promise this is a secret?"

"Yes."

"When I make love to Suzi, I close my eyes and think of Albert Speer."

"Albert Speer?" I nearly choked on a mouthful of tea. "Why Albert Speer?"

"That piece of pigshit," Bolek said, "is maybe the same age as I am. Maybe a little older, I don't know. He sits in his prison, alive and proud. He thinks he has done nothing. He is handsome with those eyebrows. Women like him, that devil. Well, darling, this is the amazing part. Suzi and Albert Speer are born on the same street. When she is a baby, Albert Speer holds her in his arms. I *know* Suzi would love Albert Speer if he is not in Spandau." Bolek paused to catch his breath. "Every time I do it to Suzi, it is like kicking the balls of Albert Speer. It is a little crazy, no?"

"Crazy? It's better than crazy. It's perfect." How could I bear to lose Bolek? His mind had always made priceless connections. I understood them perfectly.

"This is our secret, darling," he reminded me.

"One day Suzi will get everything," I said soberly. "Albert Speer will get it all back."

"I am not stupid," Bolek said. "I will make changes. I will ask Finkelstein. Most of it will go to you."

"Not to me, Bolek. I have everything I need. Maybe you should start a foundation. . . ."

"For what a foundation?"

"I don't know. Students who want to make furs. Or paintings."

Rose announced Dr. Heller, who came in right behind her, rubbing his hands together, smiling. He was wearing a red carnation in the lapel of his black suit. His hair, tinged with gray, was cut very short. On his thick upper lip he sported a small moustache. Dr. Heller examined Bolek, smiling as he palpated, reassuring him, calling him a young man. I could see that Bolek was disgusted. He was not about to answer Heller's stupid questions: Does this hurt? Does that hurt? "Everything hurts, tell him," Bolek finally exploded.

Dr. Heller took me into the living room. "It is everywhere," he said. "there is nothing we can do."

I heard the sharp click of Suzi's footsteps in the hall. She looked tired but beautiful. "I hate that man," she said about the departing Dr. Heller. She kissed me, then we went into Bolek's room together. Suzi was weighed down by Saks parcels. She unpacked a slim box and held up another pair of silk pajamas she had bought for Bolek. He turned his head away.

"Come on, Adam," Suzi said briskly, taking my hand. "I've asked Rose to make us coffee." I sat across the living room from her, watching Suzi take her coat off, then tuck her blouse into her skirt. "When did you get in?" she asked.

"He's very bad," I said.

"Oh, I don't know. Sometimes yes, sometimes no."

"Suzi, do you know everything?"

"I'm his wife."

"It seems to be everywhere. . . ."

Suzi patted a place down for me next to her on the couch. Rose set down a tray with croissants, jams, coffee, all on silver plates, like room service at the Plaza-Athenée. "You never ask about me," Suzi pouted. "This hasn't been easy for me either, you know."

"You seem perfectly well," I said.

"Adam, I know how you love Bolek, but be fair. I am young, living with death, doing the best I can." It was her German accent that I still hated above all else.

"Why did you ever get married?" I asked.

She checked to see if the water had seeped through the filters. "You are impertinent," she said.

"He's so much older. . . ."

"So?"

"And he wasn't well even then."

"Not well? They took everything that had cancer. He was very well. And what a man he was." She pushed my coffee over to me. "Why else would I marry him?"

"The money was good," I suggested.

"I loved him. I still love him. What's the matter, a big artist like you cannot imagine a young woman marrying a man twice her age? Have you ever heard of Maggie and Jed?" Suzi's upper lip was quivering, which indicated the approach of a dark Teutonic battle. "Before I realized what was happening, he could hardly do it anymore," Suzi said. "It was just in and out, he couldn't keep it there. It's not fair—"

"I don't want to hear this, Suzi. Don't say anymore."

Her eyes sparkled like beacons now. She put her hand on my arm. "Adam," she said, "I haven't made love for a long time." Then she scratched the back of my hand with a fingernail, leaving a white line.

"Let's go back inside," I said.

Suzi took out a handkerchief and blew her nose. "It might go on like this for months, for years. . . ."

"He is still alive," I said. "Please, let's make it good for him."

"Don't leave everything to me, then," Suzi said. "You disappear in your Vermont. You are still a spoiled child."

I went back to Bolek, who was wide awake. His glasses had slipped to the tip of his nose. Today's *Women's Wear Daily* was spread all over the bed. He looked thoughtful. "All right, Mr. Big Shot American Artist," he said, "you tell me please why you are hiding in the Siberia Kingdom. No one chases you. No dogs, no police."

"We've talked about all of this before," I said. "We've talked about it many times. Don't you remember?"

"It makes no sense. I ask for guidance from above," Bolek said. "Am I crazy or is he crazy?"

"The time away has helped, Bolek. The work is more mine, really mine."

"Somebody else did it before?"

"No one else *made* it, Bolek, but often it wasn't from the heart."

"No?" Bolek said. "Somebody told you what to do?"

"I forgot my past. I took a little of this, a little of that. You know, like a salad."

"What a salad," Bolek said. "Everybody loves it, your salad, your American salad."

Now I was about to lose my patience. Bolek was still defending me from our history. "It is one of those salads with cottage cheese and Jell-O and pineapple."

"What is that? I have never seen such a salad."

"Whatever it is, it isn't mine."

"If you made it, it is yours," he insisted.

He made me feel like a child. It was like arguing my case to be an artist again. He turned his tired gray eyes away from me and looked out the window.

"All right, it is partly mine, this Jell-O," I said. "But so is the killing, the upside-down lives, the loss of everything that we loved, not knowing who we are. All that is also mine."

This was our ancient battle over again. "I am not at home anywhere," Bolek said. "Now that I am sick, I think maybe Poland is my only home. If only the Poles were not my enemies. I like what the Poles like. I like to be a hero with soft, narrow shoes. I like to make love to women. I like good air and butter and hay. Do you know what I hate? I hate to bargain. I hate everything that is tricky. I hate that I am not educated." Bolek and I were like two trains crossing and recrossing into each other's tracks. "It did all start then," he said quietly.

"Yes."

"This," he said, placing a hand in the middle of his chest, "and everything else. Your craziness, my craziness. . . ."

"Yes, the craziness. . . ."

"Dog's bone," he cursed through his teeth, "the cancer."

"There are things to do—"

"No," Bolek snapped.

"Heller said so."

"May cholera take Heller."

"Don't give up," I begged. "If you want to keep your hands in my life," I cried, "then get up, don't be sick, don't do this to me."

Bolek remained in his own thoughts. "It all began with those terrible months. I knew it then. Sickness came into my body, my eyes started to get bad, I needed a toilet all the time. . . ."

"That's not how things happen. They don't start in a moment."

"No?" Bolek said. "How do things happen? Who can stand all that? They killed and killed, but us, *us* they wounded. You are an artist, I gave my health."

"That was a long time ago."

"So?" Bolek said.

"Yes, you're right. It was the source of your illness and the source of my art. We must get back to that." I felt my heart pound hard against my rib cage. Can so much be buried back there? I took Bolek's hand.

"The Goyas on the wall," he said, "they haunt me. . . ."

"Yes, it's all about that. From the beginning, I've loved Goya. How old was I? Ten? It's all there in the Goyas."

"*Perhaps they are of another breed.*" Bolek recited the name of one of our two *Disasters.*

"Yes, that's it. It's all there."

"It is too easy to think that other people are not part of the human race," Bolek said.

"Some people *are* of another breed."

"Do you really think that?" Bolek said. "I think everybody has a right to live."

"I don't know about that," I said. "What if Germany, maybe Poland, became great holes in the ground?"

"That is wrong. I even worry about the Jews in Israel," Bolek said.

"You do?"

"I am no professor, so I don't know," Bolek said, "but they think like you. They think there should be holes in the ground all around them."

"Don't tell me that you're ready to forgive."

"Yes, why not?" Bolek said.

"Why not? Because they are all murderers. And they're not finished yet."

"So how many holes in the ground? Too many holes. You need holes everywhere. Why not France and England and Russia. . . ."

"Somebody has to even the score."

"You cannot even the score," Bolek said.

"No? Maybe you're right. Maybe you are very wise. I need to think about this, to paint about this. . . ."

"Holes in the ground?" Bolek asked.

"Death," I said. Bolek grimaced. "I'm beginning to paint dead things in the woods."

"You can paint me," Bolek said.

"Don't talk like that. Anyway, I am interested in murder, in everyone killing everyone else."

"What does that mean?" Bolek asked.

"You know, maybe anyone can be a German. There is no place to escape. Maybe even in one of those miserable desert countries where people starve, they just don't have the energy to murder. Maybe when they get enough protein, even they will get back their instinct to murder."

Bolek's eyes were half closed. "What you learn when you are close to the end," he said softly, "is that revenge is for a moment only. It is like making love. You cannot stop from coming, but so quickly you want to come again. I don't know. What difference does it make if you get revenge or if you make love?" Bolek's eyes were closed now. "Do you know what Goethe says?" he asked as from a dream.

"Goethe? My God, Bolek, when did you read Goethe?"

"He says that the only way to live a good life is to do nothing."

Suzi came in, dressed now in a plain linen suit, flat-heeled shoes, with her hair pulled back in a bun. Her kind of beauty made anything she wore look stunning. She nudged me out of my seat, her knuckles digging into my shoulder. "I want to be alone with Bolek," she said.

I moved toward the door. "I'll be back later," I told her quietly.

"Before you go," Suzi whispered, following me out of the room, "I want to tell you something." She closed his door behind her. I waited by the piano on which Suzi played simple Mozart sonatas. "I'm sick of your hiding in the country," she said. "I get calls from your dealer, from museums, from collectors. I don't want it anymore. I don't even know what they see in your junk. I see right through it. Everyone who knows can see through it. It is as deep as the skin on hot milk." She paused to light a cigarette. I felt I had to listen until she finished. "You are both dealers in skins," she said. "Covers, surfaces, wraps, masks. That's it, that's what you both have been doing all your lives, hiding things, women in animal skins, the real world in paint, pretty paint."

Suzi stubbed out her cigarette and came toward me, her teeth bared, snarling. She lifted her arms to pound on me. I grabbed her wrists. She struggled and suddenly bit my shoulder so hard that tears came to my eyes. I wanted to kill her. I barely got control of my murderous rage. I threw her down on the couch and turned to go. She screamed at me in German. In the hall by the elevators, I heard the front door slam, then the French doors to the living room.

I took a room in a small hotel in the east Sixties and called Maggie. We were both presiding over death, even though Bolek's seemed so terribly imminent. Jed was relatively well, as well as could be expected considering that both his eyes had now hemorrhaged. Renal failure would be Jed's way out, Maggie had told me. I couldn't bear the thought of Jed's dying either.

He got on the phone. "Listen, Adam, I've got this wonderful idea," he said, as upbeat and sweet as ever. "Why don't you and Maggie take a vacation together?" I was stunned. I wanted to cry. "Are you there?" he said. "She works so hard. I'm just baggage now. She looks after me, after Maria, she works her ass off for Jack Warner—"

"Do you want that really?"

"Of course I do. How else is she going to have a good time?"

"Jed, my uncle Bolek is dying, so I don't know. . . ."

Maggie got on the phone. "This man is a saint," she whispered. "What I'm learning about human decency, Adam . . ."

"Should we really go?" I asked.

"Yes," Maggie said.

"Maggie, Bolek's cancer is everywhere."

"He called a couple of days ago," Maggie said, "just to tell me that he loved me."

"Let's wait a few days," I said. "I'll call you back. Can I have one word with my daughter?"

Maria was two years old in January. The photographs Maggie sent me were of pure sunshine, always laughing, reaching with both her arms for the whole world. Now Maggie had to tell me that Maria *was* on the line. She didn't want to say anything. I recited a poem in Polish. Finally Maria laughed. "Adam, Adam," she said, melting my heart.

I stayed in the city another couple of days, trying to avoid Suzi when I went to see Bolek. He seemed better, and the day before I planned to return to Vermont, he and I sat on the balcony overlooking the East River. Rose had set up the tea, Miss Emma the suntan lotion. One of them had put a strange-looking golfing cap, open in the back, on Bolek's head. He lifted his pale face to the sun every time it peeked out from behind the clouds. Every once in a while, he winced with pain. He wasn't interested in talking. We seemed to be all talked out for now.

In the morning I went back to my exile. I reveled in the peaceful and quiet beauty of Vermont, but I still couldn't paint. My neighbor Wendell Anderson came over, as he sometimes liked to do, after his evening chores. He wasn't a drinking man, so he sat with a tall glass of cider made from his own apples in his own apple press. I sipped my first scotch of the evening.

"I'm the one who should be drinking whiskey," Wendell said, "but that woman won't let me." He chuckled quietly, his chubby face animated by thoughts of outwitting Leatrice, his wife. "Jesum, Adam," he added, "that woman could drive anyone to drink."

Most everything in Wendell's life seemed calculated to put distance between him and Leatrice. He was killing himself in the fields, hauling stones from a newly plowed meadow, or just bouncing on top of his iron monster of a tractor until well past sundown.

Wendell gulped down more cider with an oatmeal cookie he'd brought with him. "It's high time you got married, Adam," he said.

I worried about Wendell's pasty-faced complexion and the ring of fat around his middle. His life was so guileless and uncomplicated. Most of his miseries could have been fixed by eliminating white bread from his diet and Leatrice from his bed. I wished I could have found that easy a solution to Bolek's troubles.

I had fixed up one room in my Vermont house. I'd pulled down the old rotting plaster, pried up the rain-soaked floorboards, demolished two walls. I'd bought clear pine boards and cut them into doorjambs and mullions, floors and baseboards, until I'd made a haven of shining simplicity. Leatrice Anderson had made me some curtains, and I'd refinished an old drop-leaf table on which I always put a fresh tablecloth and a vase filled with flowers. The walls were white and the wood a rich golden yellow, glowing with health. In this room I drew, I painted, and I ate. As the sun moved around the house, it lit up every corner by turn.

The rest of the house was covered with layers of ancient wallpaper which, according to Wendell, entombed spaces filled with corncobs, beer bottles, and mouse nests. "Good insulation," Wendell said. These old walls were now alive with pockets of awakening, buzzing flies. My house looked, sounded, smelled like all the other farmhouses in this distant corner of the state. Its lines could not have been simpler. Not a single fanciful curve or fluted mullion or ornamental lintel, not even a coat of fresh paint to cover its rutted gray clapboards. Its one bit of whimsy was what Wendell called a "lazy window," a second-floor window that was set above and parallel to the sloping kitchen roof. It was as indigenous as the rumors of incest that hung over most of these isolated households.

I had put a couple of dead birds on the drop-leaf table. They were comical, these balls of feathers with rigid legs and *x*'s for eyes. They weren't exactly Soutine's tragic turkeys, but I felt that their lifelessness also deserved commemoration. Soutine's maggoty fowl would rise again to the heavenly sound of trumpets. These little Vermont barn swallows, now settled into my sketchbook, would never fly again. "Bury them and shut up," said Goya in one of the *Disasters*.

Wendell watched me draw as he sipped cider, one hand on his belly. He found the idea of drawing amusing, though when he had seen himself take shape on paper, the look on his face was one of childlike wonder, a Celt watching an eclipse. He sometimes displayed this look when he watched television or the caricaturist at the Rutland Fair.

There was new wonder in it for me, too. Now when I stretched a canvas in the old woodshed behind the summer kitchen, and began covering it with an image of a dead porcupine, my palette was somber and pale, my lines trenchant, to the point. Wendell had never seen my other work, not even my wild portraits, which exploded in streaks of blue and green, furious dabs of yellow and vermilion laid on like poison butterflies.

"The woods are full of dead things," I told Wendell. "Everywhere I put my foot, I kick some lump of flesh, some piece of bone."

"It's a funny time," Wendell said, "what the old-timers called a false spring. A lot of creatures come out of their winter places because it's warm for a couple of days." Wendell laughed. "They got fooled in the blood," he said.

The woods behind the house were in a kind of turmoil. Inside them, it was perfectly still except for the lonely whistle of wind in the tall, swaying cedars. But underfoot, everything was in disarray. Fallen branches and tree trunks split by lightning lay in a tangle, as the smell of rotten things rose from the ground. I had found a deer carcass with tufts of hide and hair still clinging to the bone. I sat on a rock and drew the ribs half swallowed by the earth. I drew all day, and all day I watched the carcass move about in tiny jerks, as if it were paper-thin and a wisp of wind had gotten behind it. When I kicked it over, I saw underneath it tunnels stuffed with weasels who'd been nibbling at it all winter.

This was simple, sober death, taciturn and unembellished. I resisted the temptation to translate the piles of rabbit bones at the bottom of a sugar maple into pits of human bones, or to make fantastic metaphors out of this false spring.

"Do you know why I envy you?" I asked Wendell.

"Not for Leatrice," he said.

"It's for having all your ancestors buried near you, in these cemeteries." Everywhere I looked, in all the tiny roadside plots, there were Andersons. There were Anderson women who survived several husbands, Anderson babies, Anderson men who chose their epitaphs from wandering salesmen and had them carved downstate at the granite quarries. And next to the Andersons there were Perrys, Leatrice's family, who settled this land with the Andersons hundreds of years after the Krinskys, Mandelbaums, and Kornfelds had come to Poland.

"I think you need a vacation," Wendell said. "A young man like you shouldn't be thinking about death all the time."

Later that evening I called Maggie. "Let's go to Poland," I said.

"Are you crazy?"

"I want to see the cemeteries."

"Adam—"

"The death camps, too."

"It's not what I had in mind."

"No?"

"I thought of a sunny place where we can lie around, do nothing. . . ."

"Yes, you're right."

"What is this about Poland?" Maggie asked.

"I want to see Krinsky and Mandelbaum and Kornfeld on gravestones."

"I see."

"Another time, Maggie, we'll go to Poland."

"All right."

"Now we'll soak up the sun somewhere," I said, cheerful again. "Where do you want to go?"

"We're being offered a house in Mexico. The servants are all there."

I called Bolek, who was pleased to hear that I would leave my northern paradise for a week. I went to meet Maggie near a beautiful fishing village south of Acapulco. The house was a palace on the beach. It stood alone, with the sea in front, cliffs behind, and to the south a barely visible cove where a tiny fishing fleet was moored.

Our days were lazy, idyllic. We ate lunches in a grove of palms surrounded by tropical flowers of endless variety and brilliant color. When the servants cleared up after us, we walked to the beach again, where we took off our clothes, swam, and made love. Our rare meetings made us ravenous for each other. We rubbed and stretched and penetrated each other with such ferocious hunger that our bodies stung in the ocean and stung when we cooled each other with unguents. In the process, we entered into new realms of pleasure, new boundaries of self.

It took only a day to shed the heaviness that had been shadowing me. The days ran into one another, all of them equally perfect, differentiated only by the sighting of the skeleton of a shark one day, dolphins flying out of the water on another, an all-night fiesta with radios blaring dance music on a third. We called daily to the West Coast and the East, where, happily, nothing had changed.

"I never see Maria," I complained on one of those days as we soaked up the brilliant sun. "I fear I'll never get to know her."

Maggie turned to me and explained how important it was for Jed to have Maria around, how he adored her.

"He has no idea?" I asked.

"You never know with Jed," Maggie said. "He might know, but it makes no difference to him one way or the other. He can fool himself into believing anything he wants to believe."

At night, as we walked along the white sands of the endless beach, we could hear the far-off sounds of the village, the bark of dogs, the whistle of a boat. We made plans to fix up the rest of the Vermont house, to find an apartment in New York overlooking Central Park. We shuffled streets and avenues, floor plans, furniture.

On the day of our leaving, I couldn't bear to put an end to the perfection of living in our fantasies. Nothing but death awaited us after this. I wanted to lie down and kick my legs like a hysterical child. I was ready to do anything to preserve this perfect happiness. Maggie, in a wide-brimmed straw hat and a light summer dress, walked backward to her plane, not wanting to turn from me.

After I watched her plane take off, I decided to prolong my return east by making a quick jaunt to Las Vegas to see Lou Kaitz. For two days he wined and dined me. Lou seemed to own all of Las Vegas, though he took special pride in his newest hotel, the Skylark. As we walked down its long vaulted corridors, I was astonished to see some of my freestanding pieces inside large glass cases, the kind of elegant showcases usually reserved for furs, gowns, and perfumes. I was happy to be reunited with my *Baby Carriage with Tuba*, my *Sagrada Familia*, my *Family Unit*, surprised at the pleasure they still gave me. "I call this corridor 'The Krinsky Esplanade,'" Lou said, and indeed those very words were carved into the marble lintels on both entrances to the corridor. "I bring some of the dumb thugs who work for me here. It's part of their initiation. I hold them by the scruff of the neck and make them look. I tell them to talk about the pieces. I ask questions. How else are they going to know how to deal on the East Coast if they don't know shit about art?"

I couldn't stay away any longer, and as soon as I returned to my house in Vermont, I was catapulted in more ways than one into the cold, cold world. A letter from Kor was waiting for me in my mailbox. He and Lala had gone to Europe again. The letter was from Warsaw. It was mostly about Treblinka.

Only a monument remains, but what a monument. It is probably art in its finest moment. You must come to see it. The Poles have taken over Auschwitz and Majdanek as *their* graves. Treblinka, they admit, is entirely Jewish. They don't advertise its existence, although, unbelievably, *they* built it. It is moving to see the gateway at Auschwitz, the cases filled with eyeglasses and crutches, but these places are museums. You can buy postcards and ice cream there. At Treblinka, there are just the woods and the fields and the wandering monument made of millions of tons of stone. What is art? I ask myself, now that I have seen this.

The monument hasn't been entirely completed yet, so you still see the occasional car full of bureaucrats come to inspect this herculean effort. I saw only one old Jewish couple. There don't seem to be many left. Imagine this: You are directed into the woods by a cobblestone path that hurts your feet. It takes you up a ramp, which, you are shocked to realize, is a station platform. Beside it, huge boulders shaped into oversize caskets or railroad ties wander over the landscape, going on *forever,* to the horizon and beyond. You walk beside them and rough-cut vertical stones, like sentinels, begin to keep you company. And then, as you reach the first horizon line, you are overwhelmed because this monument is a symbol of infinity and eternity. And this is the only way to understand what happened here. The stones go on as far as your eye can see. And then they start all over again. You walk and walk, and you think you will walk forever. You can think only of the enormity of this butchery, the endlessness of death.

Eventually you come upon a field, but the grass has been replaced by beds of poured cement. Stones of different sizes are placed all over these slabs. They are inscribed with the names of the towns and villages and cities from which these Jews were taken. In the center of this stone cemetery stands a megalith on which the words *Never Again* are written in many languages. It pulls from you more tears than you thought you owned. It is here that your mother died.

I went outside into the sunlight. I listened to the earth swallow up the last of the snow. Only small pockets remained here and there, on the edge of the woods. I could see some tufts of nearly green grass beginning to sprout in the field. Birds were chattering in the treetops. The geese I had seen flying south this morning had clearly made a mistake. My boots made sucking noises as I walked through the meadow into the woods. This place was like Poland. Bolek said so the very first time he saw Vermont. Geese must have flown over Treblinka too, animals must have died nearby, snow must have melted, just like here. I wondered if my mother lived through a spring there, if she noticed the sun arc higher and higher in the sky, if anyone noticed those things in a German death camp.

I came back and walked around the house. The ground near the foundation was still soft and spongy. I walked around it as if I were held hostage to this domestic orbit. I began to close the shutters but found that most of them were nailed open, their hinges long ago rusted out. I got my hammer and pried the shutters free, then nailed them shut. Inside my house it was dark now, except for the eerie slits of light that shone through the shutters. I closed the door behind me and sat down at the table. I heard Wendell's tractor moving up and down in the distance. I heard the birds fighting in the elm tree that towered above the house. I tried to reach back into the past again, to when they were all alive, like a tree full of birds, gliding, gobbling, mating, nesting, hunting, a tree teeming with life.

Suddenly it was dark. All was still except for the low whirr of small motors. I pulled the plug of the refrigerator, but other motors hummed. I traced the noise to the electric meter on an outside wall. The sound began to terrify me, like the sound of death, the live wire around concentration camps, the hiss of gas, the sound of my nightmares. I didn't know how to get at it. It came from *out there,* from the high wires, the far-off generators. I called the electric company. A night watchman answered and I begged him to cut the electricity coming into my house. He listened politely and said he would do what he could. Even I heard the insanity in my voice. I took the phone off the hook and buried its dial tone under pillows. The meter outside kept turning. In a sweat, I ran down to the flooded cellar and pulled all the fuses. The house was relatively still.

My mother was long and supple, like Maggie, like the flying Canadian geese. She, too, had a long neck, she, too, was beautiful and graceful. I couldn't see her on that railroad siding, in those railroad cars, but I tried and tried. All night I tried.

The sun streaked in through the closed shutters. I took a sketchbook and tried to draw my mother. I drew her like a bird, flying, contorting her long body, stretching her neck and wings. I managed to give her a human face, my face. My throat was parched and I drank some water. I sat again and felt my bladder ready to explode. At first it was hard to do, but after a while I was able to urinate in my pants. I soiled myself and I was glad to sit in my mess. I finally managed to draw her as a human form, starved and emaciated. I drew my father with his throat cut, with his head and chest torn apart by bullets. I drew a heap of bodies on a cement floor.

I didn't know how many hours or days had passed. I heard car tires crackle on the gravel in front of the house. A car stopped, its door slammed shut. There was a knock on my door, then someone tried the handle, and came in. I didn't stir. "Hello," a voice said, "anyone home?" I was jarred back into this world by Nancy, Nancy of the airplane. "I'm sorry," she said, seeing me at the table. "This doesn't seem to be the right moment." She stayed by the door. "I called and called," she said. "It was always busy."

I felt too crazy to talk. I began to laugh, and my laughter scared me. I was like the cornered vampire and Nancy was about to expose me to the cleansing light of day. Nancy came closer and sat down at the table. "Are you all right?" she asked. "Can I turn the lights on?" She seemed frightened. She got up. "Please let me help you," she said.

"Will you get me a drink?"

"I need a little light," Nancy said.

I explained about the fuses and she left to take care of the lights. When they went on, I went to splash water on my face. I smelled terrible. I scrubbed myself in the bathtub, then changed my filthy clothes.

"You look terrible," Nancy said. "Can I make you something to eat?" She stared at a small pile of bones I'd left on one end of the table, then went to the refrigerator, where everything was warm and rancid. She made tea. Nancy saw the pillows covering the telephone, and as soon as she replaced the receiver, it rang.

"What's wrong with your phone?" Suzi said, sounding angry and out of breath. "Something terrible has happened."

"He's dead," I said.

"No, he's not dead, but you must come right away. He has tried to kill himself."

"How?" I asked, as if it made a difference.

"A bottle of sleeping pills," she said.

I tried to separate things into categories. My mind wouldn't cope yet. "I have to leave," I said to Nancy.

"Tell me what to do," she said.

I remembered that Bolek and Suzi were now in their rented house in Southampton. It was one more reason why I hated Suzi. The house stood near the eighteenth tee of a golf course, in the middle of a restricted country club, no Jews allowed. I despised Suzi. I despised Southampton, that Berchtesgaden of the Atlantic coast. It wasn't like Bolek to try to kill himself. I suspected that Suzi gave him the bottle of sleeping pills.

Nancy drove me to the airport, where I chartered a plane directly to the Hamptons. Bolek was alive in the hospital. Tubes were attached to his nose, his mouth, his arms, his penis. He was breathing with great difficulty, gurgling in short, uneven spurts. His stomach had been pumped.

Suzi and I tried not to be in his room at the same time, though she kept a constant vigil. Her eyes were framed in purple. I didn't want to believe that she was grieving, but she was. As I sat beside Bolek, Suzi sat outside the room, at the end of the corridor. When I left to smoke or to pace in the hall, Suzi took my place.

At the end of the first day, Suzi and I made an uneasy truce. I stayed with her in their house because neither of us wanted to be alone. "He has been saving up the pills for a long time," she said. "He kept them in the pocket of some pajamas he never wears."

On the third day, Bolek was conscious. He looked skeletal. His expression told us that he was elsewhere, that he no longer cared to participate. In the evening, he wet his lips and told me he was embarrassed to be alive. I kissed his cold, brittle hands and tried to make him understand how grateful we were to have him back. But Bolek wasn't interested in discussing this further.

The next day, his eyes shone with a lurid glow and spit trickled down his chin. As soon as I entered his room, he let me know that he wanted to talk. I bent my head toward him. What I managed to put together from the broken fragments of his speech was this: In the terry-cloth bathrobe hanging in the closet of his room at Sutton Place, he had put away a few hundred dollars in cash. "It is there for us," he said, "for you and me. It is our escape money." With difficulty, he managed a smile. "When the city burns," he whispered, "we get out." He gave me a number to call. "It is for the *dorozhka*," he said. "He must wait downstairs." An hour later, Bolek wanted to say something more. "The money is for the driver," he said. "Tell him to cross the Praha Bridge, then on to Wilno."

When Bolek fell back into sleep again, I took a walk through the Southampton streets. I went into the candy store for a pack of cigarettes and spotted Abe Strawberry leafing through a *Playboy*. Abe now had a house somewhere in the Hamptons, as did many of the Abstract Expressionists. He puffed on a long cigar. He glowed in a shirt full of large red and black anemones. Abe was getting rich now and could wear anything he chose.

"Hey, buddy," he yelled over a rack of potato chips, "we've finally got you here." He danced over and lifted me off the floor in a bear hug. "There's a great house for sale on my road. Near the bay, walking distance to stores."

"My uncle is dying in the hospital here," I told him.

"*That* uncle?" he asked. "*The* uncle?" Abe called over to a leggy, freckled girl who was looking through a movie magazine. "This is Trudy," he said. "She's staying with me this summer." Trudy was in short shorts, a puffy halter top, bare feet. We left the candy store and went out into the street.

"I've seen your stuff in *Life*," Trudy said. She chewed her gum slowly, lazily.

"I thought I found an honest-to-God disciple when I met this guy," Abe explained to Trudy. "Then the bastard starts doing his zany stuff. Irony?" Abe said. "Right up to here. He took the family and exploded it, I mean better than the Kinsey Report." When Trudy skipped across the street to talk to a friend of hers, Abe said. "She's Guttman's daughter. The son of a bitch thinks he's such a fucking hipster, but he can't quite deal with Trudy and me being together." Percy Guttman painted primary-color circles and crosses on huge white canvases. Kor called him "the Jewish savage."

"Hey, Trudy," Abe yelled across the street, "guess who Krinsky's best friend is."

"Who?" she yelled back, not very interested.

"Maggie Coe."

Trudy squealed and ran back to our side of the street. "Maggie Coe," she chirped. "She's great. She's Polish like my dad."

"You ever going to leave your hideout?" Abe asked me. "What do you do up there anyway?"

"Paint dead things," I said.

"You don't look good, Krinsky."

"My uncle's dying, the painting's shit. I'm having a hard time."

"Again?" he said. "Listen to me, Krinsky. You suffer too much. Take it easy. Art has no *meaning*, Krinsky, only *quality*. The reason we paint is to have something to look at."

I left them, feeling drained. I went back to the hospital. As both Suzi and I sat near Bolek late that evening, he began to mouth words that I had never heard before. Neither Suzi nor I knew what he was saying. His phrasing had a strange lilt. He was chanting. It occurred to me that it might be Hebrew, which I had never suspected he knew. It was coming back to him from times before I was born. I was amazed and suddenly angry, resentful that there was a time before me in his life. I was *stricken* by his Hebrew. It shut me out and I felt unbearably alone. Suzi took my hand. She was sobbing. We had both been abandoned.

Bolek lingered for a few more days, though he was never fully conscious again. He had known what was in store for him and had wanted to spare us this pain.

In New York, he lay inside an open casket like a stuffed doll, his caved-in cheeks puffed out again, his complexion rosy, glowing with cosmetic health. These were the final touches of the fashion industry, their pink and glossy kiss of death. Bolek's friends, the Helenas and the Charlies and God knows who else, had once carried their creams and varnishes and tints to this country and made their fortunes just as Bolek had made his. They managed to even make death more palatable, more appealing, more decent. They were all there to pay their last respects, air-kissing as they glided over the too-thick carpets, among the too-many flowers, inside that morbid, awful silence. Like gagged crows, they bade a silent goodbye to one of their own, an innovator like themselves in the field of the dispensable, the frivolous, the extraneous.

I never let go of Maggie, not that whole day. I'd never needed to lean on her like that before. The loss of Bolek felt as if it would set me adrift, unattended and alone, in the endless expanse of America.

At the green and sunny cemetery, after Bolek had been lowered into the American earth he loved so much, I heard people clucking about Suzi's new millions. The accountant, Finkelstein, in the blackest suit of all, shrugged his shoulders. The law is the law, he said. Like big fish eating little fish, like the food chain itself, Albert Speer would get it back after all.

I stayed the night with Maggie in a small uptown hotel. We held on to each other for dear life, hardly sleeping, not making love, bathing each other in tears and tenderness.

After I put her on her plane back to Los Angeles, I flew to Vermont. I felt at home in this cossack country, a better, safer Poland than Poland itself. I went for a long walk in the woods, following ancient lumber roads, walking in the cool water of pebbly streams.

In the house, I didn't know what to paint. I was the sole survivor now. No need to wait for an ordeal to stimulate my art, no need to walk through fire again. Maybe Goya had it easy, I thought, for it all came suddenly: war and illness and insanity. They forced him to give up his whoring ways, enabled him to become a real *mensch*. But no one needed to wait for that. War and illness and insanity were all around, always right there. There were few respites from ordeal.

I pried my shutters open again and nailed them that way with large twelve-penny nails. I put a canvas on my easel. Many miles away, across the continent, yet on this landmass, *my* landmass right here in America, there lived a happy two-year-old whose genes contained them all, every one of them. She was my family and carried them all inside her. In Maria, Kor and Sophie lived, my parents lived, my Bolek, my Maggie, myself. My brush began to move easily over the bright, fresh canvas. With blacks and whites and dabs of ocher, as if I were taking my first steps, I began to paint them all.